Praise for *22 Britannia Road*

"Luminous . . . Hodgkinson's portrait ⌐...⌐
child . . . leaves an indelible impression.⌐...⌐
. . . lodges deep in our innermost selves⌐...⌐

"A riveting historical novel, set in post–World War II England, about a Polish couple reunited after enduring—and committing—crimes of love and war."
—*O, The Oprah Magazine*

"Can the animal horrors of war be wallpapered over? Or buried beneath the hollyhocks in a neat English terraced garden? The private terrors of two Polish survivors, who want only to bury the past in the comforting conformities of English life, are slowly exposed in this gripping narrative. A deeply felt debut."
—Helen Simonson, bestselling author of *Major Pettigrew's Last Stand*

"'What comes after surviving?' asks Hodgkinson in her ambitious, emotionally incisive first novel threaded with primitive human instincts for safety and companionship. Hodgkinson enters boldly into well-trodden, sensitive territory and distinguishes herself with freshness and empathy."
—*Kirkus Reviews* (starred review)

"Powerful . . . a sweeping tale of survival and redemption."
—*Publishers Weekly*

"Fans of novels like *The Guernsey Literary and Potato Peel Society* and *Sarah's Key*, who can never have too much of a good war story, will warm to this fine debut. Recommended."
—*Library Journal*

"An eloquent, heart-wrenching account of one couple's struggle to reunite as a family after devastating wartime experiences. A stellar example of literary World War II fiction."
—*Booklist*

"Haunting . . . This moving tale of what war has wrought on one family captures the reader from beginning to end, when these flawed characters finally come to their own fragile peace."
—*BookPage*

"An affecting story, extremely well told."
—*The Times* (London)

"Convincing and touchingly portrayed."
—*Independent on Sunday* (London)

PENGUIN BOOKS

22 BRITANNIA ROAD

Amanda Hodgkinson was born in Burnham-on-Sea, England, and earned an MA in creative writing from the University of East Anglia. She now lives with her husband and two daughters in a farmhouse in the southwest of France. This is her first novel.

Amanda Hodgkinson

22 BRITANNIA ROAD

Penguin Books

PENGUIN BOOKS

Published by the Penguin Group

Penguin Group (USA) Inc., 375 Hudson Street, New York, New York 10014, U.S.A.
Penguin Group (Canada), 90 Eglinton Avenue East, Suite 700, Toronto,
Ontario, Canada M4P 2Y3 (a division of Pearson Penguin Canada Inc.)
Penguin Books Ltd, 80 Strand, London WC2R 0RL, England
Penguin Ireland, 25 St. Stephen's Green, Dublin 2, Ireland (a division of Penguin Books Ltd)
Penguin Books Australia Ltd, 250 Camberwell Road, Camberwell,
Victoria 3124, Australia (a division of Pearson Australia Group Pty Ltd)
Penguin Books India Pvt Ltd, 11 Community Centre, Panchsheel Park, New Delhi–110 017, India
Penguin Group (NZ), 67 Apollo Drive, Rosedale, Auckland 0632,
New Zealand (a division of Pearson New Zealand Ltd)
Penguin Books (South Africa) (Pty) Ltd, 24 Sturdee Avenue,
Rosebank, Johannesburg 2196, South Africa

Penguin Books Ltd, Registered Offices: 80 Strand, London WC2R 0RL, England

First published in the United States of America by Viking Penguin,
a member of Penguin Group (USA) Inc. 2011
Published in Penguin Books 2012

1   3   5   7   9   10   8   6   4   2

A Pamela Dorman / Penguin Book

THE LIBRARY OF CONGRESS HAS CATALOGED THE HARDCOVER EDITION AS FOLLOWS:
Hodgkinson, Amanda.
22 Britannia Road / Amanda Hodgkinson.
p. cm.
ISBN 978-0-670-02263-2 (hc.)
ISBN 978-0-14-312104-6 (pbk.)
1. Polish people—England—Fiction.   2. Husband and wife—Fiction.   3. Parent and
child—Fiction.   4. Secrecy—Fiction.   5. World War, 1939–1945—Poland—Fiction.
6. World War, 1939–1945—Psychological aspects—Fiction.   7. Psychological
fiction.   I. Title.   II. Title: Twenty-two Britannia Road.
PR6108.O33A615   2011
823'.92—dc22
2010045353

Printed in the United States of America
Set in Fournier MT Std   Designed by Francesca Belanger

To my mother and father. With love.

The dead have need of fairytales too.

—ZBIGNIEW HERBERT

22
BRITANNIA
ROAD

SPRING 1946. TO ENGLAND.

The boy was everything to her. Small and unruly, he had a nervy way about him like a wild creature caught in the open. All the dark hearts of the lost, the found, and the never forgotten lived in his child's body, in his quick eyes. She loved him with the same unforgiving force that pushes forests from the deep ground, but still she feared it was not enough to keep him. So she was taking him to England, determined that Janusz would love him and keep him safe.

On the ship's sailing list she was named as Silvana Nowak. Twenty-seven years old. Married. Mother of a son, Aurek Josef, aged seven years.

"What is your profession?" the British soldier asked her, checking the identity papers she put before him.

She looked at the documents on his desk and saw pages of women's names. All were listed as housewives or housekeepers.

Behind her, hundreds more women, dressed as she was in donated clothes, stood silently with their children. Above the soldier's head, a sign in several languages including Polish, detailed the ship's rules. *All blankets and sheets remain the property of the ship. All stolen items will be confiscated.*

Silvana tightened her grasp on her son. The soldier glanced at her quickly and then looked back to his papers. She knew why. It embarrassed him to see a woman so unkempt and a child with such restless ways. She touched her headscarf, checking it was in place, and pressed her other hand into Aurek's back, trying to make him stand up straight.

"Profession?"

"Survivor," she whispered, the first word that came to her.

The soldier didn't look up. He lifted his pen. "Housekeeper or housewife?"

"I don't know," she said, and then, aware of the queue shifting impatiently behind her, "Housewife."

So that was it. She was recorded, written neatly into a book in indelible black ink. She was given a transport number, a label pinned on her lapel that corresponded with the details on the ship's passenger list. Proof that she and the boy were mother and son. That was a good start. Nobody, after all, could disagree with or dispute an official document. Only the title *housewife* looked questionable. Together or separate, Silvana was sure nobody would believe the words *house* or *wife* had anything to do with her.

All night, while the sea carried the ship and its passengers toward another land, Silvana worked at remembering. She found herself a space in one of the crowded corridors belowdecks and sat, arms crossed, legs tucked under her. Curled into herself in this way, with Aurek hidden under her coat, she breathed through the odor of sweat and diesel, the throb of the engines marking time, while she tried to recall her life with Janusz. Always, though, the same memories came to her. The ones she didn't want to own. A road she didn't want to travel. A filthy sky full of rain and planes coming out of the clouds. She shook her head, tried to think of other things, to cut off the image that would surely come. And then there it was. The wet mud shining underfoot. Trees twisting in the wind and the child swaddled in a jumble of blankets, lying in a wooden handcart.

Silvana pulled Aurek tighter to her, rocking him back and forth, the memories departing. He snaked a bony hand out from under her coat and she felt his small fingers searching her face. And how was it that love and loss were so close together? Because no matter how she loved the boy—and she did, furiously, as if her own life depended on him—loss was always there, following at her heels.

By the time the dawn sky leaked light into the darkness, Silvana was too tired to think anymore and finally closed her eyes, letting the heartbeat drone of the engines settle her to a thankfully dreamless slumber.

Morning brought with it a pale sun and salt-laden winds. Silvana pushed her way through the crowds to the upper decks, Aurek hanging on her coattail. Gripping the handrail, she let him settle in a crouch between her feet, the weight of him against her legs. Green waves lay far below and she stared down at them, trying to imagine what England would be like, a place she knew nothing of except that this was where her husband, Janusz, now lived.

She had been lost and he had found her. He must have thought he was reaching back into the past; that she would be as she was when he left her, his young wife, red hair pinned up in curls, a smile on her face, and their darling son in her arms. He couldn't know that the past was dead and she was the ghost of the wife he once had.

The heaving of the ship made her dizzy and she leaned against the handrail. She had left her country far behind and now there was no shoreline, no land to mourn, only water as far as the horizon, and shards of dazzling light splintering the waves. She hadn't seen Janusz since the day he left Warsaw six long years ago. Would she even recognize him now? She could recall the day they met, the date they married, his shoe size; that he was right-handed. But where did this awkward grabbing of dates and facts get her?

She squinted at the sea, the waves churning, over and over. She had loved him once. That much she was sure of. But so much lost time stretched between them. Six years might as well be a hundred. Could she really lay claim to a man simply because she remembered his collar size?

Aurek pulled at her hand and Silvana dropped to her knees, wiping her mouth with the back of her sleeve, trying to smile. The boy was the reason she was making this journey. A boy must have a father. Soon the past would be behind them and England would become their present. There she was sure they would be able to live each day with no yesterdays and no memories to threaten or histories to follow them. She ran her fingers through Aurek's cropped hair, and he wrapped his arms around her neck. She was on her way to a new life, and her one piece of Poland was still with her.

22 BRITANNIA ROAD, IPSWICH

Janusz thinks the house looks lucky. He steps back to get a better look at Number 22 Britannia Road, and admires the narrow redbrick property with its three windows and blue door. The door has a pane of colored glass set in it: a yellow sunrise sitting in a green border with a bluebird in its center. It's so typically English it makes him smile. It's just what he has been searching for.

It is the last house in a terrace, and although it stands next to a bomb site, somehow it has escaped any real damage itself. The only sign is a crack in the colored glass pane, a line running through the bluebird that makes it look as if it might have problems if it tried to fly. Apart from that, it is possible to believe the war has never touched this building. It's a fanciful idea, he knows, but one he likes. Maybe the house will share some of its luck with him and his wife and son.

"Don't you worry about that eyesore," says the estate agent beside him, waving his hand at the wasteland where dirty-faced children are playing. "That'll be cleared in no time. We'll have this town back on her feet quick enough." He straightens the cuffs of his tweed jacket and hands Janusz a bunch of keys. "There you are. All yours. I hope you like living here. Can I ask you where you're from?"

Janusz has been waiting for this question. The first thing people want to know is where you come from.

"Poland," he says. "I'm Polish."

The estate agent pulls out a cigarette case from the inside pocket of his jacket. "You speak damned good English. In the army, were you?"

And that is the second thing they ask: *What are you doing here?* But

Janusz is at ease in this country. He knows the manners and ways of things. Keep everything simple and to the point. Let them know you are on their side, and they're happy.

The first time someone had asked him where he came from, back when he had been anxious about his foreignness, seeing it like a birthmark, a facial port-wine stain visible to all, he had mistakenly tried to answer them. He'd not been in England very long—a year, if that—and the loud, bloody enthusiasm for war he found among his new comrades had lit a kind of fire in his heart. A rich blazing ran through his veins and flared in him an outgoing recklessness he'd never experienced before. He was in a smoky hall with a noisy crowd of RAF men, drinking beer the color of engine oil, and launched into his own story, the whole journey from Poland at the very start of the war, to France, and then England.

Too late, he realized he'd made it too complicated and in any case nobody was listening. Nobody wanted to know about the women he'd left behind. He carried on, stumbling over vocabulary, finishing up lost in his own regrets, mumbling into his beer in Polish, talking of painful things like love and honor. When he left the hall and stood in the sobering night air, looking up at a sky littered with stars, he regretted every foolish word he had uttered.

He squares his shoulders and closes his mind to those memories. "I served with the Royal Air Force," he says, his voice clear and steady. "The Polish Corps. I came over in 1940. I've been here ever since."

"Ah. Right you are." The man smiles and offers him a cigarette. "I was in the army, myself. I met quite a few of your lads. Great drinkers, the Poles."

He lights his cigarette, flicks the match onto the ground, and hands the box to Janusz.

"Stationed around here, were you?"

"No," says Janusz, taking the matchbox, giving a brief nod of thanks. "We moved about a lot. I was demobbed in Devon and offered work here or up in the North."

"Well, you'll find this is a decent enough area. Ipswich is a nice little market town. And you got this house just in time. I've a list as long as my arm of people wanting this property. If you hadn't been there, banging on my door before I'd even opened up, it would've been some other fellow who'd have got it. It's a nice family house. Have you, er . . . any . . . ?"

"Family? I have a wife and a son. They are coming to Britain next month."

"Reunited, heh? That's good to hear."

Janusz takes a drag on his cigarette, blows a smoke ring and watches it drift out of shape.

"I hope so. It's been six years since I last saw them."

The estate agent cocks his head on one side, a concerned look on his face.

"That's tough. Mind you, look at it this way, you've got this house, a job, and your family's coming over here. Add it up and you've got yourself a happy ending."

Janusz laughs. That's exactly what he is hoping for.

"That's right," he says. "A happy ending."

When the Red Cross officer told him Silvana and Aurek had been found in a British refugee camp, he had not been able to smile. "They are in a bad state," the officer said. The man's voice had dropped almost to a whisper. "They'd been living in a forest. I gather they'd been there for a long time. Good luck. I hope it works out for you all."

Janusz jangles his new house keys on his finger, watching the tweed-jacketed back of the estate agent as he walks briskly down the hill. So this is it. Peacetime. And he's got a house. A home for Silvana and Aurek when they arrive. His father would have been proud of him, bringing his family back together. Doing the right thing. Looking to the future. He can't return to Poland. Not now that his country has communist rule imposed upon it. He must face facts. Dreams of a free and independent Poland are just that—dreams. His home is here. Churchill himself said Polish troops should have the citizenship and freedom of the British Empire, and that's what he's accepted. Britain is his home now.

If he ever speaks to his parents or his sisters again, if one day they answer his letters and find him here, he hopes they will understand that this is where he has chosen to be.

He pockets his keys and wonders what life here will bring him. When he was offered two jobs, one in a factory making bicycles in Nottingham and one in an engineering works in a town in East Anglia, he sat in a library with a map of Britain and put his thumb on Ipswich. It was a small town with a harbor squatting on a straggling line of blue estuary leading to the sea. With his little finger he could reach across the blue and touch France. That's what decided it for him. He would live in Ipswich because he could be nearer to Hélène. It was a stupid reason, especially when he was trying so hard to forget, but it eased the pain a little.

He yawns and sighs deeply. It feels good here. The air is clean enough and it's a quiet place. Terraced brick houses stretch away down the hill. In the distance, a church spire reaches for the sky, the top of it boxed in by scaffolding. Whether the scaffolding is there to carry out long-awaited repair work or due to recent war damage, he doesn't know. And he doesn't care. He has stopped believing in God. Now he hopes for specific things. A job to go to. A family to care for and perhaps, one day, a small degree of happiness.

Beyond the church, rows of housing are hemmed by the river and the tall chimneys of the factories. Beyond them are fields and woodland. Above him, the sky is chewing gum gray but some blue is breaking through. Hélène would have said there was just enough blue to make a pair of trousers for a gendarme.

He lights another cigarette and allows himself to think of France. It's a weakness that he savors briefly, sweet and good as an extra spoon of sugar in bitter barracks tea. He thinks of the farmhouse with its red-tiled roof and blue wooden shutters. Hélène standing at the kitchen door. Her tanned skin and her warm southern accent, the life in her beautiful eyes.

He finishes his cigarette and wanders through the house again, planning, making a list of things that need mending or replacing. Flinging open the back door, he strides out into the garden. It is a long, rectangular piece of land. The grass hasn't seen a mower in years and there are nettles and brambles everywhere. At the end of the garden is an old oak tree. It looks just right for a tree house for his son. And when the lawn is cut and the weeds are dug up, he'll have flower beds and a vegetable plot, too. A real English garden for his family.

With his list of things to do in his hand, Janusz stands at the front door and watches the children playing on the wasteland beside the house. Hard to imagine his son Aurek will be one of them soon. Janusz is going to be a good father to the boy. He's determined to get things right. In the grainy sunlight, the children laugh and leap, shrieking through the afternoon, their shouts mingling with the sharp-edged call of gulls from the quay. When Janusz hears the cries of women calling them home for tea, he locks up and walks back to spend his last night in lodgings.

At the town hall, he fills in forms and waits in queues for government vouchers for furniture and paint. The furniture comes from a warehouse near the bus station and is all the same: solid, square shapes in thin, dark-stained wood. He buys wallpaper from Woolworths: "Summer Days"—cream colored with sprays of tiny red roses in diagonal lines. He gets enough for the front parlor and the main bedroom. He buys wallpaper for Aurek's room, too, asking the advice of a shop assistant, who says she has a son the same age.

He papers the hall and the kitchen in a pale beige, patterned with curling bamboo leaves and twiggy canes in soft green. Upstairs, rose-pink paint for the bathroom and landing. Aurek's room has gray formations of airplanes flying across its walls. It's a good-sized room. He'll be able to share it with a brother one day if everything works out the way he wants it to.

Every evening Janusz comes back from work and starts on the house, finishing only when he is too exhausted to carry on. When he lies down to sleep he has the impression his arms are outstretched in front of him, still painting and wallpapering.

Alone on his bed at night, he dreams. He enters his parents' home, running up the porch steps. The heavy front door swings open and he calls for his mother but he knows he has arrived too late and everybody has gone. In one of the empty, high-ceilinged rooms is a dark-haired woman in a yellow dress. She stands up, takes off her dress and beckons to him, then maddeningly, quick as a fish in midstream, the dream changes direction and she is gone. He wakes with a start, eyes open, heart thumping. He moves his hand toward the ache in his groin and twists his face into the pillow. This loneliness will kill him, he's sure of it.

Victoria station is huge, and even at seven in the morning the place is noisy and full of lost people who grab Janusz by the elbow and ask him questions he can't answer. He wipes the sweat from his forehead with a handkerchief and checks his watch. He has been practicing what to say to her when he sees her. "It's been a long time" is what he thinks he will say. It sounds casual and yet full of meaning.

He finds himself searching his mind for Polish phrases, but he's been immersed in the English language for so long now, he has lost the habit. It's like trying to recall the names of half-forgotten school friends, requiring too much effort and an unwilling excavation of the past. Truth is, there's too much nostalgia in his mother tongue. If Silvana can speak English it will be easier. They will be making a new life here and she will have to learn the language. "Welcome to Britain" is another phrase he thinks he might use.

The platforms overflow with crowds. Suitcases are piled high on trolleys, and rag-and-bone bales of clothes and belongings are everywhere. People blur past in grays and browns and dark blues. He scans the crowd, trying not to think of Hélène, how he had once imagined it would be her he would meet like this after the war. Then he sees a woman looking his way. He stares at her and feels a jolt of recognition. Everything comes back to him. It is Silvana. His wife. His hand goes up to take off his hat, an awful, narrow-brimmed trilby. It came with his demob suit and he swears it's made of cardboard. He smoothes his hair, spreads finger and thumb across his mustache, coughs, clasps the hat in his hands, and walks toward her. She is wearing a red headscarf and now he has seen her, she stands out in the colorless crowds like a single poppy in a swaying cornfield.

Janusz focuses on the headscarf until he is near enough to see the embroidered birds with flowing wings sweeping over her forehead and tucking themselves under her chin. She looks thinner, older, her cheekbones more prominent than he remembers. As she recognizes him she gives a small cry.

A skinny, dark-haired child leaps into her arms. Is that Aurek? Is that him? The last time he saw him he was just a baby, a plump toddler with baby curls. Not even old enough for his first haircut. He tries to see the boy's face, to find some familiarity in his features, but the child clambers up Silvana like a monkey, pulling her headscarf off, his arms locking around her neck, burying his head in her chest.

Janusz stops still in front of them and for a moment his courage fails him. What if he has made a foolish mistake and these two are somebody else's family? If all he has really recognized is the forlorn look the woman carries in her eyes and his own lonely desires?

"Silvana?"

She is fighting the child, trying to pull her headscarf back on. "Janusz? I saw you in the crowd. I saw you looking for us . . ."

"Your hair?" he says, all thought of rehearsed lines gone from his mind.

Silvana touches her head and the scarf falls around her shoulders. She looks away from him.

"I'm sorry." He doesn't know whether it is the sight of her that fills him with apologies or the idea that he has already made her uncomfortable in his presence. "Really. I didn't mean . . . How are you?"

Silvana pulls her scarf back onto her head and knots it under her chin. "The soldiers cut it."

It's hard to hear her clearly with the racket and grind of trains arriving and departing and guards calling across the platforms. He takes a tentative step closer.

"We were living in the woods," she says. "Did they tell you? The soldiers found us and told us the war was over. They cut our hair off when they found us. They do it to stop the lice. It's growing back slowly."

"Oh. It doesn't matter. I . . . I understand," says Janusz, although he doesn't. The child clutches something wooden in his hand. It looks vaguely familiar. Janusz frowns.

"Is that the rattle your father made?"

Silvana opens her mouth to speak and then closes it again. He notices her cheeks color slightly in a blush that disappears as quickly as it comes. But of course it is the rattle. She doesn't need to say a word. The dark wood, the handmade look to it: it has to be. He smiles with relief, suddenly reassured. Of course this is his family.

"You kept it all this time? Can I see it?"

He reaches out, but the boy pulls it to his chest and makes a grumbling sound.

"He's tired," says Silvana. "The journey has tired him."

It's a shock to see a child so thin. His son's face has a transparency to it, and the way his skin is tight, revealing the cradling structure of bones beneath—it makes Janusz's heart ache like a soft bruise.

"Aurek? Small, isn't he? Hello, little fellow. Don't be frightened. I am your . . . I am your father."

"Your mustache," says Silvana, pulling the boy onto her other hip. "It's different. It makes you look different."

"My mustache? I've had it for years. I'd forgotten."

"Six years," she says.

He nods his head. "And my family? Do you have news of them? Eve? Do you know where she is?"

Silvana's eyes darken. Her pupils widen and shine, and he's sure she is going to tell him Eve is dead. That they have all died. He holds his breath.

"I don't know," she says. "I'm sorry. I don't know where any of them are."

"You don't know?"

"I never saw them again after you left us."

He's been waiting for news of his family for years. He'd thought Silvana might arrive with letters from them, stories about them. Some information on their whereabouts. They stand in silence until Janusz speaks again.

"Well, you're here now."

Silvana answers in a whisper and he has to lean in toward her to hear what she is saying.

"I can hardly believe it. I can hardly believe we're here."

Janusz laughs to stop himself from crying. He presses her hand into his, curling his fingers over hers. He feels tired suddenly. It is as much as he can do to look her in the eye.

"I expect we've both changed . . . but it doesn't matter," he says, trying to sound relaxed. "We're still the same people inside. Time doesn't change that."

Even as he says it, he knows he is lying. She does, too. He can see it in her eyes. The war has changed all of them. And Silvana's hair is not just short. It has turned gray.

POLAND, 1937

Silvana

The very first time Silvana saw Janusz he was swimming. It was late spring in 1937 and all about was a feeling of listlessness, as if the sudden appearance of the sun had turned the town into a child that wanted only to play in the streets all day. Silvana had finished her afternoon shift at the Kine cinema where she worked as an usherette. The daylight was always surprising to her after the dark interior of the cinema, and she stood on the pavement feeling the breeze playing with her skirt hem, the sunlight stroking her cheek. She was eighteen years old and all she knew was that she didn't want to go home just yet. That to walk in the sun, though she had nowhere to go, was preferable to the damp silences that would creep over her the moment she entered her parents' small cottage.

She wandered down the tree-lined main street, past the square with its water fountain and tall, crumbling houses and took a dusty path into the shadows of the redbrick church and the presbytery. Once past those solid buildings she left the shade behind, the sunlight leading her down the road out of town. A few hundred yards ahead was her parents' one-story wooden house, painted the same blue as the other peasant cottages that surrounded the town. Silvana stopped and stepped off the road into an apple orchard. It had once belonged to her family but her father had sold it. He worked on other people's farms now, gathering wood, harvesting, whatever the season asked of him. The trees were loaded with white petals, big clouds of blossom, the grass under the trees soft and wildly green. A scene of ripenings and hopes. She stood in the dappled light and breathed in deeply, knowing that whatever happened to her in life, wherever she went—and she hoped it would be far away from this small town—she would always love this place.

Silvana took a footpath toward the river, glancing back at the cottage. Her mother, Olga, would be in the kitchen, drinking the vodka she distilled in the cow barn, the clear fiery liquid made from sugar beet or horseradish or, in a poor year, onions and elder. Yes, she thought. Her mother would be drunk, surrounded by all the hapless creatures she collected: kittens climbing her skirts; puppies tumbling at her feet and chewing on the table legs; the nests of blind rabbit kittens, wingless chicks, and solitary leverets that she fed every hour and nursed as she had once nursed her own dying sons.

She was known among her neighbors as a good woman who had not had things easy, having a difficult daughter to bring up. Silvana knew there was some truth in that: she had been a hard child, was still tough and inflexible, but no harder, she always believed, than her own mother had been to her. And then there were her brothers. The three boys born before her who had failed to grow up. Her mother's little princes caught in their infancy, who had blinked and whimpered through her childhood. Silvana knew their stories by heart.

Her father, Josef, had started whittling a wooden rattle when his wife first fell pregnant. He'd used a piece of cherrywood from the orchard, and somehow that wood had brought bad luck down on them. He was not a talented carver in any case. By the time the child was born, the rattle was only half finished. When the child died at three months, around the same time the potato crop failed, Josef carried on carving the rattle. He didn't notice the knife sinking into his thumb, making a gaping wound that bled and bled. When Silvana was young she liked to hold his thumb, run her finger along the jagged seam of his scar, and hear the story of how he got it.

It was after the death of their second son that Olga began drinking the vodka she made to sell to other peasants. Josef still hadn't finished the rattle. He had sold the fields by then and only worked in his orchards.

"It can't happen three times," he said to Olga. "We'll try again."

After the third child died, Olga knew the rattle must be cursed. She buried it in the garden, wrapped in a lock of her hair to ward off evil. Josef dug it up one moonless night and hid it in the unused cot. He went to his wife and told her they would try again for a child.

Cold as an unlit oven, Olga barely looked at the daughter she gave birth to a year later. Silvana Olga Valeria Dabrowski. Josef believed the curse had been broken. He finished the rattle, polished it, tied a ribbon to its handle, and gave it to his healthy, strong-minded daughter.

But Olga couldn't forget her baby boys. She kept their clothes in a locked cupboard, wrapped in tissue. Blue nightdresses with sheep embroidered upon them, white knitted booties, small blue bobble hats, three shawls crocheted gossamer thin. When Silvana was old enough, she was allowed to touch the hems and rub the tiny collars between her fingers.

"Be careful," Olga warned. "These are more precious to me than gold."

When she was ten years old, Silvana stole the baby clothes. She couldn't help herself. She took them out into the garden to play, but it began to rain so she ran in. Olga found the clothes the next day, covered in mud, tangled and torn in the raspberry canes.

"I was wrong about you," she said, locking Silvana's bedroom door. "You are a deceitful little girl. Say sorry for what you have done."

Silvana banged on her door, screaming to be let out. She would not apologize.

Olga put her mouth to the keyhole. "A boy would never behave like this."

"Your boys are dead!" screamed Silvana, full of her own furies. "I'm your child. You hear me? I'm your child!"

"You're the devil's child!" her mother screamed back. "You lived when my boys didn't."

Over the years, Silvana hardened herself against all of them, her crazy mother, her useless father, and the pressing ghosts of her dead brothers; all of them trapped within the four walls of the cottage.

In the afternoon sunlight, she flicked a wasp away from her face and stared at her home. For a place so full of complications, it appeared serene, and she wondered if all houses were capable of presenting such a good façade, looking foursquare and right while their insides were full of banging doors and raised voices. She watched smoke rising from the chimney of the cottage for a moment longer, then turned her back on it and walked briskly toward the river and the big sawmill.

Weeping willows and green sallows overhung the sparkling waters of the river, the hum of insects as loud as the continual buzz of machinery in the mill. A path had been scythed along the bank and she kicked off her shoes and followed it, the grass springy under her stockinged feet. Ahead, she saw a group of young men, all of them laughing and jumping off the bank into the river. Feeling shy, with her shoes dangling in her hand and her stockings flecked with grass, she thought about turning back. Then one of the men caught her eye. He was blond, broad, and muscular. Not tall, but strong looking.

She stopped to watch him dive into the water. He closed his eyes and straightened his body. He held his hands above his head, dipped at the knees slightly so that his calf muscles bulged, and sprang off his toes, his body cutting through the water's surface, leaving only ripples behind. As he came up out of the water, he looked at her, shook the water from his hair, and smiled. The sun caught the water droplets beading on his fair skin and turned them into tiny diamonds. He clambered onto the bank, his body shining like something brand-new. Silvana smiled back, dazzled by him.

Janusz was the only son in a family of five daughters, and to Silvana he was as golden as the rest were mouse colored. Five sisters, all anonymously plain, and Janusz, the eldest, with Prussian blue eyes and white-blond hair. A vodka bottle in a bar full of dark beer. As the only brother he was the last to carry on the family name. His father drummed that into him, hoping his son would study law at university and become someone of importance in Polish society. His mother wanted him to study to be a priest.

Silvana saw what a good son Janusz was, how hard he tried to please his family. But she also knew he had no interest in studying law. Janusz loved machinery, anything that had bits of metal and cogs and screws that he could take apart and put back together again. Really, he was the cleverest man she had ever met.

He lived in a three-story house overlooking the municipal park.

His father worked in local government, and the family prided themselves on their fine manners. So fine were their manners, they almost managed not to show their disappointment when, just months after Silvana and Janusz's first meeting, Janusz took her home and explained that he was going to do his duty and marry his sweetheart.

Janusz believed in God in those days. He never missed church, and he lectured Silvana at every opportunity on God's purpose for them all. Silvana liked to listen, though she didn't take it in much. She was too busy dreaming about American movie stars. At mass on Sundays she sat with his dull-eyed sisters, who complained of the aching necks they got from peering up at windows set high in stone walls, their brown felt hats tilted longingly toward the outside. His sister Eve said Janusz only loved God because he didn't have to talk to him face-to-face.

"You must never think Janusz is shy," she told Silvana. "He has plenty to say. It's just that growing up with sisters, and Mother being the way she is, poor Jan has been henpecked. His only defense is silence."

Eve was the middle sister, stuck between two older sisters intent only on marriage and two younger sisters who carried on like twins and went everywhere arm in arm. As a result, she said nobody noticed her and she was free to do whatever she wanted. And what Eve wanted was music. Her violin was her passion, and she practiced for hours at a time, emerging from her bedroom with her brown hair fallen around her shoulders; her face, freckled like Janusz's, creased with concentration.

She was always closer to her brother than the others, and Silvana liked her the best of all of them.

That first summer, when talk of a possible war with Germany was something neither of them took any interest in, Silvana and Janusz had spent their spare time by the river or taking bike rides out of town into the country.

"I don't want to say good-bye," Janusz told her as they lay on the grass under the shade of a cedar tree.

She laughed and took his hand in hers. His face looked so serious.

"Janusz, we've only just got here. We can spend all day together."

"Yes, but then you'll leave me."

"I won't leave you. I'll see you tomorrow."

"Why do you have to go to work tonight? I see all those men there who look at you when you take their tickets. They only go to look at you."

"Don't be stupid. I love films. I like my job." She felt annoyed with him and wanted to be mean, so she said, "Anyway, I like it when men look at me. If I'm beautiful, I can't help it, can I? Maybe you should be careful. I might get bored and go off with someone else."

He snatched his hand from hers and slapped her across the face, quickly, the way you might knock a crawling fly from somebody's cheek. Silvana turned away from him as if he had hurt her badly, but she knew it was the other way around. She had done the hurting. When she looked back at him he was red in the face and his eyes watered as though he was about to burst into tears. She was pleased. Pleased to have got a reaction. He loves me, she thought.

She pretended to be angry. She got up and walked away, and he jumped up and ran after her. When she stopped fighting in his arms he kissed her passionately, slipping a hand inside her dress. His fingers pressed against her, following the curve of her breast, the run of her ribs, as if he were looking for a way to reach inside; as if he wanted to find her heart and take it for himself.

"You've already got it," she whispered to him.

He stopped kissing her and looked into her eyes. Then he grabbed her hand and led her into the woods.

Silvana knew they had crossed an invisible line together, that they couldn't go back to how they had been before the slap. They made their way deeper into the woods and it got darker the further they pushed through the bracken, the trees growing closer together.

"We could keep going," Janusz said, holding back a bramble. "We could make a camp and live out here. I could have you all to myself."

Silvana laughed. "So that's what you want, huh?" She was a little afraid but she tipped her chin at him and tried to look confident. "My stockings are getting ruined," she said. Then she felt mischievous and lifted the skirt of her dress. "Look at this run." She showed him the rip in her black cotton stocking. "You'll have to buy me new ones."

"Let me see."

"No. No, it's nothing." Silvana pushed his hand away. She pouted at him. "I suppose you're going to hit me again?"

He shook his head slowly. "Never. I will never hurt you. I will always worship you."

Nobody had spoken to her like that before. He knelt in front of her and moved his hand up her skirt, the coldness of his fingers against her warm thigh making her gasp. He was breathing heavily by then, as if he'd been running. When he tried to put his hand inside her underwear, she pushed him away.

"Please," she said. "Wait a minute."

"What's the matter?" He was standing now, his mouth against her ear. "Have you done this before?"

She shook her head. "Never. What about you?"

"No. But I want to. Do you?"

She took a deep breath and nodded. "Yes," she whispered. "I do."

He kissed her again and they fell to their knees in the bracken.

It was as though she was the world, the whole wide world, and she let him explore her. And that was how she got her baby: the day Janusz led her into the woods. She would always remember feeling enormous that day, a giant woman, her hardness melted to softness, driven away by the sudden generosity of her body, the beginnings of their son already trawling in her juices.

"I love you," Janusz said afterward. "I love you."

They lay side by side, holding hands. Silvana closed her eyes and listened to her heart steadying. She was shrinking now, a breeze chilling her bare legs, doubts gathering in her mind over what they had done.

"Do you really?" she asked. "Why?"

"What do you mean, why? I just love you."

"I want to know why."

She wanted him to say he loved her because she was beautiful and because she was the one he had been looking for all his life. (She watched a great many films in those days and was very susceptible to American musicals.)

"Because that's what happens," he said, after a moment's pause. "People fall in love."

"Oh."

"And do you love me?"

Silvana looked at his sweet, serious face, the longing in his eyes, his unbuttoned collar, and his braces hanging loose. She stroked his cheek and he groaned, catching hold of her hand and kissing it. "Yes," she said. "Yes, I think so." "Show me," he breathed. "Show me again." So she did.

POLAND, 1939

Janusz

Janusz struggled off the crowded trolley bus, stepping down into a surging mass of people on Prosta Street. Holding his hat to his chest, he slipped into the crowds of men and women so packed together they moved like a flexing muscle, pushing him toward Warsaw Central station.

His chest felt tight, and he wondered if it was the storm-laden weather or the fear of what the future held that made him struggle for breath. A smell of sewers rose up from the grated drain holes in the cobbled streets. The heat of the day had settled like a net over the city, snagging the fumes of traffic and horse shit along with the odors of fish markets and rotting vegetables. For weeks now, there had been talk of food shortages and peasants had started bringing their produce into the city, selling it at inflated prices to families who were stockpiling supplies in their cellars. Janusz looked up at the tall buildings around him and beyond to the sullen August sun. It was glazed with skeins of gray clouds and what little breeze there was blew hot. How he longed for rain to clear the air.

Pushing past a group of girls, peasants in shawls and country headscarves, he felt a hand brushing his pocket and he dodged sideways, falling into step with some soldiers, hoping that the hawkers and pickpockets would leave him alone if they saw he was going to fight for his country.

"Bloody chaos, isn't it?" said a voice next to him.

"Terrible!" Janusz yelled back, glad to find somebody to talk to. He looked for the man, to find the eyes that belonged to the voice. "Are you . . ."

But the soldier had already gone and he was talking to the back of someone's hat.

He arrived at the station and fought his way inside, clutching his mobilization card to his chest. For weeks, radio broadcasts had urged all available men to go to their nearest railway station, where they could sign on as soldiers ready to defend Poland. For weeks, Janusz's heart had leaped and drilled against his ribs, waking him in the night with its rhythms. And there was no doubting that the war was going to happen. Here he was, standing in the middle of pandemonium—the station much worse than the crowded streets—his legs trembling while his heart still walloped his ribs in fury as if trying to beat the nerves out of him.

He looked up the stairs he had just descended, the thin section of the sky still visible above them. It would be impossible to fight his way past the crowds, back up to the station entrance and the overbaked day. He had to go on. He took one last look at the sky and then carried on forward, into the crush of people.

Trains were crowded with families trying to leave Warsaw, and whole carriages were being taken over by soldiers. Pulled back and forth, fighting for room to stand, Janusz knocked into crying children but there was no time to stop to help them. Everywhere he looked he saw bewildered infants, and it occurred to him that if anything were to happen to him, if he were to die during the war, these lost children would be his last view of Warsaw. They were surely who he was going to be fighting for, all the sons and daughters of Poland.

A harassed-looking soldier told him to hurry up and board a train.

"Which one?" asked Janusz.

The man waved his arm in the direction of a platform. "Timetable route number 401. Warsaw to Lvov. You get off at Przemyśl, 491 kilometers down the line. They need men to work on the town defenses there. Now get out of my sight."

By late afternoon, Janusz's hat had vanished, his wallet containing his identity card and a few zlotys had been pickpocketed; he had been given a uniform and a kit bag, and had boarded a diesel train heading southeast.

In carriages up and down the train, soldiers were singing and sharing jokes but Janusz stayed silent. He prayed Silvana and Aurek would be safe. He'd said good-bye casually, as if he were just going out to buy a newspaper. He'd told himself it was braver to leave like that. He'd met up with his father a few days before and that had been the old man's advice.

"Don't dwell too long on saying your good-byes. Women always cry and make a fuss. Make it quick. Good-byes are best kept short. Be strong and you'll make a fine soldier." His father had looked down then, his hand hovering over Janusz's shoulder. "Just make sure you come back in one piece."

Now Janusz regretted the way he had left. In truth it hadn't been bravery that had made him turn his back so quickly on his wife and child. It had been the hot tears that had pushed at his eyes as he'd brushed Silvana's cheek with a kiss. His father had been wrong. She'd been the brave one, standing there dry-eyed, holding their son tightly in her arms.

In the train's corridor, Janusz leaned against the door, rocking back and forth with the motion of the tracks, watching the landscape change from tall houses and industrial buildings into flat fields and dark belts of woodland interspersed with hamlets and farms.

To pass the time he composed letters in his mind, serious ones to his father detailing the regiment he was joining. He ran through arguments about the possible outcome of the war and concluded that given the strength of Poland's armed forces combined with the British and French aid promised, Germany would surely be forced to leave the Polish borders and Hitler would have to go home with his tail between his legs. Or at least that was what the newspapers were saying. Like everybody, he wanted to believe it.

As the hours passed and the flat landscape became gently hilly with rivers and forested areas, he thought of Silvana and imagined telling her about the town he was headed for. He knew it was an ancient place full of forts and flanked by mountains.

The train stopped at every town on the way, picking up more people, putting down others. As it rattled slowly toward his destination, Janusz wrote sonnets in his head to Silvana, counting the lines to make sure they were technically correct. He conjured up images and phrases and for a while he felt almost heroic. He looked at the other soldiers around him and wrote imaginary letters to them boasting about his wife. He described her red curls, the soft plumpness of her breasts, the warm width of her hips. "My wife is beautiful, shapely like the mermaid of Warsaw, our city's symbol," he told himself, and wished he had a pen and paper to hand.

He sat down on his kit bag, drank tea and ate pickled eggs and bread rolls, handed out from the samovar trolley that passed by. Finally, the day slid into star-pierced blackness and the train stopped overnight in a small country station. Janusz made his kit bag into a pillow and wrapped his arms around his knees. He was tired beyond belief. Surrounded by snoring soldiers, all of them shouldered together tight as cattle, sweat steaming off them, Janusz closed his eyes and slept.

The following morning, with a cool breeze that came off the hills on the far horizon, he composed more letters in his head, ones to the priests at the gymnasium in his hometown and letters in French to his old history teacher of whom he had been particularly fond. He was so lost in his own thoughts, puzzling over forgotten French grammar, that it was a few moments before he realized the train was pulling to a sudden halt in the middle of fields. He looked up at the sky. In the distance, planes were flying toward them.

"It's the Luftwaffe!" yelled a soldier and pushed Janusz roughly out of the doorway. "Get the hell out of the way. They've got machine guns aimed at the train."

"But we're not at war yet."

The soldier pulled the carriage door open.

"Tell that to the Germans."

Around him, men swore and women and children shrieked and cried. Doors were flung open and people stumbled and pushed to get out, jumping onto the bramble-lined railway track, running into the surrounding fields to hide in ditches and woodland.

Janusz dropped down from the train and ran after a group of men into an open ditch. There he crawled into a clump of tall reeds and squatted on his haunches, breathing rapidly. His uniform was heavy and he could feel sweat running down his face, stinging his eyes. As the planes flew over, he covered his head with his arms. There was a feeling of heat across his back and a roar of engine noise, high pitched and threatening. Then, when he felt as though the noise would deafen him completely, the planes passed overhead, rising higher in the sky and banking away toward the horizon.

"They're playing with us," said a man near him as the planes disappeared into the clouds.

"Where have they gone?"

"They'll be back. You wait. They've been doing this for the last few weeks, air attacks like this. No bombs, just machine guns opening fire on villages and train stations, picking off civilians. Scare tactics."

Janusz looked over the edge of the ditch, trying to work out where the planes had gone. In a grassy meadow, far off, he saw a peasant girl. Something in the way she moved, a certain toughness, more like a young boy than a girl, reminded him of his sister Eve and his heart gave a lurch. The girl stood in the middle of a flock of geese that began to rise up around her. Four planes came out of the clouds then and looped toward the train, dipping low over the fields. Janusz saw the girl raise a hand as if to shield her eyes. He called to her but she was too far off to hear him. There came a sound like the hammering of hailstones on a tin roof, and he realized it was machine gun fire. The last thing he saw as he stumbled back into the ditch was the goose-girl falling.

Murder was the word that flashed into his mind. He began to run along the muddy stream that lined the ditch, away from the train and the group of men who were crouched together, hands over their heads. Away from the image of the girl falling.

The ground around him shook as the machine gunners opened fire again.

Janusz heard himself cry out. And then there were no words, just red behind his screwed-up eyelids and splinters of noise like firecrackers exploding in his eardrums. He stumbled and tripped, falling forward, hitting his head as he landed, facedown in the ditch. Pain surged through him. Silver stars dazzled and died in his vision. He felt a pressure on his chest as if his lungs were being squeezed. He couldn't catch his breath. There was blackness.

He came to, lying on his belly. Coughing and choking, he rose onto all fours, gulping the air. The planes had gone, leaving blue smoke drifting in their wake, carrying the smell of engine oil and burning. He realized he was quite some way from the train now and the ditch was deep, its sides hiding him from view. He put his hand to his head and felt blood. Had he been shot? Then he saw what had hurt him: a stone sticking out of the shallow ditch water. His blood was on its flint edge. He must have been knocked unconscious when he fell. He tried to get up, but his legs felt incapable of supporting him. I'll get up, he thought. I must get up.

He was aware of soldiers nearby, and once or twice he saw them above him on the grassy shoulder. Too weak to call out to them, he stayed silent and hidden in the tall reeds. Exhaustion hit him and he fell into a trembling sleep. Within his foggy dreams he heard the sound of the train pulling away, but his limbs were too heavy to move and he let sleep overcome him again.

At the end of the day, in the dimming light, he crawled out of the ditch and lay on his back staring up at the sky. What was he going to do now? With cautious fingers he prodded and felt the swelling above his eye. The blood had dried. He sat up and then slowly got to his feet. The sound of geese honking in the distance made him think again of the girl, and he set off, walking stiffly across the fields toward the noisy birds.

The geese stood in a group around her, hissing and snaking their necks at him as he approached. He couldn't bring himself to touch the body, so he sat down and wept beside it. What kind of a soldier was he? He had lain in a ditch while all around him people had needed help. He punished himself with these thoughts until finally he took the dead girl by the shoulders and turned her over.

A wrinkled face framed by long white hair stared blankly past him. She was a tiny old woman the size of a child. He couldn't get his thoughts straight. Who was this? Where had the girl gone? Had he been mistaken? He touched her cheek. It was cold. His own face was burning hot. How could he have thought she was a young woman?

He picked up the body and carried it to the edge of the field, laying it down under a tree. He removed her bloodstained birch-bark sandals, tidied her clothes, and closed her eyes.

He was twenty-two years old and he had lost his regiment before he'd even joined it. Thunder rumbled in the sky. The storms that had been threatening for days finally broke. The sky turned dark and the rain came pelting down, needle sharp and carried horizontally by strong winds. Janusz turned up his collar and started walking. He hoped he was heading in the right direction for Warsaw. He didn't know where else to go.

IPSWICH

So far, what Silvana has seen of Britain is a country as worn down as her own. Signs of the war are everywhere, in the fire-damaged buildings they pass, the queues outside shops, and the blank faces of the people. She thought she might have been able to leave her dark sadnesses behind in Poland, but here loss squats in every corner, persistent and obstinate, calling up the past when it is obvious to her that forgetting is what everybody needs to do. But then who is she to think like this? Her own memories threaten her constantly, and forgetting doesn't come easily.

And yet, as she walks briskly behind Janusz up the steep cobbled hill past more of the redbrick houses that crowd these suburban streets, she feels determined, if not a tiny bit hopeful. The way Janusz had looked at the boy when he met them at the station had been loving. Accepting.

She wants to thank him, but he's walking so fast she has to keep encouraging Aurek to run beside her to keep up. Just as she is thinking it is warm enough to take off her coat and walk with it over her arm, Janusz stops outside the last house in a terrace.

"We're here," he says, smiling. "Here's the key. Welcome home."

She turns the key over in her hand. Aurek reaches out and touches it, and she holds it out to show it to him.

"Go on," says Janusz. "I've oiled the lock and fixed the hinges. The door was stiff but . . . well, go on. Put the key in and try it."

She slips it into the lock and it turns easily, the door swinging open onto a narrow hallway with a door leading off to the left, a staircase to the right, and another door at the end of the hall.

"Perhaps I should carry you in," says Janusz. "Carry you over the threshold. Do things properly?"

Silvana begins to protest, but he wraps a hand around her waist, scooping her into his arms, holding her tightly. She catches her breath at the sudden sensation of being lifted off her feet.

"Do you remember," he asks, his mouth brushing against her ear, "when we got our first flat and I wanted to carry you in, but you were—"

"I was pregnant," Silvana says, finishing his sentence.

Janusz staggers slightly as he tries to maneuver them both through the door, and a fragment of laughter escapes her lips, surprising her with its lightness.

For a moment she remembers the girl she once was. She thinks of her usherette's uniform, the burgundy color of it, the gold braid on collar and cuffs. Of the apple orchard behind her parents' house and the way Janusz waited there for her at dusk. The kind of useless thoughts that make her too aware of the lies she has brought with her from Poland. When he puts her down in the hallway she has barely a moment to straighten her coat before Aurek launches himself into her arms, burying his face in her collar.

"Don't be scared," she tells him. "He's your father."

Aurek whispers to her frantically, "*Nie*. No. No."

"He won't hurt us."

"Of course I won't," says Janusz, and she looks up into his frowning face.

She gives him an apologetic smile, untangles herself from her son's tight embrace, and looks around. The house feels cold and smells of new paint. The sound of their footsteps echoes as they walk through the hallway into the kitchen at the back of the house. It's a nice little room with a wooden table and three pale yellow chairs. There is a cooker, a dented-looking kettle sitting on top. Ragged lace curtains at the window.

"I washed the curtains," says Janusz. "I know they're old and a bit worn, but once you've settled in we can get some new ones."

Silvana notices how other hands have polished the doorknobs smooth and other feet have worn a small dip in the stone floor by the sink.

"Who lived here before?"

Janusz looks surprised by her question.

"I don't know. Does it matter?"

Silvana shakes her head. She knows she is the interloper here. And she is afraid the house knows it too.

Janusz picks up a package from the kitchen table. "A present for you. It's an apron."

She tries it on. A red cotton skirt with a blue band at the waist. In Poland every new wife was given an apron. Maybe it's the same custom in England. Whatever it is, she thanks him several times. Janusz runs a finger around his collar as if it is a little too tight, a gesture she remembers, one of the shy habits of his youth.

"I want you to see the garden," he says, unlocking the back door and throwing it open. "It's a bit wild, but I've cut the grass and dug some beds for roses over there. And I've got a vegetable garden started. I want a real English garden for us."

Silvana nods, although she doesn't know why an English garden should be different from any other kind of garden. The long lawn is tidy and the flower beds are freshly dug, the earth dark and rich as coffee grounds. Aurek darts past her and runs across the grass, crashing back and forth haphazardly, like a fly caught in a jar.

Janusz leans against the door watching him, a wide-shouldered man with a tired face and strong blue eyes. The suit he is wearing creases across his back. He looks foreign in it; a bit English. He looks older too. But what did she expect? They are both older. She wonders if he knows how much hope she has invested in him, in this new life, this rented house. It seems unfair to ask so much of him after all this time apart, but what choice does she have? Her loyalty is with the boy. He needs a proper home. She has to see to it that Janusz understands this.

Janusz turns and looks at her. "So you never saw my family after I left?"

Silvana feels the blood rush to her face. Was this why he found her and brought her here? So that she could give him news of his family?

"No," she says, looking at her feet. "I'm sorry. I don't know about my own parents either. I don't know what happened to them."

She unties the apron and lays it on the kitchen table as Aurek runs inside with a broken doll in his hands, a pink, armless, naked thing with rolling eyes and matted black hair. He grins and holds it up triumphantly in front of Janusz.

"Let's have a look."

Janusz reaches out to take the doll, but Aurek ducks behind his mother, making growling sounds. Silvana acts before she thinks, pushing Janusz away, protecting her son. She sees the bewilderment on Janusz's face and instantly regrets her quick movements.

"I'm sorry. I didn't mean to . . . He's not used to sharing. We've been on our own for a long time . . . He . . ."

Silvana is searching for a way to explain when a woman's voice makes them all turn around.

"Hello there, anyone home?"

The woman stands in the hallway, a cigarette in her hand. Silvana guesses she must be in her fifties. She has a middle-aged, matronly look about her. She's a tall redhead, big shouldered for a woman, and just the size of her makes Silvana feel small and out of place. The woman wears a tweed skirt and white blouse covered by yards of apron, a big messy design of faded pansies and pink roses that flower right over her hips and across the broad acres of her bosom.

"Ah," she says. "I thought I heard voices. I'm Mrs. Holborn from next door."

Silvana lets go of Aurek and he backs away and runs into the garden, the doll clutched in his arms. Janusz bends slightly at the waist as he greets the woman. For a moment it looks as though he is going to kiss her hand like a good Polish gentleman. Instead, he straightens up and shakes hands.

"Mrs. Holborn, did you say? Well, we're pleased to meet you. How do you do?"

Silvana sees Janusz's eyes upon her and realizes she is meant to say something. She remembers the English the soldiers taught her, the classes she attended in the camp.

"Good afternoon," she says carefully. "Good afternoon to you, madam."

"Charmed," says Mrs. Holborn. She takes a step toward the back door and Silvana sees her gaze settle on Aurek in the garden.

"And is that your boy?"

"Yes, he's my son," says Janusz, and Silvana hears the pride in his voice. "His name is Aurek."

"Aw—what? Sorry, I didn't get that. Can you say it again?"

"Aurek," says Janusz slowly.

"Oh, that's a hard one to get your chops around. Can't say I've heard that one before."

"In Polish it means golden-haired."

Silvana watches Aurek throwing the doll in the air and catching it. There's nothing golden about his shorn dark hair.

"He was blond when he was a baby," Janusz says, and Silvana realizes he has been thinking the same thing as her.

"Like his father," Silvana says, nodding.

"They change so much, don't they?" says Mrs. Holborn, waving a hand in Aurek's direction, a gesture Silvana finds comforting, as if the woman is already familiar with their son.

"My daughter was the same," she continues. "Born with a mop of ginger curls. You'd have thought she was the milkman's kid. If you saw her now—she's grown up and left home, mind—you'd say I was a liar, 'cus she's a brunette. Not a ginger hair on her head. But look, we don't stand on ceremony around here. You must call me Doris."

Janusz smiles. "Doris. And I am Janusz Nowak. You can call me Jan if you find it easier. My wife's name is Silvana."

"Right. Well, I'll do my best but I'm hopeless with foreign names. You'll have to forgive me if I get them wrong. I've seen you coming and going and I thought you must be moving in. You'll have to meet my Gilbert when he's back from work. You might know him already. You work together at Burtons, don't you?"

Silvana looks out of the window. The sun is turning red in the sky, casting a rosy light across the clouds. There is a chiming of birdsong through the open door, and at the end of the garden Aurek is scrambling up the lower branches of the oak tree. She thinks of the forest where she and the boy lived. Their hideout will be filling up with soil and leaves. Animals will be taking it over, the tree roots breaking through the earth walls. The forest will already be covering over her past.

Janusz touches her lightly on the shoulder and she jumps. She tries to compose her face into a smile.

"What is it?"

"She's agreed to take our photo. Come on, get Aurek."

Doris is waving a camera at her and grinning.

"I'm not very good with machinery. I hope I won't break it."

Outside the front door, Silvana stands next to Janusz. She fiddles with her headscarf, pulling it tight under her chin, and tries to relax as she feels his hand on her waist, drawing her closer to him. There is a moment of stillness when the three of them are waiting, posed, staring into the camera's eye. Frozen already into the image they expect the camera to see. Janusz is straight backed and serious. Silvana holds her headscarf in place. Aurek is clinging to Silvana's legs.

When the photo is developed, Janusz puts it in a frame and Silvana stands it on the mantelpiece in the front parlor. *Proof*, she thinks. She breathes on the frame and rubs the glass clean with her sleeve, polishing the image. There they are in black and white, a father, a mother, and their son, reunited. Her family. Nobody can take this from her. Not now.

Silvana is in the bathroom rubbing soap on her hands until they are covered with a thick layer of foam. It feels luxurious to have a whole bar of soap to herself. She looks in the mirror and wonders whether to wash her hair. Her short, gray hair. Tears come to her eyes every time she sees herself. *So ugly*, she thinks.

How can Janusz want her when she looks like this? A convict. That's what she looks like. Someone guilty of a crime. A bearer of bad news. That's what she had read in Janusz's face, when she told him she had never gone to see his parents after he'd left Warsaw. The hurt showed clearly in his eyes. She'd disappointed him.

She scrubs the bar of soap all over her head, fingernails catching against her scalp, suds dripping into her eyes, the smell of the soap so sweet and clean and renewing she is tempted to slip the whole thing into her mouth and let the suds rinse her inside as well as out.

"Are you all right?" calls Janusz, and she hears him knock on the door. The soap pops out of her hand and falls somewhere under the sink. She searches for it, water running down her face, eyes tight shut.

"Yes, yes. I'll be finished soon."

"Only you've been running the taps for a long time."

"Sorry." Silvana fishes the soap out from behind the pipes. She grabs a towel and wipes her face dry, turns the tap off and listens to the sound of Janusz padding away across the landing. She takes off her clothes and climbs into the warm water, ducking her head under, her limbs bumping against the bath.

Will Janusz want to know what happened to her during the war? Will he want to know how she ended up living in a forest? And what about him? Will he have secrets too? She won't ask him.

He has already explained to her how he arrived in Britain in 1940, though the way he told it, in short, brief sentences like a speech he has used many times, left her none the wiser as to exactly how he did it. He's explained about his soldiering, described the country he has brought her to, the cherry orchards in the south, the purple flush of the moors in the north. He hasn't asked her a single question about herself or the boy yet. It's better that way. She looks down, running her hands over her breasts and down toward her hollow belly where they come to rest, cupped together. What a pitiful body to offer him. Will Janusz still find her attractive after all these years?

Janusz is about to knock on the bathroom door again when Silvana finally emerges. She looks clean and scrubbed. Her cheeks glow pink, but there is something sad and small about her, like a wet cat, as though the bathwater has shrunk her. He takes her arm and leads her into the bedroom. This is the moment he has dreamed of and feared. Their first night together.

In the main bedroom are two single beds. Silvana climbs into one and Janusz draws the covers up over her. He sits beside her, perched on the edge of the bed, and watches her fiddle with the ribbons on the front of her nightgown.

"Do you like it?" he asks. "The house? It's a miracle, isn't it? Us, being together again? You'll like England. It's a beautiful country."

He looks down and notices her left hand. She wears no wedding ring.

"I lost it," says Silvana. She doesn't say any more than that.

"I'll get you another one," he tells her, feeling generous and good. He has to explain to her how things are in Britain. "A married woman needs a wedding ring. People look at women's hands here. They look to see who you are."

He reaches out to touch Silvana's hair and feels her flinch slightly.

"I'm sorry I don't have news of the family," she says. "I wish I had something to tell you."

"It doesn't matter. I keep writing, you know. Every time a different address, just in case somebody knows something. I think I've written to everybody in our hometown. I sent letters to your parents too."

"My parents? Did they reply?"

"No. But the Red Cross officer told me it can take years for letters to get through. I've not given up hope. And look. Here you are." He takes her hand. "Are you glad I found you? After all these years I wasn't sure . . . I have to ask. I didn't know if you had met somebody else . . ."

Silvana shakes her head vehemently and he regrets asking the question.

"I had Aurek."

There is a silence between them. Finally, it is Silvana who breaks it.

"And you?"

"Me? No. Nobody."

With that one sentence he feels as if he has crossed over a deep ravine, leaving Hélène and the past far behind him. *There was nobody.* And here he is in the present where he so desperately wants to be.

"I waited for you," he whispers, and believes what he says. He'll make this work. There are a thousand questions in his head. He is hungry to know what her life has been. He cannot understand how she survived living in a forest, although he has heard of whole villages that abandoned their homes and took shelter in the trees. Every question that comes to him dies before it reaches his lips. It is not the time for questions yet. She looks so tired. Violet shadows color the hollowed skin under her eyes. Maybe he should tuck the covers around her and leave her to sleep.

Silvana pats the eiderdown quilt. "Do you want to lie beside me?"

"Shall I? Say if it's too early . . ." He wonders at the foolishness of his words. Too early? After six years, surely he means too late?

"I used to imagine this," she says, and Janusz hears the tremble in her voice. "You and me. A house. All three of us, together again. It's all I ever wanted."

She pulls the covers back and moves to make room for him. Janusz turns off the bedside lamp. Lifting her nightdress, he slides his hands over her and hears her exhale deeply. A shiver runs through him. That sound. It is the sound of the girl he once loved coming from a woman he knows not at all.

Her hips, like misplaced elbows, rise up from her belly. Her body is all angles and depressions. Silvana takes his hand and places it on her breast. It is soft and warm and full. It is so long since he has touched a woman, and he climbs across her awkwardly.

"Is this all right?"

He is afraid to let his weight rest against her, but she opens her thighs and draws him toward her, whispering his name, wrapping her legs around him. In the darkness he grips the edge of the mattress, and then Hélène is in his mind and he shuts his eyes to get rid of her. He has to stop this craziness. Silvana's breathing hurries and the quick rasp of her voice in his ear sends a hot rush of pleasure through him, dispelling other thoughts. His loneliness falls away from him like unbuttoned clothes. Maybe this will be all right. Maybe they can do this. Live here, together. Forget Hélène. Make a family. He presses his cheek against her shorn hair, kisses her ear, licks it, folds the lobe against his teeth.

Something touches his hand. He moves slightly, vaguely aware of the feeling. His little finger is being pulled back sharply. "What the . . . ?" He starts. "Who's there? What the hell is going on?"

He tumbles off Silvana and falls between the beds, scrambling to his feet.

"Aurek?" says Silvana.

Janusz turns on the main light and the child looks at him, staring him down with wide, dark eyes. There's a possessive, adult fierceness in the boy's gaze that leaves Janusz speechless for a moment. He buttons his pajama top and glares back at the boy.

"Aurek? What are you doing here? Go back to bed."

Silvana is pulling back the covers, holding out her hands to the child.

"No, no. Let him stay."

"What does he want?" asks Janusz. "What is it, Aurek? Were you scared of something?"

Aurek looks at his mother and makes a small mewing noise.

"He's thirsty," says Silvana. "Please don't shout."

The boy climbs into bed quicker than Janusz can protest, and Silvana wraps her arms around him. He watches as the child takes his place, small hands reaching for Silvana's breast, dipping his head, taking the nipple in his mouth.

"No," says Janusz. "No. Stop. You can't do that. Aurek, get out. Go to bed."

Silvana's face is blank and impossible to read.

"I'm sorry," she says, her chin resting on the boy's head. "Next time. When Aurek doesn't need me."

POLAND

Silvana

Janusz's father found the newlyweds a small flat in Warsaw. Two rooms on the top floor of a tall town house. They filled a suitcase and a trunk with their belongings and took a bus to the city.

"I should carry you over the threshold," said Janusz as he put the key in the lock.

Silvana hesitated. He looked so handsome, his blue eyes shining at her. Nobody had ever looked at her the way he did. It was as if he saw something different in her, a truth that he had long been searching for. Of course he wanted to carry her into her new home. That's what a husband had to do.

"I'm not sure, Jan," she said. "Is it safe? For the baby, I mean? Look, why don't I give you my gloves and hat. You could carry them inside for me instead."

She saw the disappointment in his face, and her optimism gave way to doubt. Perhaps he thought they had got things wrong, the baby coming along so quickly. Had he married her out of duty? By rights Janusz should be at university now, not offering to carry a pregnant peasant girl over the threshold of an attic flat. Perhaps he was disappointed by the turn of events. Certainly his parents had been against the marriage.

But if Janusz was frustrated by his new life, he showed no sign of it.

"Come here," he said laughing, and picked her up, making a big show of groaning and puffing out his cheeks, as if she were a huge burden to lift. He walked one step and then stood her down inside the door.

Silvana looked around the tiny flat. She finally had her own home.

Janusz jumped onto the kitchen table. "Can you climb up here? I want to show you the view. I'll hold you tight, I promise."

Through the skylight window it was possible to see the tops of the trees in the park.

"It's wonderful," she breathed, the table rocking slightly under their weight. "The city is wonderful."

"We have a fine view. The best in Warsaw, I'd say."

He helped her down and handed her a present wrapped in gold paper.

"Here. My wedding present to you."

It was a necklace. A silver chain with a disk of colored glass hanging from it, a small circle of blue no bigger than a one-grosz piece. Within the blue was a tree made of tiny circles of green and gold glass.

"It comes from Jaroslaw, where the best glass and crystal comes from. It's a tree. To remind us of our . . . of the first time we . . . That day in the woods . . ."

"I remember," said Silvana. She held the little pendant up to the light, and the tree sparkled. She had a new life now with a man she loved. And she was free from her parents and her ghostly brothers at last.

Silvana loved the city from the moment she arrived. It felt alive and vibrant. The city women had short hair and wore tiny veiled hats, velvet cloches, or berets perched on the backs of their heads. They even walked differently. They took up more space on the pavement and led with their chins. Silvana, dressed in a straw hat and country clothes, led with her belly.

Janusz bought her a book, *An Album of Film Land: A Pictorial Survey of Today's Movie Stars*. In the Café Blikle, where she ate Viennese pastries every morning at eleven, Silvana pored over the sepia images of actresses and actors, her fingers tracing high cheekbones and smooth skin, arched brows and Cupid's bow lips. Finally, she walked into a glass-fronted hairdresser's shop and held out her book.

Her long chestnut hair was cut off, curls corkscrewing on the wooden floor. Silvana looked at recurring images of herself in the beveled mirrors. She copied the other women in the salon, turning her head this way and that, nodding her approval while the hairdresser swept the piles of hair on the floor into a dustpan.

At home, undressing in the cramped bedroom of their flat, in front of an oval mirror, a pink satin slip straining over her stomach, Silvana looked at herself. She tossed her head back, her short bob shining. She was nineteen years old and thought she knew all there was to know about the world.

Janusz

The cottage was made of split logs, unpainted except for the tiny windows, whose frames were white. A rat-ruined thatch roof, like a hat pulled down at the brim, gave the building a dark, squat look. It was a simple peasant home, shabbier than some, not worse than others. What Janusz's father would call a "one-acre starveling's dwelling."

Janusz had seen it from the brow of a hill, and walked down in the hope of finding someone who could tell him which way to get back on the road to Warsaw. He knocked but there was no response. He walked around the cottage several times and finally opened the front door, stooping to step inside.

There were two rooms with pressed clay floors, one with a blackened fireplace, a kitchen table, and chair. Potatoes were stored in a wicker basket by the door. The only decorations in the room were some handmade paper icons, carefully cut and folded forms representing different saints, lined up along the windowsill. They were yellowed by age and thick with dust.

The other room had a long bench against the wall on which a cat and kittens slept. In a corner he found a decorated wooden chest with linen and blankets inside. A dowry chest painted with bouquets of flowers and small birds. Something a young girl would be given by her family on her wedding day. There was nothing else except the mildewed smell of poverty and loneliness.

In the yard, geese honked and chickens waded through thick layers of goose shit, scratching at the ground. The rains of the night before had turned the yard into a muddy mess and there was a stench in the air that made Janusz cough, pressing his hand over his nose. The place was empty. It was, he guessed, the home of the dead goose-woman.

Despite his vow to return to Warsaw, he felt compelled to stay. He would do something useful here in this dead woman's home. He washed and bandaged his head wound with a strip of cotton sheet he found in the wooden chest, then he lit the fire in the hearth and cooked himself some potatoes.

The next day, he fed the geese and cleaned out the filthy henhouse. After that he walked around, noting the other jobs to be done. Every day he worked. He swept the yard and mended broken fences. He cleaned the two-room cottage and laid down branches of rosemary from the vegetable patch across the floors, to sweeten the air.

At night he slept in the chair by the hearth and dreamed of Silvana. By day he kept busy. He wanted to make things right. He didn't ask himself any questions. He organized and tidied and brought in vegetables from the garden.

Out at the back of the cottage, hidden by a thicket of elder trees, he found an overgrown grassy mound marked with a birch-wood cross. The cross was worn and old, silvered by the weather to a pitted gray. There was no name, no way of knowing who was buried there. He sat down beside it, thinking of the old woman, her body still under the tree where he had left it, and felt weighed down by a loneliness that made his mouth taste bad and his eyes itch with salty tears.

There'd been an old woman in his small town, a bent creature with a downy beard that had the local kids laughing till their sides split. She was crazy, spitting and swearing whenever they taunted her. His father had explained to him once, when Janusz and a group of boys had thrown stones at her windows just to see her come out screaming, that the old lady was lonely. His father had sat him down and said the word cautiously, as if it were an improper word to use in front of his son.

"Loneliness is a disease anybody can catch. When your grandfather died in the war against the Bolsheviks, your grandmother caught the disease. She died of it when I was just a boy."

"But she had you," Janusz had replied. How could his grandmother have been lonely if she had children?

"You can be lonely in the biggest crowd," said his father, and Janusz looked up at his steady face, settled in its white starched collar like an egg in an eggcup, not sure whether his father was telling him now about himself or his grandmother. Was it just that all the grown-ups in the world were lonely? That when he grew up he'd get the disease too?

"She didn't have her husband," continued his father. "That was what destroyed her." He sighed, stood up, and patted Janusz on the shoulder. "Now, stop tormenting that old woman. One day you might be lonely and you'll regret your behavior here today."

Janusz looked again at the unmarked grave. He knew what he had to do. He found some fencing wood in the log pile and, with a ball of twine, strapped a new piece of wood to the old, until he had the cross standing more or less upright. Then he set to, chopping back and clearing away the elder trees until he was so tired he could only stagger back to the house and sleep.

Janusz mended the water pump in the yard. He found a pot of whitewash and decided to repaint the window frames. Some days he just sat in the yard and watched the geese, thinking of his son and wife all those miles away and trying to work out how he had managed to become so lost and why he quite liked this numb state and this anonymous place. Over the weeks he lost track of time until finally one morning he woke up and realized he still had one more thing to do.

He started at dawn the following day, digging a hole beside the unmarked grave. By the time the afternoon threw long shadows across his back, the hole was deep enough. He drank a cupful of water from the pump in the yard, lit the fire in the hearth, took a blanket from the dowry box, and went back to find the body of the old woman.

He knew he was near to it by the cloud of flies that flew up to meet him. Her body was covered in them, a metallic blue mass moving in glistening shivers. He retched at the sight of them. It was his fault for leaving her there so long. He realized now that all the tidying and mending had been a way of putting off this moment. He lifted the blanket and threw it over the body, bundling it up, flies and all. Carrying her back to the house he was half afraid the old woman was still alive and it was her, not the flies, pushing and pulsing under the blanket.

He dropped his burden into the ground and began shoveling the earth on top of her, working as fast as he could, until the noise of the flies became muffled and he could slow down and take his time.

When he had finished, he recited the Lord's Prayer. He leaned on the spade, looking out across the fields. Now this final act was done, he knew he couldn't stay much longer. There was nothing else to do here. He figured he'd stay for another week. Then he'd have to leave. He had to go back to Warsaw.

His best plan would be to find a village and get news of the war. Then he'd go home and see Silvana and Aurek. He'd see his family. Let everyone know he was safe and start again as if none of this had happened. He'd fight for his country and nobody would ever need to know about the train and how he had stayed behind when it left.

He stood up and was about to cross himself when he saw something that made him take up the spade in his two hands again. Two men coming across the fields. Two men in uniform.

He met them in the yard. Close up they looked all wrong to be soldiers. One was a lanky kid, bony-faced with hands that were too large for his wrists. The other one was stout, with heavy black eyebrows and a nose big enough to be Jewish. Short-legged and barrel-chested, he walked heavily. Their uniforms didn't fit them properly. The boy's jacket was too short in the arm; the other man's too tight in the chest.

"*Dzień dobry*," said the boy. "Good day to you."

"You can put that down," said the older man, holding his hands up in mock surrender. "We only want a bit of food and then we'll be on our way."

Janusz didn't lower the spade. "Where have you come from?"

"Lvov. We escaped from the Russians."

"Russians?"

"They're against us now," the boy said. "Didn't you know?"

"I don't know anything. I lost my regiment a while ago." He frowned. Exactly how long had he been here now? He looked at the other man. "So what's happening?"

"The Germans took Warsaw three weeks ago. They came across the borders from Pomerania, East Prussia, Bohemia, Moravia, and Slovakia. We weren't prepared at all. Now the Russians want a piece of the action too . . ."

"We've been betrayed. Poland's been pissed on from both sides." The boy rolled his eyes when he spoke, showing the whites, like a horse about to take flight.

Janusz looked at their stubbled faces, saw the tiredness in their eyes. He couldn't understand how things had moved so quickly. The older man must have seen the confusion on Janusz's face. He spoke slowly and carefully, explaining what was happening. Warsaw had surrendered to the Germans. The Russians had first entered Poland as allies and had quickly become occupiers, too quickly for anybody to understand. Now the country was being divided up between the two of them.

"Bruno Berkson," said the older man, holding out his hand. "And this is Franek. Franek Zielinski. We were part of the defense on the eastern border. When the Russians came, our officers told us not to attack. We laid down our guns and the Russians took everything, our weapons, tanks, food. They took it all. Franek and I escaped when they were marching us to a prison camp. We've been on the run ever since. Hiding in woods and barns. If you could give us something to eat we'll be on our way."

Janusz put down the spade, dusted mud off his trousers. "And Warsaw? What do you know about Warsaw? My wife is there . . ."

"From what we've heard, the city's in ruins."

Franek sniffed. "And full of *szkops*. Overrun by Germans."

Janusz turned to Bruno. Already he preferred the older man to this boy with his hurried speech and uncoordinated limbs.

"But how did it all happen so quickly? What date is it?"

"October 8th," said Franek. "My mother's birthday. I wanted to send her a postcard, but Bruno says we'll have to do it when we get to France." He nodded at the freshly turned earth behind them. "What are you doing up there? What're you digging for?"

Janusz looked at the old woman's grave. He had no wish to tell them the truth.

"I was burying a dead dog. If you're hungry you'd better come this way. I can find you something to eat."

He led them to the cottage, thinking about what they'd said. Had he really spent over a month here? He glanced back at the mound of earth. A mass of flies still buzzed above it. How he hated those insects. If it was already October, the coming Polish winter would soon kill them and he'd be glad. The old woman would be able to rest in peace. Then she might finally stop haunting his dreams.

"Come in," he said to the men, holding the door open. As they entered the cottage he realized he was glad they were there. He'd been alone too long.

IPSWICH

Aurek has his own room. His mother told him it was just for him, and he wonders what he's going to do with it. He doesn't understand why he can't share with her, why she has to sleep in another room where he is not allowed. He pulls his sheets into a ball, drags his eiderdown up to the headboard of his rickety iron bed and makes a nest. He'd rather sleep under the trees. He misses the feel of the shelter he and his mother had squeezed into for so long.

With his knuckled spine pressed hard against the wall, sheets twisted around him, his eyes follow the upward tilt of hundreds of small gray airplanes flying in formations across the bumpy walls. There is a dark wardrobe he won't open in case a man with an ax is hiding in it, and a bookshelf with heavy-looking English books stacked on it. The one thing he likes is the picture on the wall: a black-and-white print of puppies crowded into a basket with ribbons around their necks. That's the image to concentrate on when the night comes and the wardrobe starts mocking him for sleeping alone.

He climbs out of the muddle of bedclothes, takes a leap past the wardrobe, and is up on the windowsill, face against the window.

There are other houses across the way, redbrick with outhouses just like this one and long rows of gardens where washing lines flash and billow. The tree at the bottom of his garden is covered in new leaves tight as children's fists. It's a perfect tree for climbing and already a towering friend to Aurek. He can almost smell the earthy, beetle-shell scent of its bark and he longs to climb into its branches.

But he can't go into the garden. His mother is down there, kneeling in the earth, planting seeds. The man she says is his father is working alongside her, digging a trench for potatoes. That's the man who has taken his mother away from him.

The glass is cold against Aurek's cheek.

"You're not my father," he breathes, a circle of mist appearing on the windowpane. "*Pan jest moim wrogiem.* You are *enemy.*"

In the garden, Janusz stops his work and wipes his face with his sleeve. He looks up at the sky, and Aurek wonders if he has heard his whisperings and is considering what he said. As Janusz slams his spade into the ground and begins turning over the soil again, Aurek leaps back onto the bed, pulling the covers over him.

Beyond the closed knot of his folded limbs, he is sure he hears the wardrobe door creak. He is shot through with fear. He huddles deeper into his nest and croons to himself, a soft birdsong to keep the enemy away.

In the first few months, Janusz struggles to find an order to their life. He leaves home early for work and when he returns, he teaches Silvana and Aurek English. They read together and then listen to the radio, mimicking the crystal-clear accents of the presenters.

He's surprised and pleased by the way Silvana picks up the language. She looks better week by week. Her skin is still pale but she has put on a little weight and he's hoping she will soon lose the watchfulness in her eyes, the constant look of mistrust. What he hadn't bargained for was the amount of time he would spend teaching Silvana and Aurek not to do things. Not to take a bath in their clothes. Not to fidget when they listen to the radio. Not to steal vegetables from the allotments by the river. After coming home from work several times to find the front door open and the house empty, he also teaches them not to wander off into the town and spend hours getting lost. Aurek has to learn not to hide food around the house; that it belongs in the kitchen. He must not go into his parents' bedroom. Ever. Nor must he touch his mother's breasts. Ever. That's something Janusz has lost his temper over, sending the boy wailing to his room. The boy also learns not to bring animals of any description into the house after Janusz finds a nest of harvest mice wrapped in a tea towel in his bed.

"You have to get used to living in a house again," says Janusz. "Put the past behind you both. The war's over. This is peacetime. A new start for us." He tries to soften his voice. He is aware that he sounds harsh. "I know it's hard. You must miss Poland. I did too, to begin with."

He watches their faces: his wife's nervy stare, the boy's silent eyes, blank as carved stone.

"There's a club in the town. A group of twenty or so Poles like us. Displaced people who have ended up living here. Some of them have children. You could speak Polish there, make some friends . . ."

"No!" Silvana replies, and he is surprised by the fierceness of her response.

"I don't want to see any other Polish people," she says. "They'll just remind me of what I have lost."

"What we've both lost," he replies, and she turns away from him, as if he has said something stupid.

Janusz brings home pamphlets. They have pictures of smiling families waving British flags on the front of them. He reads to Silvana from a booklet called "Learning the British Way of Life."

"Home Entertainment for Foreigners" brings a smile to his wife's face when he shows it to her. It has a picture of a housewife holding a tray of tarts on the front page. The woman's frilled apron rises up around her ears like the fluted ruff of her pastry.

"How to Learn British Manners" is Janusz's preferred reading. The illustration on the front cover is of two men shaking hands and lifting their hats to each other. Janusz insists they read it together.

"There are ways of doing things here," he says. "You need to learn them if you are going to fit in." He clears his throat, lifts an imaginary hat from his head. "Good morning, Mrs. Nowak. How do you do?"

"How do you do?" Silvana repeats dutifully, a small smile playing around her lips.

"Lovely weather for the time of year."

"Yes, *eezn't* it." Silvana giggles.

Janusz's eyes crease at the corners. "Yes, *eezn't* it." He laughs a little.

Silvana bites her lip and concentrates. "Lovely vezzer," she repeats, her voice breaking into laughter.

"Weather."

"*Vezzer.* Wehhzer?"

"Wait a moment," says Janusz. He comes back from the kitchen with a bottle. "I got this today. It's called sherry. You should try it. It's what they drink here."

Silvana takes the glass he offers.

"Oh, no, no. You mustn't drink it down in one. It's not like vodka. Here they sip it slowly and say, 'Chin chin. God save the King.' "

It is sweet and cloying but they drink the bottle dry and dance around the room, the wireless playing Glenn Miller, Aurek lying on his back on the rug, making small, off-key noises to himself. Janusz puts a porcelain bowl on his head and pretends it is a bowler hat, while Silvana waves an umbrella in the air. Their voices are loud and full of laughter.

Swinging Silvana around in time to the music, Janusz thinks they must look to the outside world like a couple of newlyweds. People who have never been touched by the war. He holds her close and feels . . . young. A young married man. A husband and a father. Something he has not felt for a long time. He will make up for the years they have spent apart. The war and all its horrors will be forgotten in this house. He has been given a second chance. It's all falling into place, this new beginning. *Yes*, he thinks, as he watches his wife's face. *This is a lucky house. And if it wasn't before, it is now.*

Most nights the dreams still come to Silvana. She cannot stop them. Being with Janusz has brought her to a kind of calmness, and yet his nearness brings back memories that she has kept from herself for years. Memories that threaten to undo her. Their son before the war; Janusz's parents' garden with its smooth lawns; Eve playing her violin for Aurek and his delighted, high-pitched laugh. It was there Aurek had taken his first steps, the child grinning with a smile only Janusz could have given him, father and son inseparable as a cloud's reflection in a lake. Memories like this seem to pour out of her, and she finds herself crying for those lost days.

Her dreams are dark and terrible. Her son is swimming in unfathomable waters, and try as she might to save him, he always slips from her grasp, falling back into the inky depths. She wakes, trying to scrape the skin from her fingers, thinking of lost children, the groups of homeless street kids she saw, the orphans at the camp. Where are they now? Still searching for their dead parents? She cannot get the children out of her head. They haunt her nights. And all the women searching for their babies call to her in her dreams, begging her to help them.

She knows she disturbs Janusz with her night frights, but he says nothing. He is quiet and patient, but already she wonders whether he regrets bringing her to England. It is surely not the reunion he must have had in mind. Have they both made an awful mistake?

One morning, she knocks on the door of Doris, the neighbor who always waves hello, the only one in the street who acknowledges them at all.

"I need to learn how to be a good British housewife," says Silvana, smoothing her hands over her apron front, trying to ignore the way Aurek is pulling on her sleeve. "Can you help me?"

"Show you how to be a housewife?" says Doris with a look of surprise, as if Silvana has asked her the daftest question she has ever heard. "Come on in, dear. Bring the little lad in too. I've got some toys he can play with."

Doris is hard to follow. She bustles around, filling the coal scuttles, beating rugs, washing curtains, counting her housekeeping money. She scrubs her kitchen floor on all fours, bare armed, sweating with exertion, tendrils of red hair sticking to her forehead. When it's finished, she grabs a basket of wet clothes by the back door and strides into the garden, where she hangs the washing out with deft precision, shaking Gilbert's overalls into shape, slapping the creases from wet sheets, already talking about peeling potatoes for the evening meal. Keeping up with her is like trying to run after a departing train.

According to Doris, a good housewife should keep her home clean, do her washing on Tuesdays, her ironing on Fridays, make sure there's bread and jam on the table at weekends, and bake Victoria sponges on high days and holidays. Surely Silvana can do these things.

In her own home, Silvana spends hours wandering through the rooms in a daze. She forgets to fill the coal scuttles and doesn't find the need to sweep or dust. When she makes the beds she often lies down and falls asleep on them.

Janusz doesn't give her housekeeping money. He says he is waiting until she understands pounds, shillings, and pence. The money is strange, the notes bigger than Polish currency, the coins thicker. And she'll never get used to ration books, no matter how often Janusz explains them to her.

Janusz is a good husband. More than she deserves. He takes her shopping and teaches her the names of household goods: corned beef, flour, Pears Soap, Bovril. He patiently writes her shopping lists in English and stands next to her when she reads them to the man behind the counter at the greengrocer's, correcting her when she makes mistakes.

"I want to buy flower seeds," Janusz says in Woolworths. They are looking at rows of brightly colored seed packets. Silvana can recognize some of the flower illustrations, but the English names mean nothing to her.

Janusz hands her a packet with a brightly colored picture of an orange flower on it.

"Coreopsis. A few years ago, I saw a garden in Devon filled with them. And look at these hollyhocks—what a lovely red color. Do you like them? Lady's mantle grows well here. The English use it for ground cover. What do you think? Is there anything you would like to plant?"

Silvana studies the packets, their rich designs, the showy flowers they promise.

"Herbs," she says. "I'd like to plant herbs."

She searches the bright packets, looking for an illustration of a delicate white flower.

"Do they have *czosnek?*"

Janusz frowns. "Garlic? No, I don't think so. The English don't like strong flavors. But how about mint? Or parsley? That grows well here."

Silvana is distracted by Aurek, who has picked up a brown paper packet of beans and is rattling it against his ear. He begins to hum and dance, twirling around, tapping a rhythm on the wooden floors, grinning at the sound the dry seeds make. People are beginning to stare.

"Come on," says Silvana, taking the packet from him gently. "Stop making all that noise."

"Do you want to choose some flower seeds?" Janusz asks him. "You can help in the garden too."

Aurek shakes his head. He waves his arms and sways. "Trees," he croons. "I want trees."

Silvana can see Janusz is confused by the boy's behavior, so she leads Aurek outside and waits in the street while Janusz pays for the seeds. By the time Janusz joins them, he has a smile on his face again and the earlier red flush of embarrassment in his cheeks has gone.

"Let's look in the jewelry shop," he says, taking Silvana by the arm. He wants to buy her a wedding ring, but the salesman tells him there is a national shortage. Too many weddings going on and not enough gold. Silver, yes, but not gold.

"We're already married," Janusz tells the salesman. "This is our son." He takes Aurek by the shoulders. "Surely you must have a gold wedding ring you can sell us. Can I see the manager, please?"

The manager is a long-faced man with a dirty shirt collar and worn cuffs. He comes out of his office shaking his head with a kind of weary patience that suggests they are not the only people who have asked him for the impossible that day.

Janusz explains again that they are married. Silvana stands beside him, trying to look like a good wife, clutching her wicker shopping basket to her as though it's a velvet evening bag. She watches the manager's polite disinterest in their marital history, Janusz's confusion when the man tries to sell them a watch instead.

"We'll wait," Silvana says as they step out onto the pavement. "I don't mind waiting. I don't really need a ring."

She sees the stiff set of Janusz's mouth and knows she has said the wrong thing.

"I really don't mind," she says, pressing her hand into his. "I have you and Aurek. All I want is that. Let's go home."

Walking up Britannia Road, they pass a parade of women kneeling outside their front doors as if on prayer mats, heads bent toward their stone steps. Their aproned hips swing in almost perfect unison as they buff their steps to a shine. It's a sight that makes Silvana feel awkward, all those backs turned to her as she walks past.

"Morning," calls Doris when they stop outside their home.

"You've got to polish your steps," she explains, standing up. "It's a matter of pride around here. You need a donkey stone. Don't ask me why it's called that. All I know is how you keep your front door shows how you keep your home. You don't want everybody thinking they're better than you, do you?"

Silvana nods uncertainly. "Donkey stone?"

"Put your hand out. That's it."

Silvana turns the stone over, examining it as if she has been handed a piece of rock from Mars.

"Come on then, you have a go."

Silvana kneels and rubs the stone against the step. It's a pleasant movement, the stone running circles over the step, an ice-skater tracing patterns in the ice. Even the noise is like the sound of skates cutting through watery ice, a soft crunch and a whoosh as it glides in arcs under her hand.

Doris runs her fingertips over the step.

"Well. You did a good job there. That's one thing you can say. Don't you worry, dearie. You'll soon fit in. Keep the stone. Look after it. It's a good one."

Janusz slips his arm around Silvana's waist.

"My wife has always been very house-proud," he says to Doris.

Silvana looks sideways at him. Was she really? She can't remember, but she's pleased to hear him talk like this.

"We lived in Warsaw before the war, you see. A beautiful city. It was known as the Paris of the east."

"Was it now?" says Doris. She laughs loudly. "Well, Ipswich is in the east too, but I don't think it's quite gay *Paree*. I'm glad I saw you in any case. Gilbert told me to tell you there are jobs for women going at one of the textile factories by the canal. All you've got to do is sew in a straight line. I thought of you, Sylvia. You should get down there quick."

"Me?"

"Well, yes. It's a good job. Not like the munitions factories I had to work in during the war. See this yellow color on my face?" She turns her cheek briefly to Silvana and it's true: there is a dirty yellow tint to her skin. "That's from filling shells. I cover it up with a bit of panstick but it's still there. I did my bit for the war effort. Nobody can say I didn't."

"It's very kind of you to help us," says Janusz. "Very kind. Aurek will be going to school soon and we have been thinking about finding work for my wife. We'll go down to the factory today."

Silvana can't remember any conversations about finding her a job.

"School?" she says, and feels her legs go weak. "Aurek has to go to school?"

POLAND

Silvana

Silvana loved the early summer evenings in Warsaw. Janusz came home from work and they ate together quickly, Janusz telling her about his day while she listened and nodded and enjoyed feeling like a perfect urban wife. Afterward, they went out into the streets and walked in the park, feeding the ducks on the pond and watching children pushing their wooden sailing boats out on the green water before their nannies took them home.

One night they stayed longer than usual. It was a hot night and Silvana didn't feel like going back to the flat, so they sat on a park bench and watched the dusk sky deepen to violet and then a greeny blue before the streetlights were lit and it was dark.

The animals in the menagerie began to call, weaving fretful paths through sawdust bedding. Monkeys howled and chattered in their cages. Clouds of moths circled the streetlights. Silvana felt restless. The doctor had told her that the birth was not far off, a week at most. She was filled with energy and wanted to walk.

A group of women in feathered hats walked past and looked at Janusz. They put their hands across their lipsticked mouths and whispered to each other. Silvana gripped Janusz's hand and pretended not to notice them.

The park at night was different—like wading out from the shallows into suddenly cold, deep water that pressed on your chest. Silvana noticed men sitting on benches where no one had been before. Even in the shadows of the magnolia trees behind them, Silvana could see some of them were holding hands. Ahead of her a woman took the arm of a man and walked away into the trees.

When Silvana and Janusz got home they didn't speak. They climbed the narrow staircase to their flat and once inside, Janusz guided Silvana to the bedroom. He sat her on the bed and she watched him take off his clothes, unbuckling his trouser belt, pulling his shirt off over his head.

She had never seen him naked. Their courting days had been in fields and woodland and their lovemaking had always involved creased clothes and a fear of being discovered. Since they had married, Silvana had felt unsure of the new legitimacy of their lives together. She was careful to look away when Janusz undressed at night and made sure she was always in bed first, under the safety of the bedcovers. Tonight, though, was different.

"Wait," she said as he moved toward her. "Stay there. I want to look at you."

She got up and walked around him, studying him, touching him with her fingertips, like an artist slowly exploring the shadows and curves of a sculpture. Janusz caught hold of her hands and pulled her to him.

"Now you," he breathed. "Let me see you."

Silently Silvana took hold of her collar and unbuttoned it. She let her dress slip to the floor.

"You're beautiful," Janusz whispered, and ran his hands over her belly as if he were polishing its domed surface.

When they climbed into bed, Silvana felt as though she could make more babies. That the one in her belly could be joined by another. She was too big and heavy to lie on her back, so she knelt on all fours. Silvana felt an urgent, deeper love for Janusz than she had ever felt before. She bowed her head and imagined the dark world inside herself where the child must be, curled under her cathedral ribs. Then she was swept away from her thoughts and there was only Janusz and the unstoppable, silent language of their love.

By the time she woke the next day, Janusz had already left for work. The bedsheets were wet and twisted around her. She unraveled them and tried to work out why she was lying in such dampness. Then the pain hit her. A sudden hurt like a rope pulled tight around her hips. The baby was coming. It must be. The pain faded and she struggled out of bed, reaching for her clothes. The doctor's house was a couple of blocks away and she was sure she could get there if she went slowly.

She dressed and left the flat, edging down the narrow staircase, hands pressed against the wall. When she got to the landing, the rope tightened again. She let out a groan of pain, a low, animal noise she didn't recognize as her own voice. She leaned against the wall, sweat beading on her forehead. She'd never make it to the doctor. When the pain lessened enough for her to think again, she knocked on a flat door. A woman answered, a crowd of small brown dogs yapping around her feet. They rushed into the corridor and began nipping at Silvana's heels.

"Come here!" the women yelled at the dogs, trying to usher them back inside. A man came out behind her, asking what all the noise was.

"My God," he said on seeing Silvana. "You're the girl from upstairs, aren't you? Are you all right?"

Silvana fell forward into his arms. Here she was, bigger than a house and moaning like a cow and he wanted to know if she was all right. "I'm fine," she managed to reply before the pain across her belly tightened and she doubled over.

After a while the pain was all there was. Silvana forgot she was giving birth; she believed she was fighting for her life. And then, just as she had begun to welcome the idea of death, her body began to call her back.

"I need to push," she told the woman. "Oh my God, I need to push."

"Already? The doctor's not here yet. Can't you wait?"

Silvana shook her head. She began to moan.

"Get on the bed," said the woman. "Get on the bed. The doctor won't want to see you on the floor."

Silvana batted the woman away. "I can't," she panted. "I don't want to. Leave me alone."

With her eyes tight shut, crouching in the corner of the room, she gave a long, drawn-out moan and felt heat burn through her. She screamed. Then, just as she could bear no more, a sense of relief flooded her. When she opened her eyes and looked down, a blood-smeared infant lay between her trembling legs. Her body convulsed and she felt the urge to push again. Was there another child? Twins? She cried out in fear.

"It's the afterbirth," the woman said sharply. She leaned over and Silvana felt her hands pushing down hard on her belly. Silvana tried to reach for the baby but the pain made her cry out and she closed her eyes tight. Then came a second warm rush of relief, and she sat back on the floor, exhausted.

She was aware of the baby being lifted in a sheet, of being helped into bed, of someone wiping a cool cloth across her forehead. She heard the woman fussing about her sheets being stained, a man's voice telling the woman to be quiet, and the sound of dogs barking in another room, and then she slept briefly, absolutely spent.

When she woke, the pillows were plumped under her head, and beside her, swaddled in a blanket, was her son.

She studied his face. He kept his eyes tight shut, his eyelids creased and purple, as if he didn't want to see what the world had to offer him. A feeling of awe crowded her lungs and took her breath away. She felt suddenly afraid of the silent creature in her arms. It was such a tiny thing, a screwed-up, boiled-red scrap of a beginning, but she knew its strength; that the love she felt already for this stranger could undo her entirely. Was she capable of looking after him? She thought of her mother and the losses she had suffered. What if her son died like her brothers had? What if he were to be ill?

"Can you take him?" she asked the woman.

"Take him?"

"I don't know how to care for him. Please. It's for the best. Take him. I can't be his mother."

"That's enough of this nonsense," said the doctor, coming between Silvana and the woman. He put a hand on Silvana's forehead. "This is your son. He needs you."

"Will he live?" Silvana grabbed the doctor's sleeve. "If there's something wrong with him I want to know now. I need to know he'll live . . ."

"The boy is well and so are you. All he needs is a good feed."

But Silvana wanted answers. She tried to push the child into the doctor's arms.

"I need to know he's healthy. My brothers died. It's in my family. Boys in my family . . . Please tell me if there's something wrong with him."

And then the baby opened his eyes. He unfurled his fists, moving them as though dragging them through water, a drifting movement like pondweed in a slow river. She put her finger against his palm and he closed his own fingers around it. She stroked his face, took off his swaddling clothes, and counted his tiny toes. She kissed the soft dip of his skull.

"My darling," she whispered, and was embarrassed by her outburst. How could she have been so crazy? It was obvious. Her life was always going to be about this child. In that room, with the day turning into evening, Silvana lifted the child to her breast and he started to suckle, surprising her with the strength of his grip. She didn't know how long she stayed like that, but when she looked up again, Janusz was standing beside her.

"Can I hold him?"

She held the baby out, though in her heart she was unwilling to give him up.

"So I have a son," said Janusz, his face full of surprise.

Silvana felt her body relax. Perhaps her mother's bad luck was not going to pass on to her. She'd done it. She had given birth to a healthy baby boy.

"Aurek," said Janusz, grinning. "We'll call him Aurek, after my father."

"Can I have him back?" she asked, and closed her eyes with pleasure as the weight of her child filled her arms once more.

Janusz

"Franek, why don't you go and catch us a chicken?" said Bruno, smacking at the boy's head with his army cap. "I'm starving."

"I might catch a goose or two," Franek said. "I could eat a bear, the way I feel."

"Don't touch the geese," said Janusz. "Leave them alone. A chicken will be fine."

Janusz had invited the two men to share a meal with him. He was still trying to make sense of how the weeks had passed so quickly since he had been at the cottage. He watched Franek lope outside and begin running around the yard after the chickens.

"What's wrong with him?"

"He's a child," said Bruno. "A child in a man's body. He joined up with his elder brother when he should have stayed at home. He wasn't bright enough to go to school, but he was good on the family farm. That's where he should have stayed. He's not a soldier. He did all right with us until the Russians came across the border. They just kept rolling past. Hundreds of them. We knew we couldn't fight them, but Franek went running up to one of them, yelling and shouting, telling them Poland would always be free. Nearly got himself killed. Tomasz—his brother—wanted to escape so he could take Franek home.

"We had a plan to get him back to his family. Tomasz and I were going to take him home and then join the underground movement. We were being marched to a camp when we ducked out and ran into woodland. Franek fell over. The boy's got two left feet. Down he goes and I stop running to help him.

"The Russian guards came after us. I was trying to get Franek up, but his ankle was twisted badly. The guards were coming closer, so

Tomasz turns around and goes back toward them, picking up rocks as he goes. He hurls them at the guards. Just stands there, aiming them while they open fire on him. I got Franek away, forced him to run. The boy won't talk about what happened. He's never mentioned Tomasz since."

In the yard, Franek was still chasing chickens. Finally, he caught one, lifted it high in the air and swung it, smashing its body against the water pump again and again. The chicken went limp and he dropped it on the ground. He stood over it, as if he thought it might just get up and run away. Bruno walked out into the yard and Janusz followed him. Franek had hit the bird so hard it was a bloody mess of feathers and smashed bones.

"Is it dead?" Franek asked.

Janusz kicked the bird gently with his foot. "Yes, it's dead."

"Do you want another one? I can catch us another one."

"You catch it," said Bruno, pulling a penknife from his pocket, "and then give it to me. I'll kill it."

Janusz saw the penknife glint in Bruno's thick hand. He saw the same flickering shine in Franek's eyes as he turned on the chickens once again. It made him feel afraid. The boy looked quite mad.

Janusz went into the cottage. He piled sticks in the hearth and set a fire. He could hear Franek shouting and yelling in the yard. The sooner he left for Warsaw, he decided, the better.

IPSWICH

The school is a large, redbrick building with a playground in front and black metal railings around it. Two entrances have heavy lintels over the blue doors with the words *girls* and *boys* carved into weathered limestone. Girls play hopscotch and skip and boys kick footballs or stand in secretive groups swapping cigarette cards.

Aurek clings to Silvana, sinking his fingers into her coat and wrapping his skinny legs around her so tightly she yelps in pain. His cheeks are flushed and his eyes plead with her, but Silvana knows she cannot help him. Janusz is firm on this matter. Aurek has to go to school.

"It's only for a month," Janusz tells them both. "Then the school will break up for the summer holidays. He's got to go sometime."

The first day, the teacher tries to prize Aurek out of Silvana's arms.

"He'll be absolutely fine," she says. "Come along with me, young man."

By the time the woman has him in her grip, her face is red and the veins on her skinny neck stand out blue and angry looking. Her voice is full of the strain of holding the boy. After a week of the same scenario, the teacher rolls her sleeves up as soon as they arrive, grabbing Aurek before he has a chance to wrap himself around Silvana.

"Just go," she snaps at Silvana. "The boy will be fine if you just go. It's always the mothers who are the problem, not the children."

Silvana leaves, her heart broken by the sound of Aurek's cries.

The second week, things are no better.

"Come on," she says, trying to sound sure of herself. "Please, Aurek? Let go now. We can't do this all the time."

"Nie."

"Please?"

The teacher comes out into the playground ringing the school bell, heaving it up and down in a two-handed grip as children flow past her.

"Good morning," she says putting the bell down and clenching her fists, like a farmer approaching a difficult calf, arms already tensed for a fight. "Still don't want to come to lessons, young man?"

Week after week, the other mothers act as if they have not noticed Aurek and his high-pitched screaming or the spectacle of Silvana and the teacher trying to hold on to the furious child. Silvana alternates between wanting to cry or take an angry bow in front of her audience. She and the boy might as well be starring in a theater show for the parents and children at the school; a tragedy—*Polish Mother Abandons Son*. Please bring cotton wool to plug your ears.

By midterm, she finally manages to find a way to change the one-act play. She gives Aurek her headscarf at the school gates, and if he has that to hold, he lets her walk away. It pains her to reveal her gray hair to the world, the unruly kinks and curls that are forming as it grows longer. But it is the only way.

She walks briskly, head up, back straight, past the other mothers. Ten agonizing minutes down the road, she stops, her heart racing, and runs back to the school, staring at the empty playground. She allows herself a few moments like this before she has to hurry across town to get to work, knowing already that she will be late.

Paris Fashions factory gates are high and wooden, held between two tall redbrick pillars. They are always shut, except when the lorries bring fabric and take clothes away. There is a door in one of the wooden gates that opens to let the women who work there come in and go out.

Silvana notices the other women chatting as they walk along the road to work, but they never talk to her. As they enter the factory gates, they all fall silent, concentrating on not bumping their heads on the frame of the small entrance or tripping over the wooden step; if anyone does, they become the first joke of the morning. Then the laughter, breaking the silence on either side of the big wooden gates, lasts until they are all sitting at the machines and the foreman walks among them, nodding approval as their sewing machines rattle into life and each woman watches her needle stitch a path through the day.

Several times now, Silvana has had to knock on the door and wait for the foreman to open it for her. He looks at his watch as if it is a filthy thing, and then at her as if she is responsible for its state, and her cheeks burn as she apologizes for her lateness, trying to seem as though she cares about the job.

She hunches over her machine and does her best to look industrious. Around her, the women's talk is easy and full of jokes and gossip about people she knows nothing about. Occasionally another woman tries to make conversation with Silvana, but she doesn't answer. She pretends to be having problems with the skirt band she is sewing, and hopes they will leave her alone. The work isn't too bad. She remembers how to sew. She'd made all her own clothes when she lived with her parents, but still, looking as if she is concentrating on something makes it easier to be left alone with her own thoughts.

Every day, she fights the desire to leave her work and take Aurek out of school. As she stitches she imagines the day with him: how they will stay in bed curled up for warmth in the mornings; how she will trace the narrow dip in the small of his neck and breathe the damp child smell behind his ear. She will tend the herbs she and Janusz have planted in the garden while Aurek plays until it is time for dinner, which they will prepare together, Aurek shaping dumplings and Silvana cutting potatoes.

Then she will tell Aurek stories. Stories about Pan Zagloba, the lackadaisical nobleman, and Jan Skrzetuski, the virtuous knight. Stories of aristocrats and beautiful maidens saved by bravery and courage from evil barons. Horses gallop through the stories, arrows are fired, wild boars caught, bears hunted. Now she is far from home, she tells him stories of her family, of her grandmother, and her childhood. She resurrects her brothers, giving them long lives and summers spent fishing in the lake and climbing trees, and reinvents her parents as loving, sober people.

Janusz never mentions his sisters or his family. She doesn't blame him. Not knowing where they are is a terrible thing. She wishes she could have given him some news of them. Janusz has told her he thinks they must be in Russia. As a functionary in local government, it is quite likely his father was arrested. More than that, Janusz will not say. And she doesn't push him. While Silvana tells stories of her childhood, Janusz prefers to read Aurek facts from the boys' annuals he buys him. *How fast does a bullet move? Why does iron go rusty? What are sun spots? How many stars are there?*

She is jolted from her dreams by the sound of the siren. The sewing machines stutter to a stop and Silvana joins the movement toward the doors.

"Miss?"

Silvana looks up to see the foreman looking at her.

"Can I have a word?"

His eyes are neutral, his expression slightly bored. He folds his arms and Silvana feels herself shrinking under his impassive glance.

"You think we make enough money here to pay you to daydream all day? I've got my eye on you. No more lateness and no more sitting idle. Understand?"

"Of course. I'm sorry. I'm very sorry. Do I still have my job?"

"Just about. Go on, and stop looking at me like that. I'm not a bleeding monster. Just make sure you do your work."

He steps aside and she dips her head to go through the wooden door, thankful that she has been given another chance. Bent over like that, for a moment she is reminded of Sunday church visits with Janusz's family. She instinctively lifts her hand to cross herself. She will work harder. No more daydreaming. She's so fired up by her convictions, she turns back and asks the foreman if she can stay behind and sew for a few more hours.

"Go home," he says, not unkindly. "Go on, get on with you."

"I don't want anyone looking at my son."

Janusz sighs. "It's just a doctor."

"There is no need to get other people involved," insists Silvana. "There is nothing wrong with Aurek."

Janusz will not be talked out of his decision. He explains they need to know how to stop the child fighting at school, how to stop him making odd noises and acting crazy. What he really wants to know is how to make the child love him.

When Janusz looks at Aurek it is as though he sees the boy through a curtain, a fine curtain that you cannot take hold of in your hands, a curtain like a fast falling flurry of snow that changes landscapes and blocks out all chance of understanding. He wants the doctor to show him how to see through it, how to bring the child into the light.

In his mind he sees a lively, chatty little English lad with his pockets full of cigarette cards, conkers, string, penknives, and homemade catapults. He wants a boy who asks him to explain how airplanes work and machines turn.

Somewhere behind that snowy, hemmed-in world Aurek inhabits is his real child. Of that Janusz is sure. A doctor will know what to do. Modern medicine will give Janusz back his son, and he will be able to teach him how to ride a bicycle and make model planes. They will play cricket together in the back garden and go to soccer matches.

Janusz and Silvana sit in a crowded waiting room with the child between them, surrounded by the sounds of legs crossing and uncrossing, magazine pages being turned, the wet gurgles and wails of babies, and the dry misery of hacking coughs and stifled sneezes. Janusz checks his watch.

"There is nothing wrong with him," insists Silvana.

"That's what I hope."

Aurek has started humming, a rumbling purr, like the drone of bees. Janusz tries to catch Silvana's eye, wanting her to stop the boy making that noise, but she is staring at the exit as if she is planning to escape at any moment.

Beside the door, a young woman sits, swinging her foot. Her tan stocking is darned at the ankle. She reminds him of Hélène. He can't help staring. The woman looks up from her magazine and their eyes meet. But she is nothing like Hélène. It is a mistake he makes all the time, seeing her in other women, tiny fragments of recognition in the brim of a hat, the movement of an ankle, a collar, the curve of a neck, a wave of the hand. It's a weakness in him that won't go away. A shameful hunger in him, like a man who has long ago stopped drinking but still dreams of the taste of vodka burning his lips.

Janusz can feel the woman's gaze shift to take in his wife and son beside him. She turns back to the magazine on her lap and he feels suddenly foolish. It is a relief when they are finally ushered into the doctor's office, a small, dark room lined with books in glass cabinets.

The doctor is a tall man with a stooped back and a head of thick gray hair. He moves methodically, steadily. Janusz has confidence in him. Like so many Englishmen of the middle classes, the doctor's clothes are shabby but still look expensive: a thick wool jacket wearing thin at the elbows, overwashed white cuffs, discreet gold cufflinks. Polished black leather shoes that shine like oil.

He is gentle with Aurek, approaching him slowly, spreading his hands as if to show he has nothing to hide. No sudden movements. Calm and steady.

Blood pressure, weight, height, head circumference, pulse.

Aurek, in his vest, nervous as a stray dog.

"Nothing wrong with him as such," says the doctor, taking off his stethoscope and laying it on his desk. He fishes in his pocket and pulls out a sweet. "There you are, young man. A barley sugar for your troubles. That's it; let your mother get you dressed again."

"Is it normal . . ." Janusz hesitates. He doesn't know how to say this. "Is it normal that he doesn't seem to know me?"

The doctor reaches for a pipe that lies on his desk and begins filling it with tobacco from a small leather pouch beside it. He glances up at Janusz.

"You've been apart for a long time. You and your wife can help him of course by showing him that you are happy together. That's important for the child's development. But, really, there's nothing terribly wrong with the boy."

"I say this," Silvana butts in. "I say this, but he won't listen."

Janusz coughs, shifts his weight from one foot to the other. "I just want to make sure the boy is all right."

The doctor lights his pipe, sucks on it, continues speaking.

"Your son is underweight and small for his age. He shows signs of having rickets; his chest, that knotted look to his sternum. But it's to be expected given his history. Unfortunately, we see this a lot at the moment."

"He hides food around the house." Janusz can hold back no longer. "He's not like other children. He pleases himself. Sometimes he talks quite normally. Other times he makes bird noises. What's wrong with him?"

"He's been through a war," says the doctor wearily. "Give him time, a secure home, proper food, and plenty of discipline and he'll be right as rain."

The doctor shakes Janusz by the hand and gives him a prescription for cod liver oil and malt extract.

"I suggest liquid paraffin for the lice. He's got quite an infestation. Leave it on his hair for thirty-six hours and take care to avoid him approaching any naked flames."

Silvana does not shake the doctor's hand. She holds Aurek tightly, guarding him in a way that makes Janusz think of the prisoners of war he has seen, the ones who fear their boots and coats will be stolen.

On the way home, Janusz tries to feel hopeful. There is nothing wrong with the boy. All he needs is a home and time to settle in. That sounds right. For all of them.

At break time, Aurek slips between the school railings, runs across the road, around the back of the cooperative dairy with its sign that says *milk* in giant glossy blue tiles, past a big house with broken glass in its windows, and stops at the main road. A policeman is walking toward him, and Aurek ducks into the garden of the empty house.

Through overgrown bushes where brown seeds stick to his clothes and weeds prickle his skin, he makes his way to the back of the derelict house. Nobody will look for him here. All he wants is to be left alone. To be allowed to wander through the easy hours of the day and sleep through the dark nights curled up against his mother.

Climbing through a window, he drops into the gloom of a large room. Cupboards full of dust and dirt stand with doors hanging from their hinges. He kicks at layers of bird droppings and old leaves to reveal a red-tiled floor. A pigeon flaps across the room and out of the window.

This is a forgotten place. He'd like to live in this house. Just him and his mother. No separate bedrooms. They stayed in a house once, a cottage in the woods. He wanders through the dim rooms, scraping lacy cauls of pale mold from damp walls. Stopping at the kitchen he finds a tall wall cupboard, its doors long since fallen off. He climbs inside, settling himself among the dust and pigeon mess.

He takes his wooden rattle from his schoolbag and sets it down beside him. He knows it's a stupid baby toy and not for a boy his age, but his mother says the rattle is full of Polish magic. It was carved from magic wood. He is sure she is wrong, but still, he is careful with it. Just in case.

He stares at his hand-me-down shoes and reties one. They are a size too big and his narrow feet slip around in someone else's footsteps. Aurek kicks at the wall, scuffing his shoe over and over. Birds fly in and out of the house and he listens to the applause of their wings, their rumbling coo. It's a lovely sound. Peaceful. There are no other children to call him names. No adults to force him to sit up straight and write his letters.

His voice starts as a vibration in his throat, like a kitten purring. He cocks his head to one side, trying out different notes, a musician tuning up. When he has the right tune, the same lilt and fall in the song as the birds roosting above him, he opens his mouth and raises his voice. The house echoes with the sound of pigeons.

When the day begins to fade, Aurek sees a man standing in the doorway of the old house, like a black shadow. The enemy has found him.

"Aurek?" says the enemy quietly. "Come with me, son. It's time to go home."

Aurek climbs out of the cupboard and follows him through the leaves and broken tiles out into the street with his hands in the air, surrendering. He's not going to admit it but he's glad they are going home because he can feel the failing heat in the hedges and pavements and smell the night descending. Aurek is afraid of the dark. He likes to close his eyes to it and keep them closed until dawn.

He picks up a stick and holds it like a gun, shooting at windows and doors. He presses it close to his side, then swings around and shoots people in the back as they pass. Sticking his head around the door of a pub, he sprays machine-gun fire into the half-empty saloon bar. A boy about the same age, sitting at a table, stares straight at him. He has a face full of brown freckles, cheeks the color of bacon.

The boy gives him a grin, nods his head, folds his fleshy chin into his solid neck. Aurek shoots him dead. A bullet to the heart. The boy gives a thumbs up and falls off his chair in a swoon, clutching his hand to his chest. Aurek is transfixed. Then the barman is shouting at him to clear off and Aurek runs ahead, waving his stick in the air the way soldiers do when they want to move people quickly. By the time he gets home, Aurek has killed everybody.

He sits at the kitchen table eating bread and drippings, and Janusz breaks his stick gun into pieces.

"No more war games," he says. "I don't like you playing like that."

Aurek thinks it's a useless thing to break his twig gun. He knows there are enough sticks and twigs in the world for him to make guns out of until he's an old, old man. Surely the enemy knows that too?

POLAND

Silvana

"Do you have to go?" asked Silvana. She was sitting on the only chair they owned, nursing Aurek, stroking his soft baby curls, idly marveling at his plump cheeks and long lashes. The boy was fourteen months old and never stopped smiling.

Janusz shrugged.

"My father says it's inevitable."

Silvana shifted Aurek on her knee. This conversation had been going back and forth between them for a week now.

"But what will we do?" she asked.

"You'll stay with my parents."

"And if I don't want to?"

"Then go to *your* parents," he said. "Whatever happens, you can't stay in Warsaw. It won't be safe."

The day he left, heading for the railway station to sign up as a soldier, Silvana stood on the kitchen table and looked out through the skylight, hoping to catch a glimpse of him walking across the park. She wanted to see him joining the other soldiers going to fight for their country, but she saw only crowds of people walking in the sunshine as though it was just another summer day in the city. She got down from the table and felt a weight in her stomach. A greasy block of fear. She was alone. She realized she should have made more of an effort to make friends. The truth was she knew no one in Warsaw. Janusz and Aurek had been her only life. And now Janusz was gone.

In the weeks that followed, the summer heat gave way to storms and the German soldiers arrived, marching in time in the pouring rain, motoring down the shopping streets and boulevards of Warsaw, bringing a cargo of terror that hit the city, tearing up buildings, raging through the streets. Silvana was too scared to risk taking her son outside, and too scared to leave him alone in the flat. She sat huddled by the stove. She received a letter from Janusz's mother telling her to hurry up and come home. They were worried for her safety. She heard nothing from her own parents.

Curfews were announced. German trucks with loudspeaker systems trundled through the streets, blasting out orders, telling people to stay inside. The trams stopped running. People were not allowed to gather in groups of more than three. The sound of gunshots woke her in the night. Silvana's days passed in a blur, sleeping, sitting by the stove, playing with Aurek, trying to summon up the courage to leave the flat and find a way out of the city back to Janusz's parents.

When the coal ran out, she went downstairs and sat in the hallways of the first-floor flats. They had radiators that worked and it was warmer there. Many people had left and the building felt empty. The Kowalskis, the couple who had taken her into their flat when she gave birth to Aurek, had stayed. They had become new Germans, *Volksdeutsche*, with red linen bands on their sleeves embroidered with a black swastika, and refused to talk to her now, acting as if she were not there when they passed her in the corridors.

Silvana was sitting on a radiator when she saw a family from one of the ground-floor flats leaving. A man and a woman with a little girl. The man carried two suitcases, the woman another. That's how she knew they weren't coming back.

They left the door open and she slipped inside. In the kitchen she found stale bread, a few potatoes, and some onions. There was a little coal left, so she lit the stove and made soup. She wandered through the flat. It was like stepping into a magazine picture. The piano, black wood with a shine that reflected her face in it, was covered in a pale orange silk shawl with long, delicate fringing. Silvana pressed the keys. The notes rang clearly and Aurek stirred in his baby carriage.

She stayed there a week, wandering through the empty rooms.

She dusted the ornaments and swept the richly patterned carpets. At least if someone did come, they would see she'd cared for the place. Each day she bundled up her son and went out, trying to get a bus out of the city. Each day she queued for hours and then came back to the flat again.

She was asleep in the master bedroom when soldiers came. A hand grabbed her arm and she was jerked up onto her feet.

"You shouldn't be here," said an officer, stepping through the group of soldiers. "These flats are for German citizens only."

He told the other men to leave and then, taking off his leather coat, walked around examining pictures and ornaments.

"These are nice," he said, lifting a brass candlestick from the marble mantelpiece. Silvana shrugged. It wasn't her candlestick. He could have it. He could have anything he wanted. He looked at Aurek who was sitting on the rug playing with his rattle, and she felt suddenly afraid.

"I am going to be living here," he said. "I'll need a maid. You'll have to find somebody to take the child."

He put his hands on her shoulders. "You're a pretty girl. It's very simple. If you have the right papers you can become German. It would be better for you. You can stay in Warsaw that way. You don't want to be sent to Germany to work on a farm. A city girl like you? No. Of course not. That's it. Give me a smile. I can help you."

She lay down like he told her to and hoped her obedience would save her. She would not be difficult. She would be anonymous, not interesting enough to remember and too compliant to be worth hurting. And all this decided in the time he took to unbutton her dress.

His clothes smelled of the rain. Her face was pressed against the pillows and she twisted her neck so that she could watch the curtains at the window. They were patterned with dancing children holding hands. The hem was yellowed and dirty where it touched the floor. They needed washing. Finally he rolled off her.

"Good girl," he said, panting heavily.

He straightened his uniform, picked up his coat and left, telling her he'd be back later with the right papers for her.

Silvana washed herself in the bathroom, splay-legged in the bath, wiping herself dry on her dress. In the master bedroom she found a skirt and a blouse, some stockings, underwear, and a fur coat: gingery fox with a brown silk lining. At the bottom of the cupboard were a pair of blue leather shoes with a bow at the ankle and tapered heels.

It was dark in her old flat. In a suitcase she packed baby clothes and put her album of film stars on top. She opened the cupboard in the kitchen and took their savings from it. Janusz had withdrawn their money from the bank in August.

"It's all right," she told Aurek, swaddling him in a blanket. "We'll be all right. Your daddy will come home soon."

But Janusz had deserted her. That's what she really felt. He had left her and this had happened. She wiped her eyes on her sleeve, told herself to stop sniveling. She washed her face and dried it, put on some lipstick, and tidied her hair.

It took hours to walk through the city. Everywhere, the windows of buildings were shattered and roads were blocked. Silvana walked to the banks of the river. She could still feel the soldier, the sticky itch on her thighs, the bruised rush of him inside her, the shame of it. She stood looking at the swiftly moving water. It would be so simple to let that water carry her away.

She stumbled on in the stolen high heels and arrived at the bus terminal.

"There are no buses heading north today," said the guard when she asked.

"I have money," she told him. "I can pay. It's only me and my son. I have to get to my parents-in-law."

"I can't work miracles," said the man, eyeing the banknotes in her outstretched hand.

He found her standing room on an overcrowded bus. Yelling at the other passengers to move down and make room for one more, he took her money and wished her luck. The bus was going the wrong way, heading east, but Silvana didn't care. Janusz was gone. Her home was gone. All she had was her son, another woman's clothes, and a strong desire to leave the city.

The bus passed through wooded countryside and villages, market towns and open fields. When it broke down, Silvana hitched a ride on the back of a cart. She found another bus. When that ran out of fuel, she got off and walked.

On the road ahead stretched a long line of people with handcarts and farm carts loaded with mattresses, pulled by horses. Silent women pushed perambulators, bicycles weaving through them all, avoiding the crush of the slow-footed crowds.

Silvana swapped the high heels for a pair of wooden clogs and walked for days. She had no idea where she was going, but then nobody else seemed to either. Aurek howled at the wind and dribbled miserably. Around his lips an angry red scab appeared, worsening every day. He caught a cold. Green snot bubbled in his nose and he was hot to the touch. Nothing she did could make him happy. When a woman walking beside her offered to nurse him for her, she only hesitated for a moment before she took off her fur coat, wrapped him in it, and handed him over, glad of the rest.

A storm had been gathering in the skies all afternoon and a biting east wind began to blow. Silvana looked up to see a black cloud to the west. It moved fast and began spreading out, rushing forward like spilled ink, covering the sky, shutting down the daylight in minutes. The first splatter of rain fell, icy and needle sharp. With a crash of thunder the storm was over them.

Silvana was soaked through in moments. She looked around for the woman carrying Aurek, but she was nowhere to be seen.

Over the sound of the whistling wind and the rain came another sound. It grew louder until it became a deafening drone. Silvana turned her face toward it. A low-flying formation of planes cut through the sky, their undercarriages gleaming.

Silvana swung around in panic, calling for her son. How could she have given him to another woman? How could she have been so stupid? People were dragging children down from the carts they were traveling on. Men and women ran through the rain. Horses were driven off the road into the fields, heading for the trees.

Then she saw her. The woman with Aurek. She was crossing the road toward the fields. The hum of the planes grew louder. The air changed and a gust rushed over her. Silvana began to run toward the woman. She heard the sound of screaming and the crash of thunder, smelled something burning. Looking up, she saw one of the planes spiraling in a high-pitched dive. Then there was only a great heat like a furnace door being opened, and she fell.

She opened her eyes and felt a shooting pain in her leg. Her hands were cut and bloody, and her ankle had a deep wound in it. The storm had passed over and the water lying in puddles all around gleamed darkly. Silvana stumbled over the bodies of women and children and fallen horses. She was barefoot, and slipped and fell in a pool of blood slicked like oil across the road. On hands and knees she crawled. She pulled herself to her feet and searched for Aurek, offering up her life to any number of saints if she could just find the woman who had her boy.

Her mother's words were in her head. *Just don't love the baby too much. You don't know what it's like to love someone and lose them.* For the first time she understood. And she grieved for her. She grieved for her mother terribly.

She saw the coat first, the orange fur up ahead of her, like a wounded animal in the mud. The woman lay beside it, her legs twisted, as though she had jumped from a height and landed badly. Silvana touched the coat. It was sticky with blood. Her heart leapt, thudded and slowed as she opened the coat.

"My baby," she whispered. He was lying in the coat's silk lining, his face quite calm.

Janusz

"Come with us," said Bruno, and Janusz shook his head.

They were sitting at the kitchen table in the cottage.

"You can't stay here. The Russians will pick you up. The government wants all Polish troops to resist. We can make our way to France. I've got money. If we can get to Budapest without being picked up, the Polish consul there will arrange a passage to Marseilles and we can join the French and the British. Come with us."

Earlier, Bruno had picked up the basket of potatoes under the windowsill and proclaimed himself the cook. Franek had plucked the chickens and Janusz had got water from the well. Now they had eaten and were sharing the remains of a bottle of vodka Bruno had produced from his rucksack.

The two men had been curious about what Janusz was doing in the cottage on his own. They'd asked so many questions he found himself telling them the truth just to get them to be quiet.

"Dog!" said Franek. He laughed, slapped his knees, and spat on the floor. "You said you were burying a dog! I knew you were lying. I knew it. You're a deserter."

Janusz glared at him. "You weren't there."

"You did the right thing," said Bruno. "You'd only be in a prison camp by now if you had stayed on the train. You can still fight. That's what we have to do. We Poles have always fought for our freedom."

"Fight or run away. You'll end up dead either way," said Franek. "That's the way things are now. You might have the angel of death riding on your shoulder. You look like you have. You're going to be called soon enough."

Janusz ignored him. They were sitting back after their meal, the heat of the fire on their faces, an oil lamp burning on the table.

"I don't care," said Franek, belching loudly. "Eat, drink, and loosen your belt. Nothing better. Who knows when we'll be able to again, hey, Bruno?"

Bruno picked through the remains of the chicken. "We'll fight for our country and when we come back, we'll go to my house in Toruń. I was the manager of a soap factory and I have a large house. We'll drink Polish vodka until we fall down dead drunk. Then we'll wake up and do it again. Of course, that's if the looters haven't stolen everything. The crime rate in the city has gone up crazily this summer. I can only imagine it's worse in Warsaw?"

"There were stories in the papers," said Janusz. His head was throbbing and his throat felt dry. Sleep was weighing down his eyes.

"Thieves like wartime," said Bruno. He finished the last drops of vodka in the bottle and threw it on the floor. "All of them: Polish thieves, Jews, Lithuanians, Russians, Germans, Slovakians. They're all at it. Don't believe the newspapers who talk of our brave people working against the Germans. There are spies and criminals who are profiting from this war already."

"I've never been to France," said Franek. He was cleaning his fingernails with the blade of his pocketknife. "I'd never been out of my village before I joined up. What about you, Janusz?"

Janusz looked at the fire burning in the hearth. "I have to get back to Warsaw. I have to see my wife."

"Be my guest." Franek waved his knife in the air. "Warsaw is in that direction. Just follow the German tanks and the guns. Nice knowing you, dead man."

Bruno wiped his hands clean on his trousers. "The best you can do is get out of Poland. There are truckloads of men heading to Romania and Hungary. Come with us while you can. The borders are still easy enough to cross, but they won't stay that way for long."

Janusz stood up. He didn't feel like having this conversation. "I'll get some logs in. It's cold tonight."

He stepped outside and felt the night air clear his head. He trudged across the yard. Out there, under the starless night with the damp smell of vegetation, it was possible to believe that the men sitting in the cottage were just figments of his imagination. They'd leave tomorrow and it would be as if he had never met them. And then he'd go home. He began to pile logs into his arms. Footsteps came across the yard and he stopped, peering into the blackness. Bruno stepped toward him, smelling of chicken fat and woodsmoke.

"I thought I'd give you a hand. What I was saying inside earlier? I meant it. I can't get to France with Franek on my own. I need someone with me who's got his head screwed on right. You can't stay here. Franek's right about you being judged as a deserter . . ."

"I got separated from my unit."

"And then you hid up here. I've seen what happens to deserters. Nobody knows what the hell is going on anymore. People are scared. They don't know who to trust. I saw an execution just days ago. A lad in civilian clothes wearing military boots. He was picked up by a lieutenant. He was made to stand in the middle of the road as the troops went past. The lieutenant said deserting was a sign of cowardice. Then the crazy bastard shot him. There was no court-martial, nothing. The lad had military boots and civilian clothes and that was enough. There are army units marching all over the country. If they find you here . . ."

Janusz picked up a log and balanced it with the others in his arms. "I'm not a deserter."

"That's for them to judge. Come with us. I've got money. Enough to get us to France."

Janusz didn't want to ask how Bruno had got his money. He thought it would be better not to know. As he straightened up he saw a flash in the darkness.

"There's a light. Over there."

A soft yellow beam moved through the trees. The sound of an engine echoed in the distance.

"It's a motorbike," said Bruno. "It must be about a kilometer away. There are troops nearby."

"Polish?"

"Russians, I'd have thought. There it is again. Look, you can stay here and get picked up by them. Or come with us."

"You make it sound like I don't have a choice."

"You don't."

Franek opened the door to the cottage, holding up the oil lamp. "What are you two doing? This fire's nearly dead. I'm freezing in here."

The lamplight twinkled in the dark. Janusz dropped the logs and ran toward him. "Put the light out."

"Get your boots, Franek," said Bruno, coming up behind him. "We're leaving. Hurry."

Janusz stepped inside the cottage behind Franek, and Bruno shut the door. Just before he cut the oil lamp, he caught a glimpse of Bruno and Franek pulling on their boots and coats: an overweight man who was surely too old to fight and a scared jackrabbit of a boy. Bruno touched his shoulder.

"So? Are you coming with us? Will you come to France?"

Janusz nodded. He saw the reality of the situation. If he was captured as a deserter he might be killed. If he managed to get to Warsaw, he'd be taken prisoner.

"Well?" said Bruno.

"I'm coming."

He would go with these men and fight for his country. He pulled on his coat and stepped out into the night.

IPSWICH

Janusz goes into the kitchen, opens the pantry door, and takes out a wooden box filled with shoe polishes, boot brushes, and soft cloths. He glances out of the window. Silvana is in the garden, Aurek prancing behind her like a shadow.

Pushing a hand through the brushes and cloths, he pulls out a bundle of letters. He picks through them carefully. The first letter Hélène wrote him. That's the one he wants to read again, although he knows every word by heart. Written on thin blue paper, her handwriting is spidery, as if she rushed to get the words on the page. Accented and punctuated with a leaking ink pen, her letters have the look of handwritten bars of music.

The words are hopeful and plain, simple as only love letters can be. She has covered the page on both sides with her inky thoughts, and Janusz reads, his fingers tracing her words. He is on a farm in the hills behind Marseilles. The stone buildings around him are solid and glow honey-colored in the sunlight. Hélène stands in the distance waving to him and begins to walk toward him. He wills her to come closer, but he can't do it. His imagination always keeps her at a distance.

Janusz looks up to see Silvana coming across the garden. A piece of hair has escaped from under her headscarf and Janusz stares at it, watching it coil over her forehead like a small gray question mark. He hurries to put the letters back and replaces the box in the pantry, his movements quick and furtive.

"The washing will never dry in this weather," says Silvana, opening the back door. "Does it always rain like this in summer?"

She dumps the basket of clothes on the kitchen table. Aurek trails in behind her, and she closes the door after him.

"Here," says Janusz. "Give them to me. I'll light the fire and we can dry the clothes that way."

He reaches out and as she picks up the basket to hand it to him, he feels the brush of her hand against his. The thought of the letters hidden in the pantry burns him like a flame, and the worst of it is that he knows he cannot be without them. As long as he has the letters, he still has Hélène. The sound of her voice, the pattern of her thoughts, the touch of her fingers in the folds creased into the blue papers.

"Are you all right?" Silvana looks at him, her face full of concern.

He drops the washing basket and pulls her to him, folding her thin shoulders into his hands. The weight of her head against him feels heavy, obedient, as she bends to his insistent embrace.

"Sorry," he whispers. "I'm so sorry."

"So am I," she says, wrapping her arms around him so he feels her gather him in.

He wants to love this troubled wife of his. She stands in a heap of wet clothes, holding him up, when it is he who should be strong for her. It is all he can do to stop himself from telling her he still loves Hélène, as if confiding in Silvana would release him from the pain he feels. The only person he could imagine telling is the one person who must never know.

He lets her go and picks up the washing.

"Do you want tea?" she asks.

"Yes," he replies. "A cup of tea. That's what we need."

He looks up and meets her eyes. "It's hard to know how to go on." He searches for words, a way to explain how he needs her to make sense of his life. He can understand nothing of the last six years. All that happened, the way he left Warsaw and didn't go back, the love he feels for another woman, the war and all its bloody awfulness; all of it is a jumble of jigsaw pieces and he never knows which he will pick up.

All the time, he was hoping for peace; now it's here, he's like a man coming up to the light after years of living underground. It should be wonderful, but it's not. He keeps pretending everything is all right, but the truth is his son hates him, his wife cries every night, and he still dreams of the woman he left.

"You and me," he says. "It's like we've been given a chance to get something right, but after the years we've spent apart I don't know how to do it."

"We're a family," Silvana says, as if this fact alone will see them through. "You're Aurek's father."

He glances at the boy crouched behind his mother. Janusz's heart feels as heavy as the wet washing he has scooped up off the floor.

"What happened?" he asks. "Why did you hide in a forest with the boy? Why did you do that?"

Silvana bends to help him pick up the clothes. "You know what happened. Why must you ask again and again? I tried to get to your parents' house, but the bus I was on broke down. I was afraid I would be picked up by soldiers and sent to work on a German farm. Lots of women were. I didn't want anybody taking Aurek from me. When the bus broke down I joined a queue of people and followed some of them into the forest, where we hid. Then the war ended, we were in a camp and you found us."

She hands him a damp towel and asks him again if he would like tea.

"Yes," he says. "A cup of tea."

There must be more than that to the story. Something terrible happened to the two of them, that much he knows.

"Aurek," he says. "Go to your room. I need to talk to your mother."

The boy slinks past him and Janusz shuts the kitchen door.

"Tell me what happened to you during the war. I just . . . Sometimes I look at Aurek and I wonder if he's the child I left behind."

Her eyes darken with tears. "He's been through a war. Can't you understand that?"

Maybe he is wrong to let things go like this, but Janusz lets the conversation end. He apologizes. He takes three cups out of the cupboard, puts them on the kitchen table, and calls Aurek back.

"There you are," he says as the boy comes into the room. "Come and have a cup of tea with us. You like lots of milk, don't you?"

Aurek takes a seat at the table, elbows splayed, his head in his hands. The child has no manners whatsoever. Silvana catches hold of him and kisses the top of his head. It's a fierce action and full of ownership, like a cat might grab a kitten.

Janusz's mother would never have let him sit like that as a child. He has a sudden image of his parents' dining room, the table set for lunch with all the best silverware and he and his sisters sitting straight-backed in their chairs. The strained formality of his own upbringing. He looks around the room, at the shabby curtains, the kettle boiling on the gas ring, Silvana holding the teapot, waiting, just as he taught her. Bring the pot to the kettle, not the other way around. He sighs. Let the boy sprawl.

"Give Aurek an extra spoonful of sugar," he tells Silvana as she pours the tea. He smiles at his son. "And a biscuit if we've got any."

The best day of the week is Sunday. That's when the family has breakfast together in the kitchen: bread, tea, milk, a boiled egg each.

Silvana and Aurek finish the remains of a pint of yellow, soured milk. She and the boy drink lustily, as if the curdled liquid is still fresh and creamy. Thank God there is no one else to see this display of poverty. And yet it makes Janusz want to care for them, to protect them like fragile plants from hard winters. He picks up the newspaper, a pen in his hand, a battered Polish–English dictionary at his side.

Silvana and Aurek have a map spread out on the table.

"Look," says Silvana, putting her finger on a green area outside the town. "There's a forest. A real forest. Can we go there?"

Janusz puts the paper down. "What's wrong with the park? We can go for a walk in the park this afternoon and Aurek can meet other children and make a few friends."

Aurek is leaning against his mother's arm, and Janusz feels an urge to pull them apart.

"Or we could walk along the canal. Surely that's a better idea? Come here, Aurek. Come and sit with me. Leave your mother alone for a minute."

Aurek doesn't move and Janusz lifts his newspaper to his face, pretending to read. He lowers it again. "What would we do in the woods? People walk their dogs there. We don't have a dog. We'd look strange just walking around. In the park, people walk with and without dogs."

Silvana draws circles on the tabletop with her fingers. Aurek is eating the stale bread Janusz put to one side to feed the ducks in the park. The child looks strangely beautiful, his small upturned nose, his neat mouth. Janusz would like to take his dainty chin between finger and thumb. He tries to meet the boy's gaze, fails, and sighs.

"If you really wanted to, we'd have to get a bus out to the paper mill and walk the rest of the way. It's up to you."

Aurek grins. A wide, urchin grin that fills Janusz with a swift and sudden joy.

Well, he thinks. *At least I can make the boy happy. That's a start.*

They catch the bus at the bottom of the hill and Aurek sits by the window watching the town, the rows of houses, the shops, the narrow streets, and the men and women, mechanical people who walk at the same pace. Aurek can see into the windows of terraced houses. A woman ironing. A man staring straight ahead. Front parlors full of old people and crying babies. What must it be like to be one of the children living here? To have always had a house to live in and a family sardined into it, full of brothers and sisters and aunts and uncles?

He imagines the noise: the yelling and the banging, the laughing, the lung-pumping cries, thumping of feet, plates, doors. These are the sounds he hears when front doors are ajar and he dares to pause in front of them. His own home is quiet in comparison. Nobody makes a noise there. The enemy says he likes peace. His mother never says much to anyone.

The bus finally arrives at Papermill Lane. They get out beside the mill and are met by the sound of water churning under a small bridge. The enemy is smiling at him. He shows Aurek how to drop sticks over one side and watch the current take them under the bridge, emerging on the other side. It's a game he could play for days if they let him. In the swirling water below them he can see green algae swaying over pebbles and rocks, all smooth and long and full of crystal air bubbles.

Aurek's stick is bent in two. The bark is dark and the snap in the stick shows the new wood as pale as bone within it, sharp against his fingertips.

"It's so you know it's yours," says Janusz. "Ready?"

The three of them stand with their sticks held out over the bridge.

"One, two, three, go!"

Aurek lets go with his eyes screwed shut, hope boiling up in his body. The stick disappears and then comes under the bridge in front of the others. When he wins, he screams with joy.

Silvana and Janusz join in, laughing. The more Silvana laughs, the more Aurek likes it. Her laughter is warm and safe, like the days in the forest when she used to wrap him in her coat. The game is so much fun, Silvana has to drag him away from it, promising him trees to climb, squirrels to find.

Grudgingly, he leaves his stick glories and they walk along country lanes, cutting across fields toward the trees. Aurek throws his cap off his head and runs, tumbling through brambles and nettles, splashing through puddles and jumping over fallen trees, screaming with excitement.

Nobody can catch him. No evil spirits or wood sprites or any of the revenging fairies and ghouls that live in ancient forests can touch him. He moves faster than sticks in a river current. He is freewheeling away from everything. Away from school, where the children call him a dirty refugee. *A crazy Polack. The dumb boy.* He is faster than them all and doesn't need anyone to teach him. He can do it himself.

Aurek taught himself to whistle, to swim, to catch and skin rabbits.

He can climb any tree. He can build a fire, kill snakes, and the stars are his compass. Nobody can touch him. He's a child of the woods.

Bright with energy, Aurek whoops and hollers, slipping and falling and scrambling to his feet. A cock pheasant rises in front of him, a brilliant sheen of red and gold, and Aurek lifts his arms like wings, sure he can follow the bird in its ungainly flight toward the sky.

Behind him, his parents stand side by side; his father holding his hat in his hands, his mother with an armful of wildflowers. They seem lost. Like two people trying to remember the way home. But Aurek cannot stop to help them. He chases through the woods away from them, faster and faster. Further into the trees. He windmills his arms backward trying to slow himself down, but his legs are too strong. Nothing can stop them. If he knew where he was going, he'd direct his runaway legs and get there. But he doesn't. He only knows that he cannot stop running.

Janusz takes Aurek to school on Monday morning. Aurek says good morning to his teacher and lifts his cap just like Janusz has told him to.

"Good lad," says Janusz. "Don't get into any fights today, hey? You be a good boy and make some friends."

"*Las?*"

"Speak English, Aurek. But yes, we can go to the woods again. You've only a week left at school and then you'll be on holiday and we can do lots of things together."

Aurek watches the enemy walking away. When he is gone, he follows the other children walking into class and at the last minute ducks around the side of the school and hides in the boys' toilets, a cramped cold place where nobody will find him. He curls up against the brick wall watching a spiderweb flap gently in a draft. It's nice and quiet.

The door to the toilets bangs open and Aurek jumps.

A fat boy stares at him.

"You'll be for it if Mrs. West finds you in here."

He lumps down beside Aurek and offers him a wheel of licorice.

"Do you speak English?"

Aurek nods. He picked up English from the soldiers in the refugee camp before he and his mother took the boat. His knowledge of English swearwords is comprehensive. He tries out a few and the boy laughs and slaps his leg.

"Don't let the teacher hear you talking like that. So what's your name? I'm Peter."

Aurek looks at him. He's seen this boy before. In the pub. It's the boy who fell down dead.

The licorice tastes sweet. Aurek pushes it all into his mouth and chews, black spittle dribbling pleasantly down his chin.

The fat boy laughs. "My old man has a pet shop. We have loads of animals. I've got a dog that catches rabbits. He killed somebody's cat once. A ginger tom. Ate it, guts and all, and then sicked it up over my grandma's carpet. The fur changed color when the dog sicked it up. It came out brown."

"Shouldn't eat the guts," says Aurek. "They're bad. That's why your dog was sick."

"How do you know? Have you eaten cat?"

Aurek shrugs. "Maybe."

"What does it taste like?"

"A bit like chicken."

Peter's eyes widen.

"Do you want to bunk off school? We could go to the park and chase ducks around the lake."

Aurek and Peter slip through the railings at the back of the school. They run through the streets, hiding behind cars, and sidestepping into alleys until they reach the park.

The lake is at the bottom of a green hill. Aurek runs down the hill and skids out into the water. He stands knee-deep in it, his legs turning purple with cold.

"Do you want to play war games?" Peter asks. He picks up a stone and throws it at Aurek.

"Kill the Nazis!"

Chop them down, thinks Aurek. He slices a hand through the air and steps out into the lake. Peter is laughing, throwing more stones at him. A stone hits him on the shoulder. Then another flies past his head and Aurek stumbles, wishing he had stones to throw. He steps back and his feet float as he searches for the ground beneath him. Slipping sideways, the lake claims him, the cold water grabbing at his heart, shrinking his lungs.

Everything feels heavy. He thrashes with his arms, face upward, trying to swim but he just keeps sinking. Then hands are pulling him to the surface and Aurek is gasping and coughing and his lungs are on fire. Peter is beside him, pulling on his shoulders so that they both tumble over and over as they crawl their way back to the edge.

"Somebody threw a baby in the lake last year," says Peter.

They are under a tarpaulin in the boat shed by the lake. "Divers came and got it out. It was wrapped in weeds and the fish had eaten its fingers. It was covered in blood and its face was all mush."

Aurek wraps the tarpaulin closer around himself. He's not impressed with Peter's stories. He could tell far worse ones. He wonders if Peter knows about *rusalkas*, the ghost women who live in lakes or hide in trees and pull men to their deaths.

"I don't reckon it's time to go home yet," says Peter. "I can't go too early. My old man would know something's up. Have you got a mother?"

Aurek frowns. What kind of question is that?

"My mum's dead," says Peter. "She had a wasting disease. I'll probably get it when I'm older. I'm weak. What did your dad do in the war?"

Aurek considers. He doesn't know, and anyway, he is trying to work out how Peter lives without a mother.

"My dad was a spy for British intelligence," says Peter. "He's got medals and all. I lived with Gran and Grandad while he was away and I couldn't tell anybody where he was. Everybody's dad went away. Lizzie Crookshank's died and her mum went mental. Lizzie's in an orphanage and wets the bed every night. My gran says Lizzie'll go mental too, one day. You don't remember me, do you? You shot me. In the pub. I fell off my chair."

"I remember," says Aurek, but Peter isn't listening. He's holding his hand out like a gun, shooting off imaginery rounds into Aurek's chest.

"So," he says, when he's shot Aurek for long enough. "Shall we go to your house, dumb boy?"

They run through the park, their faces shiny red with cold. Aurek's throat is still burning and he has a headache, but he feels happy running alongside this other boy. *Friend*, he whispers to himself, trying out the word. That's what the enemy said he should have. *A friend*.

Silvana is in the road looking for Aurek. When she went to pick him up from school today the teacher told her that he and another boy had played truant. Janusz will be furious when he finds out. And who is the other boy?

She sees Aurek coming up the hill and runs to meet him, hugging him to her, kissing him, the relief of finding him overshadowing her anxiety. He is safe. That's all that matters.

The other boy is short and square. It surprises her to see such plumpness. It is rare to see a child that looks so well fed. Perhaps he is a farmer's child. Doris says the Suffolk farmers are the only ones not to have suffered from rationing; that they fill themselves up on eggs and pies and home-cured hams and sausages. Yes, that's it. He is a peasant's child. A prosperous peasant's son, and his family will be furious when they find him here with Aurek.

"Your teacher says you were not at school," Silvana tells Aurek. "She says she will get the police next time. The police!" She shakes him by the shoulders. "Do you want them to take you away from me? And you bring another boy with you. What will his parents say? What will your father say? Come in and get out of those wet clothes and get by the fire. You look frozen. Go on. Hurry up."

"What did she say?" Peter whispers to Aurek.

"We have to go in."

"Yes," snaps Silvana. "Yes. In. Go!"

In the front parlor, Silvana undresses Aurek and asks the other boy his name.

"Peter Benetoni."

"In Polish, you are called Piotr. But because you are a boy and not a man we say Piotrek." She pauses. He is not listening to her. He's looking at Aurek as if they are sharing a private joke, laughing at her accent.

"You too," she says to Peter, more sharply than she means to. "You take your clothes off. They are soaking wet."

She hands him a towel and leaves the room, coming back with dry clothes when she thinks enough time has elapsed for the fat, sniggering boy to undress and dry himself.

She is helping Aurek into his pullover when somebody knocks at the door.

"If that's my dad," says Peter, "he's going to kill me."

"Nobody will kill you," says Silvana. "I will talk to him. Tell him you boys made a mistake."

She stands in the hallway, the shape of a man darkening the colored glass pane in the door. She ties her headscarf tight and opens the door, preparing words in her head. She will explain that the boys meant no harm.

"Good afternoon," the man says, lifting his hat. "I am Peter's father. Mr. Benetoni."

Silvana forgets her words. Something in the man's smile makes her forget to speak. Everything about him, from his polished shoes to his trilby hat and even his thick head of hair, shines like something brand-new. If the price labels were still attached to his clothes she wouldn't be surprised at all.

She realizes she is staring like an idiot and looks quickly at the ground, as if she has dropped something. His shoes are brown leather lace-ups. Elegant shoes. They must be handmade. Her eyes take in the

turnups of his sharply creased trousers. The man is the newest-looking
thing she's seen in years.

"I'm Peter's father," he says, extending his hand to her.

They shake hands and still she doesn't look up because she's blush-
ing now. His hand is wide and fleshy and he encloses her own small
fingers gently, the way you would hold a small bird.

"He is here, isn't he, Peter?"

"Yes," she says, trying to pull herself together. "Yes, he is here."

She invites him inside and he fills the hallway. He looks well fed like
his son, a double chin framing a large-nosed face and bright, concerned
eyes. He has dark curls that glisten with hair oil. This is not a peasant
farmer. Not at all. Silvana looks at his broad chest and imagines him as
an opera singer.

"I'm very sorry, Mr. Benetoni," she says. "Please do not be angry
with the boys. Aurek is very sorry."

"Call me Tony," he says. He speaks slowly, his voice careful and
steady. "I'm not angry. What does a day missed from school matter?
Peter is often in trouble at school. He hasn't had an easy life."

And then he launches into his own story, which is not at all new.
They stand in the hall with the door half open, and Silvana has not even
asked him if he would like to take his coat off, and he is telling her about
his wife who died.

"I lost her just after Peter was born," he says, holding his hands out,
splaying his thick fingers as if sand is spilling through them.

Silvana would like to stop him talking. She doesn't need his sad stories. She has enough of her own, and anyway, the world is full of sad
stories. But this man carries on as if he has come to the house explicitly
to tell her, and she is drawn in by him. She can feel her head tipping to
one side as she listens.

He is a foreigner too. Italian parents who came to Suffolk and
worked in the cider orchards. He was born and brought up in England,
and lost his mother when he was just a child. When he was old enough
to leave school, his father moved to Kent but Tony stayed in Suffolk and

married a local landowner's daughter. Her parents were furious. She had married down.

"Down?" Silvana is not sure what this means.

"Down. She was upper-class. They thought I wasn't good enough for her. Once we had Peter, they changed their minds. They've been very good to me. And then, after the birth of Peter, my wife became ill and died."

He tells her how, when Italy entered the war, he was interned, separated from his parents-in-law and his son, and sent to prison despite all the influence his father-in-law wielded in town.

"Local politics," he said. "A lot of people profited from the war, and my father-in-law was on the wrong side of certain people at that time. He got me out eventually, but it took some time."

Silvana struggles to keep up with his story; it is long and winding and involves different places, the Isle of Wight, a prison in Kent, other places in England she has never heard of, and the machinations of local councils and crooked government officials. She finally edges around Tony and shuts the front door. Then she finds she is stuck between him and the staircase. Peter opens the parlor door.

"Hello, Dad."

"Peter, what are you wearing?"

"I got wet. These are Eric's clothes. He lent them to me."

They are so obviously small for him that Silvana wants to apologize for making the boy look ridiculous. "Not Eric," she says. "*Aurek.*"

"Well," says Tony. "We must make sure you give them back to him. Peter, what am I to do with you? Why are you getting other boys into trouble?"

"Oh, no," says Silvana, climbing the stairs slightly to give herself a better vantage point to look at them all. "Don't be angry with Peter. Aurek doesn't like school either."

"He's my friend," says Peter.

Silvana likes the boy suddenly. If he is a friend to Aurek then he is a friend to her. No matter that he is a child with no obvious graces.

"I blame myself for his misbehavior," says Tony. He addresses her as if they are alone. "I never liked school and I have always told Peter that. It's my own mistake."

Silvana suddenly remembers she has not offered him something to drink. Janusz would think this unforgivable. What should it be, tea or sherry?

"But I must make you tea."

She takes a hurried step down, misjudges the stair, and swings into midair, falling forward. Peter's father catches her.

He has strong arms, this man. She can smell the lemony scent of him. Clean and soapy. What on earth is she thinking? His cheek shows a shadow of dark stubble. Dashing. She read that word on a cinema poster just the other day.

This man is dashing.

He carries on talking, setting her upright, ignoring her excuses and discomfort, as if women always fall into his arms, telling her how he breeds canaries and owns a pet shop.

Not an opera singer then.

"No, it's very kind of you but we mustn't take up any more of your time," says Tony. "I must say, it has been a real pleasure to talk to you, Mrs. . . ."

"Please, my name is Silvana."

"Silvana. What a beautiful name. And I will make sure Peter brings back the clothes you've lent him."

As Silvana and Aurek walk them to their car, Janusz appears, walking up the hill, back from work, a newspaper and his dictionary under his arm, his face grimed with oil and dirt.

"This is my husband," she says, glad to see Janusz's welcoming smile. She feels exhausted by Peter's father and all his talk, exhausted by her own girlish reaction to him earlier. She wants her husband beside her. He knows how to talk to people. She has long ago lost the skill.

"What a view you have up here," Tony says to Janusz after they shake hands. "I've always liked this street. I know a couple who live up here, the Holborns?"

"Doris and Gilbert? The Holborns are our neighbors," says Janusz. "Yes, we know them very well." He sounds proud. "Everybody keeps to themselves here, you know how it is. But the Holborns are very friendly."

"I should call in on them again. I haven't seen Gilbert in ages. If you see them, say hello from me. Tell them if there's anything they need they can give me a call."

Janusz doesn't get angry with Aurek that night. Nobody mentions the truancy. Instead Janusz says he is pleased Aurek has found a friend.

"A black Wolseley? That's a lovely car to own. I wouldn't mind a car of my own. Hey, Aurek? That's what we'll get one day, and I can drive you out to the woods to play."

Silvana remembers Janusz as a young man, always mad about cars. It reminds her of who they both once were. He hasn't changed. She feels something move within her, as though someone has put his hand on her heart and squeezed it. It is love. Not just gratitude but real love.

"You look different," he says.

"Do I?"

"Yes. There's something about you today."

She laughs, a womanly sound. She can feel a warmth inside her, as if the sun has been shining on her. Janusz puts his arms around her waist and kisses her. She closes her eyes and breathes in the scent of his skin. It takes her back to the riverbank where they met, to the dusty seats of their hometown's cinema where their hands touched in the dark.

Is it really possible that meeting Peter's father, the man with a brand-new smile, has nudged the block of coldness wedged inside her for so long?

POLAND

Silvana

Silvana walked away from the wreckage of the plane and sat down at a crossroads beside an abandoned wooden handcart and a pile of spilled blankets. She sat there for a long, long time. The rain had turned to sleet. She put on her fur coat and cradled her child inside it. He was crying lustily and the sound was something wonderful to her.

Someone stopped in front of her and she looked up. A woman stared down at her.

"Go away," Silvana said. "Get away. Get away from my baby."

"Don't be ridiculous," the woman said briskly. "I don't want your child. I want you to get up. You're going to die sitting here in the cold."

She was older than Silvana, and even in that terrible weather, wearing, as she was, a man's overcoat and peasant boots, she had a worldliness about her, an aura of sophistication that made Silvana see her not as she was, with her ragged clothes and thin pale face, but as she could be, as she probably had been, a red-lipped pouting beauty with diamonds in her hair.

"Come on," the woman said, frowning so that her pencil-thin eyebrows creased. "Get up off your arse and get moving."

Silvana sat up straighter, tried to tidy her hair. "Leave me alone. Just go away."

"I am not going away. You and the child will die of the fucking cold if you don't get up. And what is the point of leaving those blankets in the mud? Pick them up and wrap them around him. He looks half frozen."

Something in the woman's voice, the clear commanding sound of it, made Silvana get up, picking up the blankets as she did so.

"His name's Aurek," she said. She lifted the boy so that the woman could see him. "This is my son. I'm his mother. I lost him and then I found him."

"Did you? Well, you're the sorriest-looking mother I ever saw."

The woman held out a pair of flat, lace-up leather shoes. "Here, take these. You can't go barefoot, you'll get frostbite. They're all I have. They're dance shoes, although with that wound on your ankle, you don't look like you'll be dancing for a while."

The woman's name was Hanka. She said she sang in clubs in Warsaw, and named places Silvana had never heard of.

"I was going to get my big break and sing with an American orchestra, then Hitler messed things up for me."

Hanka laughed. "You're lucky I met you. I'll look after you. You and your miserable baby."

They walked together along muddy roads and endless tracks, until Hanka finally persuaded a farmer to let them stay in his barn.

"Do you have any money?"

Silvana shook her head. She'd spent the savings she and Janusz had on the bus journey and food along the way.

"Jewelry?"

Silvana looked at her wedding ring. She touched her throat and felt the small glass medallion Janusz had given her.

"No," she said.

Hanka frowned, hands on hips. She grabbed Silvana's hand.

"Give me your ring. We need food, right? Then give me your ring."

Silvana watched as Hanka handed over her wedding ring to the farmer.

"Is that all?" the man asked.

Hanka put her hand on her hip and looked slyly at him. "What else do you want?"

She walked away and he followed her into a stable. Silvana stood in the farmyard waiting. The farmer came out later, pulling his belt tight on his britches, telling them they could stay as long as they liked.

"Oh now, don't look so worried," Hanka told Silvana afterward when the farmer's wife had silently brought them dishes of beetroot soup and cups of hot tea.

"He won't touch you. I've told him you're out-of-bounds. You need to wise up. *Hart ducha.* It means strength of will. That's what you need, Silvana. I can sell myself if I must, but I am my own person. I do what I want. Look at you. Let me guess. You married a peasant and this is your child, whom you believe will make your fortune one day."

"My husband is not a peasant," Silvana replied. "He is an engineer."

"Ah, a clever peasant," she said. "And where is he now?"

"I don't know," Silvana said. She tried not to think of Janusz and focused instead on the warm cup in her hand, the steam rising from it.

"And what about you?" she asked Hanka.

"*Szlachta,*" Hanka said, tossing her head back. *Nobility.* And the subject was closed.

The barn Silvana lived in with Hanka, the daughter of nobility, was a small thatched building made of wood and plaster. The farmer and his wife kept rabbits in it for meat. There were rats that came around the cages at night, but by making beds on stilts, the women managed to keep away from them.

They cared for the farm animals and were fed and given shelter. Sometimes, when it was very cold, Hanka demanded that the farmer let Silvana and Aurek sleep in the house with them. Silvana didn't want to. She knew the farmer's wife didn't like her, and she feared the farmer might like her too much.

The farm was isolated, miles from any villages, but still, every time the farmer's wife spoke to her, it was about German troops and how she wouldn't hide the two women if they arrived at the house. Silvana felt it was only a matter of time before they were found. The farmer's wife told them women from the next village had been sent to work on German farms. Their children had been taken from them.

Hanka said it was all talk and nothing more than that. "Listen, that woman needs us. We do as much work as both of them on the farm. She won't hand us over to any soldiers."

"It's the way she looks at me," said Silvana. "Like she hates me."

"Well, of course she does. You're younger and prettier than she is. Look, stay in the barn if you want. But if you do, you'd better stop moaning in your sleep. I am not going to be woken up by your bad dreams every night."

Silvana blushed hotly and the other woman put her hand out and touched her cheek. "It's all right, *moja droga*. Don't listen to me, my dear. I don't mean to be harsh. We all have nightmares. This war is the worst one of all. Tell me, what is it that makes you cry?"

Silvana stroked Aurek's head and tried to stop the tears pricking at her eyes.

"I don't know," she whispered. "I think I miss my husband, that's all."

Janusz

Flat river plains and wide fields stretched ahead of them. It seemed to Janusz, in those early weeks of their journey, that the air itself was filled with unease and danger. The weather turned vicious, gales blew and raged, uprooting trees, shutting down the landscape in folds of gray rain so that Janusz could often only see a few meters in front of him. Snowstorms came, the cold gnawed into him, and whiteness burned his eyes. And every step took him further away from Silvana and his son.

They passed towns filled with Polish army units, groups of men giving up their weapons to the Russian units that came from the east. They saw the Red Army soldiers marching, singing their beloved national songs. So many tired-looking men and thin horses. Bruno always led them away from the crowds even as Janusz felt they should step forward and join up with the other soldiers. In villages and towns, the snow-banked roads were clogged with men, horse-driven wagons, artillery pieces, and dismal field kitchens.

Janusz longed for Warsaw. He wanted tall buildings and wide urban streets, pavements beneath his feet, the sound of the trams, the theaters, and glass-fronted shops. The things he hated before, he now missed: the gangs of dippers, the thieves, the Jewish street hawkers, the *koniks*, and cab drivers. He missed the colors of the gypsies with their violin-playing and their red trousers and rainbow scarves, selling their wares off the Royal Way, looking like they belonged to the last century.

But most of all he missed Silvana. The touch of her, the hard frown she wore like armor against the world, her arms tight around him at night, the sound of his son's breath as he slept on the cot beside them. Instead he was stuck on this journey, and he followed Bruno and Franek silently, like a dog follows a cart, hypnotized by the metallic clink of its wheels.

They stopped at farmsteads and were hidden in attics and barns. Bruno had been telling the truth when he said he had money. Where he could, he bought sugar, salt, vinegar, and soap. These became precious commodities and worth more than cash. He bartered and got them all civilian clothes.

Slowly they became aware of an underground movement of men and women. The Home Army, they were called. Men and women who were proud to be Polish, who wanted to fight any way they could. These people sent them on to safe houses and told them which towns and villages to avoid.

There were men from other regiments trying to get across to France, and news was swapped and speculated upon. Stories filtered through to them via secret whisperings and illegal pamphlets, and it was always bad news. There had been large-scale arrests by the Russians in the east: government officials, police, clergymen. Always at night. Nobody could ever be sure he would sleep through a peaceful night.

Janusz slept lightly. He woke at the slightest noise, ready to move. He saw himself in a mirror in a house and didn't recognize the stubbly, red-eyed man looking fearfully back at him. The loneliness of the journey made him short-tempered. He felt sure arrest was just around the corner. Each new day brought more kilometers to cover. His feet hurt. He had blisters that, unattended, turned to sores.

Bruno was stronger. He said they owed it to Poland to stay free. If hiding was the way to do it, so be it. France was their only chance. There, they'd be trained to fight and they'd whip the Germans and the Russians both.

"I have my mother's medallion to protect me," explained Franek. He held a chain on his neck and showed them the small silver disk hanging from it. They were in a barn waiting for a guide to come to take them to the next safe house. Outside, a gale blew and the barn creaked and rocked like a boat in rough seas.

"St. Sebastian will see me through. God won't be calling me yet. He calls those he loves, but he's not ready for me yet."

Bruno patted his duffle bag. "I've got my insurance. Some nice gold watches and cuff links to barter with. And a kilo of flour. What about you, Janusz? What will save you?"

Janusz stared down at his feet. "I have my boots," he said. "But I don't think they'll save me. In fact, I think they're killing me."

Bruno and Franek looked at him. Bruno started laughing and Franek joined in, too. A full thirty seconds behind the joke, Janusz suddenly coughed up a laugh.

It had been a long time since he had found anything funny.

Weeks later, they stood on the banks of a frozen river, preparing to leave Poland and cross into Romania. They had avoided the towns filled with soldiers, and a guide had taken them along the riverbank for miles during the night. Now, at dawn, Janusz felt numbness creep across his chest, as if his shirt bound him too tightly. He undid the buttons on his coat and loosened the necktie around his throat, but the numbness spread to his head, tightening around his eyes. He was leaving his country and didn't know if he would ever return. Flat fields lay behind him, and thick woodland welcomed him across the narrow river. He thought of turning back. Making his way across Poland again, working his way north, back to Silvana.

"We'll walk across," said Bruno, tapping Janusz's arm and waking him from his thoughts. "The ice will hold us."

It took only minutes, stepping out onto the ice, feeling it solid under them, and then they had crossed over and were running for cover into the trees.

Janusz stopped and looked back at the border to his country. He stood quietly for a moment as though at the graveside of a friend. How surprising then, when he found in his heart a strong fluttering, a surge of hopefulness. No matter what he expected to feel or how he tried to make this last image of his own country fix in his mind, the thrill of adventure overtook him and he ran after the others, into the trees, toward the future.

IPSWICH

It smells of tree roots inside the underground shelter and Aurek likes it.
He's hidden away here. He hears his mother calling for him, but he stays
put. She can come and climb in with him. They can sit in here together,
just like they used to. He still misses the feel of her against him.

Yesterday, the last day of school before the holidays, his teacher
called him a brat. A heathen child who needed punishing for his rude-
ness. She told him to take his shoe off, and then smacked his legs with
it. He had bitten her hand, grabbed his shoe, and run away. She came to
the house after that, with her hand in a bandage. The enemy told her he
was sorry and that Aurek would be punished.

Aurek doesn't care. They are all wrong. He is not a heathen child,
whatever that means. He is a wild boar. All thick black hair and wet
snout, scraping the earth, finding tree roots in the dark.

He spits on the ground, rubs a finger in it, and wipes mud across his
face. Through a gap in the metal he can see Silvana frowning, looking
up the garden.

She walks up to the shelter but doesn't crawl inside to be with him.
She bangs on the boards and starts an avalanche of water droplets that
fall on him. Aurek digs into the muddy ground and curls up.

"Aurek," Silvana calls. "Peter is here. He has brought your clothes
back. Why don't you come out and say hello?"

Aurek ignores her. He longs for the encircling safety of the trees
of his past. In the forest the trees spoke to him in green whispers, telling secrets that could crack the bones of those that did not belong. He
walked among them and felt their words like falling leaves, soft and

understanding. He does not like this England where he must wear his school cap straight, sit up, and recite the Lord's Prayer from memory. He does not belong in a country where he must not swing his legs on the bus, where he mustn't eat with his fingers, must endure the smart of a ruler across his knuckles in class and not fight back. He digs the ground with his fingers again, angrily scraping away at the earth.

"Is Aurek in there?"

Aurek stops still. It is a man's voice he has heard.

His mother replies. "Yes. Yes, he's hiding. But he will come out soon."

"Don't worry. We can come back another time. Perhaps he'd like to come to play at the pet shop?"

Through a gap, Aurek sees Peter and his father standing together.

"Why don't you crawl in with him?" Peter's father says.

"Dad, you know I can't fit through that gap. Hey, Aurek! You coming out?"

Aurek considers what to do. He'd like to see Peter, but it's not easy to change out of his pig shape. He can't bring himself to be a boy just yet.

He watches Tony Benetoni grinning at his mother. He can see the man's slicked shiny hair, his large nose, his white teeth in his open mouth. Peter is sucking on a pink stick of rock. Aurek hears his mother apologizing and watches them walk away. He grunts, snarls, lets out a yell, and rolls over in the dirt like an animal in pain.

After they have gone, Silvana puts the flowers Tony brought in a jam jar on the windowsill, arranging them for a while, shifting first one dahlia and then another as if she is organizing a complex color scheme, when in reality they are all white.

She can't remember the last time anybody bought her flowers. In her grandmother's village, dahlias were always known as bachelor's flowers. Giving white ones was a single man's way of telling a girl he liked her. She allows herself to dwell on this and then dismisses it as ridiculous. Of course he wouldn't know about Polish traditions.

She had white flowers for her wedding, an armful of peppery-scented carnations. Janusz's father had grown them in his garden. She moves the flowers from the windowsill onto the kitchen table and climbs the stairs with a cup of tea for Janusz.

"Are you awake?"

Janusz stirs in bed and sits up, yawning.

"I'll be glad when I don't have to work the night shift anymore. I don't like sleeping in the afternoon. Did I hear voices downstairs?"

She puts the teacup down, perches on the edge of the bed, and thinks of the flowers again.

"Tony brought Peter to play with Aurek. But Aurek was in the shelter at the bottom of the garden and refused to come out. Tony and Peter left a minute ago."

"I wish Aurek would be more polite. That boy is the only friend he's got. I think I'll get rid of the shelter."

"Is that Aurek's punishment?"

"For his behavior at school? No. I'm not going to punish him. I thought I'd knock down the shelter and build him a tree house."

"A tree house?" Silvana smiles. "He'd love that."

"Where is Aurek now?"

"Still in the garden. Why?"

"Because I want you all to myself for a moment."

He kisses her, pulling her down onto him.

"You're all I want," he whispers. "You know that? You and the boy."

His eyes are so blue and clear, they shine with a kind of truth that shames her.

She closes her own eyes and silences him with a kiss, pressing against his warm body, but memories circle her, like wolves in a forest, the same ones that attack her in her dreams. She moans and Janusz misinterprets the sound for pleasure. He pulls her under him and she wills her body to follow his. Only her mind lags behind. She clings to him, gratitude moving her toward a place of unexpected desire. A place where her memories leave her alone and she is fleetingly full and whole, just like she was before the war.

"Thank you," she says afterward.

They are lying side by side, breathing heavily.

"What do you mean?"

She wonders at it herself. What is she thanking him for? For making love to her? Or for helping her forget, no matter how briefly, the memories that live under her skin?

"I don't know. For finding us, I suppose."

She gets up, wrapping the sheet around her, and lifts the curtain to look out into the garden, checking Aurek is still safe.

"I love you," says Janusz, sitting up and reaching for his cigarettes. She turns and looks at him.

"Thank you," she says again, and they both laugh.

"Come back to bed."

She folds herself into his arms and watches him smoking, a small smile playing on his lips.

I love you too, she thinks, and closes her eyes.

Later, when Janusz has gone to work, Silvana slides an arm into the shelter like a cat searching for a mouse. Aurek strokes her hand. She catches hold of his fingers and pulls him through the broken wooden boards, her hands cupping his head, drawing one shoulder then the next through the gap until finally his legs slip out onto the damp grass. He cries out, and when she has him in front of her, slimy and wet with mud, she holds him tightly to her.

"You don't have to hide anymore," she whispers. "This is a new life for us. We are safe here with your father. I promise."

She feels his grip relax and realizes with a soaring sense of gratitude that she actually believes what she is saying.

The next day Janusz dismantles the shelter, pulling and pushing, digging sharp-edged metal out of the soil.

"Do you want a hand with that?" Gilbert Holborn is looking over the fence.

Janusz shakes his head. "I've nearly finished. I'm making more room for flower beds."

"Oh, yes, quite right. Out with the old, eh? Mind you, Doris won't part with ours just yet. We had plenty of singsongs in it, me and her and Geena. Our Anderson shelter is a firm favorite. Crazy, innit?"

"Yes," replies Janusz, mimicking Gilbert's country vowels. "Crazy, innit."

"And what about your son?" says Gilbert. "What's he going to do now he's not got a den to play in?"

"I'm going to make him a tree house."

"That's a beautiful tree," says Gilbert, looking toward the oak. "Must be hundreds of years old, I reckon. Not many houses around here have got trees like that in their gardens, I can tell you. And you're right. It's perfect for a tree house." He pulls out a packet of cigarettes and offers one to Janusz. "A tree house *and* a flower garden. That'll keep you busy. I've got some dahlia tubers you can have, if you're interested. We've got a club going, shows and whatnot. You could join us if you wanted. Where were you based before, Jan? In the war, I mean. I was in the Home Guard myself."

He passes a box of matches over the fence and Janusz takes them, lighting his cigarette in cupped hands.

"I moved around. Scotland, Kent, Devon. Engineer corps."

"Bit of fun that was, I imagine. Next time you need a hand, let me know."

"Thank you, I will." Janusz tries to think of something else to say, something to keep this conversation with his neighbor going.

"I know a friend of yours," he says. "Tony Benetoni?"

"Tony the Wop? Ah, now he is a real gentleman. I haven't seen him for quite a while. And he spoke about me?"

"He said to tell you that if there is anything you need to get in contact with him."

"Did he? He said to tell me that? Oh, yes, he's well known around here. Local businessman, he is."

"His son is Aurek's friend."

"Is he?" Gilbert grips the top of the wooden fence with his hands. He lowers his voice and Janusz steps closer.

"Tony's a useful bloke to know. Doesn't understand the meaning of rationing, if you see what I'm saying. Anything you want, Tony can get it. He's not a spiv. I wouldn't want you to think that. No, Tony's an absolute gentleman like I said. But he can get you anything you want off ration. Look, I've got half a bottle of scotch in the garden shed. Come over when the women are out shopping. I'll show you my seed catalogs and we can have a great old chat about the war and all that."

Janusz does not want to remember the war.

"That would be nice," he says, handing Gilbert back his matches. "Thank you very much."

It is a hot and humid summer's day, but English houses don't have shutters on their windows so Silvana cannot shut the heat out. Instead, she does what the English do and opens the windows and doors, hoping for a breeze. The kitchen is filled with the sweet smell of cooking and a plate of biscuits steams gently on the table, a dishcloth covering it to keep off the flies. She checks the time on the clock. Aurek and Janusz will be back soon. They left an hour ago to watch a game of cricket being played in Christchurch Park. She hopes Aurek won't be difficult. The last time Janusz took him to the park, Aurek ran away and came home on his own.

She is washing up when she hears the metal-on-stone sound of horses hooves, followed by a harsh, whining cry, "*Ragg gannnddbone, ragg gannnddbone.*"

In the street, a black and white horse stands in front of a wooden cart piled high with clothes, broken bits of furniture, and pots and pans.

The rag-and-bone man climbs down from his cart and gives Silvana a black-toothed grin as she rushes out of her front door, wiping her hands on her apron.

"Can I have a look?" she asks.

"Course you can, Miss."

She sees a pair of men's leather shoes poking out of a porcelain chamber pot. Black lace-ups. They look practically new. All they need is a clean. The leather is hardly worn. She holds them out to the man.

"How much?"

"If you let me have a quick drink of water you can have'em for a florin."

"Yes. Wait one moment please. I'll be right back."

Janusz keeps money in the kitchen drawer; money he uses to buy himself a drink at the British Legion bar with Gilbert after work on a Friday. She finds the right change and takes the man a glass of water and some biscuits on a tray. The more she looks at the shoes, the more she is sure Janusz will like them.

"Thank you very much, Miss," says the rag-and-bone man, wiping his mouth with his sleeve. "You're a real lady."

In the kitchen she lays the shoes on newspaper on the table, opens the pantry cupboard, and takes out Janusz's shoe polish box. It is a large wooden box with a brass catch on the front. She wants Janusz to be able to see his reflection in the shoes. She wants him to have something brand-new.

She dips her hand happily into the box, reaching for a brush, and catches sight of a pale blue airmail envelope, just the corner of it. She pulls it out. The writing on it reminds her of the perfect copperplate they used to have to learn at school. She reaches back inside the box and pulls out more letters, lots more.

Sitting down at the kitchen table, she begins to take them out of their envelopes, one by one, unfolding their sharp creases. There are a few French words she knows. *Je t'aime* is an expression she understands. The letters are full of that phrase. It jumps out at her. Silvana struggles to think straight. She tries to steady her breathing. She must not panic.

So that is what he did during the war.

He fell in love.

She doesn't understand. Why did he bring her here if he loves another woman? It can't be true. This can't be true. Just when she thought she and the boy were safe. She folds up the letters, making sure her tears don't fall upon them. Her fingers tremble as she puts them back under the dusters and soft brushes, as carefully as she'd put eggs back under a broody hen. Her stomach churns, and she thinks she might even be sick, so terrible is this feeling of hurt.

She stumbles through the hall and out into the street, slamming the front door behind her, hurrying down the hill into the heat-hazed town, sweat sticking her hair to her forehead, and tears stinging her eyes.

In the narrow streets of the town center, she walks aimlessly, past the grocer's and the hardware store where new saucepans, jam boilers, and pressure cookers, preserving jars and canning machines glint at her. All shining, silvery and bright and brilliantly necessary. And why not a wedding ring in silver? That preserving pan with its practical heavy bottom—a sliver of that would make a ring. Why hadn't she insisted upon a wedding ring when she had the chance? She's not a proper wife without a ring. Maybe the other woman has a ring? And then another thought comes to her. A terrible thought, worse than all the others. What if he leaves them, and Aurek loses his father? She can feel tears pricking her eyes again when somebody calls her name.

"Silvana! Doing a bit of shopping?"

Tony stands beside her. He is wearing brown overalls and his sleeves are rolled back to the elbows, revealing forearms covered in thick black hair. He waves an arm to show her a sign painted above a shop doorway: *Benetoni's Animal Emporium.*

"Why don't you come in and have a look around? Mine is the best pet shop in Suffolk."

She casts around for something to say.

"I'm thinking of buying pots. For the kitchen."

"Tell me what you want and I'll get it . . . Hey? Are you all right?" He steps toward her, his arms reaching out to her. "You're crying."

For a moment she is tempted to tell him why. But she can't. Of course she can't.

"I'm sorry, I have to go."

"But wait . . ."

She begins to run, not caring that nobody runs in the streets here. She is a foreigner. She will always look out of place. Why not pick up her skirts and run if she wants to? She hears him call her again as she rounds the corner, but she doesn't look back.

She has no idea of where she is going, and finds herself at the docks. Ahead of her are semi-demolished warehouses, piles of brick rubble, and official-looking signs warning the public to stay away, that many of the buildings are bomb damaged and structurally unsafe. Some of the warehouses are still in use, and men are unloading sacks of grain into them. Coils of thick rope lie everywhere on the ground, and dust and debris drift on the breeze.

Picking her way over ropes and stacks of burlap sacks, she walks along the quay, past the sailors and warehousemen, ignoring the looks they give her, to where the water drifts away into the horizon and seagulls swagger and wheel in the sky.

Heavy wooden barges with red sails move slowly on the greeny waters. The salty smell of river mud is thick in the air, and seabirds wade across the gleaming black mudflats in the dry docks. Some way out, there is a ship covered in orange rust and peeling paint. A metal warship, held in place by huge chains, as if whoever moored it there was afraid the ship might try to escape to sea.

She remembers the terrible seasickness she suffered on the journey to England. How, when she finally staggered down the gangplanks onto English land, she knew she would never return to Poland.

She is as out of place as that ship on the river. Lost. Wanting a country that doesn't exist anymore. Poland is under communist rule. She can never go back. That's the truth of it.

She heads toward home, her mind clearing. She has been so sure of her own role as villain in this marriage, she never imagined Janusz could be capable of hiding things from her.

But she must harden herself. To ask him about the letters would be to risk their family, and Aurek must have a family. It's what she promised him. It's likely that the affair is over. A wartime foolishness. And if Janusz is still involved with this other woman, she must not interfere. She must be hard and serious and stay silent. She has no choice. She must go back and be a good wife. Let Janusz have his secrets. At least now she is not the only one in the marriage with something to hide.

When she walks through the hallway and into the kitchen, Janusz and Aurek are waiting for her.

"They're a perfect fit!" says Janusz.

She looks at his face blankly.

"The shoes! It was you that left them on the table?"

"Oh. Yes. Yes, I got them from the rag-and-bone man."

"I've cleaned them. Aurek helped me. A bit of shoe polish brought them up like new. English leather. You remember the doctor we took Aurek to? He had the same shoes, I'm sure."

"I'm glad you like them."

"I'll keep them for best, of course."

"That's right," she says, sinking into a chair and beckoning to Aurek to come and sit on her lap. "Keep them for best."

POLAND

Silvana

As the months went by, Aurek delighted Silvana and entertained Hanka. Full of energy, he played in the rabbit cages and ran with the farm dogs, his back bent, shoulders rounded, touching the ground with his hands for balance, pushing himself off from outstretched fingers. He was fast like that.

Hanka called him a little bear. She told Silvana a story about a boy brought up by bears in a Lithuanian forest. The three of them were wrapped in blankets in their straw bed, Aurek curled tightly against Silvana's breast.

"Nobody knew where he had come from," said Hanka, tickling Aurek's fingers. "The bears took him as their own. He went about on all fours and grew hair down his back. He lived on a diet of crab apples and honey. A hunter caught him and gave him to the King of Poland who tried to teach him to speak, but he never learned to do anything other than grunt."

Aurek laughed at the story. Hanka grunted and growled like a bear until Silvana was worried Aurek would hurt himself laughing so hard. They giggled and growled and roared and finally, when they fell back on the straw exhausted by their laughter, Silvana pressed her face against the top of her son's head and felt tears run down her cheeks.

"My little bear," she whispered to him. "My lost little bear."

"Here," Hanka said one night when the stars looked sharp enough to slice the black velvet sky into icy ribbons. She held out a dried plum, dark and wrinkled. Silvana's mouth watered at the sight of it.

"Would he like this?"

Silvana looked at Aurek, curled up in her arms, head tucked in. She wasn't sure. Hanka tutted.

"All children like them."

She held the piece of fruit out to Aurek and he pushed it greedily into his mouth.

"See? I knew he would."

"What will we do when the summer comes?" Silvana asked. "Will we stay here?"

"Warsaw." Hanka leaned across her and wiped a dribble from Aurek's mouth. "I'm going to Warsaw. You can come if you want."

"You're going to the city?"

Silvana was surprised. She had thought Hanka would go home. Hanka had told her about her family home: a white stucco house with an avenue of lime trees leading to it and Virginia creeper trailing across its facade. A *pavillon de chasse*, she called it. She had described the shooting trophies in the hall, heads of boar and roe, glass domes containing blackcock and capercaillie and the floors made of marble. Outside were kitchen gardens, a lake full of carp, a dairy, and a laundry. It sounded like a wonderful place.

"Why don't you go home?" she asked.

Hanka shook her head.

"I was a child during the Great War. The Germans took over our house. They had their motor repair shops in the barns alongside the vegetable gardens. My family hid almost all our possessions, the paintings, sculptures, the silver, and so on; all walled up in the cellar. At the end of the war, all the valuables were safe but my mother died. She caught typhus from one of the soldiers. And now another war, and our house is taken over again. My father didn't bother hiding the family heirlooms this time. The only thing he asked was that his children would be safe. He's forbidden any of us to go near the house until the war is over. I can't go home and I can't carry on living like this. I need to be in the city."

It was true that Hanka looked like she belonged in the city. Her limbs were too fine for farmwork, her hands too soft.

"I'm going back to see my lover," continued Hanka. Silvana watched her face grow still, the tiredness settling in the shadows under her eyes.

"He's a musician. He plays American jazz, and the last time I saw him he told me to get out of the city. He said he didn't want me having to sing for a German audience. So I left. But I miss him. I have to go back: I have to see him again. And I don't care who I sing to. I just want my life back."

Silvana rocked Aurek on her lap and Hanka smiled at her.

"So, little Silvana, will you come with me?"

Silvana felt her heart ache. "Yes," she said. Though the thought of returning to Warsaw filled her with dread.

Janusz

On a moonless night, a guide took Janusz, Bruno, and Franek to the Hungarian border. They were used to each other now, and Janusz had even begun to feel fond of Franek and his mad ways. The boy's heart was in the right place and he was as brave as they came. They'd been given papers, but it was still best to cross at night, in secret. They reached a rocky promontory and watched as border guards with dogs patrolled the path below them.

"The guide said we've got about fifteen minutes before they come back," said Bruno as the guards rounded the corner out of sight.

"I need a machine gun," said Franek.

He was shivering and shaking, and Janusz wanted to tell him to stop bloody moving.

"I'd take them all out," Franek said. "Bang, bang, bang. Shoot them all down. If I had my old gun from home, I could do it."

"When do we go?" asked Janusz. He felt sick, and realized he, too, was shaking.

"We go now," said Bruno. "The guards won't be expecting any-thing tonight. Nobody would want to be out on a night like tonight. Even the wolves would find it too cold. One at a time. Every three minutes. That gives us plenty of time to make it across. You go first, Jan. Then Franek and I will follow him. Don't worry, we'll be right behind you."

Janusz couldn't feel his legs anymore. He doubted his ability to run. His breath was coming in quick gasps. He was trembling with tiredness and his heart was hammering.

Bruno nodded. He gave Janusz a push. "OK, it's time," he whis-pered. "Good luck. Go!"

Janusz got up and started running, scrambling down the rocks.

He didn't look back. If he was going to die, so be it. He stumbled. His legs were not listening to his brain; they buckled under him, but he forced himself to keep going. There was no one on the road. He crossed it and threw himself into the deep snow, where he rolled downhill. He slithered and slid and slammed into a fir tree. Getting to his feet, he ran. Finally he reached the shelter of trees and, on hands and knees, crawled into a forest of dark pine trees, and lay there. He could taste blood on his lip, and a pulse thumped in his neck. He could feel it: the blood pushing through him, the feeling of being alive. He lay still and his heart pumped, fear twitching his eyelids, pulling at a nerve in his cheek. He worked his way further into the trees and dug himself into the snow. Shivering, he heard noises around him. Cracking branches and scuffling sounds. He hoped Bruno was right. That the night really was too cold for wolves.

Franek came into view, running and jumping through the snow, smashing full pelt into Janusz, knocking him in the face with his elbow.

"Sorry," panted Franek. "I didn't see you."

"Jesus, Franek," whispered Janusz. "I think you've broken my bloody nose."

"Christ, no, I'm sorry . . ."

"Forget it, you big oaf. You made it. We both did."

"We made it," said Franek. "I'm a good soldier."

He sounded so proud, Janusz only just managed to stop himself from hugging the boy.

IPSWICH

The pile of wooden planks underneath the oak tree gets bigger all the time, and Aurek climbs it, jumping up and down, feeling the wood wobble underneath him. If the pile keeps on growing, it will be even easier to climb his tree than before. He will jump on the wood stack and be able to leap into the tree's lower branches. Hop onto them, just like a sparrow hunting insects.

He sees Janusz walking up the garden and stops jumping. For once, he's not treading on any precious plants, but still, he knows the enemy doesn't like to see foolishness in his neat and perfect garden.

The enemy stands with his hands on his hips, surveying the scene. He is frowning, his blue eyes hooded by his eyebrows. Aurek mimics Janusz's stance, hands on hips. He knows he has only a limited amount of time before he will be berated for this kind of cheekiness. He furrows his brow just like the enemy. Tries to feel what it is like to be his father.

Before they'd come to England, Aurek had imagined his father would look different. Mama had told him he had blond hair, but he doesn't. It's an ashy color; when he rubs hair oil over it, it turns a shade darker, like metal. It makes him look old, older than Silvana. Maybe he isn't his father. Maybe his mother made a mistake? Sometimes, Aurek wonders if his real father isn't still in Poland searching the forests for him and his mama. He studies the enemy a little longer. He's not so bad. Sometimes, Aurek finds himself forgetting to hate him.

Janusz moves, folds his arms. Aurek does the same. He feels laughter warming him, but holds it back. The enemy salutes. Straight-faced,

Aurek does the same. Then Janusz cocks his leg like a dog and farts loudly.

The laughter escapes from Aurek; it bursts out of him quicker than fizzy lemonade in a shaken bottle, shooting down his nose, making his eyes water. He laughs and holds his sides.

"You're a funny little lad," says Janusz. "But it's a pleasure to see you laughing. Be careful climbing on the wood. I don't want you to get splinters."

He turns and walks toward the house, and Aurek wishes he'd come back to play the game again.

"*Ojciec*," he calls. "Father?"

But Janusz doesn't hear him, and goes into the kitchen. Aurek salutes him again anyway.

The following Saturday, Tony brings Peter around and Janusz invites them into the garden, pleased to be able to show them his family working together on their flower borders and lawn. He points to Aurek crouching among the roses, scratching at the ground.

"Aurek has his own little vegetable patch over there," he explains, wishing the boy would look less furtive in his actions. The child has been digging up the carrots he has been asked not to touch. Janusz has explained many times to the boy that it's too early in the season and the carrots are too small, but Aurek still loves to pull them up, brush the earth off them, and eat them. Janusz glances at Tony, but he doesn't seem to notice Aurek's behavior. He is looking at Silvana.

Silvana is kneeling on the lawn, a small knife in her hand, digging at weeds, just as he showed her. She is muttering to herself, a concentrated liturgy of Polish words and their English translations: *jaskier ostry, powój polny, mniszek pospolity, cieciorka pstra; buttercup, bindweed, dandelions, daisies.*

Janusz calls her name and she looks up from her work, her red headscarf fluttering slightly in the breeze. She stands up hurriedly, wiping her hands on her apron, apologizing for not seeing they had visitors.

"Don't let me disturb you," says Tony. "Your flower beds are marvelous. All these Victory gardens left over from the war are so depressing. This is a real peacetime garden."

"Exactly," Janusz says.

Silvana extends her hand. "Good morning, Tony."

"Silvana, lovely to see you. I was just saying what a beautiful garden you have."

"Janusz is very proud of it. Today he is building a tree house for Aurek."

"A tree house?" Tony claps his hands together. "What a wonderful idea. Can I help?"

"Of course," says Janusz, delighted by Tony's enthusiasm. Tony reminds him of Bruno: the kind of man who always knows a way out of a scrape. He is a loner, as far as Janusz can see, a man too taken with his business to worry about a home and a settled life. Not like Janusz, who needs a wife and a family to make sense of his days. Janusz wants the polished key to his front door in his pocket, a hook on the wall for that key when he comes home, his newspaper and dictionary beside his chair in the front parlor, his family gathered around him at mealtimes. But still, he looks at Tony and likes him for being different.

At the bottom of the garden, Janusz saws planks and Tony pulls out old nails from the wood with a claw hammer.

"I'm going to show you how to make a dovetail joint," Janusz says to Aurek and Peter. He holds his hands up, makes a fist with one. "This is the mortice. The tenon is like this." He holds his other hand like an arrow, fingers straight. "They fit together like this." He pushes his straight fingers into the hole in the middle of his fist.

Peter does the same. So does Aurek. Janusz smiles at Aurek. He's pleased his son has a friend at last. The two of them may get into quite a bit of trouble at school, but it is just schoolboy pranks. A bit of tomfoolery. Normal for their age. And Aurek speaks good English now, without a hint of a foreign accent. That makes Janusz proud. Children learn so quickly. The boy has even stopped making bird noises. Janusz knows he's a bit hard on him about that, but the boy has to learn. When he goes back to school in September, he will fit right in.

They pull the wood up into the tree, Janusz and Tony doing the heavy lifting while the boys are allowed to hammer in nails. The tree house has four sides, its roof made from corrugated iron. A perfect den for a boy at the bottom of a perfect English garden.

The garden is the key to everything. A place for them all. Janusz has planted herb beds and roses for Silvana. Sage and hyssop, marjoram, sprawling mint and low-lying clumps of thyme sit under pink rose blossoms. The lawn is flat, rolled and velvety green. Borders are filled with dahlias, hollyhocks, yellow and white irises, lilacs, and love-in-a-mist. Beyond these is the vegetable patch. Here potatoes grow in leafy rows. Onions are pushing up pale globes out of the soil. Marigolds have seeded freely through them all. They keep the vegetables happy and ward off insects. And now, in the oak, Aurek's tree house will look down on them all. He'd like his father to see this garden, his grandson playing in his den.

"You're a clever man, Janusz," says Tony, breaking his thoughts. "I can't put up a stack of shelves on my own."

"I had a tree house when I was a boy," says Janusz. "I hid up there with my slingshot and I could hit a bird's nest right across my parents' garden." He pauses and then, seeing the way Aurek is listening, his gaze concentrated upon him, he continues.

"I had a tin whistle my father gave me. I sat in my tree house and played it for hours. I made a terrible noise with it. I'm not musical. Not like my sister Eve. She plays the violin like an angel. And I collected snails for racing. I loved that. My friends brought their snails along and we raced them down the trunk of the tree. The first to reach the bottom was the champion."

"Well, that's not so far away from my own boyhood," says Tony. "I had a whole stable of champion racing snails. My father loved them. I bred the snails and he cooked them in garlic butter."

Peter pulls a face.

"Don't look like that, Peter. Give the boy a choice and he'd eat roast beef and Yorkshire puddings every day of the week. One day I will take you to Italy, young man, and you'll learn about real food."

Janusz is intrigued. "I was in southern Italy. Only for a month or so, back in '44. We flew over the countryside dropping propaganda leaflets. It looked beautiful. What part of the country did you come from?"

"My parents came from Genoa. I was born here, but my heart is in Italy. I eat like an Italian. I love my food." He thumps his belly and then opens his arms wide. "And look at this," he says. "Your good wife coming down the garden path with a tray of tea things. What could be better?"

They sit at the foot of the oak tree on a tartan blanket. Silvana pours the tea and Tony helps her, passing around the teacups. Janusz lies on his back looking up into the green branches and the blue sky beyond.

"What are you looking for?" Peter asks. "Enemy fire?"

Tony takes a cup of tea from Silvana. "It's certainly a beautiful view from here."

"Enough blue up there to make trousers for a dozen policemen," says Janusz.

"Ah, we say trousers for a sailor here," says Tony. "A bit of a poet, aren't you? But of course you are; you have Silvana. Your beautiful muse."

Janusz glances at his wife. She doesn't seem to be listening. She has been lost in her own world recently.

"You were in a hurry the other day when I saw you," Tony says to Silvana.

"What other day?" asks Janusz. She has not mentioned seeing Tony.

"A week or so ago. I saw your lady wife out shopping."

"I was busy," Silvana replies. "I didn't have time to stop."

"Next time I insist you come and have a look at the pet shop."

"All right," she says. "I will."

Tony turns to Janusz. "What a lucky chap you are, having a wife who takes such good care of you."

Tony laughs and Silvana blushes. Janusz leans back on his elbow, pleased to see his wife looking happy for once. He stops himself from reaching out to her. Even though she is right there beside him, Janusz feels she has become distant from him. Further away from him than the blue sky above.

POLAND

Silvana

When the spring came, the farmer told Silvana and Hanka he couldn't risk hiding them any longer. He looked nervous, as if afraid the women might make a fuss. Hanka shrugged and said it was time they were moving on in any case.

The farmer gave Silvana a pair of boots and Aurek a blanket. His wife handed them a parcel of food for the journey and told them never to come back or she would see to it herself that the Germans would find them.

It was May when they left, and the sun had started to dry out the muddy roads and meadows. Walking away from the farm, Silvana watched Aurek toddling ahead of her. He had grown and his baby curls were gone, revealing a thick head of hair as straight and dark as summer shadows. The sun tanned him and the boy looked happy, gamboling down the road, chasing butterflies, and dancing this way and that.

They camped near a river and washed their clothes in the water, drying them on the bank in the sunshine.

"My necklace," Silvana said, putting her hand to her throat. She was sitting naked on the riverbank. Hanka had told her nudity was glorious and she was trying to show that she believed her, although all she wanted was to put her clothes back on.

"My glass pendant. It's gone."

"That old weasel back at the farm," replied Hanka. She stroked Silvana's neck. "He will have stolen it for his wife. You can't trust peasants with anything. Do you want me to go back for it? I'll get it for you."

"No," Silvana said. "No. It's gone."

Hanka made a daisy chain and gave it to her.

Silvana put it on and felt grateful once again for her friend's kindness.

"Here," she said. She held out her fur coat. She wanted to give Hanka something, a gift for her friendship, and she had nothing else to give. "You should have this."

"Really?" Hanka slipped it around her shoulders, stroking the fur.

She gave Silvana her greatcoat in exchange. That afternoon, Hanka walked up and down the riverbank in the fur coat, head held high, like a model. She didn't seem to notice the matted, dried bloodstains in the fur and the rips where the silk lining showed through.

"I thought about stealing it off you anyway," Hanka admitted. "Fur doesn't suit you. You're too thin to wear it."

They sat together on the riverbank.

"We'll go back to Warsaw," Hanka said. You can come to the Adria club where I used to sing with the Henryka Golda orchestra. I'll take you dancing. You can hear me sing and I'll show you how to dress properly. Pearls! We'll have pearls and diamonds!"

Silvana laughed. "But what would I do?"

"Do? You could sing. Learn to dance. Use that body of yours."

Silvana shook her head. "I don't think I can really go to Warsaw."

"You don't want to come with me?"

Silvana remembered the soldier in the flat, the smell of rain on his clothes, and the bruises he left on her thighs.

"Hanka, I can't."

Hanka threw off the fur coat and lay down in the sun.

"All right," she said. "We won't go." Then she turned on her side so that Silvana was left staring at her pale, naked back.

Silvana went to sleep under the stars that night. It was too early in the year for the mosquitoes to bother them, and she snuggled close to Hanka. Maybe she could go back to Warsaw? The soldier might be long gone. And she could change her name. Aurek's, too. She imagined taking the boy to Warsaw's zoo to see the elephants. And the park where he could sail a boat on the lake. Then she thought of Janusz, and grief darkened her thoughts. Was he still alive? She shut her eyes. Every-- thing was too complicated.

She woke when it was still dark with a warm feeling, as though she were lying between silk sheets. It was the joy of feeling Hanka's arms around her. She drifted back to sleep imagining it was Janusz hold- ing her.

The next morning she sat up and realized she was alone with the boy. Beside her something glinted in the sun: her glass pendant. She picked it up, held it to the sunlight, and watched the colors within it shine. She looked around for Hanka, but she was nowhere to be seen.

All day Silvana waited. The sunlight thickened in late afternoon and turned the light golden. Swarms of insects came down from the treetops and spun black clouds over the river. The sun sank onto the horizon, glowing red, its burning light turning the trees to silhouettes. Silvana knew Hanka wasn't coming back.

Silvana was still sitting by the river the next day when a man walked up the footpath toward her. He was tall with high cheekbones, a chis- eled nose, and a wide mouth. Silvana grabbed Aurek and stood up.

"Good morning," he said, and his voice was pleasant, laced with a Russian accent. He held out his hand and Silvana took it.

"Gregor Lazovnik," he said. "Call me Gregor."

Janusz

Sometimes Janusz believed they would never survive the winter. The weather was vicious, always chasing them, attacking, soaking, and freezing them. The next safe house was outside a small town with a long street running through it and rows of wooden houses shuttered up against the winter. Dirty snowbanks pressed up against windows and covered the road; walking was difficult, the three of them stumbling through undisturbed, deep snow.

The house was hidden in a copse of birch trees: a three-story, clapboard property with carved wooden balconies. Milk churns and tin buckets and wicker baskets dusted with snow cluttered the front door. A tall man with a thick beard and graying hair took them in. His name was Ambrose and he helped them out of their coats and checked their cold-nipped faces and fingers for signs of frostbite.

"We're going to get you into Yugoslavia. From there, you'll get a boat to France. You'll have to be careful, of course. If anybody finds out who you are, you'll be arrested. But we'll get you through, don't worry. My God, but you men look hungry. Come on, we'll eat."

In a kitchen filled with copper pots and baskets of herbs, Ambrose made them sit at a wooden table and gave them vodka, boiled fish heads, and a hot meaty gruel that Janusz thought the most delicious he had ever tasted. Even when it gave him the shits that night, and he ran out into the snow too many times, unbuckling his belt and dropping his trousers, he still wished he could eat more of the hot stew.

The next day, they walked along the edge of a frozen lake, hunting deer with Ambrose, rifles slung over their shoulders. A thick fog was coming in across the lake, rolling toward them over the ice. Janusz watched Franek play with the hunting dogs that trotted obediently beside them all. They were rough-coated, long-snouted dogs that nipped at each other's heels and wagged their tails so busily they knocked shards of silver frost into the air like tiny snowstorms everywhere they went. The boy looked as happy as the dogs at his side, and Janusz wondered if it wouldn't be better to leave him here in this remote village where surely he would be safe until the end of the war.

"I had a dog like this one," said Franek, stroking a big orange hound that beat its tail enthusiastically beside him. "My brother gave him to me."

He stopped patting the hound and looked at Bruno, his face suddenly serious. "I want to see my dog. When are we going home?"

"That ice looks thick," said Bruno, and Janusz watched to see if Franek could be that easily distracted.

"It's solid here, but further out it's thinner," replied Ambrose. "This lake never freezes over completely. It has weak spots."

Franek walked out onto the edge of the lake. "Look at this," he laughed. "Look at the dogs."

They all laughed. Each dog was trying to run on the ice beside Franek, claws scratching for grip as they flipped onto their sides and slid along on their bellies.

Ambrose lifted his hand for silence. "Shhh. Deer. Over there. In the trees."

He raised his rifle.

Franek hurried off the ice, pulling his rifle off his shoulder. He and Bruno cocked their guns and waited. Janusz didn't move. He had never enjoyed hunting. He didn't want to shoot anything.

The men fell silent, their breath steaming in front of them. Janusz looked at them all, guns lifted, cheeks red, the sparkle of frost on their eyelashes. What if they stopped traveling? What if they came to a rest right here in this snow-covered world and waited until the war was over? Surely they could hide up here?

Ambrose sighed loudly. He lowered his gun and put the safety catch on. "No. I heard them but I can't see them."

Bruno did the same. He coughed as the tension left the small group and began stamping his feet, as if he had grown stiff standing motionless for too long.

"I haven't eaten venison for a long time," he said.

"I've venison sausages back at the house," said Ambrose. "The trick is to make them with plenty of paprika."

Janusz rubbed his hands together. "They sound delicious. And I'm starving."

"Those deer are around here somewhere," said Franek. He still held his gun, cocked, ready to shoot.

"It's not safe hunting in this fog," said Janusz, wondering when they could get back and eat the sausages.

Franek balanced his gun on his shoulder, broke a small branch from a tree and threw it onto the ice for the dogs to retrieve. The big orange-colored hound ran for it. It turned with the stick in its mouth and slipped and slid onto its side.

Everything happened very quickly after that. Janusz saw the dog floundering, trying to get up, and then he heard the ice creak and groan, and watched in horror as the dog fell through a small gap into the lake.

"Burek!" called Ambrose. "Burek, you stupid dog!"

Ambrose pulled his backpack off his shoulders and stepped out onto the frozen lake, lowering himself quickly onto his belly and sliding out across the ice.

"We need to smash the ice!" he yelled. "Get the dog out from under it."

"I'll get him!" yelled Franek. Janusz saw the excitement in Franek's eyes, the determination in the way he ran out onto the lake, past Ambrose.

"No!" Bruno shouted. "Get off the ice! It's not safe!"

"Burek!" yelled Franek. "Burek! He's here! I can see him. I can get him out."

Franek hammered the ice with the butt of his rifle. He struck it hard twice, maybe three times. As he did so, a shot rang out and a flock of black crows in the treetops rose into the air. The gun sounded again and Franek fell to the ground, his body twisting. Ambrose slid along the ice beside him, sank his arm into the hole that had appeared, and pulled the orange dog out of the water.

Something caught Janusz's eye, a movement behind him, and he turned. Four red deer, their breath smoking in front of them, broke into the open, cantering past into the snowy woodland. Janusz watched them go. When he looked back at the lake, Franek lay motionless, his discharged rifle beside him, a red pool of blood spreading across the ice.

IPSWICH

Carrying her laden shopping bags, Silvana crosses the road at the tram station, walking through one busy street and then another until she finds herself outside Tony's pet shop. She hesitates. What is she going to say to him? She doesn't even know why she is there except that he asked her and she said yes. She pushes open the door, stepping into a cacophony of birdsong. The place smells of wood shavings and disinfectant, and Silvana tries not to cough as she breathes in the warm air.

It really is an emporium. There are puppies asleep on straw in cages, kittens, rabbits, even ducks, and chickens. White mice scurry in large wire mesh cages, and a whole wall is given over to an aviary filled with noisy parrots, canaries, budgerigars, and thumb-sized zebra finches. Further into the shop she sees dark tanks of fish, flashes of rainbows and oranges and golds flitting in and out of shadowy waters.

"I can get you any pet you want," says Tony. She looks up and sees him standing behind a wooden counter smiling at her, and feels glad she came. His face is full of pleasure and she can't help but feel flattered. He looks genuinely delighted to see her.

"What would you like?" says Tony, coming out from behind the counter. "A chinchilla? A tortoise? I supply zoos and circuses. An elephant for your son to ride to school on? A Suffolk ewe, a Norfolk ram?"

"I was passing," Silvana says, putting down her bags and taking off her gloves, "and I thought I would like to see the animals."

Tony gives her a kitten to hold, then a white mouse that tries to run up her sleeve. After that he puts a small black rabbit in the palm of her hand.

"You can have him as a gift. He likes you."

"He's lovely," Silvana says. "But I would have to pay you for it."

"Ah, well, this one is not for sale. It's only available as a gift."

She frowns at him, unsure of what to say. Is he laughing at her?

He leads her further into the shop, past aisles of dog biscuits and bird-seed and bins of leathery treats for dogs to chew.

Silvana looks down at a large wooden crate beside her. It is full of yellowed bones. She tries to look away but she can't; the bones have her attention. They call to her, all the polished ball-and-socket joints, the roughened shanks and nubbed ends. Piles of them, all around her. Her legs wobble underneath her.

"They're gruesome looking, aren't they," says Tony cheerfully. "Horses' bones mainly." He lifts one out of the bin and then drops it back with the others, catching hold of her as she staggers sideways. "Oh my God, I'm sorry. Are you all right?"

"I need some air. I think it's too hot in here."

Tony takes her arm and leads her through the back of the shop to a door. He pushes it open and hurries her out into a small yard.

"But you look terrible. I'm so sorry."

Silvana gulps clean air and steadies herself.

"I have to keep the place warm for the animals," says Tony. "Was it the bones? I'm sorry. I'm such a fool. I should have thought."

"Thought of what?" says Silvana, mopping her forehead with a handkerchief.

"How you might feel. Did they scare you? I understand what you've been through. What happened in your country. I've read about it. Those camps. I'm sorry. I'm so sorry."

Silvana backs away from him. "I should go now."

"Of course you shouldn't. Not yet. Please, at least let me offer you a cup of tea. You can't go home yet."

His eyes are dark brown and fixed on her. If she fell he would catch her. She knows it. That is why she is here. She has to place her trust somewhere, now that Janusz has hurt her so badly.

He cups her elbow in his hand. "Forgive me, but you look lonely, Silvana."

"I . . ."

"Don't misunderstand me. I'm glad you came."

"I should go . . ."

"Not until you tell me what makes you so sad. Do you need something? I can get you anything. Will you tell me what's troubling you?"

Silvana thinks of the letters. "Can you speak French?"

"French? No. Why?"

"Could you read French? It's like Italian, isn't it?"

"I don't think so. But I have a French-English dictionary somewhere. Would that help?"

"Yes. If I could borrow it."

"You can have it."

"And . . . And please don't tell my husband."

Tony's arm is around her waist and she feels the heat of it through her clothes.

"I won't breathe a word. Will you tell me one day why you want a dictionary? You're not planning on a holiday in the Côte d'Azur, are you?"

He lets go of her, laughing gently, and she tries to relax her face.

"No. Not a holiday."

"Good. I don't want to think you're going away. Well now," he says, stepping away from her, the intimacy between them vanishing. "May I get you that cup of tea?"

When he offers her a sandwich in his flat above the shop she realizes she has been hungry for days.

The foreman's office feels crowded with just the two of them in it. Silvana stands on one side of a wooden desk covered with paperwork piled high in untidy, slippery heaps. The foreman sits on the other side, puffing on a cigarette that hangs in the corner of his mouth, as he searches through his papers. Beside him a window looks out onto the shop floor, and Silvana wishes with all her heart she was still at her machine, working alongside the other women.

"I'm sorry, love," says the foreman, finally pulling a page out of a stack of documents. "Do you understand? We're laying you off. We're paying you now but you can't come back."

"Please. I can sew faster."

"You're not keeping up with the workload. We can't pay workers who can't keep up."

She thinks of pleading, of getting down on her knees. But she knows it would do no good. She has been a hopeless worker. Instead, she nods and apologizes.

Walking across the yard, she is surprised by the sense of relief she feels. The sun is warm on her face, and she is free of that dusty, dark factory.

When she arrives home, the house is empty. Janusz must have picked up Aurek from school and taken him for a walk. And how will she tell Janusz her news? He will see it as a failure.

She wanders into the garden and hears Janusz's voice drift over the fence. Peering over, she sees him with Gilbert and Tony sitting at a card table. Their heads are bent over it, almost touching, elbows splayed.

She walks out into the street and up to Doris's open front door.

"Hello, love," says Doris. She is standing in her hallway smoking a cigarette. "You've seen the men, have you?" She hoicks a thumb behind her. "Out in the garden, playing at cardsharps. Tony turned up with bottles of booze and organized an impromptu get-together. I've got your little lad in the front parlor with me. Go on through. He likes his grub, doesn't he? I don't know where he puts it. He's been eating bread and jam like it's going out of fashion."

The front parlor is a dark room filled with more furniture than she and Janusz have in their whole house. The walls are papered in white and olive green stripes. A mirror hangs above the fireplace with two large red and white china dogs sitting either side of it. There are ornaments on every surface.

Aurek is playing with a toy tractor, pushing it up and down the floor, weaving it in and out of the chair legs.

"He's been playing, happy as Larry, all afternoon. I'm glad you called around because I've got something for you. Here. Hair dye. Don't take this wrong, but I thought you could get rid of all that gray. My Geena gets 'em from Leslie's hairdressers. He got them cheap from Woolworths after they were bombed out. Chestnut Harmony. Looks lovely on the packet, doesn't it? Now, you sit down and we can get on with it."

Silvana hesitates. "I don't know." She touches her headscarf. "Perhaps I should ask Janusz?"

"Oh, leave him to his cards. This is just between us women. In this country you don't have to ask your husband's permission to do your hair. This isn't the Dark Ages, you know. It's best not to ask your husband anything. What they don't know they don't grieve over. Come on, I did a stint at a hairdresser's before I married Gilbert. I know what I'm doing. Let's get rid of that headscarf and bring you up to date."

Having her hair washed and her scalp rubbed makes Silvana feel sleepy and relaxed.

"I had long hair before," she tells Doris. "Long chestnut-red hair."

"Did you? Well, we're all a bit older now. There comes a time when it's better for a woman to have her hair short."

Doris wraps Silvana's hair in a towel like a turban, and they drink tea while they wait for the color to take. From the garden they can hear the men's voices, a rumble of talk and laughter. Silvana can hear Tony's laugh, louder than the other two.

"Have you known Mr. Benetoni a long time?" she asks.

Doris picks up a bag of curlers and starts sorting them on her lap.

"Tony? Years. I remember his mother. She was a lovely lady. Died when he was quite young. And then the poor man loses his wife. Terrible tragedy, that was. Tony went away during the war. People say he did something a bit hush-hush, but I don't think so. Gilbert says more likely he was banged up in prison somewhere when all the fuss about foreigners being spies went on. A couple of years ago he came back and opened up a pet shop. It was very nice to see him back. He's a real gentleman."

"And did you know his wife?"

"Not really. She was such a pretty young thing. She came from a very good family. Far too posh for Tony really, but she fell for him hook, line, and sinker. He was a real looker. Still is, or haven't you noticed?" Doris laughs throatily. "I must say, whoever wins him will have done very well for herself. Quite the eligible bachelor, Tony is. Pity the little boy didn't get his father's charm or his mother's looks. Funny kid, isn't he? He's the apple of his grandparents' eyes, though. They dote on him. Right little Billy Bunter. Your lad could do with a few of his pounds. Now—let's have a quick peek at your hair. Yes. That looks just right. Come on, let's get some curlers on."

When Doris has curled and set Silvana's hair, she moves the china dogs and calendars on the mantelpiece so that Silvana can look at herself in the mirror.

"Do you like it? That's what we called the 'victory style' during the war."

Silvana turns her head from side to side. Her hair is a dark shade of mahogany, curled tightly at the front and looser at the back. She doesn't recognize herself.

"Wait a minute." Doris scrabbles through her handbag and pulls out a small gold lipstick case. "Here. Put a bit of this on."

Silvana laughs. Doris is so excited for her. The woman is clasping her hands together, as if she is an artist who has just unveiled her latest masterpiece. The Polish woman remade. And why not? She kisses Doris on her powdered cheek, feeling pitted skin beneath her lips, and realizes life has taken its toll on Doris, too. "You are a good person," she whispers.

"Don't be daft."

"You remind me of a friend I once had," Silvana says, reaching down to stroke Aurek's head. "Hanka. She was very kind, like you."

"Oh now, stop. I'm just your neighbor. To tell you the truth, I like having you around. Since our Geena left home, I've missed out on female company. I used to like having my daughter at home. But they grow up so fast. Look at your little lad. He loves you, doesn't he? I've never seen a mother and son as close as you two. Gilbert calls you the Russian dollies, you know, those wooden toys that fit one inside the other? And the boy's the spitting image of you."

"Do you think so?"

"He's got your looks completely. Now, let's call the men in. I want to show them how I've got Vivien Leigh in my front parlor."

"No. No, don't. I'll show Janusz later."

"Nonsense. They may have had a few drinks this afternoon, but they can still appreciate my handiwork."

And Doris has left the room before Silvana can say another word.

The three men crowd into the room and Doris takes Silvana by the shoulders, turning her one way and then the other.

"So, what do you think?"

"I didn't recognize you," says Janusz. He is swaying on his feet slightly, and it is easy to see he has drunk too much.

She is embarrassed by his vagueness, the way he smiles sleepily at everybody. She looks at Tony and realizes that she cares what he thinks of her hair. She is anxious about his reaction. What if he thinks she looks ridiculous? She keeps her eyes fixed on Janusz, his slumped figure, the cigarette in his hand, the smoke from it rising lightly over his hand and wrist.

"You're beautiful, Silvana," says Tony, as if he has read her thoughts. He catches hold of Doris's waist, swinging her around the room in a waltz. "And so are you, Mrs. Holborn."

"Oh now, stop that. Put me down."

"Don't get her dancing," says Gilbert. "That's how she caught me. I was only a young lad. She took me in her arms and that was that. I was hooked like a sprat on a line."

"You do talk nonsense," laughs Doris. "Our Geena is the one that likes dancing. You should give her a call, Tony. I'm sure she'd be free one evening to go dancing in town with you."

"I'd be glad to," says Tony. "I haven't been dancing in a long time." He catches Silvana's eye and winks.

"Aurek?" Silvana turns to her son. "Look. Look at Mama. What do you think? Aurek?"

Aurek shakes his head. "Tractor," he says, and pushes it over the carpet, crashing it into the chair leg, knocking over a brass coal scuttle, and sending a pair of fire tongs flying into the hearth.

"Mind what you're doing, young lad," says Doris.

"Well." Gilbert rubs his hands together. "Shall we get on, gentlemen? Another round of cards?"

Tony stops swinging Doris around. He salutes her. "Good idea. Another game. I'll get some more refreshments from the car. I have presents for the ladies, too. Would you excuse me for a moment?"

"All right," says Gilbert. "But if you're any longer than five minutes, we'll send a search party out."

Tony comes back with two boxes of chocolates and a sugar mouse.

"There we are. Milk Tray and something for Aurek."

"Oh now," says Doris, as he hands her a box with a red ribbon tied across it. "It's been years since I got a box of chocolates from a man."

"Don't go spoiling her," says Gilbert. "God only knows what she'll be wanting next."

"At least I'm not slurring my words," says Doris. "I'll make you all a cup of tea. Jan, you look like you need one. Come through to the kitchen."

Doris ushers them out of the room, and Tony and Silvana stand together in the front parlor, Aurek wheeling the tractor around their legs.

"Open it," says Tony, handing her a box of chocolates.

Silvana takes off the ribbon and the lid. There are no chocolates. Instead a small red book nestles inside. A dictionary.

"It's what you wanted, isn't it?"

She nods, trying to think of something to say.

"Shhh," he says. "Not a word." He touches her cheek with his fingertips, gives her a crooked smile, and leaves the room.

That night, after Janusz has gone to bed, Silvana sits at the kitchen table with the red dictionary open on her lap and Janusz's Polish-English dictionary beside her on the table. Slowly, she translates the first few lines of one of the letters. It takes her a long time, flicking through the books, writing down words in English, then finding them in Polish. Finally, she has something she can make sense of.

> *My Dearest,*
>   *It is necessary that you do not feel bad. If you have no news of your wife, perhaps she find someone else? And remember, you never want to fall in love. It just arrives. I read something today. Where love is, there is forgiveness. I believe this.*

Silvana walks to the pantry and puts the letter back in the box, turns out the light and climbs the stairs to bed in the dark. She knows the number of stairs, the turn on the landing, the feel of the banister under her hand. This house has become her home. But it is a home full of lies.

And if Janusz knew Silvana's secret, would he forgive her? She has no words for what happened. No: it is better to guard her secret, to keep it dark, pickled, and slippery, like a jar of something forgotten, pushed so far to the back of the pantry that not even she can remember what is floating in there.

In the bedroom she puts the red dictionary in a drawer along with her headscarf. Silvana thinks of Doris as she slips into bed, of what she said about Aurek. How he looks like her. She closes her eyes. Sometimes it feels as though Doris knows everything and absolutely nothing all at the same time.

She hears Janusz stirring in the bed beside her.

"What have you been doing?"

Silvana starts at the sound of his sleepy voice.

"I was having a cup of cocoa. I didn't mean to wake you."

She pulls her blankets around her and shuts her mind to the letters. They hurt her too much to think about.

"Janusz? They sent me home. I lost my job."

Silvana turns on the bedside lamp.

Blinking in the light, Janusz looks hungover, his eyes bleary, his hair standing up in tufts. He asks her to turn off the light.

"You never liked the job anyway," he says. "We'll talk about it later. I have to sleep now."

Silvana listens to Janusz's breathing settle. She thinks of Tony. The way he looked at her when he gave her the dictionary, the touch of his fingers against her cheek. Her hand rests on her chest and, slipping it inside her nightdress, she cups her breast, fingers tracing circles over the nipple. She's come this far. Her goals for the rest of her life are clear to her: marriage, motherhood, this house. A third of the rest of her life for each of these. With these thoughts turning in her mind, she buttons her nightdress, sinks back onto the pillow, and lets sleep pull her into the darkness of her dreams.

POLAND

Silvana

Gregor was a handsome man who knew it. Long limbed and lean, he wore a tailored tweed suit under a long trench coat and a mustard-colored scarf tied tightly around his long neck. He said he was a doctor. He'd worked in Russia, living in backwood villages in the Urals miles from any towns. He was a *znakhar*, a practitioner of folk medicine. He had a small group of people with him now: three women and a man. The first day Silvana joined them, Gregor instructed her to look out for anthills. The old man with him suffered from arthritis.

"I need to find the ants that build their hills up out of the ground. If you find them we have to gather the nests whole. The secretion the ants use in nest building is excellent as a cure for crippling diseases."

"He knows what he's talking about," said one of the women to Silvana. "He saved my baby." She stroked her stomach. "It's early days. I'm just eight weeks, but I'm as sick as a dog already. I come from a village fifty or so miles north of here. I met Gregor a few weeks ago. I was bleeding and he gave me medicine that stopped it. Now look at me. I'm fine. He's an amazing man."

Her name was Elsa. She had a round, freckled face framed by a thick bob of dark, shiny hair. Her eyes were large and long lashed and her lips plump and given to pouting. She followed Gregor everywhere. When she was too tired to move from the camp she sat and watched for him.

There was an old couple. He was fond of complaining of the cold, rubbing his bald head, and making jokes about needing a haircut. She was wide hipped, loose skinned, her hair plaited and piled on top of her head like gray sausages. She took charge of cooking whatever Gregor brought them. The rest of the time she fussed over her ailing husband.

The last was a dark-haired woman called Lottie. Silvana called her the pianist. She wore her hair in a tight bun and had elegant hands, which she stared at for long periods at a time.

Gregor showed Silvana how to use a knife to skin animals and how to set traps, and she was surprised how quickly she learned to survive in the trees.

"Here," he said, handing her a dead rabbit the first time they went hunting. "Don't be afraid. Take one of my knives and I'll show you what to do."

They were deep in the forest, among bracken and thorny brambles.

Silvana nodded. She had already skinned rabbits with Hanka when they wintered at the farm. She would show this man she knew just what to do. She took the knife he offered her, a short-handled, stubby hunting knife. Aurek crouched beside her.

Gregor smiled at her, as if she were his favorite student.

"Start at the hind legs. We want to keep the pelt whole. You'll be pleased with rabbit skin gloves come the cold weather. You make a cut across to the thigh. Be bold with the knife. Don't be scared, it's quite . . ."

Silvana took the knife and cut swiftly. Minutes later, she held up a bloody rabbit skin. "Like this?"

Gregor laughed. "So what have we here? A peasant? And I thought you said you came from Warsaw? You're no city girl. But you're not quite a peasant either. What are you doing alone in the forest with your dark-eyed gypsy child?"

She looked him straight in the eyes, hoping he would look away. He didn't.

"My husband is a Polish soldier. While he is away, I am trying to keep our son safe." She drew a protective arm around Aurek. "The forest is a good place for hiding him. After the war my husband will come and find us and we will live in Warsaw again."

"Hmm. That's your story. I think you're a forest sprite. A lovely maiden who walked through the trees. Gathering herbs, plucking roots. The moon she stole, the sun she ate."

He picked up the skinned rabbit and shook it free of the flies that were beginning to gather. "That's a Russian incantation. It scares away witches. But you don't look scared, so maybe you are who you say you are. Whoever you are, it's good to have somebody who can handle a knife. Come on, we can see if our other traps have caught anything. You might get those rabbit fur gloves if you're lucky."

Sometimes, she woke to find Gregor beside her.

"Are you sleeping? If you're cold I can lie beside you."

"Please go away."

"Come on, let me warm you."

"Go away."

"It's your loss," he whispered as he got up. "Not mine."

Late at night, when the sounds of sleeping people were louder than the noise of the forest, Silvana heard him with first Elsa and then Lottie, his feet cracking twigs as he crept from one woman to the other.

Over the summer months, he took Silvana hunting with him, saying she was quicker and more cunning than the other women. She liked those days, the two of them with Aurek, moving quietly through the trees. They found a wicker basket in a ditch and propped it up with a stick, a long line of string attached to it. They caught squirrels, weasels, even a baby wild boar once. Gregor snatched the hairy, squealing little creature into his arms. Silvana grabbed Aurek and they ran as fast as they could, afraid that the mother would be somewhere nearby and angry.

One day in late summer, Gregor took them looking for mushrooms and they discovered a deer, eyes clouded with death, head stretched out as if it had fallen running. Gregor bent over it.

"It's been shot. Help me lift it. Whoever shot it will be coming to look for it. We've got to get it away from here. This will feed us all."

Silvana grabbed the forelegs and helped Gregor lift it onto his shoulders. She walked beside him, carrying Aurek. The boy was light and he clung to her with a strong grip, so she could have her hands free to help steady Gregor's burden.

He stopped in a clearing and dropped the carcass onto the ground.

"I can't carry it any further. It's too heavy. We have to cut it up here."

Silvana set Aurek onto his feet.

"Here?"

He pulled two knives from his coat and handed one to her. Then he bent over the body and slit open the deer's belly. Its guts spilled, a rush of silken crimsons and blues, and the body seemed to sigh, as if all its air was suddenly lost.

"We'll throw the innards away," Gregor was saying, as he stuck his hands into the bloody body. "And we have to bury the meat now. If we leave it in the open, flies will lay eggs in it. We can't eat maggoty meat, no matter how hungry we are. Once it's covered up it will keep. We have to make sure the flies don't get to it, that's all."

Silvana turned away, her stomach contracting at the smell rising off the flesh. Gregor glanced up at her.

"Can you do this?"

She nodded. This was no time for weakness. They needed meat. Aurek needed to eat.

"Yes," she said. "Yes, of course I can."

She knelt and he told her what to cut, how to dissect the body. The guts were hot and she could feel her own heart pulsing inside her, quickening as she hauled the innards away and dug a shallow grave for them.

"Have you ever seen a wounded man?" Gregor asked. "Someone bleeding badly?"

"No. Why do you ask?"

"There are men in these forests. Men who are fighting the Germans. They need people like you. You could join them. You're tough enough to fight with them. I could take you to their camp. You could learn how to use a gun. And if you didn't want to fight, they still need nurses. Women who don't flinch at the sight of blood. You could do it."

Silvana was cleaning the cavities of the deer with grass. She stopped for a moment, wiped her sleeve across her cheek, and looked at Aurek chasing butterflies, his face and clothes daubed with deer blood.

"I have my son to look after. I'll do what I have to for him. I'm not capable of more than that."

Gregor wiped his knife clean on the ground. "Who knows what we're capable of in wartime. Come on. We'd better dig a hole quickly. We need to bury most of this."

One moonlit night at the end of the summer, when everything was bathed in blue and silver light, Silvana saw Gregor lie down with the old woman. She oozed flesh from beneath his large-framed body, and Silvana was sure she could hear the old woman's tired bones creaking as Gregor moved slowly on top of her, back and forth like a rolling pin pressing pastry. Beside them, pretending to be asleep, her husband curled up like a baby and sucked his thumb in an impotent sulk.

Silvana closed her eyes, unsettled by the desire that stirred within her.

Janusz

Janusz wanted to stay. To try to make sense of what had happened. Ambrose said there was nothing they could do. Franek would be buried in the village. Ambrose would write to the family and tell them the boy had died in a hunting accident.

Bruno grew angry and insisted he write the letter himself. The family would not receive a letter from a stranger. They would be told that Franek had been a war hero. There was no need to say that Franek had been carrying a loaded gun and had shot himself.

Janusz watched him sitting in the kitchen composing the letter, throwing away attempt after attempt until he had it right.

A sledge arrived in the early hours of the morning loaded with goat-skins, and they said good-bye to Ambrose in the dark.

"Send my letter to Franek's family," said Bruno as they left. "Promise me you'll send it today."

It was a long, sorrowful journey, weaving through small villages, along roads lined with huge snowbanks, tunnels of white which turned the air blue and the trees black. Neither Janusz nor Bruno spoke. The smell of the skins they sat upon permeated everything, a greasy stink of goats that turned Janusz's stomach.

They arrived at a school, where they were given glasses of vodka mixed with duck fat.

"*For strength*," somebody said, handing Janusz a glass of the cloudy infusion. "It's a good medicine after what you've been through."

He drank it straight down and asked for another. And then another.

That same day, two girls accompanied Janusz and Bruno to the train station, kissing them good-bye as though they were their girlfriends.

"Remember," said the girl standing with Janusz, "you must sit in another carriage to your friend. You must travel alone. Two men together will be stopped by the police."

"Good-bye," said Janusz. His head spun with the effect of too much vodka. A wind swept along the station platform, snow spiraling and circling within it, and Janusz tried to put himself between the icy blast and the girl, sheltering her from the worst of the cold.

She had brown hair, short and curly under her woolen hat. Her eyes were slanted and small and her eyebrows heavy. The cold nipped her nose red. She stood on tiptoe and kissed him. "Make a good show," she whispered. "You must look like a local. Pretend you are saying good-bye to your sweetheart."

"I'll miss you," he said obligingly, and thought that in fact he would miss her.

"I love you," he whispered, his words misting into clouds in the frozen air. And it seemed believable. He pulled her into his arms. Loving a stranger might be the easiest thing in the world to do. He was filled with a force of wanting that came from somewhere other than the heart and was clear and uncomplicated as a result. He kissed the girl, pulling off his gloves, risking the cold, unbuttoning her coat, trying to push a way past her layers of clothing. He wanted only to take this stranger and go back to the school and undress her. She pulled away from him, pressing her hand against his chest.

"You're drunk."

"What's your name?"

"It's best you don't know."

"Please?"

"You don't really need to know."

"I do. I want to see you again. After the war."

The girl shook her head.

"My name is Roza."

"Roza. When the war is over, I'll come back."

She kissed him gently on the lips. "You think you're the only one who has told me this? It's what every soldier says. Romantic fools, every one of you. Go. Don't forget to wave at me from the train. Make it look good."

Janusz got on the train and tried to wave at her but the snow was falling too thickly and he couldn't see her. He studied his hands in his lap and felt foolish for letting his emotions rise up as they had done. He wondered if Bruno had seen him, pushing his way into the girl's clothes. He thought of Silvana and knew that he would never have felt this way about another girl if he could have stayed close to her. It was loneliness driving him mad.

At some point, the police must have boarded the train. Afterward, when Bruno told the story of their escape, there were always police, but Janusz could never remember them. He'd been told to keep his head down and not make eye contact with anyone.

Memories of home carried him forward as the train rattled and lurched: his mother playing the piano; his father coming home from work, talking of politics and local government. He remembered the apple orchards behind Silvana's parents' house where he had waited for her when they were courting. He thought again of the old woman and the mistake he had made, thinking her just a girl. The blood on her feet. Her white hair. He thought of Franek and wanted to say how it felt to see the boy lying helpless on the ice. But there was no one to confess to. He leaned against the window and watched the day turn into night. When the train stopped early the next morning, Bruno walked past and Janusz got up and followed him.

Strangers met them on the platform. They were passed among these people. They crossed a frozen river in silence and took another train. Janusz realized Roza had been right. It had been foolish to suggest he would ever see her again. And Silvana and his son? Bruno told him to forget them. He would probably never see them again either.

IPSWICH

In September, Aurek starts back at school. Now that he has Peter to accompany him into his classroom he doesn't make a fuss, and Silvana experiences a sense of dismay as he lets go of her hand and walks away. It's a strange feeling, no longer being governed by the need to stay together. The boy doesn't need her like he used to. It hurts to see him walk away so easily.

Peter, who, Silvana learns from Tony, stays with his grandparents during the week, joins Silvana and Aurek in the park on their way to school every morning. His grandmother walks him to the edge of the park. She is a thin, gray-haired woman in a tweed skirt and high-necked blouse. Narrow as a knife blade, sideways on she almost disappears. When she takes the boy in her arms, though, her thin face glows. She swells, becoming solid, warm, and startling, her needs as obvious as a baby's. The old woman kisses Peter's plump cheeks fiercely, as if she is afraid she might never see him again.

Silvana knows that the old lady's hands contain the fear of loss in them. She has lost a daughter. No wonder she clings to the boy. And no wonder Peter shrinks from her touch. He must feel the weight of his mother's death every time his grandmother's bony hands fold around his face.

Silvana would like to talk to her, tell her she understands, but the old woman always ignores her. She turns her head and sets her body metal-thin once again. The woman only has eyes for her grandson.

On Friday afternoons, Tony collects Peter at the school gates to take him home for the weekend. Just the sight of the man standing, waiting for his son, makes Silvana's heart race. It frightens her how she hopes to see him, and she often tries to hide among the other mothers collecting their children. He always finds her though, his hand lifted high in greeting, as if he has seen her in the middle of a much larger crowd than there really is, and has to attract her attention with an extravagant gesture.

They walk through the park with the two boys racing ahead. Talking to Tony is so easy. With him she can leave her past behind. She believes he understands her. Every time Silvana searches for a word, he has it already, finishing the sentence for her.

It used to be like that with Janusz when they were young. They could look at each other and know what the other was thinking. Even their dreams overlapped sometimes. These days, there is a cool politeness between them.

"I miss certain foods," she says in response to Tony's question about her homeland. He often asks questions about Poland, and she is happy to answer as long as he doesn't touch on the war. When he tries to ask her about the years she spent in the forest, she changes the subject, or diverts his attention, pointing out a squirrel scampering along the path, or finds her coat sleeves need straightening, a button needs buttoning, her handbag clasp checking.

"Pierogi," she says. "I miss them. Dough filled with cabbage and cheese, or mushrooms and onions. Anything you like. We always ate them with sour cream. You can have sweet ones, too. Honey and apple and nuts. When I think of pierogi, I feel . . ."

"Nostalgic?"

"*Tesknota.* Yes. Nostalgic. That's why I don't think of these things very often."

Tony holds his hands in front of him, a politician about to give a speech, playing to the crowds. Silvana likes this self-important way he has about him. As if he is out to impress her. And it has been years since a man has tried to do that.

"Do you ever think of going back?"

"Janusz thinks we'll be able to go home one day, but how can we?

There's nothing to go back to. Our homeland is communist now. We couldn't go back even if we wanted to."

"But Aurek has the right to know where he came from. Everybody should know who they belong to and where they come from."

Silvana looks at him. "Aurek belongs to me," she says firmly.

On the edge of the park, they turn to watch the boys playing behind them.

"Well, I had better go," Silvana says.

"Must you? Why not let the boys play a little longer?"

Tony holds her hands for a moment, gently, as if they might break if he grips them too firmly. She looks at them when he lets go, to see if they are as fragile as he thinks. But no. She has tough hands. Small and muscular and always searching for something to fill them.

"I'd love to walk you home," he says. "But people might talk if Janusz isn't back from work and they see us arrive together. I wouldn't want to set tongues wagging. The British are narrow-minded and sharp-tongued, and the inhabitants of this town are the worst of a bad bunch."

"Well," she says as they wait for Aurek to come down from the tree he is climbing. "I'll see you again soon."

"Perhaps you and Janusz would like to take the boys for a walk this weekend. Or we could go to the boating lake with them?"

"Yes, that would be nice."

She is used to Tony making suggestions like this. Sometimes he shows up, but more often than not he doesn't. Then he turns up out of the blue, days later, with gifts for them: oranges and glassy green grapes; a freckled banana each; pork sausages that they have to cook right there and then, because they are, as he says, slightly on the turn. Things so unexpected and delicious, Silvana forgets all about the missed outings.

"Tell me," he says. "Before you go. The dictionary? I know I shouldn't ask, but I am curious. Was it useful to you? You've never said."

Silvana considers the question, fidgeting with her hair. She makes a comment about Peter, how he is growing tall for his age.

"Yes, he is," says Tony. "But the dictionary? What was it for?"

Silvana casts a look around. There is nothing to distract him from his line of questioning. The park is empty, the squirrels have already been pointed out, and if she fiddles with her clothes and hair anymore he will think she has lice.

"Silvana?"

She takes a deep breath and tries the truth. "I had some letters I needed to translate."

"Letters? Just some letters?"

Tony's brown eyes are steady on her, inviting. *Talk to me*, they say to her. And she wants to. She is tired of carrying Janusz's secrets. She has enough of her own. She coughs nervously and tips her chin toward him, trying to look as if she is amused by this conversation.

"The letters belong to Janusz. They're from another woman."

"Another woman?"

"Isn't it silly?" she says, trying to sound as English as she can. "Just so silly."

"Oh, Silvana. I'm sorry." Tony takes her hands in his again but this time he is forceful, crushing her fingers. A sudden, horrific thought comes to her: what if he confronts Janusz?

"It's complicated," she says, wishing she could speak Polish to him now. She itches to unroll her own language, to taste it on her lips, all its nuances and figures of speech, all the subtle dips and turns her own tongue could produce. She could explain everything to him in Polish. "It's nothing. I only told you because it's so tiring keeping secrets all the time. Janusz is a good husband, really he is. And he's a good father to Aurek."

Tony pulls her to him, pressing her hands against his chest, and this time there is no mistaking the way he holds her.

"Silvana, darling. I had no idea . . ."

She looks into his eyes, and for a moment she thinks he is going to kiss her. And yet she doesn't pull away from him.

"What if I tell Janusz I know and then he leaves me? What if he goes back to her? What will Aurek and I do then?"

Tony leans toward her, his voice hot against her face. "But you must know . . ."

"I don't know anything."

"You must know I will always help you. You must realize how I . . ."

Behind them, Aurek tumbles down from the tree and wraps his arms around Silvana's legs. She pulls her hands free of Tony's grip and steps away from him.

"Really, I must go."

"Don't. Come to the flat. Now. We can talk. Please don't go like this."

He looks so sad that she is sure one of them or perhaps both will start to cry, and crying is pointless. Crying would be a sign that it is all too much. Crying would show Tony that she is a woman with no control over her life. She has already been a fool telling him. It would be better to explain that she is just a mean-faced survivor who came to England to give Aurek a father.

She whispers, "Janusz and I . . . We don't know who we are anymore. So much happened during the war. The past won't leave me alone. During the war, I thought Janusz was dead. All those years apart. I never imagined he would find me. Too much happened . . ."

She looks into his eyes again. She has no idea what she is doing, telling Tony about her life. She might as well be out on a window ledge, about to fall to her death. She is risking everything, and for what? The chance to tell him the untellable? Or to feel the heat of this man's eyes upon her?

"Please forget I said anything. Aurek needs his father. I . . . Please, just pretend I never said anything. I have to go."

With a residue of strength still within herself, Silvana turns on her heels, hoping Tony will see only the back of a strong woman walking away from him. He calls after her, urging her to wait, but she does not turn around.

Aurek hurries to keep up. Silvana knows he doesn't like it when she walks too fast, but it is all she can do not to break into a run. Aurek is whining but she cannot slow down. She grabs his hand and pulls him along. At the edge of the park she stops.

"Aurek. Look behind you. Can you see them?"

Aurek shakes his head.

"Good. Come here. I'll carry you. We have to hurry home."

Aurek struggles in her arms and she knows he is too old for this kind of embrace, but she begs him to be still and finally he wraps his legs around her back and snakes his arms around her neck.

By the time Silvana puts the key in the front door, she has convinced herself that Janusz will be there, that he will know everything she has said. But when she steps into the hallway, the house is empty and the only sound is the clock ticking on the mantelpiece in the front parlor.

She opens the back door for Aurek, who runs outside and climbs the rope ladder into his tree house. In the pantry, the wooden box sits on a shelf. Just the sight of it brings on anxiety. She will burn the letters. She'll take them out and burn them, and then the three of them will be able to live like they had done before.

She picks up the box and sets it on the kitchen table. Carefully she pushes her hand through the cloths and brushes and tins of polish, but the letters are not there. She yanks everything out of the box, shaking it, turning it upside down. What now? Slowly she refills the box, picking up the things she threw around, tidying the contents. She puts it back in the pantry and closes the door, leaning against it as though afraid it might spring open of its own accord. Then she steps out into the garden, gulping lungfuls of damp air.

The vegetable plot below the tree has yielded onions and carrots; she and Janusz harvested them together. There are more onions to be lifted. Janusz planted ones that keep growing. *Everlasting*, they are called. Silvana sighs. What kind of a fool is she turning into where even the name of an onion can make her feel weak?

She runs a hand over the heads of rust-colored chrysanthemums. The holly bushes Janusz planted are still tiny, but they sparkle with bloodred berries. In Poland they'd say those berries were the sign of a hard winter to come. Blue Michaelmas daisies and white anemones tumble over each other, and the last of Janusz's giant pink and purple dahlias, staked and supported, proudly rise up toward the sky, glowing in the late afternoon light.

Silvana picks a few flowers until she has a small bunch in her hand. If Janusz knew she had found the letters, surely he would have said something? He must have moved them thinking she knew nothing about them. She feels a sense of relief that the letters have gone. As if some tight knot within her has been straightened out.

Maybe she feels better because she has told Tony about them? She persuades herself Janusz has thrown the letters away. This means the affair must be over. It was a wartime thing, that's all. And what about herself and Tony?

She is a master at lying to herself, pretending certain things happened in one way and not another, and she manages to settle the story in her mind. She might have had a small infatuation for Tony, but it is over now. He is just a friend of the family. Nothing more than that. A man with a boy the same age as their son. She looks down at the bunch of flowers in her hands and realizes she has plucked all the petals off and is holding only a few stalks and leaves. She lets them fall onto the lawn.

As the sun sets, the garden becomes somber. The sky turns turquoise and the first star appears.

"Come down," she calls to Aurek in his tree house. "Come inside and we'll make tea for your father."

Father is such a good word. It fits with *family, mother,* and *son.* Safe words. Standing there, on the lawn Janusz has lovingly mown and rolled, looking up at the back of their house, she knows she must never see Tony again. Their friendship is over.

POLAND

Silvana

A cold wind installed itself, sweeping through the forests, blowing the leaves off the trees. Silvana watched the leaves tumbling down, circling and dancing around her. It had been over a year since she had left Warsaw. Over a year since she had last seen Janusz. She heard a noise of cracking twigs and sat up as Gregor lumbered into view, carrying a sack, which he dropped in the middle of their camp.

He made a great show of emptying it, handing out black bread and apples to everybody.

"And I have . . . salt!" he said.

He dipped his finger in a paper parcel and licked it. "We will need it for the winter. We should make a store if we can. There's a woodsman who has a cottage a mile or so from here. He's friendly and willing to give us food. I treated his wife for stomach pains. I used *chaga*, a fungus that grows on birch trees. She's promised me she will kill a couple of chickens for us. Then we can have a feast."

In dribs and drabs after that, Gregor brought other things, some milk in a can, more bread, some potatoes. The now heavily pregnant Elsa ate first. She wasn't far off giving birth, that was obvious. Gregor sat beside her until she had enough. Silvana pushed Aurek forward.

"After her, he must eat. He's a child. He needs the food."

She sat him on her lap and guarded him while he ate. The others talked about her but she didn't care. The boy had to eat.

They reorganized the camp for winter, weaving wild clematis and the bark of the birch trees into panels to make walls for their huts.

Branches were bound together to make shelters which Silvana padded with moss and dried bracken. Gregor walked among them, undoing mistakes and handing out sheaves of willow canes he had gathered. Without him, Silvana doubted any of them would survive.

He came to her again one night, pushing his rough hands into her clothes, disturbing the small amount of warmth she had, sending cold air against her skin. His breath smelled sour.

"Who are you keeping yourself for?" he asked. "Your husband is never coming back. He's dead on a battlefield somewhere. Stop this ridiculous show of independence. It's not worth it."

His words broke something in her and she gave a sob as she opened her arms to him, pressing her lips against his.

It was over fast. He was on her and Silvana was bucking under his fingers, already finished with him as he pushed himself inside her. Afterward she lay in his arms, aware of Aurek next to her, fidgeting in his sleep.

"You'd better go," she whispered.

"I like you, forest girl," he said.

"Please, just leave. I made a mistake. I'm sorry."

Silvana heard him pissing against a tree. Gregor was a dog, a wolf with his pack. She felt like a fool.

Janusz

Janusz and Bruno left Yugoslavia in a fishing boat and arrived in Marseilles, sitting among piles of netting and baskets of fish. France was more beautiful than Janusz had imagined. Dusty yellow mimosa spread a buttery light across the hillsides. Stumpy palm trees and leathery blue agaves shimmered in the heat of an early spring.

They and the other men with them were told they should catch a train to Lyon, where they'd be given uniforms and an army rank. Bruno didn't want to. He had plans to get to England. When the boat docked and they felt solid ground under them, Bruno pulled Janusz away and they slipped into the shadowy, labyrinthine streets of the old city.

The first thing they did was swim. They stripped off their filthy clothes and ran into the sea. While Bruno splashed and yelled, Janusz dived into the waves and swam out as far as he could. He drifted in the swell of the waves, looking back at the coastline. The water was crystal clear. He was in a country he had only ever seen in books.

It was Janusz who strung enough French together to get them some rooms, and they ended up in a ramshackle, skinny building in Marseilles's backstreets. Each day they walked to a small curve of beach near the port and sat in the sun.

"You look like a lobster from the fish market." Bruno grinned through the smoke of a cigarette hanging from his mouth. "I've never seen a man so sunburned."

Janusz ignored him. "We can't do this, just sit around all day. We need to join a French unit."

"Maybe, maybe not. I'm in no hurry right now. We can afford to stay for a week or so. If they want us, they can come looking. We can have a couple of weeks before we risk our lives again."

Each day they hiked to different beaches. Each evening they walked back and ate in bars, plates of grilled octopus and orange sea urchins. Janusz pushed them around with his fork.

"I don't know how you can eat this," he said. "Why can't we just have a steak?"

"It's cheap and it's good," said Bruno. "Look over there." He nodded toward the waitress. "She's pretty." Bruno pushed back his chair and got up from the table. "I don't know what you are going to do tomorrow, but I think I'll be busy."

"With her?"

"Why not?"

Janusz turned his head away. "Do what you want." He didn't think the girl would be interested in any case. Bruno barely spoke a word of French.

The next day, Bruno was still with the waitress and Janusz set off on his own. He found a beach and walked for miles until the sand gave way to rocks and boulders. Seagulls squealed as Janusz found their nests and took their eggs, large blue-white ovals. The seagulls wheeled and dived at him until he was forced to run, his hands above his head in surrender.

He walked in the tide, trouser legs rolled up, shirt tied around his waist. A heat haze rising off the waves made him dizzy and his head began to throb. Sitting down by some rocks, he made a pillow out of his shirt and closed his eyes.

When he woke the sun had shifted around and he was in the full heat of its rays. Dizzy and thirsty he wandered back to his room, where he drank a jugful of water and poured another over his head and neck. He lay down, soaking wet, cocooned himself in a sheet, and thought of Silvana. He staggered up and hunted around until he found a pen and a scrap of paper by the side of Bruno's bed. But he couldn't think what to write. What could he say? I am in France in the sun and I hope you are safe with my parents? He dared not even think of her in Poland. He felt dumb and thickheaded. He put the pen and paper down and collapsed on his bunk.

That night he dreamed in his airless room that his tightening, burned body had split open like a chrysalis. That another man, another Janusz, emerged from his skin and stepped slowly out into the airless night, eased from his shell by the sweat that poured off him. That this other man stood in the moonlight and loped through the streets until he came to the sea.

The Mediterranean, so clear and fresh by day, had turned silky black, and he paused for a moment at the water's edge before wading out into it, letting the waves lick his raw new body. He was somebody else. He had been reborn from the air into water. A birth in reverse.

He woke with a terrible thirst. He tried to move, but the pain across his back stopped him.

He heard Bruno's whispering voice, "Jan? Are you getting up today? Listen, there's a camp in the hills above the city. I met some men last night. The Germans are making their way south. They should be here in a matter of months, maybe weeks. The men I met say we can join a military unit and get a boat to England. We need to move on. What do you think? Jesus, look at you."

He held up the sheet.

"God, man, you look awful. Can you hear me? Look at you, covered in blisters. Jesus help you, you're sunburned all over."

Bruno opened the windows, coughing. "You need air in here."

Janusz opened his eyes. The wallpaper swirled. He tried to speak, but his lips cracked and he tasted blood again.

"He cannot stay here."

The landlady stood in the doorway, black and gray hair piled high on her head, coral pink lipstick and spidery black eyelashes.

"Stupid boy. You are too fair for the sun. Look at you. You're dried out like a piece of salt cod."

Janusz heard Bruno pleading in a broken mix of French and Polish. He forced his dry lips to whisper: "I am sorry, madam. I'll leave. It's not safe for you to have me here." Levering himself off the bed on an elbow, he gestured to Bruno. "Hand me my clothes."

"No, no, no." The woman sighed. "You speak French; that makes it easier. I'll find somewhere for you to go. I have a friend with a farm. You can rest there."

She stared at his naked body. "When you're better you can work for them. You're stocky enough. You look like a peasant."

A day later, Janusz set out, clothes sticky and uncomfortable, body stiff and painful. As the cart carried him higher into the hills beyond Marseilles the air became sweeter. The smell of the sea faded and was replaced by the scent of pine trees and hot greenery.

IPSWICH

Silvana refuses to think of Tony. She avoids walking through the park and stays away from the pet shop. It is hard to keep him from her mind, but she manages it. Every time an image of Tony comes into her head—his brown eyes, his curling black hair shiny with oil, his hands moving as he talks—she clamps down on it, concentrating on the duster she is holding or the coal she is shoveling in the small coal store in the backyard. Like a tailor using only what material they have in their hand, she fashions her life with Janusz.

"You're not to play with Peter anymore," she tells Aurek one evening as she prepares their supper. She busies herself at the stove, banging saucepans together loudly, scraping at their bubbling contents with a wooden spoon, her voice rising over the noise. "Aurek? Did you hear me?"

"Why?"

"Why?" She throws the wooden spoon into the sink and faces the boy. "What do you mean why? You will do as you are told, do you hear me? He's not your friend anymore."

She doesn't mean to, but the way the boy looks at her, defiantly, as if she is someone to be hated, makes her lash out at him, her hand connecting with his shoulder. He staggers and falls sideways, knocking himself against the table, then scrambles to his feet, backing away from her.

"Aurek! No," she says, horrified. She has never hit him. Never. "No," she cries. "I'm sorry."

Aurek darts out of the kitchen, through the hall, fumbling with the front door latch before she can reach him. She grabs the door as he opens it, trying to catch hold of him, but he slips outside into the dark evening, straight out into the pouring rain.

She knows there's no point in going after him but she walks the streets, splashing through puddles, the blackness of the night pressing against her eyes. For an hour she searches, although she knows it is no use. He will not come back until he is ready.

"Where on earth have you been?" says Janusz when she comes back into the house.

She stands blinking in the hallway, her hair dripping water into her eyes. The house smells of burned food and she remembers the pans she left on the stove. The kitchen door is open and she can see a pall of cooking smoke drifting just above their heads.

"It's Aurek," she says. "He's outside. He'll come back. We have to wait."

Two hours later, there is a knock at the front door and Aurek stands there, his clothes soaked through, hair plastered smooth and dark as an otter. It's more than Silvana can stand. She pushes past Janusz, ignoring the way Aurek shrinks from her.

"Aurek, let me dry you . . ."

Janusz puts his hand out and pulls her back.

"Leave him to me. Come on, young lad. Let's get you dry."

Aurek looks darkly at Silvana and then puts his hand in Janusz's outstretched palm. He might as well have stabbed her with a knife.

Silvana sits on the top stair listening to Janusz talking to the boy in his bedroom, explaining that he must not run off. Slowly, it occurs to her that this is something she should be pleased about: the fatherly tone in Janusz's voice, the quiet sternness. Instead she feels bereft. They don't need her. Neither of them. They don't need her at all.

A week later, when Aurek has still not forgiven her, he comes down with a fever. His temperature rises and by the following evening he is as floppy as a rag doll. Silvana pulls dried herbs from jars in the pantry: thyme, stonecrop, willow bark, lavender, all the plants she has gathered and dried through the summer months. She runs a cold bath and throws the herbs into it.

"Get in," she tells Aurek, who is staggering weakly beside her.

Janusz stands at the bathroom door.

"He's shivering. Are you sure it's a good idea? We've got aspirin. Can't you give the boy some aspirin and put him to bed?"

She is not listening. Aurek is ill and it is all her fault.

"Let me at least look after my son," she snaps as she lifts the boy into the bath. "This will bring his fever down. But I need birch bark. The fever has to be broken. You'll have to find some trees. Get me some bark and I can boil it and then add it to the bath. It's the only way to bring a fever down."

"Where the hell am I going to find birch trees?"

"I tell you, I need birch bark. *Brzoza*. There's a copse of birches in Christchurch Park. I've seen them. If you won't go, I'll do it."

Silvana knows she sounds like a mad woman. Maybe that is what her time in the forest has done to her. The war has turned her into a Baba Jaga, an old witch of the forests. And it is her fault the child is ill. Worse, she does not know what to do. She looks at Janusz and waits to hear what he has to say. He's the English one here.

Aurek wraps his arms around his knees and coughs. His ribs shine under the water and he coughs again, sending a spasm though his shoulders.

"I can't go into the park at ten o'clock at night," Janusz says. "For God's sake. That's enough of this. Get Aurek into his pajamas and wrap him up in bed. I'll go for the doctor."

"A doctor?"

"That's what he needs. Get him out of the bath. His lips are turning blue."

She turns her eyes on the child and nods. "Yes. You're right. A doctor. A doctor will know what to do."

She lifts Aurek, water dripping down the front of her dress, and the child, still burning hot to the touch, faints in her arms. Memories rush toward her, panic rising in her chest. The mud underfoot. The fur coat covered in blood. She is a terrible mother, cursed just like her own mother.

"Janusz, hurry!" she screams, but he has already gone. She holds her son tight in her arms and sobs into his neck.

It is raining hard; icy rain that is turning to sleet. Janusz nearly tumbles off his bike, freewheeling down the hill, skidding through freezing puddles. He pumps the pedals, bent over the handlebars, wanting to get to the doctor's house as fast as he can. Silvana's fear has taken him over. He no longer thinks the boy just has a bad cold. Now other diseases crowd his thoughts. *Polio. Tuberculosis. Pneumonia.*

The sleet stings his face and he turns off the main street, hurtling up a gravel driveway. Nothing is more important than the boy. Pedaling like a fury, energy surging through him, he can feel a tight knot of love for his strange son, lodged in his heart, snug as a bar of metal in a lathe. The relief he feels when he sees a light still on in the doctor's front rooms is so great, he throws his bike to the ground and takes the steps onto the porch two at a time, banging on the door with his fists so that the doctor's wife opens the door angrily, scolding him for scaring her half to death.

The bedroom is cold. It is the first thing Janusz notices when he shows the doctor into Aurek's room. He doesn't bother to take the man's coat. The way he has left it buttoned up suggests he doesn't want to part with it.

"There's nothing to worry about," says the doctor, rubbing his hands together briskly. "He's going to be all right."

Janusz realizes he has been holding his breath. He sighs with relief. Silvana has tidied the room in the time he was absent: Aurek's books are lined up; the picture of puppies in a wicker basket hangs straight;

the rug looks like she might have swept it. She has forgotten her wet dress and it clings to her. Janusz finds himself studying the line of her suspender belt, which shows clearly against the soaked fabric. It's been so long since he last touched her. He turns to face the doctor, hoping he has not seen him staring.

"It's chicken pox," says the doctor. "It's going around. Half the youngsters at the school are off with it. The fever will be gone by tomorrow morning. Then the spots will come."

"Chicken pox?"

"My own son had it two weeks ago."

Janusz relaxes. Aurek has something other children have. Something normal and curable.

"Your son?"

"A bit late really. My boy's twelve and I do think it's better to get these illnesses done with earlier rather than later."

"So Aurek is a good age for chicken pox? He's the right age for it? It's a normal thing to have at his age?"

"Well, yes, you could say that. If his temperature is still up tomorrow, let me know. But I'm sure it won't be."

Janusz looks at Aurek lying in bed and strokes the boy's forehead. He is a normal child. Just like any other. The doctor has just said so. There is a whole world of renewed hope in chicken pox.

When Janusz wakes again at dawn and goes to see the patient, Aurek's temperature has disappeared and a rash covers his body. The sight of these miraculous spots makes Janusz laugh out loud.

"Hungry," says Aurek, picking at a row of tiny red blisters on his cheek.

"Are you? Well, that's a good thing. Come here and look out of the window. I've something to show you."

Silvana is sitting on the edge of the bed looking dazed, as if the blue light of the morning beginning to edge into the room confuses her.

"There," he says as they look down on a white world. "Snow. Lots of it. It must have snowed all night." He turns to Silvana. "You look exhausted."

Silvana nods, yawns, and rubs her eyes. She falls back onto Aurek's bed, and curls up into herself, arms wrapped around her knees. Janusz pauses, looking at her pale cheek, her long-lashed eyes closed as if she is sleeping. He remembers her when she was pregnant with their son, all those years ago, the way she liked to sleep in that position, her arms around her belly as though it were something she was guarding.

She opens her eyes. "Thank you for last night. You got the doctor and all I could do was act like a mad woman, calling for birch bark."

"You made me think of your grandmother."

"She was a good woman."

"So are you."

Janusz takes her hand. This is the closest he has felt to her for months. Aurek being ill has brought them together. And it is right that the boy is the bond between them.

"I'll never leave you again," he says. "Even if there's another war. I won't go."

The moment is obvious to him.

"Silvana. I think we should try for another child. Give Aurek a little brother."

Silvana doesn't reply and he leans over her and kisses her, feeling her stiffen against his touch.

"You're tired," he says, pretending not to notice. "You should sleep. I won't disturb you."

He covers her with a blanket, tucking it around her.

"Come on," he says to Aurek. "Let's get you breakfast. Brush your teeth and wash and I'll make you porridge."

While the boy is washing, Janusz goes out into the garden. Everything is covered in white and the sky looks full of more snow to come. Feathery flakes fall steadily around him. In his tiny potting shed he checks his dahlia bulbs are well covered with sand. He is about to shut the door when he stops, lifts the crate of bulbs and pulls a bundle of

letters out from under them. One day he will get rid of them. He puts
them back under the crate. One day soon. He loves Silvana but he can't
let go of Hélène. Not just yet.

Aurek sits in the kitchen, his eyes sticky with sleep, eating a bowl of
porridge. He feels quite well but he can't understand where the spots
have come from. He keeps lifting his pajama top to look at them. He'd
like to ask the enemy to look at them too, but he is busy. Janusz is sitting
with his back to him, polishing his boots, buffing black leather, holding
up a shining toe cap to the light and then furiously rubbing at it all over
again, his elbow sliding back and forth like a fiddle player.

"Are you cold?" Janusz says, turning his flushed face to Aurek. "I
can get you a blanket if you're cold."

Aurek shakes his head and gives the spots on his cheek a scratch.

"Don't touch them," warns Janusz. "Come on, eat your porridge."

Aurek takes a spoonful.

"We're all right together, aren't we?" says Janusz. "You and me?"

Janusz puts his boots on the floor and rubs them over with a cloth.

"Would you like a brother one day? Or a sister? Aurek, are you
listening? A new baby would be fun, wouldn't it?"

Aurek considers this. He thinks of his mother and shakes his head
again. He doesn't want to share her with a baby.

"Well, we might one day. One day we might give you a brother and
you'd be the eldest. You'd have to help look after him."

Janusz pulls his boots on.

"We don't get much time on our own, do we? Your mother keeps
you all to herself. Tell me. Do you remember the forest you lived in?"

Aurek frowns. He hates these kinds of questions. He digs his spoon
in his porridge and stirs it.

"I'd like to hear about it," Janusz says. "When I get back from work
you can tell me, hmm?"

Aurek's mother never talks about the forest, and the enemy always
wants to. Between them Aurek feels like he is a secret neither will share

properly. But the enemy is smiling at him, and Aurek tries to think of something to say that will keep the smile there.

"When I was a baby I swallowed a button."

"What?"

"I swallowed a button. You turned me upside down so I didn't choke."

The enemy smiles crookedly. "That's right. You swallowed a button. I'd forgotten. But you can't remember that, surely?"

"Mama told me. Do I go to school now?"

"No. You'll have to stay home until all the spots are gone. I'm off to work. You be a good boy for your mother."

Aurek follows Janusz to the front door, the tiles icy under his feet.

When Janusz does up his coat and opens the door, a blast of wind nearly knocks Aurek over.

"A button," Janusz says. "Fancy that. I'd forgotten. You were always putting things in your mouth when you were a baby."

Janusz stares out at the day steadily, like a horse that has suddenly lifted its head in a field and looked into the distance. Aurek shuffles closer. He stands behind Janusz's legs and peers at the fluttering snowflakes outside, at the houses on the other side of the road, their gray windows, the frozen milk bottles on the doorsteps. He touches Janusz's hand. Perhaps the enemy will try to hug him today? If he does, Aurek will let him.

"Would you like to make a snowman when I get back from work?" says Janusz, looking down at him.

"Now?"

"No. Not now. After work. Men have to work, you know. You will too, one day." Janusz pulls his hat tight over his ears and rubs his hands together. "Shut the door behind me," he says, and then he is gone, marching away with his shoulders hunched against the cold.

"Hurry back," whispers Aurek.

He goes upstairs, climbing into bed beside his mother who looks like she is sleeping, her eyes shut, hair across her face.

"Am I going to have a brother?"

Silvana opens her eyes. "What?"

"A baby?"

"No," she says, slipping an arm around him. "You're everything we need."

Aurek curls up beside her and feels glad. She's right. They don't need a baby.

POLAND

Silvana

It began to rain and the camp turned muddy underfoot. Silvana had almost forgotten the war. Here it was as though they were far from everything, in another world. They lifted their beds higher off the ground, making pallets out of branches and fallen trees, but everything was soaked through and there was no way of drying anything.

The old man stopped getting out of his blankets, staying wrapped up in his own mess day and night. His wife let Gregor take his share of the food. Gregor sat chewing on dry bread while the old woman fussed over him, picking nits from his hair, smiling like an indulgent mother. Elsa and Lottie watched her, and Silvana saw the jealousy in their eyes. The old man stared at the canopy of branches above his head. Maybe he never saw the sky at all. Maybe he wasn't looking that far.

Silvana took to wandering during the day, walking miles with Aurek on her back. Some nights she couldn't bear the thought of Gregor so she stayed away from the camp at night too, taking her rabbit skins, and making bracken beds for her and the boy. One morning she came back to find the old man staring harder than ever at the sky. The old woman was crying.

"Is he dead?" Silvana asked.

"What?" The sad-faced Lottie looked up. "Him? God, no. He's not dead."

"Why do you ask a question like that?" the old woman shouted. "Don't I look after him? Is that what you are saying? I've cared for that man all my life. What would you know? Who are you anyway? You never speak to us. You creep around with that child of yours like a thief in the night. What use are you to us?"

Silvana looked around for Elsa. Then she understood. Gregor had gone. He and Elsa had left in the night.

The women left the next morning just as it was getting light. They didn't speak to Silvana, and she watched them gather their blankets and belongings. Lottie, the pianist, had stopped wearing her hair in a bun. Instead it hung down her back in thick coils. She and the old woman were bent over with the cold, moving like mirror images of each other. Two hags of the forest with twigs in their hair. Silvana was glad to see them go.

The old man died a week after they left. She tried to dig a hole to bury the corpse, but the ground was too hard and the old man was rigid. Besides, his blankets smelled bad, even in the cold. Silvana dragged him out of his shelter and let the snow that had begun to fall cover him. In hours he was frozen under a blanket of white. She wrapped Aurek in his rabbit furs, picked him up, pulled her coat tight around her, and walked away. When the thaw comes, she thought, we will be far from here and the wild animals will have taken him. What she and the boy would be doing though, she had no idea.

Janusz

The farmer and his wife were quietly welcoming to Janusz. They gave him a room at the back of the house, helping him onto the metal-framed bed where he lay flat on his back and stared at the cracked ceiling and dark beams, wondering if he would ever be able to move freely again. The farmer's wife covered him with a damp sheet, dropping it lightly over him so that it covered not just his body but his face too. He blinked under the white cotton and felt like a corpse being laid to rest.

On his sunburned skin, the sheet felt heavy. Just as he was about to move his stiff arms to lift it off him, two hands touched his face and folded the sheet back. He stared up at a girl in a yellow dress. The color reminded him of the buttercups that grew alongside the river back in his hometown.

He smiled at her and though pain cracked the peeling skin on his face, he didn't care.

"What's your name?" he whispered.

She leaned over him. "Did you say something, Monsieur?"

He swallowed, tried again to speak. "Your name?"

"Hélène," she said. "Hélène Legarde, Monsieur."

For a week he lay in bed with a fever brought on by sunstroke. Hélène smeared olive oil onto his burns and gave him tiny sips of water. Her kindnesses made him dizzy with gratitude. She popped the blisters on his back and spread dressings over the raw skin. When she leaned across him, her breasts rested briefly against his chest, sending a bolt of electricity through his spine. He could smell the scent of her, the musky smell of her sweat. It made him want to reach out and touch her. At night he waited impatiently until dawn, when she checked him again.

Once a day she helped him outside to the middy, the ditch at the back of the old stone farmhouse. Hélène left him with a shovel and a bowl of ash and he squatted in the blessed shade of the stone house, thinking about the simplicity of this family's life and the sense of peace he had found here.

He walked back into the courtyard, lizards rushing through scorched grass at his feet as he interrupted their sunbathing. In the yard, dogs slept, noses resting on stretched legs. Chickens gathered by a barn door, lying in dirt to keep cool, spreading wing feathers out like fingers. Hélène was there too, her back to him, sweeping the terrace steps. He watched sweat spreading wetly across the back of her dress, making the summer print darken. She turned around, her breasts sliding toward each other as she grasped the broom with both hands and dipped her head, concentrating on her job.

Janusz walked toward her. "It's too hot to work. You must be thirsty. Can I get you a drink?"

She looked up and he took the broom from her.

"A drink?" she asked, her cheeks shining with heat. She walked over to the well in the middle of the yard and began pulling on a thick cord that dangled into its depths. Finally a metal bucket swung into view. She reached into it and pulled out a bottle of red wine.

"Nice and cold," she said. "We have a drink together?"

IPSWICH

Christmas at Number 22 smells of cabbage, baked fish, and calamine lotion. They open their presents on Christmas Eve and Janusz says next year they'll wait and do it on Christmas Day like the rest of England.

"Of course," says Silvana, who is too tired to argue, let alone think of another year. "Whatever you want."

There is a secondhand Raleigh bike for Aurek and a promise from Janusz to teach him how to ride it. Silvana doesn't want the boy riding a bicycle. She fears he will fall and hurt himself. Every time she looks at the bike, she imagines Aurek falling. She says nothing. Aurek leans it against the stairs in the hallway and polishes its wheel spokes with his handkerchief.

Silvana gives Janusz a brown paper bag of dahlia bulbs in sawdust. Janusz gives her perfume: Yardley English Lavender. She opens the bottle, breathes in, and has a sneezing fit.

With the extra coal allowance the doctor gave them for Aurek, Silvana insists that they stoke the fire and keep the house warm. The snow hasn't let up and the whole country is freezing. It's on the radio and in the newspapers. The worst winter in years. She tells Janusz he should be proud: she read in a newspaper that it is Polish miners in Britain who are working around the clock to keep the coal supplies coming.

"The British moan about foreign workers," she says to Janusz. "But they would be stuck without our miners, wouldn't they?"

Even cheered as she is by this thought, she has to admit the Polish miners seem to be failing to keep her warm. She is wearing two pairs of stockings, a petticoat, a thick tweed skirt, two blouses, and a cardigan, but it makes no difference.

She shivers and shakes with cold.

"Come on, Aurek, pay attention," says Janusz. He is sitting in his chair by the fire with Aurek on the rug, trying to finish a jigsaw puzzle. "That's the cowboy's scarf. It's blue. See? Look at the picture on the box. There's a piece like that somewhere else in here. Look for the same blue."

Silvana wonders what Tony is doing, whether he is with Peter in the grandparents' big house by the park, doing jigsaw puzzles in front of the fire. She sits back in her chair. She hasn't seen him since October, when she told him about the letters. She should be pleased. Surely it makes her life easier not to see him, and yet she feels angry. How can he step in and then out of her life so easily?

She watches Janusz searching for the right pieces of the puzzle, steadily, logically, while Aurek piles up the wooden pieces into small towers.

"Time for a glass of sherry," says Janusz after he has dismantled Aurek's pile of jigsaw pieces and put the last section of the sky in place. "Aurek, no. Don't touch it. It's finished. Go and put the radio on. The King's speech will be on soon."

The three of them sit listening to the radio, Silvana sipping her sherry. It tastes terrible so she gulps it down, eager to finish the glass and be excused. Her head is thumping and she longs only to be in bed.

"And we should raise our glasses to the Royal Family," says Janusz. "And a toast to our own son. Aurek, do you want to try some sherry?"

When the national anthem plays, Janusz looks at Silvana expectantly but she does not move. She is sure that she will fall over if she attempts to stand. Janusz stands up, stiff and serious. His faith in the King is touching. Or is it just that she is too tired to be annoyed right now by his constant desire to be a perfect Englishman? Then Aurek surprises her by leaping to his feet and saluting as the anthem plays on.

"I've taught him the words," says Janusz. "Come on, Aurek. Sing with me."

To see Aurek singing the British national anthem with his father, both of them standing to attention together, Aurek breaking into crow calls and dog howls as he sings, makes her laugh and then cough and splutter, and finally retch and vomit.

Janusz turns the radio down. "Are you all right?" He bends over her and pulls his handkerchief from his pocket.

Christmas is a terrible time of year, she thinks, wiping her mouth. It leaves her defenseless.

"I want to go home," she mumbles.

Janusz leans toward her, pushing a lock of hair away from her eyes. "Me too," he whispers into her ear. Or at least she thinks that is what he said. She looks into his eyes.

"*Wesolych swiat,*" she says. "Happy holidays."

Then she lets Janusz help her up to bed.

The rest of Christmas and New Year pass by in a blur. The doctor is called and says she has the flu. Her head feels like a steam iron, clunky and heavy, and her body is something she would gladly give up if she could.

During the day, when Janusz is back at work, Doris takes Aurek to school. She brings Silvana beef tea and Easton's tonic, a sticky brown syrup that Doris swears by and Silvana silently swears at. And all the time, while Silvana lies in bed recovering, she has the feeling that Aurek is slipping away from her.

In the garden, the light is fading. Trees are frosted with white. The rickety garden fence is soft gray against the freezing snow that clings in ice-beaded lines along the top of it. On the ground the snow is the same dry white as a sugar loaf. On the old oak tree at the bottom of the garden the snow is a different color again. Against the tree's black trunk it is as blue-white as breast milk.

Silvana turns away from the wintry scene outside her window and looks at Aurek sitting at the kitchen table. Doris has just brought him back from school.

"Are you still friends with Peter?"

She has promised herself she will not do this, but here she is.

"I never meant it when I said you shouldn't be friends, you know. I'm sorry for what I said. He's a nice boy. Why don't you ask him over to play?"

"Peter's not at school."

"Not at school?"

"The teacher says he's not coming back. He's gone away."

So it really is true. Tony has left. And to think, she had nearly told him everything. Aurek looks as if he might cry. His only friend, and she has forced him to leave town.

"You can have the day off school tomorrow," she whispers to him.

As it is, the school is closed. The snow keeps on falling and the roads become impassable. Everybody talks about it being the worst winter in living memory. Janusz stays home for a week when his factory closes and they live on soup with dumplings because even if the shops had any food in them, which is doubtful, they are all closed.

Every morning, Silvana goes walking. She knows she should stay in the house, but her legs won't let her.

"We have snow like this in Poland every year," she says to Janusz. "I don't know what the fuss is about."

"People are freezing in their homes," says Janusz. "Don't you read the news? The country is on its knees. And you can't take Aurek with you. It's too cold for him out there."

"I just need to walk," she says. Truth is, she is ashamed of what she feels when she sees Janusz and the boy together. She has what she wanted, a father for Aurek. He loves the boy and Aurek, she can see, is beginning to trust him. She should be happy, but instead she can't bear to see them together.

She trudges through the blue light of sleet and ice, her lungs burning with cold, and pretends she is back in the frozen Polish winters of the war, back with her own memories and the importance of survival, of having nothing else to consider.

She walks past sheep huddled in fields. She sees a train buried in snow, glassy icicles hanging like daggers off shopfront windows. In the center of town, Tony's pet shop is shut, blinds over the windows, a *Closed* sign in the door. She stands in front of it, looking up at the windows of the flat above the shop and wonders where he could be.

The estuary freezes over and Silvana walks out onto the ice, listening to the low moan of wind skating across its surface. She feels the ice bow and creak under her feet. If the ice opened and she fell into the dark waters, her secret would be gone with her. Only Aurek would be left. Just a boy and his father. But the river doesn't take her. She is as dry and weightless as the wind itself, and the constant snap and shiver of ice as she steps out toward the middle of the river becomes companionable, like sticks breaking on a forest floor.

The town stays frozen for weeks and then the thaws come, causing the river to flood and the canals to fill with surging brown waters. In the center of town, the buses and trams start running again, people walk the streets in Wellingtons and sou'westers and the schools are all open.

On a bright morning, after taking Aurek to school, Silvana walks through the backstreets of Ipswich. She passes by the Methodist church with its bleak yellow brick front and sees a small passageway she has not been down before. She enters it, running her fingertips against narrow moss-lined brick walls, marveling at the darkness that gathers at her feet like blackened leaves.

The passageway comes out into a cobbled street full of garages and repair shops. Cars, trucks, vans, and buses are parked in an orderless jumble, blocking the road. She makes her way through them and at the end of it she finds a yard. A painted sign hangs over the wooden doors: *Harry Goldberg & Son. Rag & Bone & Scrap Metal Merchants.* The man who sold her the shoes. She is curious, drawn to the place.

The next day she bakes gingerbread. Half of it she puts on the kitchen table for Aurek and Janusz. The other half she wraps in a tea towel and takes to the rag-and-bone man. He remembers her. He pushes the gingerbread into his mouth and smiles, showing sticky teeth and receding gums.

"Have a look around. I've got everything here, antiques an' all. I have dealers coming down from London to look over my stock. My father ran this place before me. He used to buy bones an' all. Boiled 'em up right here."

"Bones?"

"Rag and bone. That's what we dealt in. We sold bones for fertilizer. No money in it now. Have a look around."

The stables are full of clothes and bric-a-brac. Dining room chairs are piled to the ceiling of one stall. Bales of damp-smelling linen fill another. Dozens of cats, sleeping in among the linen, wake at Silvana's approach and watch her with sharp eyes. She looks into dark stalls filled with carpets and silk parachutes, beds, and blanket boxes. For the first time since coming to England, she feels a moment of recognition. She is surely part of this jetsam of human life.

The following week, Silvana bakes more gingerbread for the rag-and-bone man. He has a sweet tooth and, she suspects, nobody in his life to feed it. The simple exchange of cake for time to wander through his barns and stables pleases her.

"It's my birthday," she tells him, encouraged by the obvious pleasure with which he greets her. "Today."

It is probably not the kind of thing you say to a stranger, but Silvana wants to tell somebody. Janusz went off this morning without a mention of it. Not that it matters. She is twenty-eight years old. Too old for cakes and singsongs.

"Well then, you just help yourself," the man tells her. "Happy birthday, Miss. You go on and take what you want. Most of these clothes go to charity in any case. I sort them and they get sent off to people who need them. Foreigners mainly. Poor beggars who've got nothing."

For a moment she thinks he is insulting her. But then she stares at his hooded eyes and sallow face and realizes she sees him in the same way, as just another lonely foreigner who has nothing.

Silvana helps him sort the clothes. Bed linen and cotton for rags. Musty-smelling coats in one pile; men's clothes in another; women's and children's in a third. She thinks of the refugee camp, the long lines of people who came and went and disappeared just like she did onto trains and buses and boats heading for other countries. The clothes they were all given must have started their journey in places like this. Sorting clothes with the rag-and-bone man is like moving among lost people, and they are the kind she knows best.

Silvana opens a burlap sack filled with blouses and imagines the women who once wore them. The stains and cloudy marks on bedsheets are a registry of births and marriages and deaths. Sweat rings on collars make her sigh. She puts her hands in sleeves and traces the roughened seams of stitching pulled open by bodies that must have, day after day, strained against the cloth. Buckets of shoes leave her trembling. The hardened leather shoes and boots are like the misshapen feet of the dead.

She notes the repairs and the slow decline of garments and feels like she is in mourning for the people who once wore them. Yet she can resurrect these clothes. She will package and parcel and sort them. They will travel on, into the arms of men and women and children who have arrived at the end of the war with nothing but the curious realization that they have survived something and a dull sense that they might not survive the beginning of something else.

She finds a black cotton dress with wide skirts, the kind her mother wore. She imagines her mother in the gown, head bent in sorrow or annoyance, her hands holding the shape of her dead sons. Silvana lifts the dress by its shoulders and shakes the creases out of it.

"I'm your daughter," she says, holding it at arm's length. She gives it another shake and its sleeves flap aggressively, black and sullen, like the wings of a cornered crow.

"So, what shall I do, Mother?" she asks the dress. "I think of Tony all the time. Tell me, what should I do? What would you do? Why can't you help me when I need you?"

The dress gives her no advice. Of course it wouldn't. When did her mother ever help her before? And yet she misses her.

She walks home carrying it over one arm and finds Janusz and Aurek sitting in the front parlor with Doris.

"Happy birthday!"

They break into song. "Happy birthday to you, happy birthday to you . . ."

Silvana cannot move to take her coat off. Her frozen fingers throb in the sudden warmth, tingling as if they are coming back to life. Mottled red and white, they sting and swell so she couldn't unbutton her coat even if she wanted to.

"You thought they'd forgotten," says Doris. She takes a drag on her cigarette and coughs heartily. "Jan's been doing things behind your back!"

"Here." Janusz hands her a large white box with a blue ribbon across it. "Doris helped us choose it."

"Me," says Aurek. "Me, me, me."

Doris laughs. "All right. You chose it. Go on, Sylvia, open it."

Silvana opens the box and lifts out a dress. It is a dark blue fabric with a white polka dot. Three-quarter-length sleeves edged with lace and a wasp waist with a boned girdle over a wide skirt.

Janusz hands her another box. He speaks quietly so that only she can hear. "I've missed too many of your birthdays."

Inside the box is a pair of court shoes and kid leather gloves.

"I've kept those boxes in my spare bedroom for weeks now," says Doris. "And believe me, it's lucky you're smaller than me or I'd have had that frock and worn it myself! Come on. Give us a fashion show. Let's see what you look like."

In her bedroom, Silvana puts the black gown in the wardrobe. She changes into her new dress, spinning around to feel the skirts swirl. The skirt is gathered. Imagine that! Folds of fabric all around her. And new! Bought for her, never worn by anyone else. She can't remember the last time she wore a brand-new dress. She slips her feet into the shoes and puts the gloves on, pushing her fingers into firm leather. In the bathroom she looks in the mirror. The dress is beautiful, but the woman staring back at her looks blank-eyed, harsh. When, she wonders, will I look less like a stranger to myself?

She goes downstairs and Janusz nods his approval.

"You can wear it on Friday."

"Friday?"

"We're going to the cinema. Doris and Gilbert are coming with us."

"The cinema?"

She thinks of Warsaw and the film theaters where she went to see matinee performances. Sitting on velvet seats in the dark, her pregnant belly almost touching the seat in front, she had been carried through her favorite American movies on a wave of hopefulness. She'd gone every week and thought that the child when he was born (despite her mother's craziness, she had always believed her prophecy that she was carrying a boy) would grow up to love films.

Doris claps her hands together and Silvana is woken from her reverie. She is grateful to Doris for snapping her out of that line of thought. She pulls Aurek to her, folding him into her skirts.

"We've even got a babysitter arranged," says Doris.

Janusz nods. "It's only for a few hours."

Silvana shakes her head. She is not leaving the boy with a stranger.

"Who's going to babysit Aurek?"

"Tony!" says Doris. "I bumped into him the other day. He said to tell you he's looking forward to seeing you. He'll be here on the button at 6 p.m., Friday night."

Janusz runs his finger along the inside of his collar. "That's all right, isn't it?"

"There you are," says Doris. "All fixed."

"Silvana?" says Janusz. "Are you all right?"

"You look like you've seen a ghost," laughs Doris. "White as a sheet, you are."

Silvana sits down, her stiff skirts rising up around her. She clasps her hands together and forces herself to smile.

"I'm fine," she says. "Absolutely fine."

POLAND

Silvana

Silvana spent days wandering through the forest. It was without end. After Gregor left and the women followed him, she didn't understand the trees. No matter how far she walked, she never found the edge of the forest and she never saw any other signs of life. She looked for men, for the partisans hiding out in the forest, but there was no one. She and the boy were alone. Perhaps, she thought, she should have been more friendly with Gregor? Wherever he had taken Elsa, maybe he could have taken her and Aurek as well.

It was the tiredness that got to her. She was too tired to be cold anymore. Too tired to notice the ache in her teeth and the pain in her back from hunching against the icy wind.

She imagined lying down on a bed, one that she and the child could stretch out on. She thought she wanted sleep. After a while she knew it was death she hoped for. Silvana understood everything then. She was her mother's daughter. Unlucky, incapable of bringing up a child.

She remembered the snow in the apple orchard when she was a child and told Aurek about it, hoping to bring some magic to the ice around them. She had made angels in the snow. She and the other children searched for untouched snow then lay down in it and stretched their arms and legs so they appeared like semaphore stars spread-eagled on the ground. Carefully, the child lying down would be pulled clear of their imprint and a magical shape like a cutout angel would be left in the snow with no sign of how it had been made.

She hadn't expected the winter to be so terrible. It wasn't like the snow she remembered from her childhood at all. It was brutal. The trees glowed blue with hoarfrost and the bare branches glittered. Her teeth ached with cold. Her hands stiffened; her jaw froze. Fingers swelled. Trying to do anything with them was difficult.

Aurek stopped crying. He lay in Silvana's arms with his eyes half closed and his mouth open. His apple-red cheeks turned frost-white. She could feel him giving up.

She discovered a small clearing in the forest, a dip in the landscape where only fire-scorched tree trunks remained. A bomb must have exploded there, scooping out earth and trees like a giant hand, leaving a bowl-shaped area sheltered from the winds by high banks of snow. Silvana sat on the crater's edge and slid down the bank on her back with Aurek between her legs. At the bottom, in a flurry of snow, she saw something that made her rub her eyes and blink.

It was then she knew she would never leave the forest again. She stared at it, taking in its beauty. It was the most colorful thing she had seen for a long time. The gold fringing beckoned her like a friend. Tightly sprung, button-backed in red velvet, a chaise longue sitting on a carpet of white like something enchanted.

Silvana had found other furniture before: tables, broken stools, cupboards. She'd never found anything as beautiful as the red chaise longue.

Black crows flew through the bare branches of the sky. They were urging her on, she was sure of it. For days she had heard them calling her name. At first she'd thought they were mocking her, but then she'd understood. She was part of the forest. The crows were telling her that. They had been leading her here. This was the end. The boy was already fading in her arms.

Silvana walked toward the chaise, her eyes fixed on the roll of carved mahogany at its back. With numb fingers she traced the smooth shine of wet wood and pitted woodworm, black circles against the white crystals of ice that clung to its outline. Dusting off layers of snow, she sat down. Aurek leaned against the red velvet. He put his mouth against it and tasted the color on his tongue. Silvana bent forward and lifted him onto her lap where he whimpered, curling tightly into her. She leaned her head back. It felt good to be giving up. To know she wasn't going to have to walk any further.

It wouldn't take long for the cold to crackle through her. For the glacial sleep to come. Aurek's body, normally as insubstantial as the powdery snow that drifted in the wind, began to feel heavy against her. This way, she reasoned as she let go of consciousness, they would be together forever. She and the child. She whispered to him, explained how sorry she was to fail him. Twice she said it. Two sorrows, banked up against her, cold as the snow.

Janusz

When his skin began to peel in dry white flakes, Janusz dozed in a shaded barn, the scent of thyme, sage, rosemary, hot in his nostrils. Gradually he felt stronger, his skin healed and he began to help Hélène water the animals, collect eggs. They worked quietly together. She showed him how to milk the goats and stack the hay in the barn. Their hands touched as Hélène passed him eggs.

"How old are you?" she asked one morning.

He had wanted to ask her the same question but hadn't wanted to be rude.

"I'm twenty-four," she said. "*Vingt-quatre*. Here, catch!" She threw an egg in the air and he caught it. "Bravo!" she cried and threw him another.

"Twenty-four years old and my mother worries I am too old to find a husband. She thinks I'll be an old maid all my life."

"And you, what do you think?"

"I think I'm waiting for the right man to come along. Here, catch!"

The egg hit him on the chest and broke in his hands.

She took a twist of hay and wiped his shirt clean.

"Take it off," she said. "I'll wash it for you." She reached out to unbutton it and he backed away, feeling foolish.

"Suit yourself," she said, and walked out of the barn.

She came back to find him hanging his shirt up to dry in the sun. He saw her watching him, leaning against the barn door, her arms folded, a smile playing on her lips.

"Hey, *soldat*. If you've finished being a washerwoman, I want to show you something."

She led him into the barn, shooed the roosting chickens away and pulled a tarpaulin off a red car covered in dust. She untied her apron and wiped it over the hood, revealing shiny paintwork.

"Whose is this?" He ran a hand over it, tried not to think of how he wanted to take Hélène in his arms. Tried not to look into her eyes.

"It's Pascal's. My brother. It doesn't work. He came back from Marseilles with it a week before he joined up."

"Where is he now?"

"Normandy. He's the reason you're here. Madam Agut, who runs the boarding house where you were staying, is a friend of his."

Janusz could smell Hélène's soap, the heat of her skin. He lifted the hood and peered inside. The spark plugs were probably worn. He pulled one out and held it up to the light. Hélène took it from him.

"Kiss me."

She put her hand on the back of his neck and pressed against him: He pushed her away.

"I'm married."

He was an idiot to say it, but the words tumbled out. A defense against his own desperate desire to tell her he loved the sight of her, the sound of her.

"So where is your wife?"

"Back in Poland."

"Exactly."

She kissed him and he felt warmed through, as if he hadn't known until that moment how much coldness still dwelled in his body. He tried to speak, to make her see sense.

"I'm not . . . This is all I can give you. And I have to leave soon."

"So we should be together, while we can." She kissed him again. "We only live one life. How can you let this pass?"

And he couldn't.

She slipped off her dress and pulled his head down, cramming a brown-nippled breast, sweet as a sun-warmed apple, into his mouth. He was crazy for her. He dropped to his knees, pulling her down with him, and she climbed across him, strong and determined, her thighs smacking his ribs, hands pulling his hair, the bowl of her hips spread across his face, knees knocking his ears.

He tasted her, but when he tried to hold her she flicked her hips and was away again, sliding down his body. He caught her tightly in his grip and held her as they rolled together, bumping and bucking, on the barn floor, bruising elbows, buttocks, faces, knees.

They looked like a couple of wrestlers when they had finished, covered in sweat and dirt. He held her in his arms and she sank her head against his chest. They dozed for a while, then he looked down at her and kissed her, his arms scooping her up, drawing her into his embrace. She wound her body around him.

She was a blanket then, against the world. He didn't have to think of murdered old women and young men shooting themselves for the sake of drowning dogs. All the cold and the fear that had brought him here was gone. There was nothing more in his life than her, this warm, beautiful girl, the tough southern sunlight, and the pungent smell of sex in his nostrils.

They sat together on the backseat of her brother's car. For an hour they didn't speak. There were no words for how he felt about her. He traced the lines on her hands, kissed the tips of her fingertips, the calluses on her palms, the span of muscle between her thumb and forefinger. Her stubby fingers and calloused palms delighted him. No matter what happened, no matter where he went after this, he knew he would always remember her hands. She asked him about his life and he told her about Silvana and Aurek.

"Wait." He pulled a photograph from his trouser pocket. "There. That's them. My wife Silvana and that's our son."

"She's pretty. And the boy looks like an angel. I'm very happy for you."

"Are you?"

"No. I'm jealous."

He looked into her eyes. She smiled, shrugged her shoulders, and kissed him.

"Don't look so worried," she said when she pulled apart from him. "I know I can't keep you."

Janusz allowed himself to think of being lost. Of being forgotten up there on the hill. Weeks passed. Hélène told him love was something that nobody could guard themselves against, and he liked to believe her. She visited him at night, slipping naked between his sheets.

"We should be careful," he whispered, though the thought of her carrying his child was pleasurable to him.

Hélène sighed and stroked his forehead. "Don't worry about that. I can look after myself."

She climbed across him the next morning. He lay in bed and watched her go into a small back room, fingers of sunlight reaching in through the half-opened shutters and playing patterns across her long back, her short, strong legs. She left the door slightly ajar so that he could see her bent over, one foot up on a tin bath, talking to him about vinegar and lemon juice douches. He'd never met a woman like her.

IPSWICH

"Bellissima" is the first word Tony says when Silvana opens her front door. She blinks at the sound of his voice, as if someone has shone a dazzling light in her eyes.

Tony lifts his hat and smiles.

"Silvana, it's wonderful to see you. What a lovely dress. You're a woman made to wear beautiful clothes. If only you could have met Lucy. She loved fashion. But how are you? Doris told me you had the flu a while back? I hope you're better now. You certainly look radiant."

She'd forgotten how broad he was, taking up the door frame with his size. Her first instinct is to throw her arms around his neck. Then, when he mentions his dead wife, she folds her arms across her chest instead. He steps back and Peter comes into view carrying paper bags in his fists.

"I've got sweets," he says. "Licorice wheels and humbugs."

Tony laughs. "We bought out the sweet shop, didn't we, Peter?"

She smiles at the plump, red-faced child. "Why don't you go up, Peter? Aurek is waiting for you in his bedroom."

"I'm sorry I haven't seen you for so long," says Tony as they watch Peter climb the stairs. "I have a house in Felixstowe by the sea and I've been there. Peter's grandparents got him into private day school, so I'm afraid he hasn't seen Aurek for a while, has he? Anyway, here." He lifts up a string shopping bag. "I brought you a birthday present. A bottle of Tokaji and a fresh rabbit."

"Tokaji?" It's been years since she saw a bottle of Hungarian wine. "We had Tokaji at our wedding party," she says, turning the bottle over in her hands. "It's very generous of you. And rabbit will make a change from horse meat. I find I can get nothing else at the moment. It's a lovely present. Thank you."

"A pleasure." Tony lowers his voice. "How are you, I mean, really?"

"I'm sorry," says Silvana, desperate to change the subject. "I haven't asked to take your coat. Here, let me help you."

She almost cries out when his hand brushes against her wrist, and she is glad she has put the wine down because she would surely have dropped it.

"Oh, it's heavy," she says, taking a handful of coat. Was it an accident, that touch, the way his fingers rested on her skin? Is she imagining things?

"This is wool, no? It's the quality of cloth that is important." She can hear herself babbling like an idiot, but silence would be worse. "So, here is your coat and I . . . I haven't seen you since . . . since . . ."

"The park?"

"Yes, that's it." She sighs. *It is remarkable,* she thinks, *how this man can always finish a sentence for her.*

Tony leans toward her. "I didn't want to make your life more complicated so I—"

"Hello, Tony!"

Gilbert is standing at the parlor door.

"Gilbert, good to see you."

"Well, are you coming in for a drink?" says Gilbert, laughing. "Or are you having a top secret chin-wag out here?"

"We were just coming," says Silvana, and she follows Gilbert into the front parlor, Tony close behind her.

"Tony," says Doris through a haze of cigarette smoke. "We haven't seen much of you for a while. You up to no good again? What're you selling under the counter today? Snow to the Eskimos?"

"Hello, Doris. No, I don't think they're rationing snow yet. Janusz, I was just saying to Silvana, I have brought you a rabbit. And a bottle of wine to go with it."

Silvana watches Janusz's face crease with pleasure as he takes the bottle in his hands. "Tokaji? Silvana, have you seen this?"

"Wine, is it?" says Gilbert. "Very posh. I prefer a pint myself."

"Or a nice glass of cider," says Doris.

"You might prefer vodka," says Tony. "Next time. I have contacts at the docks. The sailors bring things in to sell. I'm sure I can get you vodka."

Janusz holds the bottle out to let Gilbert and Doris look at it.

"No, no. I like this wine very much. We'll keep it for a special occasion. We're drinking sherry tonight. Would you like one?"

"Better not get the babysitter drunk," laughs Doris.

"I'll put these things in the kitchen," says Janusz. "Silvana, can you pour our friend here a drink?"

"No, not for me," says Tony. "Doris is right. If I'm babysitting I had better keep a clear head."

"Oh, a cup of tea perhaps?" Janusz says. "With a currant bun?"

"No, nothing. Thank you."

Silvana watches the way Tony smiles at them all. He should be a politician. He has all of them eating out of his hand. And her, too. He leaves and then comes back into her life as if she is a doll he can pick up and put down at will.

"I'll have a top-up," says Gilbert. "Rabbit, eh? I haven't had rabbit for quite a while. Doris, you used to do a lovely rabbit casserole. Do you remember?"

"Gilbert, sometimes I wonder if you look at what you eat. We had rabbit just last month. Got it from a lad that works over at Chantry Park."

"How could I forget? You had any luck getting potatoes lately? Doris stood in line outside the Co-op for hours the other day."

"Hours, I stood. Doesn't it craze you? We fought Hitler for six years and had all the spuds we wanted. End of the war comes and not a spud in sight. We've not even got proper fish for fish and chips. I tell you, things can't get worse."

"How do you manage to run that car of yours, Tony?" Gilbert asks. "You still getting your petrol on the black?"

It is always the same talk. The shortages of this and that and the government letting people down. Sometimes Silvana imagines herself telling them to shut up. To put a sock in it, as Doris would say. To belt up good and proper.

"Liverpool are at the top of the first division," says Tony, who appears not to have heard Gilbert's question. Silvana notices how carefully he changes the subject. Janusz comes back into the room.

"What do you think?" Tony asks him. "Do you support them?"

"I prefer cricket," says Janusz.

"I'm an Ipswich Town fan myself," says Gilbert enthusiastically. "Got to support our local lads. They're the middle of the third division and climbing. They'll give Liverpool a run for their money one day."

Tony laughs. "I won't hold my breath."

"Ah, you wait. When I win the soccer pools I'll buy Ipswich and train them myself."

Doris looks at her watch. "We should go. No more soccer talk, please, gentlemen. We don't want to miss the beginning of the film."

And then they are all gathering up coats and out of the door, an icy wind hitting them full in the face. Silvana turns to look at Tony. He doesn't meet her gaze. Janusz steps up beside her.

"It's very decent of you, Tony. We appreciate it."

"Yes, yes we do," Silvana says.

"Have fun, children," says Tony jovially, waving them away.

Silvana looks up at the bedroom window. Aurek has pressed his face to the glass.

"I think Aurek wants something," she begins to say, but Doris takes her arm firmly.

"Come on, Sylvia. You've got to leave him sometime. Let him grow up."

A night out without Aurek. The first since they arrived in Britain. She doesn't know if it is leaving the boy or the way Tony brushed his hand against hers, but even in all her splendor, her new dress and gloves, she feels exposed and vulnerable.

Janusz is wearing his demob suit, the one he was wearing when he met her at the train station, a single-breasted jacket and trousers with turnups. He looks handsome. A good man, solid and respectable.

"Smile," he says. "You look as though you are in pain."

"I don't like leaving Aurek."

"Why? What could happen? This is a good town. We're safe here."

"Sometimes I don't feel safe."

"Well, you should. I'll get a promotion at work soon. There's a man retiring and I'm in line for his job. I've worked overtime and extra hours to make sure I get it."

"Think you will?" asks Gilbert, coming up alongside them. "Sorry, couldn't help overhearing. Think you'll get it then?"

"I don't see why not. I work hard. I deserve it."

"That's just it, isn't it? You foreigners work too bloody hard."

"We finish when the work is done."

"That's why you're unpopular. It upsets the system."

"In the mood for a film?" says Doris loudly, and Silvana sees the way she jabs Gilbert in the ribs with her elbow. "And I want to watch it all, Gilbert Holborn, so don't even try to get me to sit at the back with you."

"Me?"

"Yes, you," says Doris. "You won't get me sitting with the courting couples. I'm too old for all that."

They are going to see *Top Hat*. It's an old Fred Astaire musical, and Silvana's choice. Gilbert says he'd rather see a war film, but Doris reminds him it is Silvana's birthday treat, not his. The four of them walk through town, past Woolworths and Lipton's with its pretty green-tiled shopfront, Smith's the butchers, the dry cleaner's, and the drugstore, toward the Odeon cinema.

"There was a dirty great crater here," says Doris as they pick their way along a temporary path of gravel with muddy earth either side of it. "A parachute mine right at the end of the war. They filled the hole in pretty quick. It looked like someone was trying to build a tunnel right through to Australia. A ruddy great hole. It was a miracle nobody was hurt."

The Odeon is a grand-looking building with long windows like a church and lots of peeling pink paint. Gilbert tells them all how he was one of the workers that built it back in '29. Doris shows them shrapnel damage on the front steps, and Janusz and Gilbert follow the pockmarks on the stone, bent over like doctors examining old scar tissue. Silvana just wants to get inside. It has been years, too many years, since she was last in a cinema.

Inside, a blue neon light glows and thick velvet curtains drape over ribbed plasterwork. An usherette in a neat-fitting navy suit with white piping and a hat to match takes their tickets and shows them to their seats.

"I was one of those," Silvana whispers to Doris.

"What?"

"An usherette. In Poland. That was my job before I married."

"Really? Not a big cinema like this though?"

"A beautiful cinema," says Silvana. "And the usherette uniforms were smarter. You see that girl? She has holes in her stockings and her jacket is too tight."

Doris purses her lips. "Give her a chance. We had a war here, you know. Mend and make do . . ."

"Do you remember my uniform?" Silvana asks Janusz, whispering to him in Polish.

He answers her in their mother tongue. "Burgundy with gold ribbons on the sleeves. You looked wonderful in it."

"The uniforms were much better in Poland."

Janusz is quiet for a moment. "Yes," he says. "I think you are right."

"So you had cinemas all over Poland?" Doris asks.

"Everywhere," says Janusz. "Much bigger than this one."

Silvana is grateful to him for defending her memories. She can't stand the way the English think everything they have is bigger and better. If you listened to Doris, you'd think wild bears ran through the ruined streets of Europe.

The moment the red curtains part and the screen comes to life, Silvana is entranced. The story is simple. Fred and Ginger are in love. Anyone can see it—except for them. Every word that falls from their lips is the wrong one, and they argue their way through the first two-thirds of the film. Finally, just when it seems they have really lost each other, the right words come to them and the truth tumbles out.

"I love you," says Fred Astaire. "Despite everything."

"I love you too," Ginger Rogers replies.

And they never lose sight of each other again.

"Beautiful," whispers Silvana as the credits roll. "Just beautiful."

By the time they are walking back home, up the hill to Britannia Road, Silvana's new shoes have given her blisters. Doris and Gilbert are up ahead, Gilbert complaining about the pubs closing early and not getting a drink, Doris talking about sponge cakes and whether her grandmother's recipe is better than Gilbert's mother's.

Silvana stops walking. She takes her shoes off and feels the pavement wet under her feet.

Janusz takes her shoes from her. "Did you enjoy the film?"

"I loved it. It's been so long since I last went to the cinema. Fred and Ginger are wonderful together."

"Wonderful. And what about us?"

"Us?"

"Silvana, why don't we try for a baby? It would be good for Aurek to have a brother or a sister."

She tries to think of something to say, but all she can think of is the impossibility of having another child.

"Look," he says. "I went to see the doctor . . . I went to ask him about . . . about us. I know you're not happy. You hardly let me touch you these days, and the thing is, the doctor thought that what would do you good—that what might make you happier—is another child. I told him I agreed. Another child would be right for all of us."

Silvana can see Janusz is waiting for a response, his face lit by the streetlamps.

"I have blisters," she says.

Janusz hands her back her shoes. "Is that all you have to say?"

"Yes."

He turns his back on her and walks on. She hurries behind him.

"I'm sorry. Give me more time. Aurek is still so young."

"He's nearly nine. He needs a brother."

"But we can't afford another child."

"We can if I get this job as foreman."

"Isn't Aurek enough for us both?"

"So you don't want to try?"

Silvana shakes her head. The thought of another child terrifies her. She mustn't have one. She doesn't deserve one. And how can he ask this of her when he loved another woman—indeed, might still love her?

Janusz shoves his hands in his pockets and hurries his step. She watches him catch up with Doris and Gilbert and begin a discussion about the film. The moment is over. Silvana has ruined it. She walks behind them, her shoes in her hand. She'd like to return to the darkened cinema. To sink into a velvet seat and lose herself again in the film's plot.

"Are you coming?" calls Doris. I want to get home before it rains."

Silvana looks at Doris, Gilbert, and Janusz waiting for her, their breath misting in the night air.

"Of course," she replies, and quickens her pace, the feel of the cobblestones under her bare feet cold and wet.

Aurek is asleep by the fire when they get back, Peter curled up in the armchair and Tony reading.

"Hello," he says, putting down his book. "Had a good time?"

Silvana stands dejectedly behind Janusz. Her stockings have holes in the toes and one of the blisters on her heel is weeping.

"Very nice," she says. "I'll just put Aurek to bed."

"No." Janusz bends down and takes the sleeping boy in his arms. "I can do it."

Silvana's heart splinters slightly at the sight of him holding the boy. She watches him carrying Aurek out of the room, the way he presses his cheek tenderly against the child's face.

"So, have you forgiven me?" Tony asks her. He crosses the room and shuts the door quietly.

"Forgiven you?" Now she is alone with him, Silvana can feel her heart beating too fast. She was so sure she wouldn't weaken like this, but the nearness of him is overwhelming.

"For not seeing you. I've missed you. I tried to stay away. I didn't want to complicate your life. Will you meet me?" He steps closer to her. "When you get Aurek from school? Meet me in the park? I have to talk to you."

"I can't."

"Silvana, I need to see you. I can't pretend anymore."

Silvana is desperate to escape his gaze. She can feel it slipping over her hair, across the bodice of her dress. I am a housewife, she wants to tell him. Not a character in a film.

"This is impossible. Peter is in the room."

"He's asleep. Next week," he says. "Tuesday. I'll be at the school gates. Will you come?"

She doesn't get a chance to answer. The door swings open and they both look toward it.

"Can I get you something to drink, Tony?" says Janusz, coming back into the room. "A cup of tea? Or wine or sherry?"

Standing between the two men, Silvana can feel the heat of Janusz's controlled displeasure toward her.

"A nightcap," says Tony, who acts as though he is completely unaware of the cold wind that has just blown in with Janusz. "What a good idea."

There they all are, Tony talking with his hands, gesturing to an imaginary audience; Janusz holding his hands firmly behind his back, speaking of work and the weather; Silvana turning a blank gaze toward the fire, the mantelpiece, the door, the sleeping form of Peter by the hearth, the area just above Tony's right shoulder, the crease in his elbow. The corner cupboard behind his head.

"I was just asking Silvana if you would like to take the boys to the woods after school next week," says Tony.

"I don't think we have time," Silvana says, trying to sound calm.

"Well, if you do, I'd be delighted to meet up with you all on Tuesday."

"I don't know if I can make it," says Janusz. "I'll try, but we're changing hours at work at the moment. I may be on nights again."

"Oh well, we can wait until you're free, Jan."

"No, don't wait for me. I'm trying to get in as much overtime as they'll let me at the moment. I'm hoping for a promotion, in fact. But Silvana can go with Aurek. I know Aurek's missed having Peter to play with. Silvana?"

"I don't know. Perhaps. Please excuse me," Silvana says, rubbing her eyes. "I am tired. I think I'll go up to bed."

"So I'll see you and Aurek on Tuesday?"

Janusz and Tony are both looking at her.

"Not next week," she says. "Perhaps another time, when Janusz is not working."

She slips out of the door and hurries up the stairs, deciding she will sleep in Aurek's bed tonight.

When she brushes her teeth and washes her face, she tries not to look at herself in the mirror. She doesn't use her jar of cold cream. Her face can feel dry and sore. And she won't brush her hair out tonight. Satisfied with the small punishments she metes out to herself, she takes off her new dress and lays it carefully on the chair in her bedroom, smoothing the fabric with her hand. The dress means no harm, after all. And it is new. It carries nothing inside it but the possible beginnings of her downfall.

She goes into Aurek's bedroom and climbs into his bed. She waits for sleep to take her. *No dreams of Poland*, she thinks. *Please, no dreams of planes and snow and the sound of children crying tonight.* Aurek stirs in his sleep, throwing an arm around her, his skin hot against her neck.

Her intentions have always been clear to her. To give Aurek a father. If the boy is safe, she is safe.

"I've got you, my darling," she whispers to Aurek, and she knows it is he who holds her. In the rough seas she feels she is floating in right now, it is the boy who is the life raft. Try as she might, she cannot lose this image. This floating in dark waters. But it is not her watery thoughts that bother her; it is the knowing that as surely as the boy holds her up, he is also pulling her under.

POLAND

Silvana

Silvana woke to find an old man grinding snow into her chest. It was such a ridiculous sight she closed her eyes again, but still he went on, pushing and pummeling her until she couldn't ignore him. She had snow in her mouth, and as she woke again she thought of the boy and tried to speak, to ask the man where her son was, but words wouldn't come.

The next time she opened her eyes, Aurek was bundled onto her chest. She wasn't lying on the red chaise longue but on a pile of logs on a sledge, a goatskin wrapped around her and the boy, being dragged through the forest.

They arrived at a cottage where a dog barked and two women stood watching them. Silvana tried to focus, to see who they were, but she kept drifting into a light sleep. She saw one of the women bend toward her and Aurek being taken from her. Then she was picked up herself and carried into the cottage, where she was laid on the table, her clothes stripped from her.

"Mama," said one of the women. "Maybe we should get them by the fire? She's like a wet stone."

"No, too much heat's bad for them. Antek, keep rubbing the boy with that towel, especially the skin that's gone yellow. We've got to get them warm from the inside."

Silvana heard them talking as she drifted in and out of consciousness. *Had she been lucky?* she wondered. *Should they both have died? Or was it the boy's luck that had saved them?* She shut her eyes. Her head burned and her body felt like dough, but her heart filled with love for the child.

They were poor peasants, these people who saved Silvana and Aurek's lives, their clothes no better than rags. Several times when Silvana woke from the deep sleep she kept falling into for the first few days, she thought she was at her parents' home again, her mother standing over her.

The woodsman was delighted by his rescue. He looked in on them each day as they began to recover. He was called Antek, and his wife, a smaller, sober version of Silvana's own mother, was named Ela.

Ela stood crookedly, shaped by her meager life like a tree shaped by the wind. When she walked she carried her head low, her back bent like a shelf for the snow to settle upon. She complained of stomach pains and drank bottles of medicine the color of charcoal.

They had just one daughter, a stocky young woman called Marysia.

"There are soldiers in the village an hour's walk along the river," Ela said as she sat massaging Silvana's legs with goose fat. "You should stay close to the house."

"Germans?" Silvana asked. She had been at the cottage for a couple of weeks and was just beginning to feel strong enough to take notice of where she was.

"A few hundred of them. We have no problems with them."

"The villagers call us kulaks because they think we're on the side of the Germans," Marysia said. "But they're jealous because we don't have to work for the soldiers like they do."

"The Germans are not so bad," Marysia told Silvana when her mother had left the room. "Some of them are better than the animals that call themselves men in the village."

"Such gentlemen to take our country," Silvana replied.

"Let them take it," Marysia said. "They're welcome to it. Before they came we were hungry. Now I have food whenever I want. And look—" she lifted her skirts and turned an ankle, showing off a pair of laced brown boots with a small heel. "These come from Paris. I'd let you try them, but I don't think you'd get them on."

Silvana looked down at her swollen feet. Her toes were scarlet, her feet covered in a red rash that marbled up her legs, stopping just below the knees.

Marysia tutted. "You'll have scars. What were you doing in the woods anyway? Were you hiding? Are you Jewish? The boy looks Jewish."

"My son is Polish. So am I."

"I don't care either way," Marysia said. "My father thinks you and the boy are a couple of miracles. He'll let you stay here as long as you like. I'll let you stay as long as you pull your weight."

Silvana stood up stiffly. It seemed as though she had lived many lives, that the day Janusz left her in Warsaw was the day one life ended and another began. And now here she was, starting again. A miracle no less. But she was nothing of the sort. She and the boy were foundlings from the forest, mysteries even to herself. In the kitchen, Aurek was sitting on Antek's lap, wrapped in oilcloths. Antek was teaching him a song: "*Oto dziś dzień krwi i chwały*," "Today is a day of blood and glory."

The old woman sat watching in a chair by the fire.

"Ah, there you are," Antek said. "Come and sit down." He handed Aurek to Silvana.

"I was just saying how I thought you were nothing but a pile of old clothes when I found you. That's all I thought you were: a heap of blankets. I found the chaise a few days before. Thought it might be useful. There's lots of stuff in the woods now. People trying to get to the Russian side. They carry their furniture and belongings as far as they can, then abandon them. See that clock?" A wide-hipped grandfather clock stood against the whitewashed wall. It had a hand missing and the front was made of a different colored wood from the body. "Mended it myself. I reckon it came from the same house the chaise longue came from. And then I saw you and I thought you were a pile of clothes."

"Do you think you could show me the chaise longue again, when the weather improves?" Silvana asked. "I had a bag with me. I'd like to go back and try to find it. And a necklace. A glass pendant. It's probably lost, but my husband gave it to me."

"I didn't see a bag and I never saw a necklace. There was nothing but you and that broken seat."

"The things that come out of the forest," said his wife in a hushed voice. "You hear such stories."

"The drowned woman," said Marysia. "Tell us about the drowned woman."

"That's a stupid story," grumbled Antek.

"Go on, Mama, tell the story. I'm sure our guest wants to hear it."

"All right," said Ela. "She was a drinker, this woman. She had a son but that didn't stop her. Her husband chucked her out. Kept the baby and threw her out in the street."

"She slept with different men," said Marysia. "Nobody knew who the father of her baby really was." She stared at Silvana. "Do you like a drink?"

"Marysia!" snapped her mother. "Are you telling the story or am I?" She shifted in her seat and continued. "The woman went straight to the Jewish tavern in the village. When the bar closed, she wandered around in the dark and stumbled into the forest, where she fell into a deep pond. They found her there the next day, drowned. The child screamed and cried and nothing would silence it."

"So what happened?" Silvana asked.

Ela sat back in her chair. "She came back from the dead. Three days later she came back to suckle her son. The sound of him crying brought that wretched woman back. After that, she never left her cottage, never spoke a word, spun wool every night, prepared the meals, and raised her boy. Her husband said he liked her better dead than alive."

"And it really happened," said Marysia.

"Of course it didn't," said the woodsman. "It's a stupid tale you women like to tell. Why don't you quiet down with all your nonsense and let me talk? At least I can tell God's truth and not some story put about by women with too much time on their hands."

He stood up and warmed himself by the fire.

"You couldn't have been there long. I found you just in time. I rubbed you down with snow as fast as I could. I used up so much snow I was sweating by the time I brought you around. Sweating in all that snow! It made me laugh out loud. I cleared an area this wide. Back to the earth. If I hadn't decided to take that red chaise home, you would have died. Like I said, it's a miracle I found you. Like God had left you there."

Marysia snorted with laughter. "Either him or the devil."

Silvana shifted Aurek on her knee and pretended not to hear.

Janusz

Every morning, at first light, Janusz breakfasted with the family before they worked the fields together. He learned how to manage vines and grow crops, and took charge of the vegetable garden. The famer's wife showed him how to tend roses and care for the fruit trees in the orchards.

In the afternoons when the heat was too much to work in and everybody slept, Hélène pulled Janusz into the barn where they made love, salt settling on his lips, sweat stiffening his hair and dripping into his eyes, rivulets running down his back, between his buttocks. She seemed to turn the air thick with the heat of her lovemaking, always wanting more from him, always desiring him, loving him.

He couldn't bear to let her out of his sight. He was so full of her he couldn't understand his joy. He knew the war continued, but it didn't matter to him anymore. It was all somebody else's business. He was not part of any of it.

The farmer asked Janusz if he was going to marry her. He didn't want to know about Janusz's past. He needed a man to work the farm. He wanted grandchildren. Lots of them.

"If the Germans come down here, we'll hide you. I know what war is like. I was a poilu in 1914. Stay here. Hélène's a good girl. She'll make you a good wife."

"I will, sir," said Janusz. He was so serious, he saluted the old man. And the old man stood to attention and saluted him back.

IPSWICH

Janusz is counting on his promotion at work. He wonders if they will choose another man, a British man, over him. He is wearing his best shoes, the ones Silvana gave him, polished and bright. His hair is oiled, his face clean, and his collar starched. There is not a man who works as hard as he does on the shop floor, of that he is sure. But will that be enough?

He waits in the office where the secretaries work, listening to the chatter of typewriters, and when the boss comes out of his glass-fronted booth, cigar in hand, Janusz asks him whether he has made a decision about who will replace Mr. Wilkens as foreman. The boss tells him not yet, but he believes the Poles are all damn good workers. Janusz runs a finger around the inside of his collar, clears his throat, feels suddenly hopeful and says so.

The boss says he should be. He has a factory to run and doesn't give a pig's arse what the locals think of foreigners stealing their jobs.

"But just don't touch their women. We know what you Continentals are like. Young Lotharios, the lot of you," he laughs, and pats Janusz on the shoulder. Then he strides out, leaving Janusz alone in the room with six silent typewriters and six giggling secretaries looking at him as if they think he might be a Polish Casanova in blue overalls. It takes most of the afternoon for his normally pale cheeks to lose their red glare of embarrassment.

Janusz has always believed in things falling into place. He knows patience and a sense of duty will always be rewarded. This belief comes from his father and his grandfather. He is one of Poland's sons and has a steady understanding that right will somehow or other always be rewarded by right.

Like a stream trickling over pebbles will smooth and shape them, so Janusz's hopefulness is a slow and unending force that runs coolly through his life, rubbing, rolling, and forming it. So when the chance to buy a car falls into his lap the same day the work promotion is almost his, he isn't surprised at all.

It is a black Rover, owned by a teacher and his wife. Made in 1940, it has a four-speed gearbox, a busted radiator, and two flat tires. In 1943, the teacher's wife drove it in a snowstorm and crashed into an oak tree. Since then it has been in a barn under a tarpaulin. Janusz overhears a man telling the story during lunch break.

He turns to the man drinking tea from a flask and offers him one of his sandwiches.

"They are cheese," says Janusz politely.

"Cheese?"

"Yes. Real cheddar. From the Co-op. With margarine and onion cut very thinly."

"Cheese, eh? All right then. Don't mind if I do."

It costs him his lunch, but he leaves work that day with the teacher's address.

He doesn't lift the tarpaulin. The rounded shape of the car underneath it is enough to make him dream of country drives, picnics with Aurek and Silvana, driving the boy to school, and trips to the seaside on Sundays.

"Yes," says Janusz.

"Have a cup of tea first, old chap," says the teacher. "There's no rush."

Janusz sits in the kitchen at a big refectory table. He looks out of the window, beyond the stone patio to a lawned garden bordered by beds of red and yellow tulips and behind them shrubs and trees. The kitchen has a black and white tiled floor, like the floor of his parents' kitchen in Poland, and a big cooking range covered in pans. Above the range hangs a drying rack covered in baby clothes.

"We've just had our fourth," says the teacher when he sees Janusz looking. "I'm afraid he's got a few problems, poor little chap. We're selling the car partly to finance a vacation for my wife. She's finding it rather hard to accept the child."

Janusz doesn't know what to say. He nods uncertainly.

The man moves the kettle on the stove. "So you'll be able to fix it up yourself, will you?"

"I think so."

The teacher's wife comes in and offers Janusz a currant bun to have with his tea. She is narrow faced and creased with tiredness. Pushing her wavy brown hair out of her face, tucking loose strands behind her ears, a gesture she repeats as she speaks, she talks about Russia and the atom bomb and Janusz tells her politely that he is Polish, not Russian.

"I think Russia having such a bomb would be a disaster. Poland will be Poland again one day, and the Russians will leave our country," he says, and then regrets the determined tone in his voice, the emotion he didn't mean to show.

"Yes, yes," says the teacher's wife. She smiles at Janusz as if he has not quite understood the complexity of the discussion. "But we have to let the people take control. Follow a Russian model whether we like it or not."

Janusz is there to buy a car, not discuss politics. His collar feels tight, but he resists a desire to loosen it.

"It's all down to understanding," says the teacher. He wears his glasses on the bridge of his nose or pushes them back over his forehead into unruly waves of ginger hair. "This country is still having a hell of a time struggling with peacetime. We need to find a way to give everyone a sense of *worthwhileness* in their lives."

The sound of a baby's high-pitched screaming floats down from another room and the teacher's wife puts her head in her hands and gives a sudden cry. The teacher takes his glasses off and cleans them.

"Susan, that's enough."

"Enough?" She lifts her head. "This is just the bloody beginning."

Janusz loosens his collar.

"Can I see the car again?"

He rolls the tarpaulin back, opens the door, dusts off the black leather seats, and gets in. He gets out, walks around the car, runs his hand over the dented hood, kicks a flat tire.

"Yes," he says again, and they go back into the house where a woman in a white apron passes the crying baby to the teacher.

"Hello, little chap," says the teacher, handing the child to Janusz. "He's abnormal, I'm afraid. Quite heartbreaking."

The child has a thick mop of brown hair, and when Janusz takes him he stops crying and smiles, a wide smile that makes his eyes disappear and his face pucker into creases. Janusz holds him on his lap and jiggles his knee to make the boy laugh. He is solid as a block of lard and not much better looking, but Janusz has to stop himself from singing Polish songs to him.

"You're good with him," the teacher says, and something in his voice makes Janusz suspect he'd like to offer him the baby along with the car.

When he leaves, with a promise from the teacher to help him move the car to Britannia Road on a trailer, the man's wife hands him a tartan blanket.

"Take this. You'll need a car blanket. Good luck with your life here."

He can see tears welling in her eyes. There's a wave of sadness coming off her that makes him feel he could drown in it.

"Your son's a lovely little chap," he says gently. "You're a good mother."

"Sadly, I'm no kind of mother," she replies. "I hope you enjoy the car."

Janusz cycles home, the blanket balanced over the handlebars, compiling a list of spare parts he needs. Apart from the brown Humber van, owned by a family that live three doors down, Janusz's car will be the first in Britannia Road.

His head is so full of his thoughts that he doesn't notice a car pulling alongside him. He nearly slams straight into it when it stops in front of him on the concrete bridge over the river.

"Evening," says his boss, winding down his window. "Glad to see you, in fact."

Janusz dismounts from his bike, smoothes his mustache, stands up straight.

"The job as foreman. You still want it?"

"Yes?"

"It's yours. Nice to give a bit of good news to somebody. Come into the office tomorrow."

He shakes Janusz's hand and drives off, waving regally.

Janusz climbs back on his bike. He reaches the bottom of the hill and instead of dismounting and pushing the bike up the road as he usually does, he feels a spurt of energy, puts his head down and cycles as hard as he can, not looking up until he makes it to the top. He comes to a triumphant stop at the top of the hill and looks back at the town, the fields bordering it, the estuary that leads to the sea and the roads that go all the way to London and beyond.

He is on top of the world up here. And this is a fine country where a man can arrive with nothing but a broken heart and make something of himself. He'd like to be able to see his father and tell him the news of his promotion. He'll write to him again. Useless, perhaps, sending letters when he has never had a reply, but he still does it. And why shouldn't he imagine he can converse with the missing? Perhaps his father, wherever he is, might be thinking of his son too?

He wheels his bike through the small alley they share with Doris and Gilbert and pushes the gate into his own backyard, taking off his bicycle clips and leaning against the wall while he waits for his breathing to come back to normal. Then he walks down to the potting shed.

Inside, among cans of oil, the lawn mower, and boxes of flower bulbs, are the letters. He takes them and lays them in a metal dish. With a match he sets fire to them, before he can talk himself out of his actions.

It is time to put the past behind him. To do things right. If they are going to have another child one day, he has to stop hanging on to the past. The letters burn quickly, all her words turning to silver and black, small dustings of them drifting in the air. When the flames die down, he presses his fingers into the silken ashes and cleans the bowl.

In the kitchen, Silvana looks up from the pot she is stirring on the stove. He smiles at her as he opens the back door and puts the blanket on the table. She always manages to look startled when she sees him, as if she is still surprised to find him there beside her. Maybe she sees the same look on his face too. Maybe she reacts to him, to the fact that he is faintly relieved to find she hasn't gone off on one of her walks and not come back.

"What's that?"

"A blanket. What are you cooking?"

"Pearl barley soup."

"Do we have any meat?"

"No. Not today."

"We'll have meat every day of the week from now on."

"How's that?"

She is wearing her best dress and the shoes he bought her, the white ones. She looks quite smart if you ignore the splattering of soup on her shoes. He slides his arms around her waist. Janusz feels glad to have her in his arms—his wife, who would do anything to protect their son. That is how she presents herself. Like a soldier who would kill for her country. And her country is their son.

And yet, no matter how Silvana juts her jaw at the world and holds her back straight as an iron bar, he knows she is fragile. She is made of the thinnest eggshell, her toughness a veneer that could be broken with a single clumsy move. He imagines her sitting in the passenger seat of his new car, the way she would hold her hands clasped together, the careful upright look of her.

"I got my promotion." Janusz feels his cheekbones move, his face settling into an unexpected grin. "Wait, that's not all. Do you want to know why I have a blanket? It's to put over your knees when I take you for a drive."

She turns, the wooden spoon in her hand dripping soup on the floor.

He takes the spoon from her and puts it back in the saucepan.

"I bought a car."

"A car?"

Aurek is sitting under the kitchen table, playing with a pack of cigarette cards.

"Did you hear me?" he asks the boy. "We've got a car. The Nowaks are going up in the world."

Aurek crawls out from under the table and Janusz holds his hand out to his son. The boy shoves his hands in his pockets. Janusz remembers being a small boy himself and his own father standing over him, the mix of fear and love he felt for him. He tries to soften his face. To be less imposing.

"A car?" says Aurek.

"That's right. We have a car."

Janusz places a hand gently on Silvana's belly. "We just need . . ."

"I know."

"And?"

She looks down, bites her lip. Then she raises her wide brown eyes to his and nods.

"All right. We'll try."

"Really?"

He is so surprised and grateful to her, he whoops with joy and stumbles through a few steps of a mazurka, kicking his legs and singing, Aurek giggling at the sight of him.

Janusz stops and regards his family, his life, the small kitchen. The table takes up most of the room, that and the three wooden chairs. The dripping tap that he must fix one day plays a repetitive, *plink-plink* tune in the ceramic sink. He looks at the suburban garden through the window. It may not be a big garden, but the lawn is smooth and weed-free, the flower beds are blooming this spring, and the vegetable patch is overflowing with produce. Aurek is making car noises, *vroom, vroom*, jigging from one foot to the other. On the stove, the pearl barley soup, brown and viscous, is gently boiling over.

"You have a smudge on your cheek," says Silvana. She wipes it with her finger and he feels the softness of her gesture. He thinks of Hélène.

"There," says Silvana. "It's gone now."

Janusz looks down at his son and ruffles the boy's hair gently.

"Aurek, I do believe you are growing," he says. He leans behind Silvana and turns off the stove.

Silvana opens a drawer and looks at her red headscarf. She hasn't worn it since Doris dyed her hair for her and showed her how to curl and coif it in the modern style. Underneath the scarf is a neat pink box. She takes it out and opens it, running a finger over the diaphragm inside. Doris had helped her get it. She'd given her the name of a doctor.

"You go and see him. He'll give you something. Some of them don't like it when you want to take matters into your own hands. They think you're trying to escape your duties. They give you all that stuff about the population and your role as a woman. This one'll see you all right. Me, I've been lucky. I had our Geena and afterward Gilbert never really bothered me for that kind of thing. We're too old now in any case. I'm looking forward to grandchildren."

"I have my son," she told the doctor. "It's enough to look after him. I don't think I could cope with another."

"And your husband treats you well?"

"Yes. Yes, he's a very good husband."

And ask about me, she thinks. *Ask me if I am a good wife and I could tell you I am a liar and a cheat.*

"He doesn't want any more children either?"

"No. We both feel our son is enough."

He nodded and wrote her a prescription. He had half a finger missing from his right hand and scarring across the back of his wrist. He held his pen awkwardly, wrote slowly.

"You're not alone," he said. "There's nothing to be ashamed of. A lot of couples feel like this. The war has affected all of us. Quite frankly, who would want to bring a child into this world?"

"You'll be all right, love," Doris said when Silvana came home. "We women always are. We have to be."

Silvana lays her headscarf back over the pink box. It's been three weeks since she agreed to try for a baby. Three weeks of feeling like she should be burning in hell and three weeks since Janusz has been nothing but kind, bringing flowers for her and toy cars for Aurek. A perfect husband when she is fast becoming a terrible wife. She can't go on like this. All her lies are stacking themselves up. Sooner or later, they will fall apart.

POLAND

Silvana

For six months Silvana stayed in the cottage. She gladly threw herself into the steady peasant life. It was a slow, hidden world she had moved into, and it suited her. Nobody asked her who she was or where she and the boy had come from. She was a young woman unafraid of hard work. That's all the family were interested in. And that suited her fine. She cooked, fetched water from the well, cleared their fields of stones, and planted out crops in May.

Each Friday, Marysia disappeared from the house for hours. She came back on Saturday morning with a flush in her cheeks and a bag of bread and meat. Once, she carried an ox tongue into the kitchen and her mother took it without a word of surprise. Silvana asked where she had found meat like that, but Ela didn't seem to hear and Marysia only laughed, a coarse laugh. She set her hands on her waist and flicked her hips at Silvana.

"Be careful. Talk of the wolf," she said, "and he's sure to appear."

Ela was often ill and Marysia left it to Silvana to nurse her. One day when Ela lay doubled up with pain she asked Silvana to bring her last bottle of medicine.

"What is it?" Silvana asked, looking at the thick cloudy mixture.

"*Chaga*. And yes, it tastes as bad as it looks. But it works. I get it from a Russian doctor who makes it for me."

Silvana held the bottle up to the light. "A Russian doctor?"

"He's in hiding, not far from here. He is a very good doctor."

There was only one person who could have made this for her.

Gregor. And this was the cottage, then, that he had got food from when they were all together in the woods. Silvana handed Ela the bottle and said nothing, but for weeks afterward, every time she looked across the fields, she wondered whether Elsa had had her baby and if Gregor might come to the cottage one day.

Janusz

Janusz and Hélène lay on a grassy mound together. Below them the Mediterranean Sea was a thin pen line of blue meeting a sky the same color. Villages, vineyards, and towns, gauzy in the heat, spread out below them. Waxy-leaved myrtle grew in clumps around them, hiding them from view.

"Stay," Hélène said, her head resting on Janusz's shoulder. "Stay here with me. We can be happy together, you and me."

Janusz smiled at her. "How can I? If I stay here I'll be arrested."

"The war won't go on forever."

Janusz pressed his fingers against his eyes.

"Janusz, are you listening? Will you? Will you stay?"

He took his hands away and looked at her.

"Stay," she repeated.

He thought of the sailors at the docks in Marseilles, unloading goods from Africa, the Ivory Coast, places where the sun mapped lines on faces toughened by sea air and saltwater. When he stepped onto the docks nearly three months ago, Janusz had envied these men their bronzed muscularity. He had listened to their voices and tried to copy their fierce vowel sounds, the questioning rise to every sentence. He felt closer to them now, as if his body turning from red to brown was part of something deeper. Janusz was warmed by their laughter, comfortable in his new skin. *I am a Frenchman*, he thought. He was wrapped in sunlight and love and a dream he didn't want to wake from.

He pulled out the photograph of Silvana and Aurek from his pocket and looked at it.

Hélène took it from him. She stood up and walked to the edge of the cliff.

"Will you stay?"

She held the photo out over the edge of the rocks.

"Shall I let this go?"

Janusz hesitated.

"I love you," Hélène said. "Do you love me? Shall I let it go?"

Janusz shut his eyes.

"If you want to."

She gave the photo back to him and he put it on the ground beside him, pulling her into his arms.

The same day, as Janusz was standing on the barn roof, setting red tiles into place, he heard the noise of a motorbike coming up the hill toward the farm. He slithered quickly down the roof, climbed down the ladder, and stood in the shadows watching as the motorbike cut up the white stone drive, sending dust clouds high into the air.

He picked his way carefully around the back of the barns and watched Bruno get off the bike and walk across the yard. The fields beyond the farm looked tempting. Nobody would find him up there. Or he could hide in the barn. He could get himself lost all day and not come out until Bruno had gone. But no, he had to see what this was about. He'd see his friend again and explain he was staying.

He found Bruno smoking a cigarette, talking to Hélène in the loud, playful voice he used with women. Janusz quickened his pace and stepped between them.

"Bruno."

"Janusz? Hélène was just telling me you weren't here. There's a boat leaving for Southampton tonight. The British are taking Polish soldiers with them."

Janusz glanced at her. "I'm not going."

"You've got no choice, mate." Bruno dropped his cigarette, stamped on it. "The Germans are moving down through France. They'll be in Marseilles before you know it. I'm sorry, Jan. You have to come with me. Pack up your stuff. We have to go now."

"What did he say?" Hélène asked. Then she backed away from him. "I can see it in your face. You're leaving, aren't you?"

"No, I . . ."

She slapped him on the chest and turned away, hurrying toward the house.

"I'm sorry," said Bruno.

Janusz ignored him. He hurried after Hélène and caught up with her by the front porch.

"Wait."

"For what?"

She fell into his arms, sobbing.

"I'll come back," he said. "I will."

"You have to," she whispered, clinging to him.

He could hear the stiff bravery in her voice and was reminded of Silvana. Was this what the war would be for him, a series of good-byes?

"You have to," she repeated. "I'll die without you."

"I swear I'll come back to you."

She raised her eyes to him. "I'll be here. Waiting."

Janusz let her go and she turned, walking into the farmhouse, shutting the door behind her. Janusz tried to fix the moment in his head, to give himself a picture of her: how pretty her hair was, the way her shoulders rounded as she hugged herself, her steady step up as she went indoors.

"I'll come back," he said to the wooden front door. "I promise I'll come back."

He had nothing to take with him. Only the clothes he stood in. He walked back to Bruno and climbed onto the motorbike behind him. They rounded a corner and tall, dark poplar trees hid the farm from view. Then he concentrated on watching the road in front of them.

A coal boat took them to Britain. It set sail with its crop of foreigners and Bruno and Janusz were billeted down in the hold, eating hard yellow cheese from the iron rations they had been given, sitting on sheets of metal, shoulder to shoulder, squashed in with crowds of men all talking about their beloved *Polska*.

Janusz borrowed a Polish guidebook on England from a group of men, the only book of its kind among hundreds of them, passed between them all like a bible. He started studying it, learning a few phrases, muttering them under his breath.

Good morning. How do you do? Do you know where I can find a post office?

He and Bruno had stilted English conversations about buying umbrellas and visiting the doctor.

"Is that all they do in Britain?" Janusz asked, handing the book over to another soldier.

Bruno shrugged. "I don't know. Here's another I learned. 'Will you please sell me a ticket for the dance tonight?' " He grinned. "That one'll come in useful. All those British girls."

Janusz put his head in his hands and thought of Hélène. He curled up, vulnerable as a child with stomach cramps, rocking himself. Then Silvana and his son entered the confused fields of his thoughts. He reached into his pocket for Silvana's photograph and couldn't find it. He remembered Hélène handing it back to him, but what had he done with it then? He must have left it behind.

A storm blew up in the Atlantic and the boat crashed and heaved in heavy waves. Janusz was sure they would never reach England, home to doctors, dancers, and umbrella sellers. That either the high waves or the patrolling German boats would sink them.

Down in the bunks, where the throbbing of the engines was deafening, all around him was seasickness and complaining. Janusz sat in silence, watching the anonymous faces, the backs of heads, the crush of men, everybody covered in fine layers of earthy black coal dust. As the ship dipped and groaned, the men shifted back and forth in the gloom, hundreds of Polish lads rolling together like a cartload of potatoes rattling across a vast furrowed field.

IPSWICH

Aurek knows it is best to look from underneath. Keep your head down and push through with your shoulders. From underneath they appear as a dark spot in the branches. Like a diver swimming toward the light, push upward until your hand touches the mossy side of the nest. Take only one egg—except from rooks' nests, where you can take as many as you like because everybody knows they are the devil's birds.

It is the enemy who taught Aurek to collect birds' eggs for fun. At home they have a box lined with cotton, full of soft-hued eggs. Each one has a label. *Blackbird. Linnet. Song Thrush. Warbler. Treecreeper. Flycatcher.* There are important rules, too. If a bird is sitting on the nest you must leave it be. Most birds nest in bushes and thick hedgerows, so expect scratches and nettle stings. These things are proof of your bravery.

When he and his mother lived in the forest, Aurek ate the eggs he found, picking holes in the top of them, sucking the soft insides into his mouth, swallowing them down in one.

"Like an oyster," his mother told him. She'd never eaten oysters but she'd supposed they were similar, fluid, and solid at the same time. "They're a luxury," she said. "In Warsaw only the rich eat oysters."

Aurek will never tell the enemy he ate the eggs he found. He won't tell him that sometimes the eggs were full of blood or the blue-skinned beginnings of birds. That they picked the shells off those and cooked them on a stick over a fire. He will not mention the fledglings he stole from nests or the strips of birch bark he chewed on in the dead of winter. Even a child knows that it is shameful to admit to that kind of hunger.

The enemy says egg collecting is part of learning about nature and every boy should be interested in Britain's wildlife, fauna and flora. In the kitchen, Aurek watches him heat the point of a needle in a flame until it blackens. He uses it to make a tiny hole in each end of a blackbird's egg, pushing the needle inside the fragile shell, mashing up the contents. Then he presses his lips to the hole he has made and blows gently until the yolk and the white slip out of the other end, into the sink. When it is Aurek's turn, he finds it hard to resist sucking in. He wants to draw the eggy mess into his mouth and swallow it. But he won't do it. Not in front of the enemy. He wouldn't want to disappoint him.

Aurek stares up at a tall elm tree with Peter beside him, thinking of rooks' eggs. They are picnicking in the woods today and there's a kind of glory in the thick spring air, the shudder of fresh leaves and the sunlight flickering through them. The grasshoppers buzzing in the nettles sound like a fanfare just for him. It's better than any orchestra at the town park's Sunday bandstand, and it makes him want to climb every tree he can see. If he could, he'd split into a hundred different boys so he could climb them all, and he imagines the boys and himself perched up high like a great cackle of magpies.

Peter's dad brought them here on this perfect Saturday. He arrived at the house in the morning with Peter and a picnic basket. Silvana told him they couldn't go out. Not when Janusz was working and she had the front steps to clean and rugs to beat.

Tony said the day was too good to waste doing housework. Then he went down on one knee, making a big show of it, begging her to give him her duster. Finally she looked at Aurek and asked him what he wanted to do. He nodded. Let's go to the woods. Please. Silvana handed the duster to Tony, who threw it into the air and declared the day a holiday.

And now here they all are in the woods and Aurek is so happy he can hardly stop himself from dropping to his knees like Peter's dad.

In the elm's uppermost branches is a big, untidy nest of twigs. Two black rooks hunker on a branch beside it, heads tucked into their wings.

"You can't climb up there," says Peter. "Those birds look evil."

"You're not to do anything dangerous," Silvana calls. Aurek and Peter look back through the trees to where she and Tony sit on a rug setting out the picnic.

"The pond," Peter says. "Let's go to the pond. We could look for the kingfishers' nest."

Kingfishers are Aurek's favorite. The birds dig tunnels in riverbanks and line them with tiny fish bones. To Aurek they are bejeweled palaces. If he could shrink himself small enough, he'd live in one of their nests.

They traipse through the undergrowth until they reach a dip in the landscape, where an expanse of water mirrors the trees and clouds. Peter finds a long stick and bashes it against the reeds. Frogs leap in the shallows. Dull-winged birds take flight, and flying insects whirl and zip across the pond's unbroken surface.

Aurek kicks off his sandals and steps into the water. His feet sink into clouds of sediment and mud sucks at his heels. He wades through clinging green algae into a bed of tall rushes, the smell of disturbed mud deliciously thick in his nostrils. Aurek is halfway around the pond when two moorhens skid across the water in alarm. He sees their nest hidden in a clump of bulrushes. It is difficult to get to, as it is in deeper water, but twenty minutes later he climbs onto the bank holding a clutch of eggs in his hands.

Peter picks up a stick and prods Aurek with it.

"*Eurgh*. Stay away from me. You stink."

Aurek sits down a safe distance from Peter's stick. Smoke wafts past his face and he wrinkles his nose. Peter is smoking a cigarette that he stole from his father's cigarette case.

"There was a murder in Ipswich last week," Peter says. He takes a drag on the cigarette and coughs. "A woman had her throat cut."

Aurek cracks an egg, sniffs it, and tips the wobbly contents into his mouth, swallowing them down. He is not in the mood to listen to Peter's story. He is too full of the woods and the sharp smell of spring.

He stares at his knees, the whiteness of them against the black mud drying like crackled lizard skin over his feet and ankles. Then he pulls on his sandals and walks back to look at the rooks' nest. Peter trails along behind him.

"It was in the newspaper. My dad says she was a call girl. Do you know what that means? There are lots of them down by the docks." Peter waves his cigarette as he speaks. "Common women. I've seen them with my dad. They wear black a lot. Grandad says they're called ladies of the night."

Aurek doesn't care what they are called. They sound like bats to him. *Ladies of the night.* Women with black cloaks flying through the air.

"So what," he says. "In Poland there are murders all the time." He hesitates, wondering whether to tell Peter the things he has seen. He decides not to. He doesn't want to think about them. He stops by the elm tree and rests a hand on its wide trunk.

"There are witches in forests. Even here. *Rusalkas.* They're the spirits of murdered girls who sit in the branches of trees and call men to their death."

Peter is impressed, he can tell. He pulls a face, grinning.

"They rip boys' eyes out."

Peter laughs. "Liar!"

He stubs his cigarette out, grinding it under his shoe.

"You going up there?"

Aurek nods. He's going to go up and get a rook's egg. Easy as that. He'll take it home for the enemy. A present for him. He's pleased with this idea. Proud of it.

He spits on his hands, accepts the leg up Peter offers him, grabs a branch, and pulls himself up. He is small and lithe and his hands and feet find tiny ledges and places to grip. It's a terrific feeling being up a tree, far away from everybody, swinging through the branches like Tarzan of the jungle. Aurek stops halfway up and looks down.

"You all right?" calls Peter from below.

Aurek waves back at him. Above him, the nest is huge, a big mess of broken sticks and branches fashioned into a globe, a dirty sun caught in the tree.

He pulls himself up to it and the two rooks swoop over him, beating their wings in his face, chattering angrily. Aurek swings his body away from the tree as far as he dares, but the birds won't leave him alone. He loses his footing for a moment and bangs against the rough bark of the tree, hitting his nose hard. Tears spring to his eyes. He touches his mouth and brings his hand away, slicked red. His nose is bleeding.

His legs feel weak and he loses his grip, snatching at branches. His right leg is hooked over a branch and it anchors him. He grabs a branch and pulls himself up again. The birds circle him, pecking at the air. Aurek closes his eyes and clings to the tree, the beating of wings loud in his ears.

"Aurek!" Peter calls. "Don't let go!"

Aurek can hear him yelling but his fingers are slipping and the birds keep flying at him. He tucks his face down, the tree bark grazing his cheek, and tries to hold on even as he knows he is going to fall.

"Mama!" he yells. "Mama!" His stomach turns in on itself. Everything is out of his reach. His legs kick and jerk, swimming in the air. One sandal slips off and he thinks he is already falling. The other shakes loose. He looks down, sees himself dead on the ground below, a bundle of bones and bright bruises, a fledgling fallen from its nest.

Silvana is up on her stockinged feet, running toward Peter, grabbing him by the shoulders. Peter points to the top of the tree, the birds circling and squawking. Aurek swings back and forth in the branches, one arm holding on, the other trying to protect his head. He must be six or seven meters up. She couldn't catch him from that height. There is nothing to spread out on the hard ground to save him when he falls. And he will fall. She has always known the world is a place that demands justice and that some day Aurek would be taken from her. This is her punishment. This is the day she loses the boy.

"Hold on," Tony says, coming up behind Silvana. He picks up a stone and aims it at the birds.

Silvana grabs his hand. "No! You might hit Aurek."

"But we've got to get the birds away from him."

"No stones! Help me get up the tree. Aurek? I'm coming." Silvana hitches up her skirts and reaches out for the lowest branch of the tree.

"Don't be crazy, you can't climb up there."

Tony tries to pull her away, but Silvana brings her elbow back sharply into his stomach. She scrambles into the lower branches of the tree. Tony tries again to grab her but she kicks him away and pulls herself up higher, out of his reach.

She climbs quickly without care, desperate to reach the boy. Her stockings rip as she clambers inexpertly in the branches, the rough bark scraping her thighs. Twigs catch in her hair. A branch whips into her eye, blinding her with pain. She feels as if her eyelid has been cut, and her cheek is wet with tears. Still she climbs, and all the time the only image in her head is of the child falling. It will not happen. She cannot lose her son. Not this time.

Her hands search out branches, and she feels the weight of her body burning the muscles in her arms as she tries to get higher. She peers at the air in front of her.

"Aurek? Aurek, don't move."

She wedges herself into a cleft and forces her one good eye to stay open. She can make out the form of Aurek above her. She takes a deep breath and forces her voice to sound calm.

"Just hold on. I'm getting there. Don't let go. You understand? Don't let go."

Her legs are trembling now, her knees slipping. She could fall herself.

She moves slowly until she can brace her back against another branch and hold herself in its grip.

"Wait, I can get nearer. Just don't let go."

And he lets go.

Aurek has jumped. He has let go, trusted the air around him and jumped toward her. He is falling, his hair drifting in the breeze of his own movement, his face triumphant above her, arms stretched like wings. She reaches out, sure she will not catch him, and he grabs a branch, swinging inward toward the tree, landing on top of her, his forehead smashing into her cheekbone.

"Aurek," she says, over and over, as stars flash behind her eyes and pain shoots through her temples. She wants to laugh with relief.

"*Ja jestem tutaj*," says Aurek, clinging to her. "I'm here, Mama. I flew. Did you see? I flew."

In the flat above the pet shop, Silvana sits on a leather sofa with a blanket around her knees, a glass of whisky cradled in her hands. The boys are in Peter's bedroom. Tony kneels in front of her, a bowl of hot water beside him, a cotton pad in one hand, a bottle of gentian violet in the other. He has a concerned look on his face, like a mother at her wits' end with a wayward child.

"He could have died," she says to him. She wants to explain, to tell him what she is so afraid of. "If he'd fallen, he could have died . . ."

"But he didn't," says Tony. "Now look, drink that whisky. We'll see to these cuts and then I'll take you home."

He pours the violet concoction into the hot water and dips cotton in it, squeezing it out. He lifts the blanket slightly and touches her leg.

"Take your stockings off." He nods at her. "Go on. They're ripped to shreds. I'll get you some more. New stockings are two a penny if you know where to find them. And I do. Let's get these ones off first. We have to clean those cuts."

She undoes first her left stocking and then the right, her hands feeling for garter straps under the blanket, peeling both stockings down to her knees.

"Two a penny," she says. "That means something is common, doesn't it?"

"Sort of. Cheap, or easy to get hold of."

She is aware of his hands on her knees, easing her stockings down to her ankles and over her feet. The soft pleasure of his attention. His fingers shape her ankles and travel gently up her leg, wiping her grazes clean with cotton wool. She watches the top of his head as he works. He doesn't look up at her.

"Children were two a penny in Poland during the war," she says. "Orphans everywhere. They had no one. I think about them. They won't leave me alone."

Tony rubs pink ointment into her cuts, his fingers touching then stopping as he asks if it hurts, if he should continue. He doesn't look up and begins to pick splinters out of her feet.

"Keep talking," he says. "Keep talking."

Silvana wonders whether he is capable of tending to all her wounds, not just the cuts and bruises but the deep ones that don't show, the ones that hurt the most and never heal. He finishes ministering to her feet and lifts the blanket, telling her, his voice as soft and liquid as honey, that he is going to wash the grit out of the gash above her knee. She sees her thigh, its pale skin already turning blue and mottled around the cut, his hands tracing the shape of the bruises as they appear.

"I heard of one village," she says, "where the houses were destroyed by bombing. Six hundred children were orphaned. Six hundred in one small village." She can feel tears running down her cheeks. "Those orphans were two a penny like you say. I don't know what happened to those children."

Tony looks up at her. He places both his hands on her upper thighs, his fingers kneading her flesh.

"Tell me. Tell me about them."

"Their mothers didn't mean to leave them," she says. She can feel her lip trembling and she swallows back tears. "I know that. No mother means to lose a child. And if you found a child who had nobody . . . surely the right thing to do is to keep it? I mean, if a child needed a mother . . ."

"A child?"

Silvana leans toward him, their heads touching.

"What is it?" he asks. "What is it you're so afraid of?"

"Aurek's not my son," she breathes. "My son is dead. I left him and he died."

He pulls her closer, his hands sweeping around her waist. She lifts her lips to his. It's a kind of oblivion, this kiss. Her eyes are tight shut, his mouth is pressing and urgent. He holds her so tight, she can hardly breathe. And she doesn't want to. She wants him to crush her. To take her last breath for himself.

With a heated needle, Aurek makes tiny holes in each end of a moorhen egg. Beside him, Peter is playing with matches, lighting one after the other. There is a softly sulfurous smell in the room.

They are not talking because when they came down from the tree, Peter told Aurek his mother was mad and Aurek threw Peter's rucksack in the pond and then hit him in the stomach.

Aurek puts the egg on a tray with three others he has prepared in the same way.

"Stop making that noise," says Peter.

Aurek looks up. So Peter is talking to him now.

"That chirping sound. You sound like a bird."

Aurek kicks at Peter and then dodges away from him, holding his tray of eggs up high.

"Get away. Don't touch me. They'll break," he warns.

"Where are you going with them?"

"I'm going to show my mum."

Peter stands at the doorway to his bedroom.

"You can't. My dad said we had to stay here."

Aurek holds the tray tightly in his hands, and Peter bunches his fists.

"My dad said we had to stay in here. You can't leave until I say so."

Aurek can see Peter is serious, but still, he wants to see his mother.

"All right," he says, holding out the tray. "You keep the eggs if I can go out there."

Peter takes the tray.

"OK. And I get to show them the eggs, right?"

They cross the landing and Aurek opens the living room door for Peter, who carries the tray in front of him, walking slowly as if he is balancing a bowl of water in his hands. Aurek trails behind him.

His mother is crying. At least he thinks she is. She is sitting on the sofa with a blanket on her knees and Tony is kneeling in front of her. He can't quite see her face because she is looking down at her hands. Aurek wants to climb in her lap and comfort her, but as he thinks of it, Tony leans forward, wraps his arms around Silvana and kisses her.

Aurek gives a yelp of pain. "Mama! No!"

"Dad!" Peter yells, dropping the tray of eggs. "Dad, what're you doing!"

The two of them pull apart. Silvana's face is white, her mouth is open and her eye, a mass of purple bruising, has already swelled. What has she done? She looks like a terrible ghost. A *rusalka*, a dead woman with eyes that could rip your heart out.

"Aurek?" she calls, throwing off the blankets she is wrapped in, standing up, grabbing her stockings off the floor. "Sweetheart, don't look like that . . ."

"Don't worry, boys." Tony strides toward the two boys, arms out, a huge shape obstructing Aurek's view of his mother. "Peter, you should have stayed in your bedroom like I asked. Aurek, come here . . ."

Aurek backs away. Tony mustn't touch him. He has to get away. He thinks of flights of starlings shifting in the sky, the mass of them blocking out the light. He sees crows circling, black branches and treetops. Lost. He is lost. He opens his mouth and his birdsong escapes, the chattering of magpies, pheasants, the strangled call of rooks.

He pushes past Peter, runs through the flat, throws open the back door and charges down the fire escape, footsteps ringing out a metallic alarm. But where can he go? He is all alone. Home. It's all he can think of. Back to the safety of 22 Britannia Road. Back to the enemy. Back to his father.

POLAND

Silvana

Silvana was airing the bedding in Marysia's room when she found her secrets. She shoved the straw mattress to one side and there, on the wooden base, was a photograph of a German soldier. A man in uniform with a smooth, round face. He had long-lashed eyes that were soft look-ing, too pretty, really, for a man. His mouth was tight set and unsmiling. Next to the photo was Silvana's book on film stars wrapped in cotton. Her quilted bag was there as well. Marysia must have found them in the forest. But did she find them after the old man had rescued Silvana, or had she picked them up while Silvana and Aurek lay dying? Either way, she had kept them and hidden them.

There wasn't much in the room. The bed, a wooden chair. An oval hand mirror. A metal trunk in one corner. Silvana lifted its lid and peered inside. It contained some dresses and hats and several pairs of black silk stockings. Silvana found a richly embroidered headscarf. Birds and flowers crisscrossing a red paisley print. She put her book back in her bag and tied the headscarf over her head. Marysia had stolen Silvana's belongings and now she would take something of hers.

She was about to step out onto the front porch, ready to confront Marysia in the yard, when she heard the sound of a vehicle driving over the uneven farm track. A canvas-covered truck was coming toward the cottage. It stopped under the big chestnut tree and a German soldier got out. Silvana turned to see the old woman, Ela, standing behind her.

Ela's face tightened. "The man outside mustn't see you. He'll think we're hiding you. You stay out of sight until he's gone."

"Is he her lover?" Silvana hadn't meant to ask. The sight of a

German soldier had frightened her more than she realized. She had to know who he was.

"What?"

"Marysia. Is that her lover? She sleeps with a German, doesn't she?"

Ela smiled and Silvana saw a viciousness in the curve of her lips that she had not noticed before. The old woman's hand went to her throat and Silvana saw a flash of color there.

"What's that?" Silvana reached out and drew Ela's hand away roughly. The old woman was wearing her glass pendant, the green glass tree sitting in the hollow of her wrinkled neck.

Now she looked at it properly, the old woman's face was harder than she had thought: her nose had a cruel sharpness to it, her eyes flinty and quick.

"It's mine," said the old woman. "Don't forget we saved your life. You should be careful what you say. Marysia keeps this family fed. She makes sacrifices for us. The fat on your cheeks is thanks to her. The soldiers take food from everybody in the village. We're not even allowed to keep our grinding stones to make our own bread. Do you think this is what she wanted?"

"So he is her lover?"

"A year ago, he came here with other soldiers. They took our grain. He came back alone for Marysia. He took her away and we didn't see her for days. Do you want to know how she cried when she came home? For days she shut herself in her bedroom and wouldn't speak to us. It wasn't just him that hurt her. There were other soldiers, too. All of them shared her between themselves."

Ela wiped her nose on her sleeve.

"You think you're better than us? You don't know how we suffer. There's an underground movement in the village. We know who the resistance members are, but we don't say anything to the Germans. And what thanks do we get?

"Marysia's had death threats from the resistance, but still we don't say anything. We could tell the soldiers all about what goes on in the

village, but we don't. So who are the bad people here? The villagers
who would kill one of their own, or my daughter who has no choice but
to do as she's told? Now get out of sight. And make sure the boy stays
quiet."

Silvana remembered the soldier in Warsaw, the one that made her
lie down on the bed, taking what he wanted from her. Maybe Ela was
telling the truth. Maybe Marysia had no choice. She ducked back slowly
into the room and stood in the shadows watching as Ela walked out into
the yard. Then she crept to the window with Aurek.

The woodsman was in the yard, and he and Ela approached the soldier as if they were greeting a neighbor, lifting their hands and calling
out cheerfully. But the soldier yelled at them. He strode toward them,
brandishing a gun, and they looked bewildered. He made them kneel
with their hands on their heads. He shouted something and the canvas
flap at the back of the truck lifted. Marysia got down from inside it.
She was crying. A man climbed out of the back of the truck. A tall,
handsome man Silvana recognized immediately. It was Gregor. Thinner looking than before and his clothes were shabby, but it was him.

Marysia was begging the soldier to forgive her.

"You know I'm yours," she was saying, her hands pulling at the soldier's arm. "I was going to tell you. Believe me. I was going to tell you
about him, to hand him over to you. Mama, tell him."

"She's right," cried her mother, lifting her head. "This man told us
he was a doctor. We didn't believe him. Marysia was going to tell you."

The German soldier strode toward the old woman and lifted his
gun. A shot rang out and she fell to the ground. Silvana gave a cry and
then Aurek screamed and banged on the window. Silvana grabbed him,
pushing her hand over his mouth.

Gregor looked up at the house, straight at her. The soldier looked
over, too, following Gregor's gaze. They had both seen her. A cold
surge of fear numbed her, made her legs as heavy as stone. She took her
hand off Aurek's mouth.

"Come out!" yelled the soldier, waving his gun toward her. "You, in the house. Come out now."

Silvana took Aurek's hand and led him out onto the front porch.

"If I tell you to run," she whispered to him, "you go as fast as you can. You just go."

The soldier was younger than she had thought. If you took him out of his uniform and put him in peasant clothes, you might have thought him a younger brother to Marysia. And yet, with his gun in his hand, and anger flushing his cheeks, he held his ground and the rest of them stood silently watching him, obedient as sheep in a pen.

She took another step toward the small group in the yard. She was aware of movement behind the soldier and saw Antek, the old man, stumbling to his feet.

The soldier was still beckoning to Silvana. He looked her up and down, and she wondered if he was imagining her as his new mistress. Someone to take over from Marysia. All the time that he stared at Silvana, his eyes creeping over her, she knew he was unaware of the old man getting closer to him. She straightened her back and pushed her chest forward, tried to swing her hips slightly as she walked. Maybe this was sheer madness, but the old man was so near to him, it was surely worth the attempt.

The soldier didn't see the old man until Antek had his arms around his neck. As Antek pulled him down like a wrestler in a fairground ring, Marysia ran over to them, hitting and kicking the soldier in the back. Silvana let go of Aurek's hand.

Gregor yelled at her. "Go! Get away while you can!"

He ran past the truck and down the farm track toward the forest.

Marysia yelled after him. And then, when it was obvious he wasn't going to stop, she began to spit and scream at him. "Fuck you! Run, you coward. Fuck you!"

Silvana stared at his retreating figure for a second. Gregor was leaving? Running away?

Aurek was beginning to cry, his face twisted with fear. Antek and the soldier were on the ground, Marysia trying to grab the gun. Silvana looked around. She had to help them. She shook herself free from Aurek, picked up a stone jar on the ground, and hurried toward the scrabbling group, smashing the jar across the soldier's back.

She knew the moment she did it, it had been a mistake. She hadn't hit him hard enough; the jar had bounced off his shoulder. It was like smacking a wasps' nest with a stick. All she'd done was drive him mad with rage and loosened Antek's grip on him.

The soldier caught hold of Silvana's skirts and pulled her down to the ground, lashing out at her with the side of his gun, hitting her cheek square on. Silvana saw stars in blackness. She could hear Marysia screaming and Aurek crying, his voice high-pitched among the rest of them. *So this was how she was going to die,* she thought as the soldier's fist smashed against her ribs. Not in snow but in the light of a summer day, grappling in the dirt with a stranger.

She tried to escape, but he grabbed her leg and pulled her back to him. She kicked out and he clutched her by the hair. It was then that she saw a flash of metal glint in the sunlight. She blinked and stopped fighting. Gregor was back, the woodsman's ax in his hand.

Everything moved more slowly then; everything seemed clear. She knew what he was going to do. They all did, all of them understanding the moment.

The soldier let go of her and Silvana crawled away. A shot rang out, then another, the soldier firing his gun into the air, hampered by Antek's grip on his arm. Gregor stood his ground and lifted the ax above his head.

Silvana reached for Aurek, crushed him against her chest, but she knew he heard it. The crack of metal against bone. Again and again.

She could feel something hot on her face, touched her cheek and her hand came away bloody. Aurek slipped from her. He was open-mouthed, swaying as if he could hear music somewhere and was letting his body move with it. Blood rained on them. Aurek let out a scream and ran toward the chicken house.

There was still the frenzy of Gregor slamming the ax down again and again. It was possible to believe that he was chopping firewood and that everything was normal except that blood and flesh were every-where and Marysia's face was full of fear and the old man lay cowering in the dirt beside his dead wife, his hands over his head.

Silvana backed away. She snatched up her bag and stumbled across the yard. When she reached the chicken house she found Aurek crouched at the back of it, half in, half out of a nest box. She dropped onto her knees and grabbed his leg, pulling him toward her and still he struggled, trying to get back into the nest box.

"Aurek," she cried. "Aurek, please. We have to go."

She gripped the struggling child tightly in her arms, crawled out of the henhouse and began to run.

She crossed the fields where the family cultivated potatoes and sugar beets and kept on running until she reached a deep stream, throwing herself into it, the cold water shocking her, setting her teeth chattering in her jaw, her legs shaking.

"It's all right," she told Aurek through gritted teeth. "It's all right. Hush, my darling. Hush."

He was shaking, shivering violently, and she washed the blood off him, rubbing at his hair, scrubbing him clean, ignoring his cries, spit-ting on his cheek, using her sleeve to clean him.

"It's all right," she insisted, tears running down her face. She looked at her dress and saw the bloodstains that had bloomed across it in the water. "It's all right," she sobbed, unsure now whether she was sooth-ing herself or the boy. "Hush now."

She carried the child across the stream and climbed through a bank of brambles on the other side. Swinging him onto her hip, she staggered on across the flat landscape, the midsummer sun high in the sky above them, its heat drying their clothes. When she fell, she picked herself up, running on until she thought her heart would burst. Finally, she came to a wide, deep ditch that separated two ripe wheat fields and slid down into it, unable to go on any further.

In the muddy water, pulling Aurek to her, hand over his mouth, afraid he might scream, she lay trying to catch her breath.

She stayed there all day and all through the hot summer night, plagued by whining mosquitoes. At first light, she and Aurek climbed out of the ditch and made their way back into the forest. She could see distant flames across the fields and a spiral of black smoke. Perhaps soldiers out for revenge had set fire to the cottage. Or maybe Marysia and Gregor and the woodsman had set fire to it and escaped.

Silvana reached the edge of the forest and the shadows of the trees, waves of dark rolling over her. The calm of pines and spruce and birch, all the trees drawing her and the boy in, letting them become part of their stillness and secrets.

"We're safe," she told Aurek. "We're safe now."

The forest was Silvana's home again. A green world that swallowed up boundaries in its pine-scented gloom. She knew enough, she figured, to live under the trees; how to skin rabbits, cook small birds, hedgehogs, weasels. She could roast rats so that the flesh didn't dry out. Set fires and build shelters. She knew where the wild fruit was and what mushrooms would be good to eat. She and the boy would learn to move through the trees like ghosts.

There were times she thought of leaving the woods, but the memory of Gregor and the others still woke Aurek when he slept. He stopped speaking, making bird noises to himself instead. They were both jumpy like deer, as nervous as the rabbits they trapped.

By the time the winter came again, they had learned to eat everything they found without wrinkling their noses in disgust. They smelled like animals and Silvana's teeth started wobbling in her jaw. Her hair grew long and tangled. Burrs wrapped themselves up in its straggled ends; leaves caught behind her ears.

Silvana stared into the stream by the camp she had made and tried to study her reflection in the rippling water. If she held strands up to her eyes she could see the gray streaks among the red. She took her knife to it all, sawing at the lumps of matted hair at the nape of her neck. It took ages. She looked in the stream again. Waited for the waters to clear, saw a shadow that was her. *That's better*, she thought. Then she did the same to Aurek's hair. Forest creatures, both of them.

Janusz

Scotland smelled of wet dogs and green grass. After a week spent in a gymnasium where they had daily showers and proper meals, they boarded a train heading south. The carriages were packed with soldiers, and girls climbed aboard at every stop, sharing cigarettes and bottles of beer with the men. Bruno got up to stretch his legs and came back with Jean and Ruby. Jean, in a beige dress, sat down next to Janusz. Ruby, a redhead with a long straight nose that made her look foxlike, sat next to Bruno. Janusz smiled politely.

Bruno tried out his few English phrases. "Welcome. God save the King. Thank you. I'd like a single ticket to Doncaster. Will you come to a dance with me?"

"He's got a way with words," said Ruby, laughing. "Jean, your one's got lovely eyes, hasn't he?"

"He has. You have very nice blue eyes." She pointed at hers and then his. "Eyes."

Janusz nodded. Ruby pulled a hip flask from her handbag. "Here, have some of this. It'll warm your cockles."

The train filled with smoke and talk and the laughter of foreign women, and Janusz sat staring out of the window, watching the undulating countryside pass, wondering how he would ever get back to France again.

IPSWICH

Janusz doesn't care about the flat tires and dented hood. His car is parked outside 22 Britannia Road looking official and proper, and he grins at it like an old friend. The paintwork shines black as coal, and the more Janusz polishes it, the prouder he feels.

When it arrived, half the street came out to watch, and men who had never said more than good morning to Janusz before shook him by the hand and told him they thought he'd got the prime minister around for tea. They joke that he must be working triple shifts to afford a car like this, and nobody mentions that it was towed up the hill or that the headlights are smashed and the front bumper still shows the shape of the tree the car smacked into.

Doris and Gilbert Holborn stand on the pavement beside Janusz.

"Lovely car, a Rover," says Gilbert. "Best of British. A teacher's car, you say? No wonder it looks so good. It'll have been looked after, won't it? You found your feet in this country, eh."

Janusz ignores him. There have been complaints among the workers since he was made foreman. A foreigner in charge. But Janusz has been hurt and surprised to find Gilbert sometimes behaving bitterly toward him.

"It needs a bit of work. A few things need sorting out, but nothing too difficult."

"I bet your boy will love it when he sees it," says Doris. "They went off with Tony this morning. I saw them go. I must say, I think it's very good of him, the way he takes them out so often . . ."

"I was thinking of getting a car," says Gilbert.

"Were you indeed?" Doris tuts loudly. "Don't be so bloody daft. You spend all our money on beer, fags, and the pools. Was it local, Jan?"

"From the other side of town. Do you want to see inside, Gilbert?"

Janusz unlocks the door and both men sit in the front seats, examining dials and checking the interior.

"You know our Geena is seeing a lad from Romford," says Gilbert. "Don't tell Doris, but from what Geena says I think it's pretty serious. I thought it'd be good to have a car. If he does pop the question, she'll be living over that way. We could visit them on the weekends. I'd like to do a bit of touring, too. Mind you, Doris says she prefers buses." He runs a hand over the dashboard. "And you'll be hard pushed to get petrol at the moment. You should ask Tony. He'd be the man to ask. He can get you anything."

Janusz lets his hands rest on the steering wheel. He'll go to the council offices and find out what he is entitled to. He doesn't want to get anything on the black. It's not his style to break the law. He adjusts the rearview mirror and imagines driving away down the hill.

"Tony? Yes, I might ask him, but I think if I'm careful I'll be able to manage."

"Would you two like a cup of tea and a biscuit?" Doris asks, leaning in the open window on the driver's side.

"I could murder one," says Gilbert.

Janusz nods. "Yes, please."

They both get out of the car and walk around it one more time. Gilbert pats Janusz on the back.

"You lucky beggar, eh? No hard feelings. Why shouldn't you be foreman? You work bloody hard. But that's the thing I don't get with you foreigners. I suppose you've got no other life." He walks away into the house, still talking, his back to Janusz. "We don't want to work all God's hours."

"I just want to do a good job," says Janusz. "If we can produce more, then the . . ."

Janusz is about to follow Gilbert inside for a cup of tea when he sees Aurek running up the street. The boy looks like he's crying. He's stumbling as he runs. As he comes nearer, Janusz can see his tearstained face clearly. He looks like he's had a fall. His shorts are sticky with mud and his shirt is stained with green.

"What's happened?" Janusz demands, but the child sinks his head into his stomach, fists banging against him.

Janusz bends down. "What is it? What's happened? Why are you covered in mud? Aurek? Tell me. Has someone hurt you? Who hurt you? Where's your mother?"

What Aurek has to say knocks the breath out of Janusz.

"I don't understand. Say it again. Slowly."

Aurek repeats the same story.

"You're sure?"

"I saw them."

Janusz lets go of the boy. He feels the blood rushing in his ears.

"Are you coming in?" Doris calls from somewhere in the house. "Do hurry up, the tea'll get cold."

Janusz takes Aurek by the hand.

"Don't worry. Stop crying. Not a word. All right?"

"The lad had a bit of a scare in a tree," he explains when they step into Doris's front parlor. "Nearly fell, apparently."

Doris ruffles Aurek's hair.

"Where's your mum, then?"

"She'll be back soon," explains Janusz. "He's come home ahead of the others. Isn't that right, son?"

Janusz keeps a steady eye on Aurek, who says nothing. Doris gives Aurek a slice of bread and jam and his favorite toy tractor to play with. Janusz drinks brown tea and eats biscuits. He talks about gearboxes and spark plugs and how to dismantle four-stroke engines. And all the while, his own heart creaks and stutters, like an engine that's sprung an oil leak.

"I think I'll take the boy home," he says, standing up.

"Tell your Sylvia to give him a bath when she gets back," says Doris. "He's muddy as a dog in winter."

Janusz doesn't bother to wash the mud off Aurek. He puts Aurek to bed in his clothes and tells him to stay in his room. The child strokes his hand, and Janusz kisses him lightly on the forehead.

"We'll be right as rain. Don't worry. Now, you get some sleep and I'll be downstairs."

He doesn't know what to do, so he stumbles into the garden and begins to weed the beds. That is what he tells himself he is doing, but he keeps breaking flower heads and treading on favorite plants. He is clumsy and careless, but it feels good to crush petals and green stems underfoot.

What a fool he is. It's probably been going on for months. He never once thought that Silvana could do something like this. How could he have been so blind?

He tries to pull up a dock weed, but its roots are stuck hard in the soil and he steps back onto a clump of his favorite irises, grinding them under his heel. One thing he is sure of: she won't take his son away. Tony will not bring up his son.

"You all right?" Gilbert is looking over the fence. "Jan? You OK, mate?"

"I'm very well," says Janusz.

"Your missus home yet?"

"No. But I'm expecting her. She'll be back soon, thank you."

He bows slightly and turns to go into the house, flattening a bed of lady's mantle as he goes.

In the kitchen he searches out the bottle of wine Tony bought them. He'd like to throw it away but he needs a drink right now, and why not drink the man's wine? He opens it, drinks a glassful, and finds it tastes bitter. He pours the wine down the sink and stumbles outside again, down to his potting shed, where he sits on the floor and puts his head in his hands. The smell of pig iron from work clings to his skin.

He looks up to see Gilbert standing over him.

"Are you really all right?"

"No," says Janusz. "I'm a bloody fool."

Silvana begs Tony to drive her home.

"I have to find Aurek," she says. "I have to find him before he sees Janusz."

Tony stops at the bottom of the hill so that nobody will see her get out of his car. She says good-bye to Peter, who is sitting on the back-seat, looking scared, the weight of what has happened that afternoon pressing on his shoulders, making him slump. He looks fatter than ever with his fists balled on his lap and his face swollen with tears.

"I want to go to Grandma's," he moans.

"Stop that crying, Peter," snaps Tony. "Silvana, will you be all right?"

"Yes. Take Peter home. Please, just let me go."

"Look, I can come with you, explain the boys made a mistake . . ."

"No. I want to go home alone. I'll be fine."

"I'll be at the pet shop," he says as she gets out of the car. "Silvana, I'll be there if you need me. Silvana?"

"Yes," she says, walking away. "I'll be fine."

She is feeling anything but fine. Her legs tremble and her eye is weeping and she bows her head, hoping nobody will see her walking stiffly up the hill.

Earlier she was carrying a picnic basket and walking with Tony and the boys in the woods. Now her world has fallen in. She should have gone home with Aurek straight away. Going back to the flat above the pet shop had been a big mistake. Her knee starts to ache and she begins to limp.

She will tell Janusz the truth. She will do what she should have done that first day they arrived and he met her off the train. It's as simple as that. No more lies. Oh, for somebody to give her advice!

Janusz will see what a gift Aurek is to them. He will see that the boy must be cherished and kept safe. They can move if he wants. Move away and start again somewhere. No more Tony. None of it. She stops outside the house and takes a deep breath.

There is a car parked outside, and she wonders who it belongs to. Her first thought is that they must have company, but she dismisses that quickly. They don't know anybody. She pushes the door open. 22 Britannia Road. This is her home. Though what sort of a welcome will be waiting for her she has no idea. She nods at the bluebird in the door, as if it might offer her some kind of luck, and walks through to the kitchen where she finds Janusz sitting at the table with Gilbert and Doris.

Silvana knows what she must look like. Her eye is swollen. She has a cut on her cheek. Her dress, the one Janusz bought her, is covered in green mossy stains and rips. She tries to tidy her hair a little and her fingers find a twig. She decides to leave it where it is. She knows she looks stupid enough, outnumbered in her own kitchen, without conjuring bird nests out of her hair.

Doris is the first to speak.

"So you've come back, have you? Why didn't you stay with your fancy man?"

"Janusz, where's Aurek?"

Doris glares at her. "Now you ask? His father put the poor little mite to bed."

Gilbert looks flushed and uncomfortable. "Doris, I think we should be getting home."

"I'll go when I'm good and ready." She dusts her hands across the front of her apron. "The poor little kid. Filthy trick if you ask me. And to think I felt sorry for you."

Silvana ignores Doris. She will not be intimidated in her own home. Not while it still is her home, at least. She turns to Janusz. He avoids her gaze.

"That poor child," insists Doris. "Thank God he's got a father, is all I can say."

"Calm down, Doris," says Gilbert. "There's no need for any trouble. I'm sorry, Jan. We're just going."

Doris makes a snorting noise, pursing her lips. She allows Gilbert to take her elbow and guide her out of her seat. Silvana steps aside to let her pass.

"I understand you all right," Doris whispers. "Oh yes, I've got you figured now. Family planning, my foot."

"Doris!" Gilbert pushes her hard.

"I tell you what. You won't get away with this. This is a respectable street. You'll get your comeuppance, you'll see."

"Doris!" Gilbert says sharply. He avoids Silvana's eyes. "We're just going."

The front door slams and Silvana can hear them arguing outside. She sits down at the kitchen table.

"I don't know what Aurek said, but it wasn't how it looked."

She knows it sounds weak even as she says it. She tries again. Hopes she sounds more convincing.

"I was scared and Tony tried to comfort me."

Janusz folds his arms. "Scared," he says. "What of this time?"

"Aurek nearly fell out of a tree. I thought I was going to lose him. I have a right to be scared. The world is dangerous, Janusz. Maybe not for you, but for me. I feel it every day."

Janusz still won't look at her. She tries to follow his gaze, and in desperation picks up her chair and places it in front of him.

He runs a finger around his collar. Stares at her coldly.

"How long has this been going on?"

She has to tell him the truth, pull the words out of herself, force them to come. It feels like she is dredging something long dead from a river.

"I have to tell you. About Aurek."

"What about him?"

"After you left us in Warsaw I got on a bus out of the city. Aurek was ill. Do you remember how he always picked up colds? He couldn't breathe properly. He cried all the time. When the bus broke down I followed women and children and old people. Everybody was walking."

Janusz reaches for his cigarettes and matches. "This has nothing to do with Tony—"

"It has everything to do with us."

Silvana stops talking. She gets up and closes the kitchen door. What she has to say must not be overheard by Aurek.

"I gave Aurek to another woman to carry. I was tired. I shouldn't have done it. I thought it wouldn't matter, not just for a minute or two. Then I heard the planes. They flew over us and one of them crashed. There was an explosion. I should have kept him with me. I should never have let him out of my sight."

She stops to get her breath. Now that she has Janusz's attention her courage is failing her. Perhaps she should stop here? Tell him yes, she kissed Tony, and leave it at that. Better to be known as an adulteress than a mother who failed her child.

Hot tears run down her face. How can she explain that she has been living with loss since the day her son slid from between her legs in a stranger's home—or that loss colors every memory she has ever had or will have. Loss fills her heart: it is there in the trees, in the rattle of the leaves in the wind, and in the living, mysterious body of a child she has grown to love. A child she calls Aurek.

"I tried to find him. I was confused. I called his name. I was frantic. I found the woman, but she was dead. Our Aurek was beside her.

"I wrapped him in my coat and rocked him. I don't know how long I stayed like that. I got up and started walking. After a while I sat down again. But he was still cold."

"For God's sake." Janusz slams his hand down on the table. "What the bloody hell is this about?"

The violence in his words hurts.

Silvana sits back in her chair, her head in her hands.

"I just wanted him to have a proper family. He loves you, anyone can see it. I'll go. I'll leave. Be a father to him, that's all I ask."

"What are you taking about?"

"Our son," she says, knowing she is about to hurt him more than he could ever hurt her. "I'm trying to tell you. Our son died. Our real son. He was dead when I found him beside the woman."

Janusz is wide-eyed. His mouth twists, as though she has forced him to taste something bitter. She stops an urge within herself to reach out to him. Her touch would revolt him.

"You're lying."

"How could I lie about that? Our son was dead in my arms. I didn't know what to do. I got up and walked with him, and then I heard a baby crying. I followed the sound and I found a child in a wooden handcart. He was around the same age as Aurek. He stretched out his arms to me. He needed me, you see? He chose me. He was crying all alone and it was me that heard him. I'm sure he had no one. He'd been left in a big pile of blankets and my boy . . . our baby, he was dead.

"The child called to me like I was his mother. What else could I do? I swapped them. I put our son in the cart and took the child and called him Aurek. I told myself it was our son come back to me."

Janusz's mouth moves but he says nothing. His cigarette is still in his hand unlit, the matches in the other. Surely now he will see how she has been surviving? Will always be surviving, in peacetime or wartime, it makes no difference. He carries on looking at her, and she is sure he understands what she has been living through. That something, per-haps everything, can be saved. She is his wife. The child can be his son. Silvana's eyes are blurred with tears, but she does not move. While they are still looking at each other there is hope.

It is Janusz who looks away.

"Go."

"You don't mean that?"

"Take the boy. Just go."

He gets up and walks into the garden. Silvana follows him down to the tree house.

"And you," she yells. "You with your love letters. Are you any bet-ter than me? You and that woman. Hélène, isn't it? You think I don't know? Why did you ever want us back anyway? Why did you bring us here if you had her?"

"I believed in you," says Janusz. "How could you lie to me about . . . about my *son*? Get out. Take the child, whoever he is, and go."

He steps into his potting shed and closes the door.

She looks back at the house and sees Aurek at his bedroom window, tapping his fingers on the glass. Silvana lifts her hand, waves at him, but he goes on, tapping the glass as if he hasn't seen her.

Aurek sits on the top step of the stairs and refuses to move.

"*Nie*," he says. "No."

"Please. Get your things."

The boy won't speak. He rocks himself on the step and Silvana takes him by the arm and pulls him to his feet, dragging him outside into the street. He growls miserably as she marches him down the hill, trying to twist out of her grip. Only hours ago she was saving him. Now what is she doing to him?

She wonders if Janusz will come after them. She crosses the road and imagines she hears the sound of him running behind them, calling them back. As she walks, she decides he will come on his bicycle, and when she reaches the high street she does hear a bike, the wheels spinning behind her. She turns, relief cracking across her face. But it's not Janusz. It's a stranger who lifts his cap as he passes and rings his bell at Aurek.

By the time she gets to Tony's pet shop she has given up hoping. She knows Janusz is not coming.

POLAND

Silvana

One morning, early, they heard men in the forest. There was a commotion of shouting and Silvana and Aurek hid in thick undergrowth and watched two German soldiers lining up three men against a row of trees.

The soldiers took their time before they killed their prisoners. One of them was never still. His chin was stubbled, his eyes sunken and empty looking. He walked around, lifting his gun to his shoulder and then lowering it again like a rehearsal, a gesture that he found funny. He was the one who touched the men's faces with the end of the barrel. It was as if the gun was part of him, an accusing finger that he pushed into the men's chest and stroked their cheeks with. Sometimes it wasn't enough for him and he slung the gun across his back as if it got in the way. Then he lifted his hand to the men's heads in turn, cocking his index finger against his thumb and pretending to jump as his wrist flung upward.

The other soldier rolled himself a cigarette and smoked it, sucking his cheeks in as he took hard drags, his face showing the structure of his skull beneath the gray-looking skin.

When they shot the men, Silvana pulled Aurek down onto the ground so that their faces were pressed against the earth. The air was filled with the sound of gunshot and the ground smelled of decay. She wiped away her son's tears. "Hush, my darling," she whispered. "Hush."

When it was getting dark, Silvana and Aurek climbed out of their hiding place and went to look at the dead men. Silvana took a jacket off one, a coat off another. One had a rucksack at his feet that contained a half-drunk bottle of vodka and some black bread.

Silvana picked up a cap from the floor and rubbed mud off the small, red enamel star pinned to it. She put the hat on and smiled at Aurek. He stared. She rocked her head from side to side and did a little dance, feet outward like a duck. Aurek began to laugh. Breaking a low branch, she used it as a walking stick, head tipping from side to side, feet splayed, kicking leaves up in the air.

"Charlie Chaplin," she whispered. "I'm Charlie Chaplin."

Aurek copied her, his laughter quiet like the murmur of a fast-running stream.

Janusz

On a concrete runway, in an East Anglian field in the pouring rain, Janusz imagined the farm up in the hills beyond Marseilles. When his squadron was moved to Yorkshire, he trudged through snow, dreaming of Hélène with her brown hair in plaits.

In Kent, he imagined her voice in his ear. Every new thing he saw he wanted to tell her about. He wrote letters to her, describing the pretty stone houses in villages, the English churches with their grassy grave-yards and big vicarages attached. He picked roses in the summer of 1943 and pretended he could give them to her.

Flying over Italy in spring 1944, dropping propaganda leaflets, he recorded the colors of the hills, the fields, the cities. Just for her.

And Hélène wrote to him. Letters that might arrive out of sequence or three at once after a long wait. He read them all; he knew each one by heart.

When a letter arrived for him in the autumn of 1944, Janusz opened it gladly, in front of the other men in his mess hall, settling down in an armchair. He was surprised to see it was written in English. And it wasn't from Hélène. It was from her brother.

Dear friend,

I am Hélène's brother. I hope you are quite well. I hear a lot about you from Hélène. My parents speak well of you. I have news that is hard to tell. I try writing before but I don't know if the letters are arriving. Our home has suffered of war but not destroyed and we live always at the farm. I must tell what happens and how sorry I am.

Hélène and I are in the city together. Le Panier near the Vieux port and German soldiers barricade us in the street. She got caught in the crowd and I lose her there. There is no one left in Le Panier. The soldiers shoot everyone. I search and I find Hélène in a hospital. I am very sorry. Her wounds were bad. She asked for you many times. She died in the hospital. I am sorry to give you this news. I think you are good man. I finish this letter with my gratitude for your fighting in this war and for your sufferings . . .

Janusz didn't read anymore. He folded the letter up and put it in his wallet. He listened to the blood running through his veins until he thought he could hear it draining from him. Blood must have been seeping from his body because he couldn't stand. His ankles, knees, thighs were closing up like a fan. His head rolled. The wind blew over him like a wail of a voice, or it may have been his own voice. Or her voice.

Or it may have been the sound of his blood and his heart beating so very loud when he wanted it to stop. He clasped his head in his hands, aware of the fragility of flesh and blood, the easy way people were killed and blown apart by guns and bombs and terribly afraid that he, on the other hand, was condemned to live through it all.

IPSWICH

"You can't stay here, Silvana. Not in the flat."

Tony is sure about that. It's the first thing he says when he opens the pet-shop door, ushering her inside quickly. She thinks she sees panic in his eyes. She is sure she knows what thoughts are racing through his mind. How has he become lumbered with this woman and her child? He is a man of the town after all. He knows local dignitaries and his dead wife's father is a magistrate. He can't afford to be seen collecting foreign waifs and strays.

She is about to apologize for coming, about to walk out. The docks, she thinks. I will go and find a ship and we'll stow away. Then Tony grabs her hands in his. She can smell whisky on his breath and his eyes have a wild look in them. Fear. That's what she can see in them. He tells her that he will look after her. He will not let her down. What about a hotel for the night?

Silvana says no. She doesn't want to be in a hotel with people staring at her.

Finally he says he will take her to the house by the sea. It's the only thing he can think of.

"Yes," she says. How can she say no? She is homeless.

She nudges Aurek, hoping he will express some kind of thanks, but the boy kicks at her shin and pinches the skin on the back of her hand, so that she pushes him away. She regrets the action immediately; pulls him back to her too fast and he falls over at her feet.

"Thank you," she says, and Tony smiles at her.

"Shall we have a drink?"

Tony steps around Aurek carefully, the way somebody might move past an unreliable dog.

"A bit of Dutch courage before we go?"

Tony doesn't talk in the car, and Silvana is happy with that. She tucks Aurek up on the backseat with a blanket and he eyes her warily.

"Where's Peter?" he demands.

"With his grandparents," she whispers. "You'll see him again soon. Now go to sleep for a little while."

The town of Felixstowe sits on the edge of pale yellow sand and rough open sea. Colored lights greet them. The sea is dark and inky, but the lights on the pier and along the seafront shine red and yellow, swaying in the wind, so that the colors smudge and blur in the rain.

"The pier used to be longer," Tony says, slowing down. "Part of it was demolished during the war. It would have been too easy a landing point for the Germans. They talk of rebuilding it, but I doubt it. Years ago, I used to fish off the end of it."

He parks the car and cuts the engine. The noise of the wind becomes louder, and rain stings Silvana's face when she steps onto the curb.

"This is the house Lucy and I lived in," Tony says, taking her bag and ushering her toward a narrow, weather-beaten house painted pink. "I moved out after she died. I use it as a store now. I'll have to tidy up a bit, but it's somewhere for you to stay."

There are two heavy padlocks on the door, and Silvana stands shivering in the rain while Tony pulls keys from his pockets and fumbles with locks in the dark. Aurek runs up and down the street and she doesn't bother to call him back. He wouldn't come anyway. Finally, Tony lets them in and feeds the electricity meter in the hall. When the lights come on, Silvana blinks in surprise.

Cardboard boxes fill the hall. Packed to the ceiling are labeled boxes of soap and washing powders, biscuits, chocolates, custard, cigarettes. The place looks like a warehouse. A staircase rises in front of them, stacked with piles of newspapers.

"We'll get the place warmed up," says Tony, moving a wooden

crate out of the way. "Sorry about the boxes. This lot'll all be gone soon enough."

He has lost his buoyancy. He seems embarrassed and unsure, and she senses that this is the side of his life not many people see.

"What's that smell?" she asks. There is a sweet odor coming from somewhere.

"Aah. I've got a crate of bananas in here. They're going tomorrow. Come on in. I know it's a bit of a mess, but it's a roof over your head."

Silvana and Aurek wait in the cold front room, sitting on cardboard boxes full of tins of corned beef, while Tony goes out to buy fish and chips. Aurek turns his back to Silvana and she knows he is angry. She tries to sound cheerful.

"This is an adventure," she tells him, and nearly chokes on the tears that thicken in her throat. "Well, I'm hungry," she says when he doesn't answer her. "Shall we get the table set for supper?"

The boy curls up into a ball and turns his back to her, so she leaves him to himself and goes into the kitchen, a narrow room, more modern than her own, with matching units in a pale yellow Formica. Opening cupboards and drawers, all of them seemingly full of tins of fruit, she finally locates some plates and knives and forks. When Tony comes back he moves a case of London Gin off the kitchen table and they sit down.

"You're hungry, Aurek," says Tony. "I didn't know you could eat so much."

For Silvana, it is nothing new. The boy always eats as if the food in front of him might be his last meal, and she has long forgotten that other children don't behave like this. She looks at Aurek. He has changed lately. He has filled out a little, and his hair is longer and thicker.

"Where do you put it all?" Tony is asking. "Have you got a tapeworm, Aurek?"

Aurek looks suddenly anxious.

"It's a long, wiggly worm that eats all your food before you can get the goodness from it. Lots of kids get them."

Silvana shakes her head and puts her hand on Aurek's arm.

"Aurek, he's only joking."

"Of course I am. I didn't mean to upset you, old man. Here, have some of my chips. Your mother's right. You do need to eat."

After they've finished, Tony smokes a cigarette and reads a newspaper. Aurek sits on the floor of the kitchen while Silvana washes up the dishes. When she's done she drifts back to the front room with its bay window and hears Aurek slip in behind her. She stares out at the night and the lights from the ships out at sea. Despite everything, it is a relief to have confessed to Janusz, to have told him the truth. He has deserved at least that for a long time now. It's a kind of relief, but it also may be the stupidest thing she's ever done. She looks at the boy and feels afraid. Where has her promise to him gone now? Who will be his father?

Silvana prepares a bath for Aurek. She twists the bath taps on full and brown water glugs out. Through the open door she can hear classical music playing on the radio. She thanks God it is not Chopin. A Polish melody would undo her. Steam rises in the room and Aurek appears at the door.

"There you are," says Silvana. "It's all ready for you. Don't stay in for too long."

She begins to undress him, but he pushes her away.

"No," he says angrily. "I do it myself. Go away."

"Don't speak like that."

Aurek pushes her away from him again and Silvana gives up. She stands looking at him. He still has mud in his hair and up his legs. Against the white skin of his calves he looks like he is wearing black ankle socks and garters. She wants to plant him in the bath and scrub him clean, but she knows he won't let her.

"All right." She sighs. "Whatever you say."

She goes downstairs and watches the fishing boats again. She doesn't know how long she sits like that, but suddenly she is aware of Aurek beside her, stroking her hand, leaning his head against her shoulder.

"I want to go home."

"Soon," she promises, wrapping an arm around him. "Soon. We'll be all right, my darling. You'll see."

She puts Aurek to bed in the camp bed Tony produces from a cupboard. He pulls it out of a green canvas bag with pale stenciled letters and numbers on the front and a stamp saying it is the property of the British Army, a clattering mix of strong cotton twill, webbing, and wooden dowelling that he folds out and assembles into a bed.

The boy climbs in and digs a nest out of his blankets, pulling them over him so that Silvana cannot kiss him goodnight. She doesn't blame him. She pats the covers and goes downstairs. In the living room Tony stands waiting for her.

"In bed, is he?"

"Yes. He's sleeping in his clothes. I forgot to bring pajamas."

"I think I've got some. In a box around here somewhere. Woolworths cotton flannel. I can have a look."

"It doesn't matter tonight."

Tony steps toward her and wraps his arms around her. He lifts a stray strand of her hair from her cheek, and she feels the tenderness in his touch. It makes her legs shake. Kindness is the last thing she must have. Her heart twists and aches. Does she love two men? Is that possible?

"Tony, do you think he heard us?"

"Who?"

"Aurek. Do you think he heard what I said to you? In the flat?"

Tony sighs. "No. He couldn't have. Look, I'll have to go to Ipswich tomorrow. I always have Sunday lunch with my parents-in-law and I need to see Peter. I'll come back in the evening. I'll get you settled in, but I will have to go back to Ipswich on Monday afternoon. I haven't got enough petrol to keep toing and froing. I can be here Friday night. In the meantime, if anybody does speak to you, if the neighbors ask you what you are doing here, I think it might be best to say you are a housekeeper. Best for you. Just to begin with."

"Housekeeper?"

"Yes. Sounds a bit more respectable, doesn't it?"

She thinks back to the ship that brought her to England. The two choices women had. To be a housewife or housekeeper.

"More respectable than what?"

"Silvana, you've left your husband. People know me around here. They know I live on my own. I don't want you to be gossiped about. I want to keep you safe, that's all."

Oh, she thinks. *Oh*. Then it dawns on her that he is afraid of people believing she is his mistress. She begins to cry, and he hands her his handkerchief.

"It'll be all right," he whispers. "Come on now, don't cry. It'll all be all right. You know I care for you."

They listen to the radio, Tony cocking an ear toward it, repeating lines and laughing as if he is alone and not sitting in a room with somebody else's wife. She can see he has the habits of someone used to living alone. When it ends, they sit in silence for a while. Silvana looks around the room.

"All these boxes. I had no idea . . ."

"That I was a black marketeer? No, I'm not really. I get asked for certain things and I supply them. Once rationing ends, I'll do something else. Lucy's father got me into it. He was offered some cheap rum from the navy stores at the docks. He's a member of a gentlemen's club in Ipswich and the club agreed to buy the rum. He couldn't do the deal himself—he's a magistrate, after all. So I stepped in and we split the cash. That's how it all started. Once you know the right people, it's easy.

"Everybody's doing it. There's a man at the Food Office in Ipswich who forges purchase permits for grocers. So, for instance, Mr. Blake at Lipton's gets tenfold the amount of sugar he should get. The surplus he sells on to me. I sell it off ration. And that's the tip of the iceberg. Like I say, everybody's doing it."

Tony gets up and goes into the kitchen. "All these boxes will be gone in a day or two," he calls out. "Don't you worry about them."

He comes back with two mugs of cocoa.

"This'll make you feel better," he says, handing her a mug. "I've put a dose of whisky in it. It'll help you sleep."

She is aware of his eyes upon her. They have a softness in them that could trip her up.

"I'm usually on my own in the evenings," he says. "In the flat above the shop. I used to think of you and wonder what you were doing. And now here you are. Right here with me."

"I won't be staying long," she says quickly, and sees the sudden alarm in his face, the way the color changes in his cheeks. She straightens her back, drinks her cocoa, and summons all the contrariness she has left in her character.

"It's very kind of you to help us in this way, but we will go home soon."

She gets up, takes his mug from him, and walks into the kitchen. Tony follows her, standing behind her while she washes up in the sink.

"Will you really go back?"

"Janusz will want to see Aurek. He's his father. I'll stay here for a few days or so and then we will have to go."

"Do you think so?" says Tony, and she can hear the sadness in his voice.

"Yes, I do."

Silvana runs the water down the sink and turns to face him.

"Shall we go up?" he says, offering her a towel for her hands.

The staircase is wooden, no carpet runner, just brass stair rods, piles of newspapers, and dust everywhere.

"Beggar's velvet," says Tony when he sees her looking. "That's what Lucy called those dust balls that gather in corners. This place needs a clean."

"I'll clean tomorrow," Silvana says, trying not to jump at the sound of his dead wife's name. This was her house and he is still proud of her. Proud, too, of the way she made poetry from skin flecks and hair and household dirt.

Tony stands with his hand on the door to the bedroom. He looks at her and she wants to say, *Please, don't ask that of me tonight*, even as she knows that she will do what he wants.

"When you kissed me today, Silvana, it was all I could do to stop myself from making love to you there and then."

So *she* kissed him? Is *that* what happened? It's not how she remembers the moment at all. Surely it was Tony who made the first move?

He presses against her, full of wanting, his tongue searching her mouth. His hands hold her hips and she feels his penis through his trousers, its insistent blunt-ended heat pressed against her. Silvana doesn't move. She is cold in his embrace and she knows he feels it.

Memories blaze through her mind. Now her secret is out in the open she is living through the death of her son all over again. She can see the woman she handed him to. Hear her offering to take him, her cheeks pinched by the cold, her eyes watering in the wind. She still can't understand how she could have been so careless. How could she have given her son to someone else?

Tony stops kissing her. He lets his lips linger on her cheek for a moment. Runs a hand through her hair and steps away from her.

"I'm sorry," she whispers.

"You can have the room next to Aurek's," he says. "I hope it's not too cold in there on your own. I can put an extra blanket on the bed."

Silvana is so relieved she even manages a smile.

"It's all right," he says, turning away from her. "You just need some time, that's all."

She sits in her room waiting for Tony to settle in the bedroom next door, listening to the sound of him undressing: the trill of a zip and the pop of buttons being released; the rustle of a shirt being eased off his back; the polite unfolding of pajamas. The creak of mattress springs as he gets into bed, and finally, the click of the lamp.

When Tony's bed springs cease their unsettled squeaking, Silvana tiptoes downstairs, picking up a few of the newspapers piled on the stairs. Tired as she is, sleep is not going to come tonight.

In the sitting room at the front of the house she flicks through old newspapers. Many of them contain photographs of children: groups of them standing in train stations and public halls, carrying boxes and suitcases, all of them labeled like lost luggage. She studies them for hours, the hollow eyes of the children staring back. What if Aurek has a mother somewhere? Did she save the boy or steal him? What if there is a woman somewhere, waiting for her son to come home to her?

She turns off the lamp and sits in the dark, staring out of the window, imagining the sea, listening hard for the sound of the waves, rolling in and out, in and out, like the breath of Tony and Aurek asleep upstairs. When a damp-looking daylight seeps across the sky and the seagulls begin noisily circling the pier, she finds a broom and starts cleaning the house.

IPSWICH

The sun is low in the sky and in the garden everything is disappearing into shadow. All Janusz's roses, his plants, and the neatly mowed lawn are disappearing into the night. Janusz leans his head against the window in Aurek's room and listens to the empty house, the gloomy weight of silence. He lies down on the bed and watches the dark reaching into the room, turning the wardrobe into a huge black cave.

His son. All these years his son has been dead and he has never known. His Aurek. He can't even think of the boy he has been loving in his place. She brought a stranger into his life and told him he was his son. And did the boy know he was an imposter? Was he a liar, too?

He tries to imagine the forest Silvana lived in. Is that where she learned to be so ruthless? He read a newspaper story just the other day about some soldiers who, unable to believe the war was over, were still stumbling around in European forests, their beards full of moss and twigs, their eyes half blind in the murky woodland light, living on rabbits, mice, and squirrels.

He should have let them be. Left Silvana to her wildness. Hélène's family would have welcomed him. He could have gone there after the war, gone to France and found work in Marseilles. Or Canada. There'd been work offers for ex-servicemen in Canada. He could have started a new life there. That's what he should have done.

He'd imagined peacetime would bring him a sense of belonging. During the war it kept him going, that thought of peace. He'd believed in it, like a season he knew would arrive one day. War had been winter all the way, years of Decembers and Januaries. Peacetime was meant to be summer. And he'd thought it had finally arrived when he'd got this house, this life in a small English town, his wife and son.

He gets up, rubbing his aching head, and turns on the light. He opens the window, breathing the night air, sniffing for the scent of woodland, the whiff of pine, the tang of mushrooms and moist earth. A faint smell of bonfires and compost heaps is carried on the breeze. Closing the window, he notices the frame is rotten around the latch.

He'll get on and mend that tomorrow. The house is the only solid thing he knows, and he'll be damned if he'll let that fall apart, too.

He tidies Aurek's bed, plumping the pillow and picking up the striped pajamas he finds underneath it.

And not even a proper burial. He can't stop thinking about that. She left his son's body in a handcart. His son. How can he ever forgive her for that?

In his own bed, he lies awake, unable to sleep. He still has the boy's pajamas in his hands. He wants to believe Silvana has made a mistake. Surely she is lying about Aurek? Janusz drops the pajamas onto the floor. He knows she isn't. He saw the truth in her eyes. His son is dead. He turns the light on and stares at Silvana's empty bed. He feels fear, a tight knot in his guts, a wartime feeling; the unsteady world Silvana inhabited has become his.

He lights a cigarette, burns his fingers watching the flame run down the match. Does it again, black soot on his thumb, the skin reddened, pain mounting inside him and so much grief it could break him open, grief for not one son but two.

FELIXSTOWE

Aurek is listening to the seagulls. It is not yet light and the sky is still laced with stars, but the birds are mewling like forsaken kittens. He opens the sash window, leans out, and copies the birds' cries until a woman a few doors down, ugly, with a stormy face, looks out of her own window and tells him she'll hang, draw, and quarter him if he doesn't shut the bloody hell up. He gets back into the camp bed and tries to sleep, hoping he'll wake again and find himself back in his own bed in Britannia Road.

They have been in Felixstowe for five days. He is still wearing the clothes he arrived in, and his mother doesn't seem to notice if he is there or not. In the evenings she sits looking through the piles of newspapers, showing Aurek pictures of children he doesn't want to see. He doesn't know them. Why should he want to look at them? And she doesn't know them either, so why does she cry over them?

Tony has gone to Ipswich. He said he had to keep the pet shop open, that he had to keep to his usual habits in order to avoid arousing any suspicion. He looks at Aurek as if he is a bad boy.

When Tony left he promised he would come back at the weekend. Aurek didn't understand why, but when he said that, handing his mother money, telling her it had to last for the week, it made her cry.

Men disturbed them last night, Wednesday, knocking on the door, taking cardboard boxes away, and bringing bales of cotton sheets. His mother told them she was Tony's housekeeper. The men lifted their hats and thanked her, and they, too, handed her money. Aurek hid from them. He made a nest in a bale of sheets.

During the day, his mother moves like a sleepwalker. She wanders the beaches and he follows her, trailing along behind, kicking sand and picking up shells and broken glass. When he is hungry she buys him candy floss: pink and green clouds of it, which make his teeth ache and his mouth water. Lovely sweetness dissolves on his tongue and he takes wild bites, the roughness of sugar on his cheek, gobs of it in his hair. If he eats it like that, his mother stops walking and watches him. Sometimes she even smiles for a moment. Then she drops her head, studies her feet, and walks on again.

He doesn't ask her about the enemy, but every time he hears footsteps outside the house or sees a man walking on the beach alone, he wonders if it is him, his father, come to take them home again.

Tony comes back on Friday night, and early on Saturday morning they drive to a forest of pine trees a half hour inland. It's a wide, evenly spaced forest of trees growing in pale soil. Tony drops them off, saying he has business to attend to in Felixstowe.

Aurek gathers the field mushrooms that grow in the grass at the edge of the forest. He can't remember learning how to hunt for mushrooms. It is something he has somehow always known how to do. He spots a cluster of smooth-skinned death caps and squats down beside them, pulling his knife from his pocket. With a steady hand, he cuts them, discarding the round puffy sac at their base that he knows poisonous mushrooms have. These cause death after a day or so. There's no cure. He lays them on the ground and looks at them. If Tony were dead, maybe they could go back home? He is already a bad child. It is his fault they are here.

"What are you doing with those?"

Aurek jumps. He hadn't heard his mother behind him. He avoids her eyes but is sure she can read his mind, and kicks at the mushrooms, stamps on them until they are a mush under his feet.

"Make sure you wipe your knife well. Those are dangerous." Silvana smiles, puts her hand on his cheek. "It's lovely here, isn't it? Just you and me. Like it used to be."

He would prefer it if the enemy were there, too, telling him how telephones work or what makes a motorcar go. The enemy could build them a tree house. He could make them a proper home in the trees. Aurek reaches out and touches his mother's hair, twisting a curl through his fingers.

"Did I do something wrong?" he asks, and she laughs loudly, as if he has told her a very funny joke.

At twilight, when Tony comes back to get them, the biggest bats Aurek has ever seen have begun to swoop through the branches. He finds a dead one and his mother persuades Tony to let him keep it.

Aurek lays it out on the porch where it dries hard like leather, but a few days later the wind snatches it up and steals it away. Aurek spends days searching for it along the seafront, crawling under beach huts and fisherman's huts, in among green nets and wicker lobster pots, his fingers searching through damp newspapers, fish hooks, and pink discarded fish guts.

"Is it good for him to run wild around town?" says Tony to Silvana when he arrives the following Friday evening and Aurek comes home stinking of fish.

"Perhaps Peter could come and play with him?"

"He's with his grandparents."

Aurek sits on the front doorstep, his fingers in his ears, pretending not to hear them talking. He tries to imagine the sound fish make underwater, wonders whether they sing to each other like birds.

"Maybe Aurek should go to school? You've been here a fortnight. We don't want the social services coming, asking questions."

"He isn't ready for school."

"What is that he's got in his hair?"

"Tar. He was down at the boatbuilders again."

"You shouldn't let him wander like he does. I could bring him a rabbit. Or a dog. He could have a pet. It might make him stay home."

"No," says Silvana. "We should wait."

"Wait for what?"

"For the right time," she replies.

Aurek takes his fingers out of his ears. He knows he won't have a pet. His mother is not happy by the sea. The right time is never going to come.

POLAND

Silvana

In the summer heat, Silvana threw off her clothes. She smeared pine sap on their bodies to keep the mosquitoes away and made circles of rowan branches around their camp to keep the soldiers out. The charm worked. There had been fewer of them since she'd been doing this.

Sometimes she lay down in a spot where the sun hit the forest floor and felt it moving across her. Ants crawled around her, big black lines of them, and she heard their legs clicking, jointed bodies rustling as they hurried. She could hear a beetle in leaf mold, its jaws crunching. Wood lice crawling under tree bark sounded like someone grinding their teeth against her cheek. The drone of a fly hurt her ears.

She was turning to wood. Her body hard as oak, skin as thin as the papery strips of silver birch bark she and the boy ate in winter. Sometimes she imagined being an old woman, dying with only a tiny view of the sky through the branches. If someone found her, they'd knock on her arms and realize she was solid.

Maybe they'd make something of her. A coffee table, a blanket box perhaps. She was certain that within her body were the rings of her life like a tree. The lean years, the healing growth circling her broken heart in fat bands.

She let her hand follow the sun's path across her ribs, her sunken stomach, her hollow thighs. She knew herself, understood herself. She had no need for any wider knowledge but the moment. She felt the heartwood of her oaken body like a lump in her throat.

Aurek danced in the sunbeams around her, leaping through dappled light, catching the dust that circled them. His head was getting too big for his body. His belly was a balloon of thin-skinned air. His arms and legs were branches, thin sticks. Her tree man. Forest sprite.

"Come here," she said, sitting up. "Come here."

She settled him on her lap and lifted her breast to his lips. He closed his eyes and she rocked him. For hours she sat, letting him suckle. When her milk stopped flowing, he pulled on her nipple until she cried out with the sharp pain of it, but still she held him, his eyelashes fluttering against her skin. A faint tingling, deep within her, began to burn in her breasts and the milk flowed again. Aurek lay back in her arms and smiled, a slack-jawed, squinting kind of smile, as though the sun dazzled him. Silvana pressed his face to her breast again.

"You and me," she whispered. "We're not dead yet."

Janusz

Janusz sat in a gloomy Nissen hut in North Wales listening to the rain on corrugated iron. Rows of barrel-shaped huts rose like burial mounds out of the earth. He and the other Poles called them *beczki smiechu*, barrels of laughs. The huts had small windows punched into their frames, and the wind blew through the ill-fitting glass. Outside, in the wet mud, glistened the tire patterns of bicycles leading out of the field onto the road beyond. Janusz sat. Waiting for Bruno.

Spring rain had soaked into muddy fields of emerald green and the hedgerows were white with blossom. If the rain didn't stop soon, it was going to flood the camp again. As it was, a thin layer of dirty water lay on the wooden floors. A drip of water splashed on his face and then another. The roof was leaking again. He inhaled deeply on his cigarette and dropped the butt onto the floor, where it sank with a fizzle into an inch of water.

All he was concerned about was the state of his chilblains and what bloody awful food the cook might be serving. He looked at his watch. Bruno would be back from duty that afternoon and Janusz wanted to go to the village pub with him.

"Not a chance," Bruno had said when Janusz asked him if he wanted to stay on in the R.A.F. "Sign on for another five years? Not a chance."

"I don't know what else to do," Janusz said. "We can't go back to Poland. I might try France. Or Canada. Get a job there. I don't know . . ."

"You should think about it. I've already got it sorted out. The war's nearly over. I'm going up to Scotland. I'm marrying Ruby."

Janusz frowned. "But you're already married. What about your family? Your children?"

Bruno sighed. "That's another life now. Another world. Jan, old man, you're so bloody decent. You must know there are plenty of married Poles here who have got themselves English girls. What are they to do? Live here like monks because they're married to women back in Poland that they'll never see again? I've been away from our country too long. Even if I could find my wife, I doubt my kids would even recognize me. They're better off without me. I can't go back. I've got a life here with Ruby now. You've got to take what chances you have." Bruno patted Janusz on the shoulder. "You've had a tough time. Why not find yourself a nice girl here? Ruby's got lots of girlfriends. We'll find you a girl all right."

The sound of other men entering the Nissen hut disturbed Janusz's thinking. They were talking about the weather. The rains had eased off and the men were discussing the fog that was coming in across the fields. Janusz stood up and pulled on his greatcoat. Bruno would be landing soon. He stepped outside and felt his feet sink into a puddle. Heavy mists swirled around him. Hands in his pockets, head down, Janusz trudged toward the airfield and waited in the mess hut for the planes to come in. He watched the fog curl and thicken outside. And what would he do after the war? Go back to Poland? Bruno was right: too much had happened to ever go back.

"A real pea-souper," somebody said.

Janusz got up. Why not live in Scotland? Start his life again? He walked out of the mess hut and nearly knocked into an officer on the steps.

"Sorry, sir," said Janusz. "I didn't see you."

"I'm not surprised. Terrible weather," said the officer as Janusz stepped to one side to let him pass.

"I hope the planes are going to come in safely tonight, sir."

"They're not landing here. Visibility's three hundred yards or less over the airfield. They've been diverted to land further north. I'll let everybody know when our crew is back on terra firma."

Janusz followed him back into the mess hut. He waited. An hour later the news came in.

The squadron had been flying blind in thick cloud base. Only five of thirteen planes had touched down successfully. Bruno's plane had crashed in a cornfield and gone up in flames.

IPSWICH

Janusz clings to his routines. He works as many hours as possible and then goes home and mends things—the kitchen chair with its broken rung, the back door, the dripping tap, next door's guttering—but two weeks and three days after he told Silvana to leave, he still cannot find enough to do to occupy himself.

Heartache burns like a fever in him. He cannot sleep. His muscles twitch, his mind races, and at dawn he throws off his bedcovers, dresses, and hurries out into his garden. So drunk with grief, it is all he can do to stop himself from roaming the streets looking for a fight.

The honeysuckle Janusz trained up the wooden fence has just begun to bud with flowers, and the holly by the shed glows dark green. Janusz grabs the honeysuckle's stem, soft as an exposed throat, and throttles it in his fist, yanking it off the fence. No more flowers. No more suburban garden. No more wife and son. He takes his spade, angrily digging at the holly's woody roots. He rips roses from the soil, slashes flowers with a scythe, kicks over shrubs, and piles their ragged remains in a funeral pyre in the middle of the lawn.

The garden was always a dream. A dream of his son playing on a green lawn and his wife cutting English roses from the flower borders. And now there are no more dreams. A splash of rain falls but he carries on his destruction, finding some kind of pleasure in digging up plants, turning the lawn over to a furrowed plot of soil. He wants black soil. Bare earth. The ground new and flecked with stones.

Perhaps he's lost his mind, but he can't stop digging in any case. His muscles are pumping like pistons. Shouldering his work like a farm horse pulling a plow through deep clay, he kicks the spade, driving it into the soil with a murderous energy.

Hours later, he leans against the fence, wiping sweat from his face.

He doesn't rest for long. Throwing down his spade, he goes inside, finds an old newspaper, soaks it in lawn mower fuel, and pushes it into his bonfire. He lights it and steps back, smoke clouding around him, stinging his eyes, the smell of smoldering plants filling the air.

The rain gets heavier but still he doesn't look up from his work. He carries on, even though the red-flamed heart of the bonfire has died, suffocated by the rain and the thick clods of green turf and plants he is piling uselessly onto it.

"What the hell are you doing?"

Gilbert is looking over the fence.

Janusz steps out of the smoke.

"Clearing up," he says. "Getting rid of it all. Leave me alone, please. This is my business."

And he walks back into the drifting, choking smoke.

FELIXSTOWE

Silvana is unsure but Tony insists. He is smiling, waving his hands as he talks, excited as a child at Christmas.

"It's all right. Come upstairs. I've got a present for you. Something special."

She steps through the open door of his bedroom. She has avoided this room so far. Avoided the memory of his wife which must lurk in the rose-patterned wallpaper and the polished wooden furniture.

"This house," she asks, "does it make you sad? Do you think of your wife when you are here?"

"No," he says as he ushers her inside. "No, we barely spent any time here together. And I've had lodgers since she died. The house has been decorated several times. There is nothing left that belonged to Lucy."

Silvana sits at the dressing table, the chintz fabric pleated around it like a tidy skirt. She presses her knees together and takes in the details of the room: the pink satin bedspread on the double bed; the bed table with a small lamp on it; and above the bed, a print of a mountain landscape, green hills rolling down to a lake where sheep graze.

Tony brandishes a key in his hand and unlocks the big wardrobe.

"Here," he says, swinging the wardrobe door open. "For you."

Colors glint shoulder to shoulder. The wardrobe is packed full of clothes. Brick red, holly green, duck-egg blue, eau de Nil, salmon, pale blue, black, coral pink, crème, gold, and silver. Furs, silks, ribbons, velvet, feathers, pearls, sequins. Evening gowns, tailored jackets, day dresses, trouser suits, silk nightdresses, blouses with tiny pearl buttons.

Silvana runs her hands over them all. Tony laughs and pulls a fur coat out for her to see.

"They're all for you."

Silvana can't believe her eyes.

"Where did they come from? You've the contents of a dress shop in here."

"I admit they're not all new, but you'll agree they're hardly worn. I've been collecting them for you. Some of them belonged to a countess. A very beautiful one."

"How did you know my size?"

He puts the coat on the bed and shrugs. "I guessed. But it was a lucky guess, right? Try something on and we'll see."

Silvana watches him push through the rails, looking for something. Had he always known she would end up in this house with him? Had he planned it all along? She dismisses the thought. There is no point wondering in any case. She is here.

"This one," he says, pulling a silver lamé evening gown from its wooden hanger. "This one is my favorite."

His hand trembles as he passes her the dress, his eyes full of expectation.

"Try it on," he says, and his voice cracks. "I want you to have it."

A thought comes to her. *Lucy.*

"These clothes. They're not . . ." She falls silent. She can't ask him that.

She looks at him steadily. "You bought them all for me?"

"Yes. Of course. Who else would I get them for?"

He turns his back while she undresses and slips the silvery dress over her head.

For one terrible moment she thought he might have been dressing her in his dead wife's clothes. But of course he wouldn't do that. Truly, she is far too morbid these days. The dress slides over her hips. It settles on her body, heavy as silver coins, fish scales rippling over her hips, clinging to her thighs. She doesn't dare look in the wardrobe mirror.

"Ready yet? Can I see?"

"Yes."

Tony smiles, opening his arms wide.

"*Bella!* Look at yourself. You're beautiful."

The woman looking back at her in the mirror wears the dress confidently. She puts a hand on her hip, twists her body so that its curves show, lifts her rib cage, turns to see her back, the round swell of her buttocks. The woman in the mirror is beautiful. Film-star beautiful.

Silvana looks into Tony's eyes. They are glassy with emotion.

"Tony? Are you all right?"

"I'm tired," he says. "My eyes water when I'm tired."

He picks through the clothes, suggests she try on a floral linen day dress.

"All right," she says, though she prefers the look of the pale green silk dress that hangs beside it. He strokes her arm, his fingers tracing her shoulder, running along the dip of her collarbone.

"You know I love you," he whispers.

Silvana nods. She takes the day dress and holds it up to herself.

"Perfect," he says, and kisses her cheek so gently, so lightly, she finds herself closing her eyes and leaning into him, lifting her lips to his.

POLAND

Silvana

Silvana started to understand the way the forest worked. It was like a compass. Spiders' webs faced south. The tops of the pine trees bent to the east. Squirrels nested in tree holes that faced west. Woodpeckers' nests had their openings to the north. The forest was a map if you could learn how to read it. She and the boy were part of it all.

One morning early, when they had put their clothes on and were trekking across the forest looking for a new place to camp, they stumbled out of the woods onto a road. Aurek sniffed the air and backed away. It was a long, straight road, disappearing into the horizon like an upside-down V. In the other direction the road disappeared at a dip where the trees rose up over it.

Silvana felt the hard surface of the road beneath her boots. She buttoned her coat and kicked at stones and Aurek joined her, picking up a handful of gravel and throwing it into the air. She heard a dusty grumble, getting louder. Standing with Aurek in the middle of the road, backs to the sun, they waited for the noise to arrive.

A line of green army trucks and tanks came into view, rising up over the dip in the road. On the first truck a flag was flying. Silvana recognized it. It was British.

"Aurek, look," she said, trying to fix her headscarf and pull the boy up straight beside her. "Look."

Janusz

Janusz took the train to Sterling and met Ruby in a pub in the village. She looked tired and her skin was pale, but she was cheerful.

"Well, it's good to see you."

She squeezed his arm. "How are things in England? Can't be as bloody awful as they are up here."

"I don't know," said Janusz. "It's been raining so long, I think we may need to build an ark. What can I get you to drink?"

"I'll have a shandy, thanks."

Janusz put their drinks down on the table and watched her pick up her glass. He might as well say it now. What point was there in waiting?

Ruby sipped her drink and put it down carefully. "Did you come here to tell me something? Is something wrong? Did Bruno send you?"

Janusz took a deep breath and started to talk. It was easier than he thought it would be. Ruby didn't interrupt. She nodded her head, listening. Tears ran down her face, making two pink streaks of clean skin through her makeup.

"Are you staying around here?"

"No," said Janusz. "I'm going back tonight."

He leaned across the table and kissed her on the cheek.

"Don't," she said, pulling away. "Don't. I'm all right. But what about you, Jan? What are you going to do now?"

He looked at Ruby's tired face and said nothing.

"You were married, weren't you?" she said. "Bruno told me you've got a little lad."

"Did he?"

"He thought the world of you. Why don't you try to find your wife and son? Put your family back together."

"I don't know," he said. "I don't know if I can."

"Listen," she said. "Life's a total mystery and I don't know why things happen like they do. The world's a complete mess, isn't it? But the way I see it, I'm sitting here crying because I've got no one, and you're sitting here with a wife and a son out there somewhere and you look more miserable than me. You're the lucky one. You've got a family. You're bloody lucky."

On the train he thought about what she had said. She was right. He had a family. Of course he had to find them.

A tall RAF officer helped Janusz fill in the missing persons forms.

"We need as much information as you can give us. Last known address, family relationships, maiden name. Work details. Just put it all down. It might take a while, but if we can, we'll help you get in contact with your family."

He handed Janusz a cigarette and lit one himself.

"I wish you luck, Mr. Nowak."

Janusz was pleased to find someone who could pronounce his name. Pleased with the man's clear, well-spoken voice. He prided himself on his own careful accent. A couple of the men on the base liked to joke that he had a better English accent than any of them.

The officer stood up and opened a cupboard, pulling out a bottle and two delicate glasses. "Have a sherry with me. You don't mind it, do you? I know you soldiers prefer beer—or in your case, I imagine, a shot of vodka. Sherry's the only thing I drink. Look, we might find your wife and son at one of our camps. Or an American camp perhaps. That's all we can do. But if she's there, we'll find her. The British will look after her. We'll do our best, I promise you."

The man's kindness was a relief. He called Janusz "old boy," "chum," "my dear man." He told him he'd follow this up personally, speed up the paperwork.

He shook Janusz by the hand, firmly.

"Good luck." He was already pouring himself another glass of sherry. "Let's hope we get you all back together again."

"Thank you," said Janusz. "Thank you very much, sir."

IPSWICH

After work and at weekends, Janusz spends his time digging the garden until he is sure there is nothing left, no fleshy, divided root, no blade of grass. Even as the sun shines down, the garden looks as barren as a field in winter. The oak tree is the only green thing in it. Janusz stands under the rope ladder of the tree house, looking up. It wouldn't take much to dismantle the whole thing.

In the garden shed, he picks up his claw hammer and a saw. He puts them down again. He can't do it. He can't bring himself to touch the tree house.

He feels tired for the first time since Silvana left. Exhausted. Now the garden is cleared, he can rest. His muscles ache, his head buzzes. He has to sleep. He staggers into the house, lies down on the boy's bed, and sleeps solidly through the afternoon and the night, waking early the next morning, sure of what he must do next.

It is a bank holiday Monday and he has a whole day free. He pulls on Wellingtons by the front door, steps outside into a drizzly gray morning, and walks briskly down the quiet streets.

The bus conductor looks at him suspiciously as he climbs aboard.

"You'll have to leave that in the luggage rack, sir," he says, pointing at the garden spade Janusz is carrying.

The bus stops at the paper mill, and he is the only person to get off. He knows the conductor is watching him suspiciously. He hoists his spade over his shoulder, gives a wave to the man, and walks away.

On the edge of woodland, between brambles and fields, Janusz turns muddy earth with the spade, bringing up worms for birds to peck at. Blisters appear on his hands as he digs. His fingernails are black with soil. The sun comes out in a blue sky and warms his back.

That first tree makes him sweat. Its roots are more tenacious than he imagined. He spends the morning digging, but it's hard work when there is so much grass underfoot. The earth is covered with a thick pelt of it. Grass up to his knees forms a matted skin that closes over the soil, refusing to allow the space for a tree to be taken.

When he manages to expose the birch's root system, he finds it is caught up in the roots of nettles, knots like tough yellow rope that he can't unravel. That's how he is, too. Caught up in English soil. He takes his spade, slams it hard into the soil, and kicks down on it, revealing the final tight root of the tree. Carefully, he pulls the sapling free from the ground.

The bus is late. When it arrives, Janusz steps up into it and the conductor shakes his head.

"You can't bring that on with you, sir."

"Oh, but surely, if I put it in the luggage rack . . ." He finds himself struggling over his words, his Polish accent getting in the way. He never has this problem. His English accent is perfect. For some reason his voice is full of Polish vowel sounds. He tries again, hears the same thick accent. "I've *vashed ʒe* roots. It's clean."

"What'll you bring next time, chickens? This isn't the bloody continent. Look at it, it's covered with mud. What would my other passengers think?"

Janusz looks down the aisle of the bus. There is only one other passenger, an old man who appears to be asleep.

"Fine," he says. "If you are going to be *obstreperous*, I will not get on your autobus."

Let him chew on that, thinks Janusz as he watches the bus pull away. He hoists the tree over his shoulder and begins the long walk home.

Later that day, in the garden, slabs of heavy soil lie all around him.

Once the hole is deep, he scatters bonemeal into it. This tree will be nurtured, cared for until its roots are deep enough for it to stand by itself. He will not fail it. This tree is just a beginning. Just a start.

He will be a part of this land, but on his own terms. He's fought for the English, worn their uniform, and learned their songs and jokes. And he's lived here long enough to know this terraced house is his castle, for him to do what he wants with. Who did he think he was anyway, trying to have a perfect English family and an English country garden? To hell with all that. Carefully, carefully, he positions the fragile sapling. Pushes the soil back, pressing down, tamping it with the heel of his boot, covering its roots deep like a secret in the ground.

He waters it every day and counts its leaves, watching over it for any signs of disease or weakness. This first tree is for Aurek. The son who died. The next will be for the son who is living.

FELIXSTOWE

Silvana, Tony, and Aurek walk along the sand listening to the screech of seagulls and the waves rushing back and forth. Tony takes off his boots and socks, rolls up his trouser legs, and stands at the edge of the water with Aurek, dancing backward when a big wave crashes toward them. Aurek shrieks and runs back up the beach.

"Right, I'm going for a swim," Tony shouts over the noise of the wind, pulling his shirt and trousers off and handing them to Silvana. "Sure you don't want to?"

"No," she says, watching him adjust the waistband of his swimming trunks. "We'll be fine here. We'll wait for you."

Silvana and Aurek sit at the bottom of a bank of silvery shingle. Shielded from the wind it is warm and quieter. Tony walks out into the brown sea, his solid, hairy legs pushing against the current as he struggles to keep upright. He drops under the water and reappears, shaking his head like a wet dog. Silvana watches him as he bobs up and down, appearing and disappearing with every wave until he is a small shape far from the beach.

She opens her handbag and takes out a postcard, a color picture of the seafront and the long pier that juts out into the water. It is a pretty card with lots of blue sky, the sandy beach tinted egg-yolk yellow. She writes a quick message to Janusz, the same message she has sent on every card. A card a week, marked with the address of Tony's house. Janusz hasn't replied. It's been two months since they left Britannia Road. This will be the last card she sends. After that, she will try to forget him. She managed it once before in Poland. She can do it again.

She pulls her coat collar tighter around her chin and her fingers sink into soft blue wool. The coat is satin-lined and feels wonderful to wear. It has decorative stitching in a creamy brown silk thread and big buttons that Aurek likes to play with. She has a pair of pearl earrings that Tony says go perfectly with it. Under her coat she wears a crepe de Chine blouse with tiny pleats and a row of buttons to the neck. Her skirt is high-waisted tweed, a little old-fashioned but good-quality cloth. The boots she wears shine like conkers. Italian leather, Tony told her when he pulled them from the wardrobe in his bedroom and suggested she try them on. She asked him about Lucy then. She couldn't help herself.

"Tony, I have to know. You can tell me. Were these Lucy's?"

He'd been matter-of-fact in his response. "No," he said, taking her hands in his. "Of course not. I gave away Lucy's clothes years ago. They are yours. Only yours."

She turns her ankle to see the leather shine in the sun. She's never had such good boots.

Tony comes back from his swim, hungry. He takes them to a restaurant and a girl serves them boiled potatoes and fish in parsley sauce, dripping the sauce over the tablecloth as she puts their plates down.

"Aurek, you're as brown as a berry, old chum," says Tony. "You could pass as a little Italian lad," he continues. "Don't you think, Silvana?"

No, she thinks. *He looks Polish*.

"Absolutely," she says, wiping the sauce off the edge of her plate with her napkin.

Tony finishes his glass of wine and orders another. Silvana sips her own wine and smiles at Tony and Aurek.

"Good health. *Na zdrowie!*" she says, raising her glass to them both.

Here we all are, she thinks. She feels such tenderness for Tony, she is carried along by it, by the feel of pearls against her neck, the silk stockings he gives her, the food he offers them. Maybe it is the effect of the wine she is not used to drinking, but she looks at Tony and her brown-faced son and believes they can be a family.

After a long and late lunch, they walk through the Massey Gardens. Tony teaches Aurek crazy golf and Silvana sits watching them. At 6 p.m., when the deck chairs on the beach are being packed away and people start drifting toward home, Tony goes to a bar and Aurek and Silvana stroll along the promenade. The two glasses of wine she drank earlier are still making her feel pleasantly numb. Necklaces of colored lightbulbs swing brightly over kiosks selling seafood and sweets and postcards. The air smells vinegary and sharp. Silvana buys Aurek a toy that whirs in the wind and some chocolate. He gives her a lump of it, popping it into her mouth. She closes her teeth on it and feels the sweet, milky texture. She laughs and throws her head back. As she does, she sees a woman looking at her from across the street. The sight of her sobers Silvana up.

"Look at you," Doris says, walking over to her. "Your bread obviously landed butter side up."

Silvana will not be intimidated. She could walk away. She'd like to, in fact. She'd like to turn on her heels and maybe even swish her elegant blue coat as she does so. A toss of the head would be satisfying. But Doris can tell her how Janusz is.

"So you're living the high life here by the sea while your poor husband goes barmy, digging up his roses?"

Silvana pushes her hair away from her face. "Have you seen him?"

Doris takes her time. She leans in close, like an actress about to speak her most important lines, making her audience wait. And Silvana is a good audience. She hangs on the woman's silence, waiting for news of Janusz. A smell of cooking fat rises off Doris's clothes.

"Your husband destroyed his beloved garden before he left," says Doris finally.

"Left?"

"Didn't you know? Your husband has left Britannia Road. He's moved away." She steps back, as if ready to take a bow now she has delivered her line. "You're on your own now, young lady. You made your bed, you can blooming well lie in it."

And she stalks away, head held high and triumphant.

Aurek pulls on Silvana's sleeve. He has eaten all the chocolate.

"I'll buy you some more," Silvana says, watching Doris disappear into the crowds. "We can stay out a bit longer."

They sit in front of a blue beach hut and watch dark clouds enveloping the sky as the sun drapes its red light into the sea. The sky turns turquoise, and Aurek says it is the color of a blackbird's egg.

When the stars come out, Silvana and Aurek curl up together on the beach. Janusz has left them. She has failed both him and the boy and her poor dead baby. She sees Tony on the pier looking for them. She can't pretend everything is all right tonight. He stands under the streetlight, looking at his watch, and then walks back toward the house. She watches him go.

Silvana pulls the boy onto her lap and they stay there until a salty dampness has soaked their clothes and Aurek asks for his bed.

The front door is open, the light in the hall left on. Silvana and Aurek tiptoe upstairs. While Aurek climbs into his camp bed, she opens the door to the main bedroom. Tony is snoring lightly. She goes downstairs, gathers up some of the old newspapers the house is filled with and hunts through the kitchen drawers. She finds a pair of scissors and carries them to the living room where she spreads the newspapers in front of her and begins cutting out pictures of children. She is businesslike about it, scanning page after page. When she finds a child's image, she stops and studies the article that accompanies it. She still doesn't read English very well, but she is quick to spot certain words and phrases. *Orphans . . . missing . . . lost . . . last seen . . . A tragic story . . . A mother's sorrow*. Sometimes the children are smiling in their photographs, as if they can see the ghosts of their families around them. Each face makes her cry for her own dead son.

She works quietly through until she has a stack of cuttings in front of her. Looking up to rest her eyes, she watches the lights on the seafront. Even in the forest, she never felt as lost as this.

POLAND

Silvana

A soldier climbed down from the first truck, hands out as if he were approaching a pair of cornered animals.

"All right now," the soldier's voice rang out. "Do you know? Do you know yet?"

Silvana backed away, pulling Aurek into her embrace.

"The war. It's over. You speak English? *Polsku?*"

"*Polsku? Tak.*"

He beckoned to a couple more men, who got down from their vehicles and walked over. One of them handed Silvana a metal flask in a harness, and she took it cautiously.

"Go ahead, it's water," he said. "Drink. Here. Like this." He held his hand to his lips and mimed drinking.

Silvana took it and tipped it back like he had. The water ran down her chin. She lifted the bottle and let the cold water run over her face.

"You go right ahead. But you can drink it, too, if you like." He put his thumb to his mouth and made a glugging noise.

Aurek snickered and snorted. He ran in circles, his thumb pressed to his lips. Silvana looked back at the forest. All along the line of trucks, men stood watching them. Aurek kept on laughing and Silvana began to laugh, too. When she stopped and looked at all those faces surrounding her, she was surprised. They looked unhappy. Like they'd seen too many sad films. Or maybe they thought she had.

One of the soldiers came toward her speaking in Polish.

"What's your name?"

She thought for a moment. Who should she say she was? *Marysia?*
Hanka?

She coughed, felt her throat dry with the effort of speaking.

She decided to be herself.

"Silvana Nowak."

"Do you have any identification papers?"

She looked at Aurek playing in the dirt beside her, pulled him to his
feet and held him close.

"My son."

"Okay," said the soldier. "Can I see your papers?"

"My son," Silvana repeated.

The soldier folded his arms, looked at her quizzically.

"Where do you live?"

"What year is this?"

"Nineteen forty-five. Where'd you come from?"

Silvana looked back at the forest and the trees. She didn't need to
hide anymore.

"Warsaw," she said, wondering if it still existed. "We come from
Warsaw."

IPSWICH

Janusz fits ten trees into the car. It seems a shame to get mud on the upholstery, but these are the last trees he will be taking. The garden is deeply planted now and although he knows birch trees are not bothered by overcrowding, he still wants to give them the best chance he can. He wishes there was some other way to get the trees than filling up his car with mud, but Gilbert says he will help him clean the car out when they get back home.

He digs up a birch from the hedgerow while Gilbert waits with an old curtain to wrap its roots in.

"I still think you should give him a thumping."

"So did I. To begin with. Now I just don't want to see him. Fighting is not my way of doing things."

"I've known Tony for years. I never thought he'd play such a mean trick."

"Can you pass me that spade, please?"

"She and the boy are in Felixstowe you know. Doris saw them."

Janusz feels the blood rush to his face. He stops what he is doing.

"She saw them?"

"Apparently."

"And?"

"She said they looked all right." Gilbert pats Janusz on the shoulder. "I don't know what went on, but Doris seemed pretty fired up. You know how she is when she gets the bit between her teeth. She told me they're moving away."

"Moving?" Janusz can't hide the panic in his voice.

Gilbert sounds unsure. "Well, I know Doris can be prone to exaggerate."

"Where are they moving to?"

"Well, that's just it. Doris won't say. Stubborn as an ox, you know. She took it all very badly. Says Sylvia betrayed her trust. But look, why don't you go and see the boy while you can? I could get you the address."

Janusz thinks of the postcards he has. He's driven past the house but never dared stop. The thought of seeing Silvana with Tony haunts him. He's not sure he would be able to cope with it.

"I already have it," he says firmly. "And I don't want to see them. Not if Silvana is happy with Tony. Let her have what she wants. Why do we even need to talk about this?"

Gilbert sighs. "All right, I hear you. I won't go on. Listen, is it legal, taking trees like this? They must belong to someone."

"They're only saplings. They're wild. No one wants them. Shine that flashlight over this way."

"Tell me again, then," asks Gilbert. "Why do we have to do this in the dark if it's legal to take them anyway?"

Back home in Britannia Road, Janusz unloads the trees, heels them into the earth in the garden, cleans the car, and then finally goes into his house and locks the door.

In the bathroom he takes off his clothes and washes himself, slowly, head down like a man caught in the rain, staring at his feet. When he closes his eyes, he swears he hears Silvana coming up the stairs, Aurek playing in the hallway. The house is haunted by the sounds of his wife and the child. And if what Doris says is true, that they're moving away, then there's no hope. He grabs a towel and rubs himself dry.

Let them go, he thinks as he dresses. He's not the one to blame. He may have sent them away, but she is the one who did the damage. He has nothing to reproach himself for. Nothing at all. If she chooses to go, then he can do nothing to stop her.

He walks into the boy's room, tidies the books on the shelf. He smoothes the bedcovers and straightens the picture on the wall. Then he sits on the bed, puts his head in his hands, and weeps.

Silvana

The ship put into port in England on an early tide, pushing through darkness and fog. Silvana had arrived in a land of clouds. Everywhere was covered in a smoky fog that banded across the landscape and blurred the shapes of buildings. She concentrated on watching her feet and the backs of the crowds in front of her as she moved slowly down the gangplank in the thick shuffle of bodies.

Land was a shock after so long at sea. As the crowds disembarked and their feet hit solid ground, Silvana and Aurek staggered and rolled like people stepping off a fairground ride, unable to walk in a straight line. They were moved along in winding queues and handed identity cards. Aurek was given a pair of red leather roller skates tied together with their own laces. A man laid them over his shoulder and Aurek sagged under their weight.

Silvana looked at the boxes of skates and toys in front of her.

The man smiled. "Does he like them?" He pointed at the skates.

Aurek was struggling, trying to take them off his shoulders.

He tipped up a box toward them. "Why don't you have a look?"

The box of toys had teddy bears and jigsaw puzzles, tin cars and dolls. A small wooden rattle sat on top of them. Plain and polished. Silvana grabbed it. The man laughed.

"Is that what you want? He's a bit old for baby stuff, isn't he?"

Silvana shook her head. She took the roller skates off Aurek's shoulders and gave the boy the rattle. She thought of her father, of the carved rattle he had made for her and how she had kept it. What had happened to it? Had she left it behind in Warsaw? She couldn't remember and didn't want to. She looked at Aurek and smiled.

"This is yours. Do you understand? It's a magic rattle. You keep it very safe now and it will bring you good luck."

She closed his fingers over the handle and held them tight for a moment. When she let go, she saw the white imprint of her own fingers on the boy's hand. He held the rattle to his chest and nodded at her, his eyes big and dark with belief.

And still the journey wasn't over. They were herded toward a waiting train crowded with people from the boat. As they pulled into London, Silvana hoisted Aurek onto her hip, holding him tightly. The train rumbled and clanked and came to a stop with a hissing of brakes. Doors began to bang open and the sound of shouting, of people calling each other and children crying, filled the air. She joined the queues to leave the train and finally got to an open door. She hesitated. The station looked huge. A guard on the platform held out his hand.

"Come on then, Miss. Down you get."

Silvana stepped down from the train. She straightened her headscarf and looked around at the crowds, trying to see Janusz among them.

"We're here," she whispered, as much to herself as to the boy. "We're here."

FELIXSTOWE

Silvana is lying awake in her bed, listening to a summer storm. There are loud rolls of thunder and the rain pelts the streets outside her window. She can hear Tony shifting in his bed, the bed springs complaining. He is a terrible sleeper, she concludes. For so many nights now she has listened to the sound of him, the slam of his body turning over on the mattress, an arm flung across the sheets, the feathery punching of his pillows, the frequent sighs.

She gets out of her bed and pulls on a dressing gown. She is well aware that he wants her. And now Janusz has gone, and she has given up hope, there is little reason for them both to lie awake trying, as Tony says, to be decent human beings.

She forces her feet into a pair of slippers that are too tight. Tony produced them out of a box for her a few days ago: black Chinese silk embroidered with red, pink, and peach roses threaded through with a leafy green stitch that might be ivy.

Padding quietly across her room, she opens the door, crosses the small landing, and goes into Tony's room. There is total silence apart from the rain outside. Is he holding his breath? She can hear nothing. Thunder grumbles and a flash of lightning lights the room for a moment. She steps toward the bed. Tony is visible briefly in the flash of lightning, his head on the pillow, lying on his back, hands folded across his chest. She stands over him and breathes in the warm smell of him.

"Are you awake?"

"At last," he says.

"Tony?"

"At last."

He seems to grow larger, rising out of the bed so that she thinks of him as a bear, his huge shadow covering her in darkness. She takes a sharp intake of breath and then he has his arms around her, his lips on her neck, damp kisses while he pulls her nightclothes off her. He picks her up and lays her down on the bed, naked except for her slippers, which, try as she might, she cannot take off.

It is over quickly, but while Tony's heavy frame presses down on her, so that she feels that he is indeed a bear of a man and she a long-awaited meal, she worries about the slippers. When the moment arises, when her feet come together briefly, she pushes one against the other, trying to free her crushed toes. She scrapes her heels along his calf muscles and at one opportune moment grabs her foot in her hand and tries to prize the slipper off. It comes away in her hand, freeing her toes, just as he groans and stalls above her.

He drops onto the mattress beside her, breathing heavily. Quickly, she pulls the other stubborn slipper off and throws it across the room, her own breath coming in short gasps.

"Are you all right?" he asks, his hand searching for hers. He grips it tightly. She has the sensation of having lived through a small earthquake. Outside the rain quickens and lightning flashes again.

"I'm fine, yes."

They lie listening to the rain and the wind and he asks her about Poland. About what she left behind.

"Tell me about your family. Your parents?"

"I can't remember," she says firmly. "I can't remember a single thing."

He turns and twists onto his side, facing her.

"I don't need to know. I think I like you being a mystery. I have something important to tell you in any case."

Janusz? she thinks. *Some news of him?*

"Somebody has offered to buy the pet shop."

"The pet shop?"

"They're willing to pay good money. House prices are rising around here. You've got to do what you can to turn a profit these days. My father-in-law thinks it's time Peter went away to board. He wants him to go to his old school. It's miles away in Wiltshire. My father-in-law will pay for it. But it's not just the fees, is it? You've got to have the whole lot, the right car, the right clothes. The accent. That's what it's all about. That's what they're giving him. Peter doesn't need me at all."

He talks about class and money and what people expect in Britain, shifting his weight in the bed, his hand occasionally brushing against her breasts or her hip.

"It won't be forever, this situation here. I don't like to leave you all week while I run the shop in Ipswich, and I've had enough of the black market stuff. It's time to get out." He caresses her hand. "I'm thinking of buying a place in London. In September, when Peter has gone to boarding school. Nobody would know us there. We could say we were married."

"What about Aurek?"

Tony is silent for a moment. He has obviously not considered Aurek. "He'll be with us."

Silvana shivers. She slips out of bed and searches for her discarded nightdress. Tony switches the bedside lamp on. He watches her.

"Come and get back under the covers."

"No. I should go back to my own bed. I don't want Aurek to wake and find me here."

Tony throws the covers back, pulls her toward him and she gives in, climbing back between the sheets. She doesn't want to go back to her cold bed all alone. The gutters gurgle and the sound of rain washing through the downpipes into the storm drains outside makes her feel as though the sea might be pulling the house into its depths.

"So what do you think?" Tony asks. "Shall we give London a go? I'll look after you like a princess. You'll have everything you want, I promise."

Silvana rests her head on his shoulder. Tony is full of these ideas.

She has learned that each week brings a new scheme, and it always involves promises.

"Aurek and I will be——" She stops herself. She almost told him she would be going home soon. She should really give up on all that. Especially now that Janusz has gone.

He strokes her hair gently.

"And if you say yes now, I promise I will get you a pair of slippers in a bigger size tomorrow."

She closes her eyes.

"Yes," she says. "Yes."

Aurek has his flashlight on under his covers. He is writing. It takes him a long time, printing each letter, trying to control the pen. He struggles but it is important and he will not give up. He has ink on his face and blue-stained teeth and lips. He is so tired by his efforts that when he falls exhausted into his dreams, his pen dribbling onto his pajamas, he sleeps soundly, curled up, knees to his chin all night, a peaceful whorl of a child.

In the morning, his mother talks to him of the storm the night before. She asks him if he heard it. He tells her he heard nothing.

"Not even the wind rattling the windows?"

He shakes his head. "Nothing."

"Good," she says. "That's very good. Why have you got ink on your face?"

Aurek shrugs.

"And you slept soundly all night?"

"All night," he promises.

He's careful not to let her see him take the stamps from Tony's writing desk. Careful to slip out of the house unnoticed.

IPSWICH

It is midsummer and Janusz has seventy silver birch trees planted in the back garden. Seventy trees in brown soil when everyone else has holly bushes, roses, pyracantha, and garden gnomes. The trees are spindly but robust and already reaching for the skies like colt-limbed young men full of the promise of the future. Every one of his saplings has taken root and grown delicate summer foliage. Janusz is going to make sure time allows these trees to become thick trunked and strong.

He waters them. Feeds them with bone, dried blood, and fishmeal fertilizer every week. Like a mother picking nits from a child's hair, he forages in the leaves and branches, picking insects off them. At their roots he clears the soil of other plants. He talks to them in the evenings and takes his coffee with them in the mornings. He is not sure why he planted them anymore. He is only aware of the fact that to survive, they need him. For now, that's enough of a reason.

He sits down under his trees and thinks of Hélène, realizing it is hard to remember her face anymore. Without the letters she is fading from his mind. Her voice has gone from him. The flutter in his heart that used to come when he thought of her is still there, but it's kinder to him now. It hurts him less. *This is how it happens*, he thinks. Memories shrink. Like a soap bar used over and over, they become deformed, weaker scented, too slight and slippery to hold.

Janusz goes into the front parlor and looks at the framed picture on the mantelpiece. He and Silvana and the boy.

He has to admire the way she went about things. Bringing up the boy the way she did. Coming to England with him in order to give him a family. She is a single-minded woman. Or she was, until she fell for Tony Benetoni. He studies Silvana's face in the photograph. Her expression is blank. Or is it? Is that her stubbornness showing in the way the corners of her mouth lift? And her eyes, so big and dark. What do they reveal, her pupils widening like a camera lens, taking in her new home, the stranger who was her husband and a life she could only guess at?

And if one day his family in Poland get in touch with him? What will he tell them? They don't know his son is dead. He has to tell his parents. They have a right to know. By the time he has found paper and a pen, he is not so sure. He starts writing, his address at the top corner, the date.

> *Dear mother and father,*
>   *I hope this finds you in good health. I have some*
> *news . . .*

He folds the paper in three and slips it into his shirt pocket, sliding the pen in beside it. Picking up his cigarettes, he lights one and wanders back out into the garden. How can he tell them their grandson is dead? If they ever got the letter, it would break their hearts. He looks at his trees and the blue sky above them and remembers the day he first held his son in his arms. The love he had felt that day.

Standing under the oak tree at the bottom of the garden, he swings the rope ladder dangling from the tree house back and forth. He takes a last deep drag on his cigarette, throws the stub to the ground, steadies the ladder, and puts a foot on its lowest rung, hoisting himself up. He's clumsy, but he manages to clamber onto the platform. He crawls into Aurek's den and lets his eyes adjust to the light. That's when he sees the wooden rattle. It's lodged against a branch inside the tree house. Is it really the one Silvana's father made? And does it matter? Now he remembers that she never answered him when he asked her. It was he who believed it to be a family heirloom.

He picks it up. A small line of writing is etched on one side of it. *Made in England*. Janusz gives the rattle a shake. The tree creaks in the wind, an answering voice.

Sitting in the tree house, knees bent, his back against the rough bark of the tree trunk, he pulls out the letter and his pen and starts writing again.

> *I have built a tree house for Aurek and he enjoys it just as I did when I had one as a child. In fact, your grandson is more agile than I remember I ever was. I would like you to be able to see how fast he can climb the rope ladder into it. You would be proud of him.*

FELIXSTOWE

The boxes have mostly gone. The only room in the house Tony stores things in now is the kitchen, and soon everything will be gone from there, too. They will be moving to London, and Tony is winding the business down as fast as he can. Silvana likes the cluttered feel of the kitchen. The rest of the house is spick-and-span, but the kitchen is filled with boxes of soap powder and Bird's Custard packets. She has moved the piles of newspapers from the stairs into it. She has to squeeze past them to get to the back door.

During the week, when Tony is in Ipswich working in the pet shop, organizing the move, she spends hours sorting through the newspapers, scissors in one hand, the other turning the pages. She goes to bed late and thinks about Janusz, trying to imagine his grief, but she has too much of her own to put herself in his place.

She takes her folder of newspaper clippings up to bed with her and sleeps with it under her pillow every night. She feels like a mother hen with all those little faces under her head. The print from the pictures smudges on the pillowcase, and the children leave their features on cotton. She never washes her pillowcase because of them. So many children, but she will gather them in.

At night her hands touch the newspaper cuttings while the faint, graveled sound of the sea and the wind outside lull her to uneasy sleep. In her dreams, the children climb out from under her hair and dance on her bed, linking hands and singing, and her own dead son rises up from his handcart grave, his blankets tumbling around him.

The bedcovers are heavy with the weight of the children. All the babies, the boys, and the girls, the innocent, come to Silvana, and she says sorry to each one of them. They rise up out of shallow graves, bombed houses, prison cells, and eyeless forests, forgetting their pasts, free and beyond harm.

In the morning they are gone, under the pillow once more, and Silvana gets up, washes in cold water, and turns her scrubbed face to the new day.

IPSWICH

The windows are boarded over and a sign pasted onto the door details planning permission for a change of use. The pet shop is going to become a hairdresser's. Janusz turns on his heels and walks briskly away. He walks on up the cobbled road and into the market square, crossing it in long, loping strides, disturbing the pigeons that settle there. He buys himself a cup of tea and a scone in Debenhams.

And if he went to Felixstowe and asked her to come back to him, what would he do if she refused? He slams his coffee cup onto the table and spills most of it. Of course he can't go. Doris said she looked well. What did that mean? Did it mean she was in love with Tony?

In his mind, he sees Silvana with Tony and Aurek, all of them smiling at him. He grunts audibly, like he's been punched in the head. Oh Christ. Why is he doing this to himself? And what else? If he's going to beat himself up, he may as well do it right.

How about Aurek sitting on Tony's knee? That image hurts. And Aurek making a tree house with Tony, all three of them laughing at him as he asks Silvana to come home. No. He can't go and ask Silvana to come back. She's where she wants to be. He gets up and walks out.

He's halfway up Britannia Road before he realizes he didn't pay for his coffee in the café and has to walk all the way back into town to put things right.

FELIXSTOWE

Silvana is cleaning the stove when the doorbell goes. She listens for a moment and the bell sounds again. Should she leave it? Nobody calls at this time of day. She hears the sound of knuckles rapping on the door and pulls off her apron, tidies her hair, and walks into the hallway. Whoever it is will not go away, it seems. She opens the door a fraction.

"Oh," she says, pulling the door wider.

Peter's grandmother steps inside without being asked. She takes off her gloves and looks around at the hallway, its polished floors, and vase of flowers on the table.

"So Tony has finally got this place cleaned up," she says.

Silvana notices Aurek standing at the end of the hall watching, and motions to him to come and stand beside her. She blushes and holds her hand out.

"I am Mrs. Nowak," she says. "I'm the housekeeper. And here . . . here is my son, Aurek."

"I know who you are," says Peter's grandmother, ignoring Silvana's outstretched hand. "I think you know who I am, too. I used to see you walking your son to school. You can call me Moira. I'm Tony's mother-in-law. And this is Peter's friend? Hello there."

She fishes in her handbag and brings out a small paper bag.

"Peter tells me you like sweets. Come along, young man. I've brought you a bag of sherbets."

When Aurek refuses to come forward, Moira simply holds the bag out. Silvana is sure she is going to drop it and so she reaches out for it, grabs it like a ball suddenly thrown in her direction. She puts the paper bag on the hall table and in the moment it takes her to do it, she sees the old woman seize the chance to look at her. There is a strong sense of curiosity in her eyes, and surprisingly a look of nervousness, too. Silvana has no idea why this woman is here. Should she tell her Tony is in Ipswich?

"Peter says they are friends, the two of them?"

"That's right."

Moira puts her gloves in her handbag. "He's shy, isn't he? My Peter is a very sensitive child, too. Goodness, it's a frightful day. Far too hot. Could you make me a cup of tea? I'm absolutely parched."

Silvana serves the tea in the front room. Moira has half closed the curtains so that the sun drives only a blade of light across the room.

She stands in the shadows, sharp and immobile as a piece of polished furniture, and her voice rises out of the folds of the curtains.

"Tell me, can you play cards?"

"I haven't for a long time."

"You never forget. Pour the tea and then sit down and have a game with me."

Moira is a canny player. They have a hand of rummy and then whist (she teaches Silvana the Portland Club rules), and Silvana teaches her how to play mizerka and tysiac, both card games she used to play in Poland.

Several hours pass and the sun tracks around so that Silvana is obliged to open the curtains to let the afternoon light bathe the room. Moira has just won another round and looks flushed with her success.

"Tony is like a son to me," she says, apropos of nothing. "I'm not used to him being so busy with his life. He usually spends more time with us. You know we brought his son up? Peter is our only grandson. My daughter died when he was just a baby."

So this is what the old lady has come to talk about. Her family.

"Tony has told me how much you care for Peter," says Silvana carefully.

"Has he? Did he tell you we bought my daughter this house as a wedding present? It's in Peter's name now, did you know that? Tony doesn't have a penny in it."

Silvana turns over her cards. She has lost again.

"Yes, I know that," she lies. She is not going to let the old lady think she is a fool. She wonders if Moira knows about London, that Tony has already put money down on a flat. Does he talk to her about these things?

"The thing about Tony," says Moira, flicking her cards faceup, "is that he is too kind. People take advantage of him."

Silvana takes the pack, reshuffles, and deals herself another dreadful hand. She stares in dismay at it.

"So tell me about yourself," the old lady says, laying a pair of queens down. She smiles pleasantly. "I gather you are married?"

Silvana blushes. "That's right."

"Are you going to be staying here long? Has Tony discussed properly your terms of engagement with you?"

"My terms of *engagement*?"

"Yes. You are the housekeeper, aren't you?"

"Well yes, but I . . ." Silvana casts around for something to say. Something to stop this conversation. She will not let this woman get the last word.

"Tony has asked me to stay indefinitely," she says. "Those were his terms of engagement." She'd like to add that he wants to pretend they are married, too, but she stops herself.

The old lady lays her cards on the table. Silvana picks up another card. For once luck is on her side. She almost laughs out loud. She can't lose this time. Not with a hand like this. She lays her cards in front of her and looks at Moira.

"I've won."

Moira clears her throat, gathers up the cards, sits back in her chair, and begins to shuffle them. "We'll play another, shall we?"

She deals the cards, picks up her own, and studies them.

"Marriages are awkward things, my dear, but one must stick at them. Has Tony talked to you about the summer holiday?"

Silvana hesitates. She says nothing and Moira doesn't seem to notice. The old lady carries on talking.

"We have relatives in Sidmouth. Normally Tony drives us down there for a fortnight. Peter adores the West Country."

Silvana tries to remember if Tony has mentioned this before. If he did, she can't remember it.

"I know all about the summer holiday," she says.

Moira puts her cards down and smiles at Silvana.

"Do you? Then you'll know that Tony says he can't come with us this year. Apparently he is too *busy*."

Silvana picks up a card. A queen. She studies Moira's face, the sharp gray eyes, the neat mouth. If only she hadn't answered the door. If only she had hidden and waited for the woman to leave.

Moira continues. "Of course, I would have thought that selling his pet shop would mean Tony has more time on his hands, not less. Wouldn't you agree?"

Silvana says nothing. She waits for the old woman to make her move, but Moira folds her cards into the pack and reaches across the table for her hat.

"I think I'm a little tired now. I have to get the train back to Ipswich and I can't stand catching the six o'clock. There are always far too many people."

In the hallway, Silvana sees the bag of sweets is still there. She hopes Aurek is not making nests in the last bales of cotton sheets Tony has stored in the kitchen. When Tony gets back, she will tell him the sooner they move to London the better. She opens the front door and steps outside, letting Moira walk past her.

The afternoon light is golden and the heated air carries the drifting scent of drying seaweed. Bareheaded girls and freckled boys run across the sands, turning cartwheels, tightrope-walking along the narrow wooden groynes of the beach, avoiding the war defenses that are still on the beach, the jumbled rolls of barbed wire heaped in rusting mounds. Silvana watches the scene for a few moments.

"Lucy always loved the sea," Moira says, as if remembering some specific day.

She turns to face Silvana. "I hope Tony manages to come to Devon with us. It would be such a shame if he didn't get to spend some time with his son this summer. Quite unforgivable."

"I don't know," says Silvana. She will not be bullied by Moira, and she is tired of these conversations. "Perhaps you need to speak to him yourself. I'm only the housekeeper here, after all."

"Yes. That's true. You are just a housekeeper. Perhaps I was mistaken."

Moira steps onto the pavement and looks up and down the road.

"By the way," she says. "The way you wear that blouse with the silk skirt? It's not very pleasant to see another woman in Lucy's clothes, but I have to concede that they suit you. You're about the same size as she was."

She gives the road another sweeping glance and steps off the pavement.

"I can see why Tony likes you. You do resemble her in a way."

Silvana feels a chill run through her. Even with the sun beating down on her, she shivers. She follows the old woman.

"What did you say?"

"The blouse with the skirt. Lucy never wore them together."

"I think you've made a mistake," Silvana says coldly. She has had enough of Moira and her haughty ways. "These are my clothes. Tony bought them for me."

"Really, I knew I had to come. This has gone far enough. You are wearing my daughter's clothes. But you know very well. Must you act so stupid? Has he given you the mink? I do hope not. It was a present from us."

"The mink? With the brown silk lining?"

Silvana can feel her legs giving way under her.

Moira is halfway across the road. A car moves slowly between them both, and her black hat with its single pheasant feather is all Silvana can see of her.

Silvana steps back onto the pavement. She steadies herself. Touches her throat, feels the tiny pearl buttons of her blouse, moves her hand away quickly, as though she has been burned.

In the kitchen she washes the teacups, swirling her hands in soapy water. Aurek comes in carrying a handful of large white feathers.

"Where have you been?"

"On the beach."

"Well, don't go off on your own like that. I was worried about you."

He pulls on her skirts until she stops what she is doing, wipes her hands on her apron, and turns around.

"What is it you want? Something to eat?"

"Home," he says, handing her the feathers.

"What about home?"

Aurek looks up at her, his face dark with freckles.

"When can *we* go home?"

"You and me. We're a home. We're survivors, remember?"

Silvana puts the feathers in her apron pocket.

"Thank you for these. You used to bring me feathers. When we lived in the trees. Do you remember?"

Aurek shrugs his small shoulders and she wonders if he doubts her. Is it possible he knows she is not his mother?

"I love you," she says, and feels, at least in that, she is honest.

There are no lies in her heart. And what is she thinking? Of course she is his mother.

That night, Silvana sits with him in the front room, watching the sea, glad of the peace in the house. When he falls asleep on her lap, she carries him upstairs and tucks him into bed. She goes into her bedroom and reaches for the newspaper cuttings under the pillow. It is time to let the children go.

She opens the window, and the sea wind that always blows catches them. Each slip of paper flies away, the wind snatching them from her fingers. She doesn't know what she and Aurek will do, but they cannot stay in Felixstowe anymore.

She changes into the dress she arrived in, the dress Janusz bought her. The one thing she owns that did not once belong to somebody else. Sitting on the bed, she goes over everything. It is clear to her now.

She will make a life on her own with her son.

IPSWICH

It is Janusz's duty as foreman to see the aisles empty of men leaving their night shifts before he is free to go. Often he stays far longer than he needs to, enjoying the few moments before the next shift clocks on and the factory starts up its work. He likes to see the machines quiet and the air clear. Despite the brief lack of workers, a muggy feeling persists in the bays like the breath of a sleeper against his collar and it makes him feel part of something. It's a great thing for him, this sense of belonging to a workforce.

He talks to the nightwatchman before he leaves, a polite discussion on the weather and football before he reluctantly walks out into the cold morning air, the dawn sun streaking the sky with red light.

He tells himself he walks home rather than taking his car because these summer mornings are too beautiful to miss. The truth is, it takes a good forty minutes to walk home. Forty minutes before he has to confront his empty house once again.

Opening his front door, Janusz sees the postman has already been. A letter and a postcard lie on the red-tiled hallway floor. He stoops and picks them up. The letter is an electricity bill. Nothing interesting there. He looks at the card. A black-and-white picture entitled "View from Wolsey Gardens."

He turns the postcard over in his hand and almost drops it in surprise. The handwriting is terrible. It's a small wonder it arrived at all. The address is barely legible. The *22* looks more like squiggles than numbers. The *B* of Britannia balloons over the rest of the letters, obscuring half of them.

There is no message, just a spidery signature. *Aurek Nowak*. The boy's name. He feels light-headed seeing it there in print. His child's name. The postmark is Felixstowe. Posted three days earlier. Janusz holds it tightly in his hand. He is tired after his night shift and his body aches for sleep, but his mind is turning too fast. He goes into his kitchen, makes himself some tea, and sits at the kitchen table. He drinks tea and looks at the postcard again, rereading it over and over, marveling at it.

FELIXSTOWE

"I know Moira's been here," Tony says when he arrives that night. He looks wary and unsure. Silvana means to be calm. She means to talk sensibly. She holds out a handful of Lucy's clothes at him. The look on his face says everything she needs to know.

"How could you!" she yells, throwing them at him. "How could you lie to me?"

He picks up a blouse, folds it carefully, turns his brown eyes to her. "They are just clothes."

"No, they're not. They are *Lucy's* clothes."

"Silvana, don't be like this. You know I love you, don't you?"

"Who?" she demands. "Who? Me or Lucy? You lied, damn it! Who do you love? Me or a dead woman?"

She regrets saying it the moment it leaves her mouth. Tony stares at her, wringing his hands.

"Can we go to bed?" he asks. "I'm tired. Let's talk tomorrow. Come to bed now. It's late. Please, just come to bed and let me hold you."

"No."

"Love me. Come to me, please."

"Throw the clothes away," she says.

"Throw them away?"

"Burn them! Get rid of them. Get them out of the house."

"I can't . . ."

"You have to."

She sits on the bed watching him move armfuls of dresses. He looks broken, as if he is carrying away the body of his dead wife wrapped in layers of silk and cotton and jersey. She pities him, but she cannot bring herself to tell him to stop. When the wardrobe is empty, he stands waiting for his next instruction but she turns on her side, pulls the covers over her head, and feigns sleep.

She wakes early the next morning, her dress crumpled and creased. Silvana opens her eyes and feels a cool sense of determination. She slides out of bed, slips her feet into her shoes and picks up the headscarf lying on the table. Lucy's house. Peter's house. Tony's house. Anybody's house but hers.

"Silvana?"

Tony is sitting in a chair in the corner of the room, looking at her. His eyes are red rimmed and his face is sunken. An empty whisky bottle rolls on the floor at his feet.

"Where are you going, Silvana?"

He has a rough blue shadow of stubble on his cheeks, and his clothes look as crumpled as hers. He obviously hasn't slept at all.

She rubs her face. "For a walk. And you? When are you going to Devon?"

"I don't have to go . . ."

But he will go with his son and parents-in-law. He will go to Devon. Of course he will. He belongs with them. Not with her. He knows that. And he knows it is over already between them. The moment she told him she knew about the clothes, she saw it in his face. Like a film coming to an end and the lights going up.

He looks at her pleadingly, his brown eyes watering, and she understands finally what that look means. The longing in his face, the desire she always thought was aimed at her. It is the longing of a man who desperately wants what he cannot have. She knows it herself. They are united in this at least: the overwhelming desire to find the dead in the living.

She wants to tell him she is no better than him. Didn't she take a child in order to pretend her own son was still living? That's what she did. The film is over for her, too. Aurek is not her dead son. He is a boy who needs loving for who he is. And Silvana is not Lucy.

"They want me to go tomorrow," he says heavily. "We'll be away for two weeks. You'll be here, won't you, when I get back?"

"I don't know," she answers. "I'm going for a walk on the beach. Do you want to come?"

Tony shakes his head. "I have to make a delivery. Those cotton sheets. I've finally sold them. I'm taking them over to a hotel in Ipswich this morning. Say you'll be here when I get back?"

She doesn't answer. She can feel the distance between them now. Overnight, a space has grown between them.

"We'll talk more this afternoon," he says, and she hears him trying to recapture the confident tone that his voice usually contains. His hands shape the air. "I must get up. Get on with things. I'll see you later. Have a good walk."

Downstairs, the kitchen is glowing with sunlight even though it is early. She turns her chair away from the window while she drinks a cup of coffee.

Silvana washes the cup, dries it, and hangs it on the wooden cup tree that stands beside the sink. She sweeps the floor, opens the pantry door, and tidies jars, packets, and tins so that all their labels face her. Then she does the same with the pots and pans under the sink, handles facing inward just like Janusz's mother used to order them in her kitchen. She wants to leave things in good order.

At the front door she breathes in the sea air, steps outside and looks up to the bedroom window. Aurek is sitting there, watching the seagulls. He waves at her and she waves back.

"I won't be long. Don't go anywhere. I want you there when I get back."

She walks on the deserted beach. She begins to run, soft sand-spray flying up. Her red headscarf flutters around her face, and she runs until she has no breath left and has to stop, hands on her knees, waiting for her heart to slow down and her breathing to come back to normal. Finally, she stands up, takes a deep breath, climbs the concrete steps onto the pavements above the beach, and walks back toward the house.

Janusz is driving slowly. He has already stopped twice, unsure of what he thinks he is doing. What if she doesn't want to see him? Both times he got out of the car, studied Aurek's postcard, and then got back in and continued on the road heading toward Felixstowe. As he comes into the town, its name proudly spelled out on a huge roadside flower bed, red flowers for the letters on a white background of daisies, a car heading toward Ipswich passes him.

It's the first he's seen on the road that morning. The driver slows as he passes. The two men look at each other.

It is Tony.

He looks tired and unshaven, his collar undone, his tie knotted carelessly, and Janusz hardly recognizes him. He wants to punch him, and slows down. They come to a stop in the road. Janusz cuts the engine, flexes his hands into fists, and gets out of his car.

Tony winds his window down.

"Get out of the car," Janusz says, lifting his fists.

Tony shakes his head. "There's no point in fighting. She's waiting for you."

The man looks so utterly wretched; Janusz forgets for a moment that he'd like to hit him. By the time Janusz remembers, Tony is already moving away, his wheels squealing. Janusz watches him speeding down the empty road. He watches until the car disappears from view.

Silvana only notices the car that passes her because it is going so slowly. It must be someone out for an early morning drive. The car is very clean, polished, a shiny black Rover. The man driving it stares at her as he passes. She carries on walking and then looks back, unsure what to do. A little way down the road, the car has pulled to a stop. She carries on walking a few more paces and then turns around. There is nothing between her and her husband now, not even a child to link them. She knows this, has told herself so, many times. But the sight of Janusz sitting waiting in his car makes her heart soar, and she walks toward him.

Janusz opens the passenger door and watches Silvana get in beside him. He tries to be calm. Silvana touches the dashboard, looks around herself.

"Aurek would like this car," she says. "He is very fond of cars."

They sit in silence, the sun glinting off the windscreen, seagulls landing and taking off in front of them. The rows of lights that loop along the seafront swing back and forth, jingling, snatched up by the wind again and again. Finally Janusz speaks.

"I met Hélène during the war."

He coughs, smoothes his thumb and forefinger over his mustache.

"She died. She died in 1944. I should never have kept her letters. I should have explained to you. Talked more. I shut it all up."

Janusz looks across at Silvana and sees her eyes are shining with tears. He pulls his handkerchief from his pocket and offers it to her.

"The thing is, the boy. I'd like to see him."

"Do you think I am a bad woman for what I did?"

Janusz shakes his head. He is not sure if she is talking about Tony or Aurek.

"Am I a criminal?" she asks.

He looks at her. Her eyes have the same hard stare he has seen in soldiers. The ones who have witnessed too much. Her lips hold more questions, waiting for his response.

She pleads with him. "Will you ever forgive me?"

He answers *No*, and *Yes, I think so*, which seem to be the answers Silvana wants to hear.

"I thought I had lost you both," he says.

Silvana touches his cheek with her hand and he feels it tremble against him.

They sit in the car, watching the wind make patterns with the sand on the road, snaking lines of yellow back and forth, and Silvana tells Janusz the story of her war. She lays it out like a book, filling in details, moving back and forth over time until the whole six years they have been apart are accounted for. Some of it is hard to hear, but he listens.

He does not turn away from her. She says she wants no more secrets between them.

His own stories of those years are hard to relate. He tries to explain things to her, but he does not want to remember the war. His memories of it are locked down, and he can't bring himself to open them. He cannot speak of Hélène. Silvana doesn't press him for details. She changes the subject. For that he is grateful.

"Maybe it doesn't matter," she says when he falters and loses his place in his own narrative. "The past—maybe we make too much of it. What we need is what's right here."

But Janusz knows she is just being kind. Of course the past matters. He looks at her and sees the country he left behind staring back at him. Her face is full of the knowledge of his own youth, and he loves her for it. He feels like he does when he mends machines, when all those engineered details that can so easily go wrong are put in the right place, when they are warm and oiled and turning over perfectly.

Silvana hugs herself. "He didn't have a mother. I know he didn't. He had filth in his hair and sores on his body. I had to care for him. He had nobody. And my own baby, our baby was—"

"Stop," says Janusz. He winds his window down, lets the sea air rush in, breathes deeply. "Not that. Tell me about him growing up."

She tells him about their woodland son and how he grew up in the forest. She tells him the boy's favorite games and the way he learned to climb trees and hunt for food.

They speak quietly together until both boys become one in Janusz's mind. It is the best way. He knows the boy he loves isn't really the boy who swallowed a button, but he will give him these memories. Aurek will own them. There will be no more mystery. He is their son. And that will be his story.

It is awkward, embracing in a car. Janusz leans toward Silvana, but the steering wheel gets in the way and the gearshift lies between them. Silvana leans further forward, shifting to the edge of her seat, and he manages to kiss her in a clumsy way, their noses bumping.

He wants her. The sound of her breathing in the night. The way she hums when she believes she is alone. All these things. Desire rises in him. His heart beats like a young man's, full of wanting. At the same time he feels old. Old enough to understand the hurt he has suffered will not disappear overnight. The thought of Tony makes him want to push her away, accuse her all over again. But he pulls her closer to him.

"Come back," he whispers. "Please come back."

"The house is along the seafront," Silvana says. "And you turn—"

"I know," he tells her, and starts the engine.

Aurek is sitting out on his window ledge when he sees the car driving up the road. He watches it stop outside the house. Sees his mother get out, and then his father. He has come! They stand by the car and look up at him. Aurek waves, slowly at first, then faster. He stands up, hanging onto the window frame, losing his balance slightly, tipping forward. He has to grab the sill to stop himself falling out of the window. Both Janusz and Silvana lift their hands to him in alarm.

"No!" they shout. "No!"

22 BRITANNIA ROAD

The car journey is long and slow and Aurek slips about on the leather backseat, sliding from one window to the other. Fields give way to community gardens and blackened railway tracks. Aurek stares at the rust and metal of the gasworks, lets his eyes skip over tangled wire fences, yellow scrubland, redbrick houses.

He feels the shade of magnolia trees and yew hedges press briefly against the window, shutting out the sun, and grips the seat tightly so he won't slip away from the view. They pass the war cemetery and Aurek glimpses the tidy lines of salt-white crosses behind the yew trees. He played there sometimes, catching lizards and slowworms, putting them in jam jars filled with bits of grass, pink quartz, and green granite chippings. He is itching to go there again, to sit motionless, waiting for the lizards to come out and bask on the graves.

They drive on, over a humpback bridge, past the newly painted wall of the house on the corner advertising Colman's Dairy in chalky blue paint, a bottle of milk nestling in the *C* of Colman's. Aurek's eyes are open wide, taking it all in. He is a sailor coming into port, watching for the cliffs of his homeland, his eyes full of the town, the broad sky, the small white clouds, the dirty haze of pigeons settling on rooftops.

They are speeding up the hill to Britannia Road, the car shaking over the cobbles. They sail over a bump in the road and Aurek flies forward, slamming into the gap between the front seats.

"Aurek!" his mother cries. She grabs his shoulder and he scrambles through to sit on her lap in the front. They arrive outside Number 22 and Aurek bounds out of the car, running to the house, banging on the front door as if someone might open up to him and let him in.

"I have something to show you," Janusz says, unlocking the door.

They walk through the hall, into the kitchen, and outside.

The light in the garden is pale. The bark of the trees is paler still, the color of new moons and baby teeth. All the leaves form a sweet fluttering of green. Aurek breathes in the smell of a warm day. He walks to the oak tree and sits down underneath his tree house. His mother sits next to him, his father the other side. The way they look at him makes him feel safe; it's like he's everything they ever wanted.

That's what his father says to his mother. *You and the boy are everything to me.*

Aurek closes his eyes and listens to the sparrows chattering in the trees. Somewhere, in another garden, or in the fields beyond the houses and factories, he hears the summer calling to him. A cuckoo's refrain, its woody voice repeating over and over. Aurek can't resist its needy cry. He opens his mouth and begins to sing.

*Forgetfulness comes softly over the years. In time, Aurek will grow up think-
ing of England as his home. But still, as an adult, when he sees his mother
staring out of the window or his father silent in his armchair, he wonders how
hard it must have been for them both, leaving Poland to give him a safe life.
A shadow of a memory will move in his mind then, quick, like a small boy
playing hide-and-seek, running barefoot through the rooms of 22 Britannia
Road.*

The shared ghost, he believes, of their old country.

Acknowledgments

Heartfelt thanks to Rachel Calder and to Juliet Annan, Jenny Lord, Pamela Dorman, and Julie Miesionczek. Thanks also to Sarah Hunt Cooke.

I am very grateful to Dr. Kathy Burrell, senior lecturer in Modern History at De Montfort University, Leicester, for generously reading the novel and commenting on the historical aspects of it.

Special thanks go to Kit Habianic for reading early drafts. Also to Deborah Goodes, Marcia Edwards, Gill Hamer, and all the talented writers who helped me at Lorraine Mace's excellent Writing Asylum. Huge thanks to Richard Butler for being my computer guru and to Delyth Potts for always believing in me. Thank you, Melanie Watson, Aimy Kersey, and Annie Benoit for your friendship and support.

And finally, thank you, darling Katya, Nancy, and Guy.

The epigraph is taken from "The Forest of Arden" by Zbigniew Herbert, *Collected Poems: 1956–1998*. With the kind permission of Atlantic Books.